Just in Time

Center Point
Large Print

Also by Marie Bostwick and available from
Center Point Large Print:

Apart at the Seams
From Here to Home
The Promise Girls

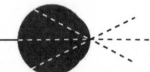

**This Large Print Book carries the
Seal of Approval of N.A.V.H.**

Just in Time

MARIE BOSTWICK

CENTER POINT LARGE PRINT
THORNDIKE, MAINE

This Center Point Large Print edition
is published in the year 2018 by arrangement with
Kensington Publishing Corp.

The text of this Large Print edition is unabridged.
In other aspects, this book may vary
from the original edition.
Printed in the United States of America
on permanent paper.
Set in 16-point Times New Roman type.

ISBN: 978-1-68324-771-5

Library of Congress Cataloging-in-Publication Data

Names: Bostwick, Marie, author.
Title: Just in time / Marie Bostwick.
Description: Center Point Large Print edition. | Thorndike, Maine :
    Center Point Large Print, 2018.
Identifiers: LCCN 2018003477 | ISBN 9781683247715
    (hardcover : alk. paper)
Subjects: LCSH: Large type books.
Classification: LCC PS3602.O838 J87 2018 | DDC 813/.6—dc23
LC record available at https://lccn.loc.gov/2018003477

For my sister, Donna,
who has the tenacity of a terrier,
the loyalty of a Lab,
and the caring heart of a Cavalier

With Many Thanks to . . .

Martin Biro, my patient, thorough, book-loving editor, for working so hard to make the story perfect and, in turn, make me look smarter than I am.

Liza Dawson, my extraordinary literary agent, sometime therapist, and friend, for courage when mine runs short and never letting me settle for less than my best.

To Cathy Lamb, awesome author and great girlfriend, for staying up late and being so willing to take panicked phone calls from blocked wordsmiths.

Donna Gomer, my creative and imaginative sister, for plot input and expertise in all things dog that made this book more fun to read, and to write.

Betty and John Walsh, my sister and brother-in-law, for first-round reading and copyediting, as well as cheerleading above and beyond the call of duty.

Lisa Sundell Olsen, my Very Sparkly Assistant, for a willing heart, sunny attitude, and wicked good organizational skills.

Amy Skinner, my creative and always on the ball publicist, for taking care of getting the word out so I can focus on getting the book done.

Davyne Verstandig, my dear friend, for beautiful poetry that inspired some of the themes and scenes in this book.

Faithful Readers, for making it possible for me to do what I love.

Just in Time

Prologue

Grace

For a long time now, my conversations with Jamie have been imaginary. That doesn't stop me from having them.

When I first met Nan and Monica and told him about the bizarre circumstances of our connection, Jamie didn't laugh, but he wanted to. I could tell from the way he worked to suppress his smile, and how his blue eyes somehow looked bluer under the disbelieving arc of his brows, the way they do when he thinks I've done something ridiculous but adorable.

"Wait. Let me make sure I'm getting this right. Your support group is made up of support group *dropouts?*" he asked.

Except he didn't say that. He didn't say anything.

Imagination has served me well, always. But it has its limitations. Or maybe we do. I do. Either way, there comes a point when you want something more concrete, a record and a response, a declaration of fact, or what you believe the facts to be. I realize there's no narrator as unreliable as one who tells his own story. But who else have we got?

Carl Sagan, the American cosmologist, once said, "We are made of star-stuff." I've always liked that quote. Jamie did too. It's such a pretty notion.

But as I sit here, perched on top of this rock in this treeless and windswept spot that isn't really close to the top of the world but feels like it could be, my lungs working to glean enough oxygen for existence, and look out across the vista of gray, and green, and granite to a spot on the horizon that might be the end of the world or the beginning, I understand in a way I never have before the limits of imagination. And everything else.

Only a thin sliver of sunlight has disappeared beneath the horizon, just a small and succulent slice from the bottom of the melon, but already its absence has brought a chill to the air. Soon this day will end. Night will resume its rightful place and purpose, giving rest to the earth, revealing the stars.

They will be beautiful this high up, so far from the lights of the city, the influence and evidence of civilization. It's strange, don't you think, that the only way for humans to *truly* see the stars is at a remove from the rest of humanity? That signifies something, I think. But at the moment I'm not exactly sure what. I'm cold and getting colder, consumed by the knowledge that the stars, while breathtakingly beautiful, are silent. They shine brightly but do not speak.

We *are* star-stuff. But more, I think.

We are what we've done, and said, and thought, and ignored. We are who we have loved and championed. Who we have failed and forgotten, and who we have forgiven. We are what we have believed, and what we have refused to believe.

We are star-stuff. But more. We are words and action, moment and place, doubts and faith. And story.

This is mine. I'd like to tell Jamie. I can't. So I'm telling you.

I'm telling myself.

Chapter 1

Grace

One night after work, just a few months after I moved to Portland, I went into the bistro near my office for a bite to eat. I was sitting at the bar because it felt less conspicuous. The bartender and I struck up a conversation and a few minutes into it, he handed me a flyer for a grief support group. Apparently, he kept it and a supply of similarly helpful publications stowed next to the highball glasses. Bartenders and social workers have a lot in common, he said.

I've never been a joiner. The idea of sharing my problems with a roomful of strangers made my pulse race and my hands feel clammy. But I knew I couldn't go on like I had been. I mean, if a bartender can peg your problems after one glass of crummy house chardonnay and ten minutes of awkward conversation, so can everybody else. And maybe I wouldn't have to talk. Maybe I could just listen. It couldn't hurt to try, right?

But when I got to the community center, I knew it wasn't going to work. The members of the group were all women, all widows. Definitely not a club I was interested in joining. And apart from two people, including a woman with frizzy brown hair that kept falling into her eyes and who kept twitching and fidgeting in her seat, as if she was having a hard time sitting still, seventy was a fond but distant memory in the minds of the other participants. The room was filled by the sounds of sniffling, and the odor of White Diamonds perfume was so strong it almost made my eyes water.

The other woman I couldn't help but notice was older but somehow not, the kind of woman who seems comfortable with her age and herself at any age. Her shoulder-length hair was a halo of curls around her head, a sandy blond color interspersed with threads of silver white. Her eyes were big and brown, and her gaze was very direct. Something about that made me feel like she saw things other people missed. Her clothes intrigued me too. I've always appreciated people who have a unique sense of style. I'd seen her blue and white skirt on sale recently, but I was pretty sure that her denim jacket, embroidered with birds and flowers, was done by hand. The fact that she'd paired it with red sneakers made me think she had a good sense of humor and didn't take herself too seriously.

She seemed to be with the group, smiling warmly at many of the white-haired women, but not of it. She quietly made the rounds with her dog, a tail-thumping golden retriever who rested her muzzle in the laps of weeping participants, gazing intently until they started to stroke her silky head, smile wetly, and calm down, at which point she would move on to a new, more distraught participant.

Still, there was a lot of crying going on and it made me uncomfortable. During the bathroom break, I got up and quietly left. I was standing in the parking lot, about to unlock my car, when I heard a voice.

"Sneaking off?"

The woman with the frizzy hair was leaning against the hood of the red PT Cruiser parked next to me. Even though she was wearing a pair of thick-heeled clogs, shoes designed for comfort rather than fashion, she stood only a couple of inches over five feet. But somehow she seemed taller, partly because of her voice—big and brassy—but also because of her face. She had one of the most expressive faces I'd ever seen; every thought or opinion she had was telegraphed through her eyes, lips, nose, cheeks, and especially her eyebrows, dark brown and bristling, capable of moving in ways I'd never seen eyebrows move before. I remember thinking that in the days of silent films, she'd have been a star.

She pulled a pack of cigarettes from her purse.

"It's not the right group for me," I said, answering her question.

She didn't say anything, just lit her cigarette and stared at me.

"I'm not a widow," I explained.

"I am. But it's not the right group for me either."

She took a long draw, making the cigarette tip glow orange and puffing out her cheeks. It didn't look like she was inhaling.

"It's a grief support group, which is fine. But I'm not feeling particularly grieved. Pissed off, but not grieved. You'd think that in the whole city of Portland, there'd be at least *one* support group for the pissed-off widows of cheating husbands. I mean, I can't be the only one, right?"

She blew out a long column of smoke and looked me up and down, eyebrows twitching and working, assessing me as if I were a dress she was thinking about trying on.

"You're not pissed off, are you?" She frowned. "No, you're sad. Really sad. I'm sorry."

Portland is not like the small town in Minnesota where I grew up. It's a city that takes pride in diversity and "keeping Portland weird," so this was far from the first strange conversation I'd had since coming here. Two days before, a homeless woman who had recently taken up residence between two concrete planters a block from my apartment stopped me as I was getting into my car and asked, politely but with the same kind of grave intensity you might use to ask someone if they believed in life after death, if I had a Twinkie in my purse. A week before that, a man with pupils as big and shiny as black marbles, wearing a tattered blue beach towel draped around his shoulders, like the cape of a superhero who had escaped a methadone clinic, clutched my sleeve to ask if I was human or android.

For a girl who grew up in rural Minnesota, those kinds of exchanges were unnerving, but I was starting to get used to them. But those people had been glassy-eyed, high as kites, and so they were easier to dismiss. This conversation was somehow more disturbing because the woman was both sober as a saint and weirdly insightful.

She took another pull on her cigarette. This time she deliberately drew the smoke into her lungs. Instantly, her face turned red and she started hacking so hard her eyes watered.

"Are you okay?"

She didn't look okay. Should I pound her on the back? Call 911?

"I hate these things," she rasped after she finally quit coughing. "I've been trying to learn to smoke, but it just isn't working out."

Really? Apart from addlebrained adolescents trying to impress their friends, who *wants* to take up smoking?

"I know," she sighed, rightly reading my

19

expression. "But every day I wake up feeling like I want to punch somebody in the face. The Paxil my doctor prescribed made me gain weight. I thought cigarettes would be better." She flicked the cigarette from her fingers and ground it out under her shoe. "This was a stupid idea."

As I stood there, trying to figure out if I should say something besides, "Well. Okay, then. Good night, Crazy Lady," I heard the chirp of a keyless car remote. The taillights of an SUV in the next row flashed. The woman with the red sneakers and embroidered jacket was walking toward us, her dog, now leash-less, padded alongside her.

"Smoke break? Or did you just have enough?" She thrust out her hand. "I'm Nan Wilja. This is Blixen."

The retriever thumped her tail against my fender and looked up as if to say hello, her tongue lolling out of her mouth.

"Grace Saunders," I said, taking her hand.

The lady with the frizzy hair pushed it out of her eyes and reached down to scratch Blixen's ear. "I'm Monica Romano."

"What were you two doing in there?" Nan asked. "Pilates meets in the same room on Tuesdays. I thought maybe you got the nights mixed up. Or you got lost."

"I saw a flyer pinned to the bulletin board at the drugstore and I thought, you know, maybe I'd give it a shot." Monica ducked her head, looking a bit sheepish. "It wasn't what I thought it would be. Maybe I should try a drum circle?"

"Hmmm," Nan murmured, which is what I later learned she did when she disagreed but was trying to be supportive. Nan says "hmmm" a lot.

"I heard you say something about being angry," Nan said. "But not grieving?"

"Not. At. All." Monica fumbled with the flap on her purse, as if she was thinking about getting another cigarette. "My husband was killed in a boating accident eight months ago. His girlfriend was driving the boat."

"Ouch." Nan winced. "I'd be mad too. And you?" She turned toward me. "Were *you* lost? Or did you show up on purpose?"

"On purpose, I guess. But it's not the group for me. I'm not a widow."

"But you are grieving."

The way Nan said it, as a statement instead of a question and so directly, caught me off guard, the same way that Monica's comment about me being sad had done. What was it about this place? Were people in Portland just unusually perceptive? Or had my expression become unusually transparent?

"It's complicated."

"It's complicated" is shorthand for "I don't want to talk about this." Most people get that and will either leave it there, change the subject, or

21

remember they're late for an appointment. Not Nan.

"Hmmm. Grief comes in all kinds of forms, doesn't it? Blixen and I have had quite a bit of experience there. She's a therapy dog. We visit hospitals, nursing homes, that kind of thing.

"I'm a widow. My husband was killed in a private plane crash twenty years ago. The facilitator called me because she's worried that some of these women have been with her for years and aren't making any progress. She thought Blixen might be able to comfort some of them." She looked down at the dog, returning her adoring gaze.

"Well, I think she did," I said, and patted the dog on the head. Nan looked up with a brilliant smile, her face glowing like a proud mother whose child has just received an enormous compliment.

"Would you two like to come over to my house for a cup of tea?" she asked, then quickly added, "I know, I know. It's sudden. And I'm a stranger. I could be crazy, a complete nut job. But trust me, I'm not. Not very." She smiled. "I just thought that . . . well, you're looking for somebody to talk to. I'm a good listener. You don't fit in with this bunch," she said, tilting her head toward illuminated windows of the big community room, where the white-haired circle was still in session. "But I have a feeling you might have a tough time finding a place where you do belong. Neither of you quite fits the mold, do you?

"I'm running a little short of human companionship myself these days. Blixen has many fine qualities, but she's not the world's best conversationalist. Maybe we can be our own support group?"

I didn't know what to say. Yes, she seemed nice, a caring, insightful, and possibly quite wise woman who liked to help, but how did I know? Denials aside, Nan could have been crazy. And if she wasn't, maybe Monica was. The signs certainly pointed in that direction.

"Gee . . ." I said slowly. "That's nice of you. But—"

"I have peach turnovers," Nan said. "And homemade vanilla ice cream."

Monica's hand shot up. "Yes, please." She turned to me. "You in?"

I knew I should say no. Even if they weren't crazy, they were definitely weird, not like anybody I knew back home. But I wasn't back home. I didn't have any friends in Portland, not one.

"The turnovers are homemade too," Nan said, adding an extra incentive. "Fresh-baked this morning."

My stomach growled, making up my mind for me, as it so often does.

"Is it far? I don't know my way around very well yet."

"Even if you did, you'd never find it," Nan laughed. "But you can follow me. I'll drive slow."

And I did. I got in my car and followed Nan home, which is *so* unlike me. But that night I forgot to be cautious, sensible, or shy. And it saved me.

I mean it. It *saved* me. They saved me.

Who could have imagined? Not me. Not then.

But the thing is, sometimes you don't know you're going down for the third time until somebody pulls you into the boat.

Chapter 2

Grace

When I was seven, my grammy taught me to sew. She'd grown up on a farm and never liked to waste anything, so every winter she'd gather up the family's worn-out clothes to make quilts. Every fall, she'd enter a quilt in the country fair and win a prize.

My mother, who wouldn't shop the sale rack because she didn't want to buy something that everybody else had passed over, made fun of Grammy's quilts, saying it was just one more way for her mother to be cheap. "As if making me wear a dress handed down through three sisters wasn't enough, now she expects me to sleep under it too."

I thought Grammy's quilts were wonderful. Always "the quiet one" and often overlooked in a family of boisterous brothers, I reveled in the attention and praise she lavished upon me during our sewing sessions.

I also loved the stories she'd tell about each block, "Now this pale blue was from the shirt your grampy wore when he came over to my house to propose. My dad knew why Ted was there. He stood on the porch and said I wasn't home, but I hollered from upstairs, 'Oh, yes, I am!' then ran downstairs, took the bouquet Ted brought for me, and said I'd marry him. That's why I picked the Lily corner block for this one, because that's the kind of flowers he brought me."

When I was nine, Grammy helped me make a log cabin quilt. I entered it in the fair and won ten dollars and a ribbon, the only prize I'd ever won in my life. Grammy died the following year, but the things she taught me stuck with me. I was always making something—doll clothes, pincushions, crocheted potholders. My mother never thought much of my crafty inclinations, or my tendency to hide inside of books; making things made me feel like there was at least one thing I knew how to do that other people couldn't.

In high school I started sewing my own clothes—dark, shapeless outfits that were designed to make me blend into the background, because nothing in the juniors department fit me. Even after I lost weight, I still had plenty of curves, so I continued to make my own "fit-and-flare" fashions, dresses with fitted waists and full skirts, partly because they flattered my figure, but mostly because it finally gave me a chance to indulge my love of color. Most every dress I sewed was made from material I found on the discount rack of the fabric store—the brighter the better.

My twirly skirts, Jamie called them, because the minute I put one on, I couldn't help but spin around in a circle, making the hem flutter around my thighs, feeling pretty, and feminine, and incandescently happy.

I haven't been doing a lot of twirling recently.

Portland's housing market is tight. If you find something you can afford in the location you want, you have to be ready to go. We put our stuff in storage and rented a tiny studio for three months before we finally closed on the condo, purchased after looking at pictures the Realtor e-mailed to us. A year and a half later, the place still looked a lot like it did when we moved in, with boxes of books shoved in the corner and unhung paintings piled against the wall. It wasn't important. By then I had bigger problems to worry about than decorating. But I wished I'd paid more attention to closet space before buying; there was only one.

Initially, I hung up Jamie's clothes along with my own. I considered it an act of faith. But after a few months, I accepted reality—Jamie was not ever going to live here. I boxed up his things to make space for my work clothes and stacked them with the books. They sat there for weeks. After tripping over one and breaking a toe during a middle-of-the-night trip to the bathroom, I realized I had to do something.

I started sorting through Jamie's things and cutting up the special items to make into quilt blocks, sewing them by hand. It's slow work, but it keeps me busy and gave me a chance to think or, depending on the day, not to think.

The longer I was at Hewlett and Hanson, where I worked as an administrative assistant for four commercial Realtors and where the atmosphere was as gray as the dress code, the less space there was for my twirly skirts. Sometimes it felt like the gray was trying to swallow up the bright colors of my old life. But the job had benefits and paid the bills, so I wasn't complaining.

And that night, for the first time in forever, I had a reason to dress up.

After trying on and rejecting half a dozen dresses, I settled on a vintage-style swing dress with a pink bolero sweater that matched the pink flamingo print. It had a kind of 1950s, rockabilly, Florida trailer park vibe, but who cared? I wasn't trying to impress anybody. I was only the third wheel in this ménage, as I explained to Nan when the phone rang.

"You're tagging along on Monica's date? Monica is what—forty-two? Isn't she a little old for a chaperone?"

"She's nervous," I said, foraging through the bathroom drawer for an eyebrow pencil. "She hasn't been on a date in years. I'm only going along for moral support. And the food. We're going to The Fish House!" I exclaimed, unable to disguise my enthusiasm.

"Well, la-di-da! Who is he? Tech entrepreneur? Stockbroker? Think he'd like to make a donation to the pet rescue?"

"Doubtful. He's some kind of carpenter, makes tables. And Monica is paying for dinner. Well, not paying exactly." I leaned closer to the bathroom mirror and filled in my brows. "Monica knows the manager at The Fish House, and he gave her gift cards—some kind of industry courtesy—but she has to use them right away."

"But why would this . . ."

"Luke," I said, filling the blank for her. "Luke . . . Pauling? Patterson? Something with a *p*. I can't remember."

"But why would this Luke want to go on a date with two women?"

"Well, I don't think he thinks it's a date— more like a sales call. Monica wants new tables and banquettes for the restaurant, and Luke came over to bid on the job. I was only there because Monica asked if I could pick Alex up from cross-country practice and then drop him off at the restaurant. When I got there, Monica said she'd like to see Luke's portfolio, then suddenly 'remembered' about the gift cards she needed to use and suggested the three of us get together over dinner to discuss the project."

"Oh. Doesn't that seem a little devious?"

"Well, yes. But I almost can't blame her. He's really handsome. And it's time Monica started getting out there. I think she'd be a lot happier if she had a boyfriend."

"Okay, but why did she have to involve you? It's bound to be awkward."

"It's all right. I'm used to Monica roping me into things. Last week she talked me into coming to Alex's school for a program on the college application process."

"Already?" Nan clucked. "Alex is only fifteen. They put too much pressure on kids. But why did you have to go to a meeting about helping Alex get into college?"

"Because," I said, exchanging the eye pencil for a lip pencil, "the forecast was calling for rain, which meant that the barometer was going to drop, which meant that Monica would be getting a migraine just as the meeting was set to start. She begged me to come along and take notes so she wouldn't miss anything. She's panicked about Alex not getting into college, staying in Portland, and making her life even more miserable than it already is."

"You don't get a headache because it rains," Nan said. "If that was true, the entire population of Portland, Oregon, would have a headache nine months out of twelve."

"I know," I said, twisting a lipstick tube open. "I wish Monica would stay off WebMD. In the last six months, she's diagnosed herself with shingles, gallstones, plantar fasciitis, anemia, psoriasis, and Lyme disease. But, really, I think she just wanted me to come along to serve as a buffer between her and Alex."

Monica does that sometimes, uses me as a human shield between herself and her step-kids, Alex and Zoe. Alex is pretty rotten to her no matter what, but he isn't quite as rotten when I'm around.

"The whole dinner for three thing does feel weird," I admitted after blotting my lipstick on a tissue, "even for Monica. Luke seemed pretty surprised by the invitation. But he's just getting his business off the ground, so maybe he's just anxious to land a client. Or maybe he totally has Monica's number, realizes she's nervous about dating and being the one to ask him out first, and is going along with it just so she won't feel embarrassed. My money's on that—he seemed too smart to fall for Monica's ruse. Or maybe he's like me, in it for the food. I'm not going to turn down free oysters."

"This Luke, he's Italian?"

"I don't know what he is, but definitely not Italian," I said, recalling Luke's handsome face, tanned but not swarthy, his wavy, sand-colored hair, and beautiful brown-gold eyes.

Huh. Weird that I couldn't remember his last name but recalled his face in such detail. Those eyes. But what struck me most was not the unusual color of his eyes, but the intensity of his gaze. When Monica spoke, he *really* listened. Not too many men know how to do that. I'd only ever known one.

"Not Italian? But I thought Monica was only—"

A dog started to whine in the background. The noise was too high-pitched for Blixen. And Blixen never whines.

"New resident?" I asked.

"He just came yesterday. Misses his mommy terribly, poor boy. I know, Nelson. I know," Nan said in a low, soothing voice. "It's all right to be sad, baby."

In addition to her many other good works, Nan volunteers with Rainbow Gate, a pet rescue providing foster care to dogs whose owners have died.

Nan may be the kindest person I've ever met. She raised seven kids—four biological and three adopted, all grown now—and is the reason the term "earth mother" exists.

Nan knits, crochets, tats, and sews. Like me, she loves anything involving fiber. That alone would have drawn me to her, but she also grows things—tomatoes, flowers, and herbs. She bakes. She cans things. She makes chairs out of bent branches. She raises chickens—for eggs, not meat. Nan's a vegetarian.

She lives simply but deeply and values people above possessions. That's why she refuses to carry a cell phone, because she says that being available to everyone at every moment makes it impossible to truly be there for the people who count when they really need you.

Nan isn't like anyone I've ever known— she's part hip and part homespun, motherly and mysterious all at once, and beautiful. Not just "for her age," but beautiful, with that glorious crown of curls and eyes that have seen everything—good and bad—and still keep smiling, enthused about whatever comes next. She's an old soul with a young heart and might be the only real grown-up I've ever met.

"Nelson is a beautiful little schnauzer," she said. "Three years old, perfectly behaved, handsome as they come. He'd make a wonderful brother for Maisie."

"No," I said firmly, because when it came to Nan and dogs you have to.

Nan has found the "perfect" dog for me about once a month since we met. Though I would never have pictured myself with a Chihuahua, in Maisie's case she was right. Nelson might have been perfect, too, but my building only allowed one dog per condo, as I explained to Nan yet again.

"But Maisie is so tiny," she protested.

"No, there's no room in my life for an emotionally needy schnauzer," I said as Nelson began whining again. "Listen to him. He'd be miserable left alone all day."

"I suppose you're right," Nan sighed. Nelson's pathetic whine became even more pathetic—the canine equivalent of keening. "Oh, dear. Oh, this poor baby. Grace, I have to go. I'll see you Monday."

I said goodbye and finished putting on my makeup, my mouth watering as I thought about dinner. I planned to dive face-first into a platter of just-shucked oysters, then follow it up with crab cakes, then lobster claws, then start all over with oysters again. Just thinking about it made me dizzy. But the fact that I hadn't eaten anything all day might have had something to do with it. I was saving room. Tonight, for once, I didn't want to feel guilty, about calories or anything else.

I slipped my feet into a pair of heels and checked the time, momentarily forgetting that my watch was broken. Seeing the hands, frozen at two and eighteen minutes past, I felt a catch in my throat.

Stop. It's too late to back out. You're going to have a good time tonight. You are. It's not like you're doing anything wrong.

I took a deep breath to collect myself, swallowing back the wave of guilt, and then reached for my earrings. As I did, I heard a *ping,* the sound of something dropping onto the counter. I looked at my left hand and saw an empty setting where a diamond should have been.

My ring! Jamie sold his motorcycle to buy that diamond!

Panicked, I dropped to my hands and knees. After five heart-pounding minutes of frantic searching, I found the stone hiding in the threads of my fuzzy white bathmat. It must have bounced off the counter.

I sat back, legs crossed underneath my skirt, and took a deep breath, trying to collect myself and swallow the wave of guilt and doubt. Maybe it was a sign. Maybe I shouldn't go. But I couldn't back out on Monica, not at the last minute.

I climbed to my feet, smoothed out my skirt, then put my ring and the loose diamond in my jewelry box before running out the door. I was *so* late and so frazzled. And I couldn't remember Luke's last name. What would I say when the hostess asked for the name of my party?

Stop. Seriously, stop. You're getting worked up over nothing. If you have to, you can go into the dining room and look for him. You'll remember Luke once you see him. And even if you don't, Monica will be there already so you can just look for her.

Say what you want about Monica, at least she's never late.

Chapter 3

Monica

When Luke Pascal showed up at my restaurant to give me a bid for new tables and banquettes, I got so flustered that I asked what kind of wood he worked with twice, only realizing I'd done it when he tipped his head to one side and slowly said, "Well, as I said before—"

"Sorry," I replied, "My stepson plays his music so loud—I think I must be going a little deaf." I laughed self-consciously and forced myself to quit staring. But, really, it was hard not to.

His eyes were the same rich, golden brown as the beef-and-bone broth I make by the gallon for the restaurant. His physique caught my attention as well—tall and lean, athletic looking but not muscle-bound, which I now consider a plus.

Vince used to spend hours at the gym—at least, that's where he said he was. It's just as possible he was out bench-pressing blondes. But he was definitely a Muscle Beach type—big biceps, thick neck, even thicker skull. I've sworn off gym rats for life.

Luke was absolutely nothing like my late,

36

hideous husband, not in manner, temperament, or looks. My first impression of him was that he was polite, capable, and smart—and undeniably attractive. But he wasn't my type.

I don't know why, but the men who melt my butter are always Italian. Always. Which is weird because my maiden name is Schiller and my roots are German/Polish and Lutheran. Yet, the men who make my heart go pitter-pat have names that end with vowels and marinara sauce running through their veins. It makes no sense, but it is what it is. And I have to tell you my track record is not good.

In high school, Johnny Zeffirelli cheated on me with my best friend and stood me up on prom night. In chef school, Anthony Esposito broke my heart, stole my recipe for bucatini alla Sorrentina, and became valedictorian because of it. Then there was Rob Russo, Joe Ricci, Matt Costa . . . And, of course, the infamous Vincente Romano.

You get the idea.

After Vince and his bimbo du jour downed four bottles of Borolo and rammed our boat into a piling (she survived: her most obvious attributes turned out to be excellent flotation devices), I decided to swear off Italian men forever, which was essentially saying I was swearing off men forever. All men. Forever.

And, hey, why not? I'm forty-two. I'm over it.

I've already done it all—the lust thing, the boy-friend thing, the husband thing, the mother thing. Okay, technically it's the stepmother thing, but still, I'm over it. Big-time. My step-kids are rotten.

I know, I know. I'm not supposed to say that. They're just kids and they've been through a lot—first their mom runs off with some guy who was demonstrating juicers at the fair and is never seen or heard from again; then their dad dies in a boating accident with his mistress. I get it. But before you go judging me, remember that I'm the one who has stuck by them, fed them, clothed them, and contributed to their college funds, even though they're rotten kids and I was only married to their father for two years.

To be fair, Zoe isn't completely rotten. She's whiny for sure. And mouthy. And a real drama queen. But so was I at thirteen, so maybe this is payback. She does seem to be entering a slutty phase that has me worried, but I still couldn't call her *completely* rotten.

But Alex *is*. Definitely.

For example, his schoolwork. I've been Alex's stepmother for three years. Since then, I've shown up for every parent/teacher conference—something Vince never bothered to attend—which translates to separate, private meetings with thirty teachers (I'm not even including the times I've been called to the principal's office because he's done some knucklehead thing or other). In all those meetings, I can't remember a single teacher saying anything about Alex except that he wasn't "living up to his potential" and then looking at me like it was my fault and I was supposed to fix it.

Look, I would if I could. Alex is smart, I realize that, and he's totally wasting his talent. But what do they want from me? I came into mothering late in the game and with zero training. If kids were like recipes and came with detailed instructions, I'd know what to do. As it is . . .

Grace says I shouldn't let Alex and Zoe push my buttons. I try, I really do. But can I help it if they know exactly where all my buttons are? Alex especially.

He's like my brother, Stevie—the Brilliant and Favored One. Stevie was smart, too, like Alex, and way more competitive. Why he felt the need to compete with me, I'll never understand. It's not like he wasn't already getting all of my parents' attention. Even so, he put me down whenever he got a chance. And my parents never stood up for me, ever. When I was little, Stevie could torment me until I sobbed and the most my mother would say was, "Now, Stevie . . ."

One day, when I was nine, Stevie called me a name and waited for me to cry. I didn't. Instead, in the sweetest voice possible, I asked if he'd noticed how that new automatic toilet cleaner

Mom bought turned the water blue and how, after somebody used the bowl, the water was the exact same yellow-green as his eyes?

He went off howling, searching for my mother, who made me do dishes for a week. But it was worth it. I had discovered Stevie's weakness and my weapon.

My brother was smart but not quick. I'm just the opposite—quick but not smart. Sarcasm worked for me and I got better at it as time went on. And now? It's gotten to be a habit, especially if I'm feeling defensive. When it comes to dealing with Alex, I'm always playing defense.

Okay, I'm getting off track here—sorry, I do that sometimes—the point is, when Vince died, I decided I was over it—over Italians, over men, over motherhood, over *all* of it.

But lately . . . I don't know. My grandmother ate herring in sour cream and kielbasa every day of her life and lived to be ninety-seven. Do I really want to be alone for the next fifty-five years?

I've had a run of incredibly bad luck, no doubt about it. But what if I was pickier? What if I refused to settle for anything less than the perfect man? Somebody with no secrets, no flaws. I'm not saying that such a man exists, but if he did, I'd be crazy to pass him up, right?

At first glance, Luke seemed to have perfect potential. Like I said, he is polite, capable, smart, handsome, and a good listener. And really passionate about his work. I could tell by the way he explained about the different decorative options for pedestal supports, options that were probably beyond my budget. All I really needed and could afford is a carpenter who could knock together a few nice tables and some benches, but Luke is obviously a real craftsman.

"Where did you learn all this?" I asked.

"I picked up my basic carpentry skills from my grandpa. He had a woodworking shop in his basement. When I was a kid, I spent all my time hanging out with him. And I put myself through college and law school doing construction for a big tract homebuilding company in the summers.

"After a few years, I figured out I hated being a lawyer, so I chucked it. After a couple of detours, I finally sold everything and went to France. I was there for three years, studying under a master furniture maker. I came back to the States two months ago to start my own custom furniture business."

He is adventurous, an entrepreneur, no stranger to hard work, *and* he loved his grandpa. How sweet is that? And though he only looked to be about thirty-five, he'd already gotten through his midlife crisis and figured out what mattered in life. Impressive. I glanced at Luke's left hand, noting neither wedding ring nor the telltale tan line of a married man who likes to cheat (after my Matt Costa debacle I always look for the tan line), so he is single too. The more we talked, the more perfect Luke Pascal appeared to be.

But still. Not Italian. I closed my eyes and tried to imagine him as Luigi Pasquale.

"Monica? Are you all right?"

I opened my eyes. No good. He was still blond and not only was my butter not melting, it was cold enough to make piecrust.

"Oh. Yes. I was just . . . uh . . . trying to picture those carved apron supports you were describing."

Dang. You can't start a fire without a spark, but a guy this good really shouldn't go to waste. When Grace arrived with Alex in tow, it occurred to me that maybe he didn't have to.

"Hey, Grace, do you have a second? Come over here. I need help figuring out what kind of tables to order for the restaurant."

I knew Grace was in a hurry and that she was already doing me a favor by dropping Alex off after practice. But I also knew she had a hard time saying no.

Grace is a good person and unfailingly polite, a product of her Midwestern upbringing. Unfailing politeness is not something I suffer from. Normally, I try not to take advantage of Grace's particular weakness. But since I was acting with her future happiness in mind, I figured it was okay.

After taking a moment to glare at me as he passed, Alex slumped down in an empty booth and started messing with his phone. He spends so much time on the phone that sometimes I feel like it's been surgically attached to his hand. But when he's texting with friends at least he's not arguing with me.

Grace sat down at our table. Her polite but pained smile told me that she really needed to go, but I pretended not to notice. Potentially perfect men don't just walk in off the street every day, you know. I wasn't one hundred percent convinced that Luke and Grace would be a good match, not yet. But if my instincts turned out to be right, an extra five minutes of her time was a small price to pay. She'd thank me later.

"Luke is new to Portland," I said, after completing the introductions.

Grace was distracted, her eyes a little glazed, probably thinking about all the things she should be doing besides helping me pick out furniture. I gave her a subtle nudge under the table and a pointed look, signaling that I needed her to focus. A bit startled, she looked at me, then Luke, and smiled.

"Oh. Really?" she said, sounding so vague that I wasn't sure she'd actually heard my comment.

"Not completely new," Luke said. "A returned former resident. Things have sure changed since I left, especially the housing market. It's completely crazy. The asking price for my little bungalow in the Hollywood District, with a workshop garage for my business, was so outrageous that I asked the Realtor if she was quoting me dollars or yen."

The joke wasn't bad, just okay, but I gave him a couple of extra points for trying. So many guys have zero sense of humor (cough, cough—Rob Russo). But the thing that put Luke over the top was his grin. When he smiled, his eyes crinkled at the corners and his lips bowed, exposing a little chip at the bottom of one of his upper teeth, kind of a snaggletooth. Totally adorable.

I was right. He was perfect for Grace.

Grace, I knew, would disagree. Ryan Reynolds could have walked in the room with a dozen roses and an indecent proposal and she still wouldn't have budged. For all her inability to say no, Grace is incredibly stubborn on this subject. But it was high time for her to find some happiness. As her friend, it was my job to help her, whether she wanted my help or not.

She'd thank me later. Or not. Either way, I had to come up with a plan to get these two together. But how?

"Look," Luke said, his expression suddenly serious, "I'm going to be straight with you. I'm trying to get my business going, so I really need this job. I know you're not really in the market for fine furniture; you just want something good

44

looking and sturdy that will do the job. But I'm willing to work with you, make you some real quality pieces at a price that'll fit your budget.

"I do good work, Monica. And I've trained with the best. But you don't have to take my word for it. If you'd come out to my workshop, I could show you."

Bingo! There it was. Luke didn't know it, but he'd just teed up the ball for me. Now all I had to do was take a swing and follow through.

"You know, that's a good idea. I would like to see some of your work. Do you have a port-folio?"

Luke nodded. "Sure. I've got a book with pictures of all the pieces I made when I was in France. I meant to bring it with me, but—"

"Great," I interrupted. "But instead of going to your workshop . . ."

I made it up as I went—the food show I never attended, the restaurant gift cards I never received, the industry courtesy that didn't exist. Luke wanted this job badly, so I knew he'd agree to anything I proposed. Grace, I was less sure of.

Besides being too polite for her own good, Grace has a couple of other weaknesses. Number one, she is loyal to a fault, will do anything for a friend. Number two, she loves to eat. I mean, *really* loves to eat. And for Grace's own good, I was willing to exploit those weaknesses.

She'd thank me later.

"Really, Luke, you'd be doing me a favor. Those gift cards expire at the end of the week. It'd be a shame to let them go to waste. So, if you don't mind coming downtown and bringing your portfolio, the three of us can meet at the restaurant.

The glazed look cleared from Grace's eyes. "Wait. The *three* of us?"

"I'll need your decorating advice."

Grace let out a disbelieving laugh. "You're kidding, right? You've seen my condo. It's one step up from a refugee camp."

I turned to Luke. "She's being modest. Grace has terrific taste."

"Monica, I don't—"

I placed my heel onto Grace's toe and pressed down, just hard enough so she'd get the message: *If you can't back me up here, at least shut up and go with it.* Grace clamped her lips shut. Then I played my trump card. I told her about the restaurant, the chef, the menu, and the oysters. By the time I was finished, she was practically salivating. I swear I could hear her stomach growl.

"Really? I never knew there were that many varieties of oysters. I've only ever had them once before—too expensive and not exactly standard menu fare if you grow up in Minnesota—but they were so, so good. Okay, count me in."

I looked at Luke.

"Sure," he said. "Me too. Sounds like fun. Saturday?"

I was about to tell him that would be fine when I remembered Grace. She knows I never go out on Saturday. I shook my head.

"The restaurant is always crazy on Saturday night. How about Sunday?"

"Sunday works." Luke looked at Grace. "Is that good for you?"

"Well, I was going to clean out the lint trap on the dryer, but you know"—she shrugged—"I guess I can reschedule."

Grace is usually pretty shy around new people. The fact that she was trying to joke around, even if the joke was pretty lame, felt like a good sign.

"What a relief," Luke said with a smile, showing off his snaggletooth.

That felt like another good sign. In fact, I was feeling very good about life in general. That is, until Alex put down his phone and pulled out his earbuds.

"Hey," he said, in his usual sarcastic snarl. "You wanna wrap it up here? Zoe texted me. Desmond got into the lasagna and is yakking all over the carpet."

I closed my eyes and pinched the bridge of my nose. The headache I'd been predicting ever since reading last week's weather forecast had finally arrived.

I hate my life.

When I opened my eyes and saw Luke staring at me, I said, "Zoe is my stepdaughter. Desmond is our dog, a Newfoundland. He weighs one hundred forty pounds, has a delicate stomach, and no moral compass. Sorry to cut this short, but I have to go."

I jumped up from the table, ticked off and with my head pounding, and yelled toward the kitchen so that Ben, my sous-chef, would know I'd be back before the dinner crowd showed up, then hissed something at Alex, who hissed something back, and walked toward the door. Grace fell into step behind me.

"Sorry," she said. "I have to go too."

"Oh, sure. No problem," Luke said, sounding accommodating but also a little confused by the abrupt exodus. "Umm . . . But should I? I mean, do you want me to—"

Grace, always so polite, turned around to face him.

"Yes, absolutely. Meeting us at the restaurant will be perfect," she said, backing out the door. "See you on Sunday. Six o'clock."

It was devious. I admit it. So was what I did later—convincing Grace that I was interested in Luke but too nervous to go on a date alone. And then, when she started to waver, texting her photos of dishes from The Fish House website that pretty much amounted to food porn.

But it wasn't half as devious as what I was about to do.

First, I called The Fish House and talked to Andrew, the manager, explaining what was going on, that there could be no check presented at the end of the meal and that the bill, however large, should be charged to my credit card.

Next, I started composing my text, salving the twinges of guilt by reminding myself that this was for Grace's own good and that everything I was saying wasn't a total lie. I really did feel a headache coming on and could tell already that it was going to be a doozy, a headache the size of a tumor.

No, I thought, deleting the tumor reference. Grace always made fun of my ailments. But people did get tumors, didn't they? And weren't raging headaches one of the symptoms? My head was just killing me.

I typed the words "brain tumor" and "headache" and "symptoms" into my phone. A bunch of pretty scary articles came up. The third one made up my mind for me—I was definitely going by Urgent Care after work.

I attached the article, hit Send, and sat there for a minute, imagining the look on Grace's face after she read my message.

She'd thank me. Later.

Chapter 4

Grace

Luke was sitting alone and drinking a glass of red wine when I arrived.

"I am *so* sorry!" I exclaimed. "I had a jewelry emergency. And the traffic was a nightmare. And I couldn't find a parking spot."

He pulled out my chair. "Take a breath. Monica's not here yet. Do you want a drink?"

I ordered a glass of chardonnay and sat down, feeling awful. He'd probably thought he'd been stood up, and by two women at the same time. In his shoes, I would have been mortified, certain that everybody was staring at me. But Luke didn't seem the least bit perturbed. Unless he was the only one who *didn't* know this was a date?

No. Not possible. Monica was so obvious. Luke had to know what was going on. A big brown scrapbook that I guessed was his portfolio was lying on one of the empty chairs, but that could have been a prop. It had to be. I didn't know Luke well, but he seemed too smart to be taken in by such an obvious ruse. He'd brought his portfolio just to play along to save Monica the embarrassment of having been the one to ask him out instead of the other way around.

That was very sweet. He seemed like a nice man. And so handsome. Those beautiful eyes. What color were they? Amber?

Luke caught me staring at him and smiled. I pretended to cough, putting the white linen napkin to my mouth to cover my embarrassment.

Where was Monica?

Luke took a sip of wine and gazed out of the restaurant's big glass window, overlooking Director Park. It's more of a square than a park but serves the same purpose. The ground is a herringbone of gray and white pavers with trees planted around the border. There's a fountain on one end for kids to splash in during the warm weather and a big checkerboard on the other end with knee-high plastic chess pieces left out for anyone who wants to play. If you look up, maybe twenty or thirty feet, you'll see an enormous glass canopy hovering over a bunch of metal tables and chairs, where people can sit and picnic. When it gets dark, the glass glows with a continually changing and unpredictable pattern of lights—blue, green, purple, pink, orange. It's eerie and beautiful, an urban aurora borealis.

"Look at that." Luke pointed toward the fountain and a young couple bundled up in parkas, boots, scarves, and blue knit caps. They were dancing—or trying to. It didn't seem to be going very well, but they were smiling, shuffling like a pair of clumsy circus bears.

"That's what I love about cities," Luke said, his beautiful eyes fixed on the dancers. "You do what you do, even when other people are around. Because you have to. You've got no choice but to get out there and rub elbows with humanity. You might not know everybody's name, but you can see what they do. And plot is character, right? People reveal themselves through actions. It's really kind of intimate, don't you think?"

He looked at me as if he expected an answer.

"I never thought about it that way."

He'd caught me off guard. Was this how people talked in France? Skipping the small talk and going directly into meaningful conversation? It was a little unnerving, but a part of me liked it. I've always sucked at small talk. And I could see he was right. The forced proximity of city life creates an unavoidable intimacy with others. You stand witness to the lives of your neighbors, whether you want to or not.

I thought about the homeless couple with the mongrel dog who lived on the block next to mine. They had moved into the neighborhood not long after I did, their belongings piled into a child's red wagon. After choosing their spot, they laid out big sheets of cardboard between the two cement planters and spread their ragged sleeping bags on top, claiming the space as their own.

Though the smell of weed hung on them from half a block away some days, they were quiet and kept their stuff from spreading out onto the sidewalk, so there was never a problem getting past. More than once I'd seen the girl pick up trash that other people dropped, load it into the red wagon, and cart it to the garbage can on the corner, like a vigilant housewife tidying up in case company came calling. I saw them almost every day of my life, yet I never spoke to them. Partly because I felt like I might be intruding on their privacy, but mostly because I didn't know what to say.

I thought, too, about the old man I saw in the grocery store the day before. He wore a dirty coat, had a long beard and bloodshot eyes. He stood in front of the coffee display with a red tin can in each hand and two more tucked under one arm. When he heard my cart coming down the aisle he spun around and grinned at me.

"Two for five bucks! I'm stocking up! Can't beat that price, can you?"

I wheeled past him, avoiding eye contact. He seemed crazy, but would it have hurt to respond? Or at least smile? Luke, I suspected, would have stopped for a lengthy conversation. He obviously enjoyed talking to people, but I wasn't prepared for conversation. I was just supposed to be the chaperone.

Where *was* Monica?

The server arrived with my wine. I took a grateful sip, then reached for my bag, fumbling around inside, and pulled out my phone. Monica had sent me a text.

> Can't make it. Dishwasher quit. Party of ten showed up without a reservation. Also, feel awful. Another headache. Terrible. Going to Urgent Care on my way home.

I clicked on a link she attached, an article from one of the more disreputable health and fitness websites, and saw a panicked headline with two exclamation points, about supposed links between cell phone use and brain tumors.

> Tell Luke I'm sorry. Have fun. Don't be mad. More crab cakes for you!

She wasn't coming? She couldn't be serious. She couldn't really believe I was going to sit here with this stranger and calmly eat crab cakes, could she?

"Monica!" I hissed, scanning the text again. "I am going to kill you. Then you won't have to worry about headaches anymore!"

Luke put down his glass.

"Something wrong with Monica?"

"*Nothing* is wrong with Monica," I replied,

which was one hundred percent true. "But . . . she can't make it. The dishwasher quit, they're short on waitstaff, and they've got a big party coming in—a wedding rehearsal dinner. She can't get away."

Okay, yes. I embellished Monica's list of excuses. And left out the part about the imaginary brain tumor. There was no reason Luke needed to know about Monica's hypochondria until he had a chance to notice all the good things about her (which I was currently struggling to remember), things that make up for the fact that she is—let's face it—a little nuts.

But I was convinced that falling in love, or even in like, with a guy like Luke would be the antidote to her imaginary diseases. The only thing she really suffered from was loneliness. There's a lot of that going around.

"Oh," he said. His expression was sort of . . . unreadable. "Huh. That's too bad."

I stuffed my phone into my bag and took a slurp from my glass, feeling ridiculous. "I'm really sorry. I'll just finish my drink and then get out of your hair."

He frowned. "Why? I thought we were having dinner? The server said the gift cards had already been entered and that we could order anytime."

"Luke," I said, tilting my head to one side. "You don't have to pretend. We both know what's going on here. I'm only here because

Monica was nervous about dating again and wanted me along for moral support."

I picked up my glass and drained it by half, anxious to save us both further embarrassment by making a quick getaway from an awkward situation.

"Don't let this discourage you, okay? Monica's life *is* complicated," I admitted. "Vince was serially unfaithful to her. Now she's left holding the bag, doing her best to take care of two teenage step-kids and run the restaurant. Monica trained as a chef, not a businesswoman. Or a mother. She tries, but she's in way over her head."

I tipped the wineglass high against my lips and gulped the contents.

"Don't give up on her. She's a good person." I pushed back my chair. "Next time, you ask *her* out. You won't regret it."

"Grace?"

"Yes?"

"Sit down."

Something about his tone reminded me of my high school history teacher, Mr. Harding, who ran such a tight ship that we didn't breathe without raising a hand to ask permission first. I sat down. The server passed by and saw my empty glass.

"Wow. That was quick. You must have been thirsty. Can I bring you another?"

"No, I'm fine. I was just—"

"Yes, please. Another round for both of us."

Luke's voice seemed to affect the server the same way it did me. She hurried off to do his bidding.

"So," he said. "Let me clear up a couple of things. I'm not interested in dating Monica. I'm here because I'm trying to get my business going. And because there was no way I was going to turn down free oysters. I developed a taste for them while I was in France. And for good wine."

He lifted his glass to his lips and took another sip.

"I'll tell you something," he said, his voice wistful, "French food"—he spread his hands—"there's just no word for how good it is."

"Really?" I said, propping my chin in my hand.

"Really. Have you ever had poached quail eggs with hollandaise? Or potatoes fried in duck fat? You should. Not too much because it's so rich. But that's the thing about French cooking—small portions but incredibly satisfying." He took a drink. "Sorry, I didn't mean to change the subject. I'm boring you."

"Not at all. I'm fascinated. I've always dreamed of going to France."

"You should. I really am glad to be back in the States, especially Oregon, but France is a wonderful place to visit. And dining out in the Loire Valley, even at the simplest little bistro, was a real experience. But," he said, taking another sip, "I hate eating out by myself."

"Oh, I hear you. Makes me feel so conspicuous.

I always think people are staring at me. At home you can at least turn on the TV for company."

Luke nodded his understanding. "Since I came back to Portland, Alex Trebek and I have become very close."

"You like *Jeopardy!*? I pegged you as more of an ESPN guy."

"I'd rather play sports than watch them. But if we're sizing each other up . . ."

He narrowed his eyes, made a show of examining my face. "PBS," he said, snapping his fingers. "You like *Masterpiece Theatre*. And *Nova*. Am I right?"

"Turner Classics. I love old movies. I like knowing good guys from bad guys and being certain that, in the end, the good guy wins."

"Happy endings," Luke said. "Real life ought to come with more of those."

He took another drink. I did the same, then put down my glass and ran my finger around the rim, trying to decide if I should ask the obvious question.

"So . . . you ran away to France for three years. Now you're back and you and Alex Trebek are besties. Divorce?"

He nodded. "Yeah, but that happened a couple of years before I went to France. I came home from the office one day, announced that I was leaving the law firm. Within a month, I opened my carpentry business. Within a year, I knew I would fail if I didn't find a way to offer something other people couldn't. I needed more training. So, I did some research and found a master carpenter in Amboise who was willing to take on an American apprentice, then sold my stuff and booked my ticket. But the marriage was really over on the day I quit the firm. She moved out the next week.

"I get it," he shrugged. "She didn't sign up to be married to a tradesman, and I didn't sign up to work in a job I hated to support a lifestyle I didn't give a damn about. We just wanted different things. No hard feelings. You?"

I put my hands in my lap, felt the indentation at the base of my finger where my ring should have been. "It's . . ."

"Complicated?"

I nodded, but not just because I didn't want to talk about it. It really was complicated. And sad. And I wasn't up for sad just then. Luke was right; real life ought to come with more happy endings. Who do I see to complain about that?

"I should go."

Luke swallowed quickly. "Don't! Stay and have dinner with me."

"I can't. This is just too . . ." The word *dangerous* unexpectedly popped into my mind. I mentally swept it under the rug. "Awkward. But thank you for the drink."

I stood up. Luke did the same but more quickly.

He reached out as if he meant to grab my arm, but I shifted to the side, avoiding his touch.

"Was it because I asked about your ex? Hey, none of my business. We don't have to talk about it. We can talk about old movies. Or our favorite books, or golf . . ."

"Golf?"

"Golf. Goldfish. Anything you want. We can sit here and exchange recipes for all I care, just please, Grace. Sit back down. You can't go."

He sounded a little desperate. I frowned.

"Why not?"

"Because of that."

He pointed across the restaurant. Two servers were walking toward our table with enormous platters of seafood.

"You were late, so I went ahead and ordered about eighty dollars' worth of appetizers," he explained. "I can't eat all that by myself. But if you leave, I'll have to. I am a product of my hardscrabble, clear-your-plate-because-children-are-starving-in-the-third-world upbringing. So I'll have no choice. Come on, Grace. Help me out here."

His voice was pleading. And charming. So charming that I had to smile a little. Luke walked around to my side of the table and pulled my chair out again.

"You said you like oysters, right?"

Chapter 5

Nan

If Nelson were human, I'd have given him a cup of tea and a peach turnover—my standard protocol for people who've suffered a loss. But dogs are different. Suffering comes as more of a shock to dogs because they can't see it coming. Even when unexpected, people have a basic understanding that tragedy comes to everyone eventually and so are more readily comforted by small acts of kindness.

Like people, dogs experience grief in different ways. Some move through it quickly, attaching themselves to someone new so easily that it seems they barely miss the someone who came before. I'm not saying that a dog who attaches quickly to a new human didn't feel love for the one who passed, far from it, but over the years I've noticed that those who had suffered more before their adoption, and were rescued from some traumatic situation, tend to grieve longer and more deeply than most.

What I knew of Nelson's history, related to me by a neighbor familiar with his situation, bore this out. Nelson was just a puppy when Helen Find, his departed owner, discovered him shivering and abandoned by some garbage cans near her garage. He was worm-ridden, flea-infested, and so skinny that Helen assumed he was feral. But when she reached out her hand, the pup got down low and scooted toward her on his belly, frightened, but so eager for love and affection that he took the risk.

From that moment on, Helen and the dog were inseparable, absolutely devoted to each another.

"When the cancer got so bad," the neighbor said, "Helen refused to go to the hospital unless Nelson could come along. Of course, they couldn't do that, so the doctors called hospice. It was too late by then anyway. Do you know that dog never left her side? Not for one minute? And when she finally passed, he whined and cried like his heart was broken. It was almost human. Never saw anything like it," he said.

Helen Find's neighbor sounded surprised. I wasn't. I'd seen it before, and not just in dogs. Nelson and Helen's story was one of true love. Most people don't understand it because they've never experienced it. Those who have, never forget. They can learn love and trust again, but it takes patience, understanding, and time. How much time? There's no way of telling. You just have to wait.

The only thing I could do for Nelson at that

moment was hold him. And so I did, stroking his black and silver head until he fell asleep; then I carried him across the room to Blixen, who had been watching patiently from her bed.

"Here you go, Blix," I whispered.

Blix rolled onto her side and I tucked Nelson up close. Blixen curled herself into a C around Nelson's body, sighed, and closed her eyes. Poor Nelson. I've fostered over a hundred dogs in my lifetime. It's never easy to see them grieve. But it's something I'm called to by temperament, experience, and circumstances.

My Jim was killed in a plane crash when I was only forty-two, so I'm acquainted with grief. But Jim and I had a good life. Apart from our time together being too short, I have no regrets. Jim left me with four wonderful reasons to go on living too.

Jim Junior, whom we called James, was twelve when his dad died. Chrissy, Matt, and Dani were ten, eight, and five. Later, I adopted three more children, Kyle, Brianna, and Emily—all teenagers when they came. Older kids can be hard to place, but they deserve stable homes too. I tried to provide that for all my kids—biological and adopted—as well as an education.

James is a radiologist and Chrissy went into teaching. Matt and Kyle went into business together, designing video games. Brianna is a social worker. Emily married Dan, who opened his own microbrewery near Bend. She's a stay-at-home mom to two-year-old twin boys.

It gets lonely sometimes, now that the kids are grown. But I keep busy; in helping other people I help myself as well. I believe that everything, the good and the bad, happens for a reason and is part of something bigger—purpose with a capital *P*. I also believe we each have an individual purpose, lowercase *p*, that fits in with the grander plan, and that part of the reason we are here is to find it, because everyone matters; each person's contribution, large or small, has an impact.

Losing Jim was just that, a loss, a terrible one. But in enduring that loss, I came to find my purpose—to comfort and nurture others, first our grieving children, then other people's children, now any person or pet who crosses my path and needs what I might have to offer—tea and a turnover, a word of encouragement, a listening ear, a way station on the path to a new home. Nurturing and comforting, that's why I'm here in this place, in this moment. That's my purpose.

And I'm fortunate to have the resources to fulfill it. I'm not wealthy. In fact, I live quite frugally. Insurance and the settlement from the airplane manufacturer allowed me to stay home with the children and keep my house and land. Acre and a half lots are impossible to come by in Portland now. Not a week passes without some developer knocking on my door. I'll never sell.

I was born in this house. My memories are here and so is my garden.

Where else would I have room to grow my tomatoes and artichokes and rhubarb? Six varieties of basil? My clary sage and elephant garlic? And I could never leave my blueberry bushes—my father planted those bushes. Even if I could find a house with sufficient land, it wouldn't have soil like mine. How many cubic yards of compost have I worked into it over the years? My garden soil is black gold. Priceless. And where would I keep the chickens if I moved?

My coop has room for twenty-five birds. When the kids lived at home, I needed that many hens to keep us in eggs. I only keep a half dozen now, but it's nice that they have room to roam. Besides the chickens, there are the dogs to consider.

Normally, I don't have more than two foster dogs at a time so they can stay inside the house. Every now and then the rescue faces a sudden emergency and I'll have to take in several dogs on short notice. That's why I converted the old goat barn into a comfy, state-of-the-art kennel with heated floors, good ventilation, a hot water bathing station, and pens for up to eight dogs. James drove up from Ashland with Leila and the kids and spent a whole week helping me with the remodeling.

That's another reason I'll never leave this house—the kids. The whole crowd and all eight grandchildren show up every summer, second week in July, for our annual Homecoming Week. When the garden is at its peak, and the grandkids are outside hooting and whooping in a wild game of tag while the grown-ups sit on the deck sharing memories and a bottle of wine, there is no place in the world I'd rather be. That's as good as life gets.

No. I'll never sell my house, not for any price. There are certain things money cannot buy. On the other hand, there are times when it comes in awfully handy, which is what prompted me to phone Monica. I knew she was out with Grace, so I only planned to leave a message. I didn't expect her to pick up.

"Why are you answering your phone?"

"Uh . . . because it rang?"

"But you shouldn't be taking calls while you're on your date."

"My date?" Monica sounded confused. "Oh. I ended up not going. The restaurant is slammed and my head is killing me. I'm going to Urgent Care later."

"Oh. Grace was getting all dressed up when I talked to her. She must have been disappointed."

"No, no, she's fine. I sent a text, told her and Luke to have fun without me."

"Wait," I said slowly, certain I must have heard her wrong. "You mean Grace was already at the restaurant when you sent a text to say you weren't coming? She'd be having dinner with a total stranger."

"So? What's the difference? It isn't like I know him either."

"She knows *you*. That would have made it less awkward. Don't you think . . ."

I let my question trail off, realizing that there was no point. Monica has a good heart, the best. Look at how she'd taken in Desmond. He's such a sweet dog, but Newfoundlands are so enormous. She'd give you the shirt off her back if you asked for it, but she's not the most emotionally sensitive person I've ever met.

"She'll be fine," Monica said breezily. "Luke's a nice guy and she needs to get out more. So, what's up?"

Between Monica's cut-to-the-chase tone and the background music of banging pots and pans, I knew the restaurant was busy and she had work to do.

"Nothing important. We can talk later," I said.

"It's okay. I've got a minute. What do you— Hang on a sec."

Monica moved the phone away from her mouth, but she was shouting so I had no trouble hearing.

"Hey! There's a piccata order for table six sitting here! Think one of you could quit examining your navel long enough to take it to the customer?"

Listening in, it occurred to me that when it came

to running a restaurant kitchen, there are worse qualities than a shortage of emotional sensitivity. Monica knows how to get things done. But the yelling couldn't be good for a headache. Before I said goodbye, I'd recommend she drink cinnamon tea instead of wasting money at Urgent Care. There's nothing better for headaches—and nothing truly wrong with Monica, I was sure of it.

Too bad I didn't have a remedy for Grace's problems. She wasn't exactly shy, but she was uncomfortable around new people. It took weeks for her to open up to me and Monica. Now, there she was, stuck having dinner with a complete stranger. Headache or not, Monica should have had a little more consideration.

Poor Grace. What was she doing right now? Whatever it was, I was sure she was absolutely miserable.

Chapter 6

Grace

If I were a prisoner on death row, requesting my last meal, I'd ask for a dozen succulent, briny, coppery-tasting Olympia Bay oysters. They are—pun intended—to die for. So delicious, so decadent that I'd *almost* be willing to delve into the sad and complicated explanation of my sad and complicated life in exchange for them.

But I didn't have to. Luke and I made a pact to steer clear of personal stuff and just enjoy a good meal and some inconsequential conversation, starting with our all-time favorite TV shows.

Luke said he liked *The Office* because sometimes you just want to laugh and not think. I like reruns of *I Love Lucy* for the same reason. Moving on to our favorite movies—I picked *When Harry Met Sally* and he picked *Star Wars*—both pretty predictable.

He told me a little bit about his work—not the business part or the details of how he'd gotten into it—but about what it felt like to actually work with wood.

"Even if you're using a machine, sanding wood

is time-consuming, but I like to do it by hand. It's almost meditative." He smiled. "Kind of magical too. Think about it—the only way to make that piece of wood smooth, to refine and reveal its true character and purpose, is by rubbing this piece of rough, gritty paper over it, again and again and again. I spend a lot of time up front, thinking about the design of a piece, but once I start in with the actual work—the cutting, and hammering, and sanding, and finishing—I don't have to think. Maybe because I've been doing it for so long now. It's like, at some point, instinct kicks in, or muscle memory. When I'm in that space where I don't have to think, just do, I'm more myself than at any other time."

He looked at me, looking at him, and laughed self-consciously.

"Sorry. It's hard to explain. And I'm talking too much."

"No, you're not. And I completely get what you mean," I said, thinking about my quilt blocks, but I didn't tell him why and, thankfully, he didn't ask. I could tell he wanted to, but he stuck to our bargain, steered clear of the complicated stuff.

Even so, I learned a lot about Luke Pascal that evening. One of the more telling parts of the conversation came when we discussed books.

I used to read a lot. Growing up, books were my refuge and the characters in them my best and sometimes only friends. In the previous two years, I'd only cracked the spine of one book and still hadn't found time to finish it.

Luke's reading list was long and literary—*No Country for Old Men, The Book Thief, The Glass Castle, The Girl with the Dragon Tattoo*. One of his choices, however, surprised me. A lot.

"*Twilight*?" I gasped, practically choking on my wine. "Seriously?"

He popped a piece of calamari into his mouth. "Hey, just because a book appeals to popular taste doesn't mean it isn't well-written or doesn't examine important themes—good versus evil, change versus tradition, vampire versus"—he furrowed his brow, pretending to concentrate—"other vampires. . . ."

He reached for the last calamari, but I beat him to it, popped the crunchy morsel into my mouth, chewed slowly, then picked up my wineglass.

"Uh-huh. Sure. I get it."

"Fine," he huffed. "You found me out. I'm a fifteen-year-old girl trapped in the body of a middle-aged carpenter. Happy?"

I choked so hard that the wine went up my nose and splashed onto my dress. Looking down at the wet spot, I started to laugh, and laugh, and laugh.

"Wow. After only two glasses of wine? Either I'm a lot funnier than I used to be, or you're the biggest lightweight in the world."

"I'm not much of a drinker," I admitted.

"No kidding? I'd never have guessed." He took

a gulp of his wine and thumped the glass onto the table. "Hey, do you want to dance?"

"What? Dance? No!"

"Oh, come on." He stood up. "The band is really good. Can't let it go to waste."

The band—really more of a combo—*was* good, but until Luke mentioned it I hadn't noticed. To me it was just background noise. Was he serious? He didn't really expect me to get up and dance. Did he? He held out his hand.

"I can't. Really, Luke. I'm a terrible dancer."

"Doesn't matter." He flashed a cocky smile. "I'm good enough for both of us. My parents taught ballroom. Follow my lead. I won't let you look stupid. Promise."

This was not a good idea, I was sure of it. My brain told me I should say good night then and there. But my body, full with food and warm with wine, hypnotized by those amber eyes, wasn't quite as sure. I reached for his hand and he helped me up, his strong arm a counterweight in my hesitant ascent.

"Nobody else is dancing," I protested, becoming nervous as we approached the shiny, pristine, possibly never-before-used, parquet dance floor.

"More space for us," Luke said, taking my left hand in his right.

"People are looking at us!" I hissed.

"They're jealous."

"But—"

"Grace. Have you ever been to this restaurant before?" I shook my head. "Neither have I. What do you care if they look? We'll never see these people again."

Before I could argue, Luke stepped off in time to the music, moving with such surety that I had no choice but to follow, trusting that he knew what he was doing.

And he did.

Which is not to say that the touch of Luke's hand suddenly transformed me into Ginger Rogers. There were several missteps, some left turns that should have been right, but Luke covered for me and, true to his word, never let me look stupid. Two songs in, I realized that the more I relaxed and quit trying to think, the easier it was. Four songs in, I was actually starting to enjoy myself—a little.

The fifth song was fun, peppy with a Latin beat. Near the end, Luke raised his hand and mine, then put a gentle pressure on my shoulder to send me under the arch of our arms. I twirled like a top, around and around, all the way across the floor. My skirt flared out so wide it looked like the flamingos were about to take flight. The song ended and I nearly collapsed from dizziness and laughter.

"See? You're having fun," he said, holding out his hand for another dance.

"Can't," I puffed, my chest heaving. "Need to catch my breath."

"One more," he urged as the band started playing. "Come on. It's a slow one."

I took a big breath. "Okay. One more."

Luke led me to the middle of the floor and laid his hand flat on my back. I rested my fingertips on his shoulder and looked into his face, watching for his silent countdown, three small and steady nods, before stepping off.

A few measures in, the keyboardist put a muted trumpet to his lips, blowing a smoky, bluesy twilight tune. The bass player plucked out a pulsing harmony, as steady as a beating heart, and the drummer circled the snare with a metallic brush, making a scratching sound that spoke of closing time. The music was slow, almost too slow. Luke shortened the length of his stride and the distance between us. Steps became a shuffle. The soles of my shoes brushed the floor, soft as a whisper.

We moved in unison, drawing closer, meeting in the middle, our bodies touching. My head turned instinctively, feeling suddenly heavy, the way it does just before sleep, sinking lower, and lower, until my cheek rested on Luke's shoulder.

The music was sweet in my ears. I felt so relaxed and good. I closed my eyes. If not for the steady boundaries of Luke's arms holding me close, I might have melted. I was aware of his breathing and my own, of the warm imprint of his hands between my shoulders and the curving swell where my waist became my hip.

I could stay here forever. Just like this. Forever.

And then I remembered.

My eyes opened, my head lifted. I was suddenly aware of my left hand and the indentation at the base of my finger, the place where my ring should have been.

"I have to go."

"Now?" Luke asked, his eyes opened too. "Why?"

"I just do. I'm sorry, Luke. I can't . . ."

I stepped backward, disentangling myself from his arms, regaining my grip on reality. I walked to the table and he followed me, asking questions that I chose not to answer, saying only what I'd said before, that I was sorry, that I had to go.

And I did. I *had* to.

I grabbed my purse and headed for the door, my stride so long and rapid that I was almost running. He followed me again but gave up after a few paces, falling away, letting me go. It was a relief. I got in the car and drove off, but not to my condo. There was someplace else I needed to be.

Twice in one day, I was late.

Chapter 7

Grace

The lobby was deserted and the reception desk unmanned, but I didn't need directions. I knew the way—left from the lobby, right at the corridor, to the end of the hall. A woman with brown hair striped gray at the part looked up from her desk.

I forced a smile. "Hi, Alicia. How's he doing?"

"Hi, Grace. I didn't think you were coming. I just checked on him. He's fine."

Fine means the same. The same as yesterday, and last week, and last month, and last year. The same, not better. Better was not going to happen. Now there were only two possibilities—the same and worse.

"Well . . . I'll get out of your hair. I'm just going to stay for a few minutes."

"Are you okay?"

She frowned, examining my face. Alicia knows me pretty well by now.

"Busy. You know how it is. But I'm fine," I said.

I was fine. I was the same. Or would be. I'd

had a momentary lapse in judgment. It wouldn't happen again. I wouldn't let it.

I tiptoed into Jamie's room, thinking he might be asleep, and felt an involuntary jolt run through my body, the kind of sensation you get from walking across thick carpeting in socks and then touching something metallic—a short, sharp shock that makes your muscles twitch and your breath catch.

Even after all that time, coming up on two years, when I saw my once-oak-strong husband, the man with deep roots, lying in bed, shrunken and dependent on the ministrations of nurses to eat, control his bowels, and simply survive, I felt that same inward gasp. Sometimes it was hard to make myself believe the body in the bed truly belonged to my Jamie.

He was awake, looking toward the doorway as if he'd been waiting for me. Maybe he was. I couldn't tell. That was the worst part of all of this. Though his eyes looked the same as they always had, deep steely blue, fringed with thick bristles of shoe-polish-black lashes, there was no way for me to tell what he thought or didn't think. Or if he could think at all. The doctors said no. At times like this, I wasn't so sure.

I stood next to his bed, but his gaze remained fixed on the open doorway. I brushed hair from his face. Still, he watched the door. Who was he waiting for?

"You need a trim," I said. "I can bring the scissors next time I come."

He didn't respond. I didn't expect him to. That didn't stop me from talking.

When Jamie was still in the coma, he never opened his eyes or responded in any way. For a time he couldn't even breathe on his own. The medical staff urged me to talk to him anyway. They said it might help him recover, so I did, telling him about the little inanities of my day—how beautiful the trees were when autumn arrived, turning orange, red, and gold; how they'd raised the cable prices so I canceled the service; how I'd met Nan and Monica, adopted Maisie, found a new recipe for chili, or a sweater on sale at Macy's; how I'd decided to stitch two dozen cardinal Christmas ornaments, made from red felt and embroidered with gold and black thread, to give to the nurses. Little things, ordinary things, the daily details of living life and passing the time, waiting for something to happen, good or bad. Stupid things that I felt stupid saying when all I really wanted to do was sob and beg him to wake up and open his eyes.

One day, he did.

I was so phenomenally happy, convinced that it was only a matter of time before he recovered completely. Talking to him was easier after that. It became a habit that stuck with me even after I was educated about the stages of recovery for brain injury and understood that the progression from coma, to persistent vegetative state, to minimally conscious, to conscious isn't always a continuous line. Some people start at A and progress all the way to Z. Others get stuck and stay there forever. Jamie got stuck.

He could breathe on his own, had sleep and wake cycles, blinked, sometimes followed things with his eyes. He could move his limbs, but not on command, laugh or cry, but not as an appropriate emotional response—it was just something he did.

I pulled a chair up close to the bed.

"Sorry I'm late. I went out to dinner at The Fish House. That's why the dress," I explained, fanning the skirt, spreading the wings of the flamingos. "Monica was supposed to come too; I never would have gone otherwise. But then she had a crisis and canceled at the last second. So it was me and Luke, and—"

Jamie made a choking sound. That happened fairly often, but I jumped to my feet, looked into those eyes that looked through me, making sure he was okay.

"Babe, listen to me. I wouldn't have gone if I'd known that Monica was going to cancel. But I couldn't walk off and leave him alone, could I? The dancing was a mistake. I see that now. But there was nothing to it. I thought it would be nice, this once, to have a nice dinner, wear a pretty dress, and spend time with a handsome—"

The words caught in my throat.

"I'm sorry. I didn't mean it that way. I just wanted *not* to be alone. Can you blame me?" I asked, lifting my head toward the ceiling, speaking to the empty air, the invisible, wordless presence I felt pressing in on me. "I'm thirty-one years old. I'm human. I miss having a man to talk to and laugh with. I miss being admired and important to someone. Is that so wrong? It's not like any of this is my fault!"

Jamie coughed again and I took his hand, feeling for the spot on his thumb where the skin was still thick, a final testament to all the things those hands were once able to do.

"I know. I know. It wasn't anybody's fault. You were just being who you are. But, don't you see? It was just dinner, a dress, a dance. I didn't see any harm in it. I was just being me, being who I was when we were still us. Do you remember?"

Jamie turned his head and gazed toward the empty doorway, resuming his vigil. He was tired, I could tell. Soon he would sleep. I would stay until he did.

I sat down in the side chair, on the seat cushion that had molded to fit my frame over these long months, and pulled out the clear zippered pouch I carried with me everywhere, filled with scraps of red, green, white, brown, and blue. My habit of carrying handwork was an old one. When

80

you spend a lot of time in hospitals, clinics, and doctor's waiting rooms, it's a good idea to bring along something to do.

I pulled out a big, eight-inch square of plain, cream-colored fabric and smoothed it out across my lap. It was more of a patch than a block, but I planned to put it in the center of the quilt. It would be the biggest individual patch of fabric in the quilt.

Measuring from side to side, I was the biggest girl in my high school. At the start of senior year, I stood five foot five and weighed 228 pounds.

Like this block, I tried hard to blend in, to go unnoticed. It's a coping mechanism familiar to most overweight kids or anyone who was bullied as a child. You quickly learn that the way to keep from being picked on is to attract as little attention as possible. And so you become wallpaper, try to blend into the background and go unnoticed because it seems the only way to survive.

Yet no one truly wants to become invisible. Everyone—no matter how fat, or slow, or tall, or ugly, or beautiful—wants to be important and loved, the center of someone's world.

When I was eighteen, Jamie Saunders saw me.

He wasn't the smartest guy in the class, or the best looking, or really the best anything. But everybody in school knew and liked Jamie. He was friendly to everyone, said hello to every single person he passed in the hall, regardless of their social standing, even me. But our first real conversation took place in the lobby of the local medical center, near the beginning of senior year.

I was sitting in a corner of the lobby, my face to the wall, crying. I felt his presence even before he spoke and was wiping away tears when he asked if I was okay, then sat down next to me on the love seat, even though there wasn't much room. He was wearing a light blue chambray shirt.

"What's wrong?" he asked. "It's okay, you can tell me."

Something about the way he said it made me believe it was true.

I told him about my failed appointment and how the doctor had denied my request, saying I was too young and not obese enough to justify the risk of surgery.

"That's the first time in my life anybody, especially a doctor, said I wasn't fat enough. Wish I'd brought along a tape recorder. I could play it back for my mom."

I tried to make a joke of it, but couldn't.

"What does he want me to do? Buy a case of potato chips so I can get fat enough to finally get thin? It's so stupid!"

Jamie frowned. "I'm sorry, Grace. That really sucks."

It did. Hearing him say so didn't change anything, but it made me feel better. I said thanks and asked where he was going.

"Orthopedist appointment. I went out for cross-country and my knees hurt. My mom wants me to get checked out."

Penny was standing with her back to us, looking out the window toward a small garden with orange mums and a fountain.

"Your mom is waiting," I said. "Don't worry about me. I'm fine. I mean, I will be."

"You sure?"

I nodded.

"I think so too," he said, and for some reason, I believed him. He seemed trustworthy. And that's how it all started.

I took some patches from the bag, the same off-white I was using in the center and some blue chambray, scraps from a shirt Jamie would never wear again. This block, a friendship star, would represent our beginning, a moment of kindness, a sea change neither of us saw coming.

I threaded my needle and started sewing, as I did every night, passing time, marking time, keeping my eyes on my stitches, refusing to look at the door or think about who Jamie was waiting for or when they might come.

Chapter 8

Nan

Monica's normal speaking voice lies somewhere between bass drum and fog horn. But with Nelson asleep on Monica's lap, I had to turn the water down so I could hear what she said when she leaned forward, searching Grace's face.

"So? Did you sleep with him?"

"Of course not!" Grace snapped. "What a thing to ask!"

"Then what's the big deal?" Monica looked disappointed. "The way you were acting, I thought you were getting ready to tell us all the sordid details. Sheesh."

"The point is that I *wanted* to sleep with him," Grace said, her expression as pained as her voice. "Or at least that I thought about it. For a minute."

"Who wouldn't? You're not made of stone, are you? Luke is gorgeous. Not my type, of course," Monica said with a shrug. "As we all know, I prefer my men short, dark, and serially unfaithful. But, aside from him being too good for me, what woman with a pulse *wouldn't* want to sleep with Luke Pascal?"

"That's fine for them," Grace countered. "Or for you. But I can't. I'm married."

Monica's smile faded. She dropped her teasing tone.

"Are you?"

"Stop it, Monica."

"Grace, it's a fair question. *Are* you?"

I shut the sink water off completely, cocking an ear for Grace's response.

"Well, I think you should sleep with him," Monica said breezily when Grace failed to answer. "Somebody should. He's too good to waste."

"Go right ahead. Be my guest."

Monica spooned a bite of baked apple into her mouth and shook her head.

"Uh-uh. He's too young for me. The whole cougar thing sounds good, but it almost never works out. Also, not Italian." She shook her head again. "Can't be me. Has to be you."

"Won't be," Grace said. "Not with Luke, not with anybody. For better or worse, Monica. Till death do us part. That's what married means."

"Sure. I get it," Monica said, spreading her hands. "And I admire your loyalty. And, yes, technically and legally, you're married. But isn't marriage more than a promise and a piece of paper? It's supposed to be a relationship, right? Thus the phrase 'marital relations.' You haven't had either of those, a relationship or relations, for close to two years. Over all this time, you've been there for Jamie, which is great. But he hasn't been there for you—"

"Because he can't!"

Grace is normally the quiet one of the group and not given to emotional outbursts. But she shoved her chair back from the table so hard that the sound of the legs scraping on the floor woke Blixen, who had been sleeping by the back door. Picking up on her distress, Blix got to her feet, crossed the room, and laid her head on Grace's knee. It didn't seem to help.

"What is wrong with you, Monica? Why would you say something like that? Don't you think that he wants to—"

Monica raised her hands. "Okay, sorry. I didn't mean it like that. I'm not saying Jamie did anything wrong or abandoned you. He didn't plan or deserve this. But neither did you. Think about it, Grace. Think about what you just said— for better or worse, till *death* do you part.

"Jamie hasn't looked at you, or talked to you, or engaged with anyone in any way since the accident. At this point, his life is like your marriage—a technicality."

Monica leaned even closer, trying to lock eyes with Grace.

"Don't say that to me, Monica. I mean it. Do it again and I'll leave."

Grace, who wouldn't look at Monica, started

stroking Blixen's head, but hard, as if she were pressing out a layer of stiff dough. Monica fiddled with her fork, then looked at me.

"What do you think?"

I took the copper kettle off the stove, carried it to the table, and filled the cups.

"I think it's time to talk about something else."

Apart from the gurgling sound coming from the kettle spout, the room was silent. I sat down, sipped my tea, and waited. You can't force these things. Nobody in the world wants to be instructed or lectured. Even when you have something to offer, it's better to wait to be asked—at least if you actually want to help someone.

Grace, who had eaten no more than a third of her dessert, pushed her bowl to Monica's side of the table. A peace offering.

"Fine," Monica muttered, picking up her spoon. "What should we talk about?"

Monica looked at me and I looked at Grace. We could talk, really talk, or we could change the subject and chat. It was up to her.

After a moment, she said, "I just don't understand what happened. All we were doing was dancing. Why should I suddenly be flooded with feelings for a man I hardly know? It felt so strange and out of control."

She looked toward me, inviting my answer.

"Could it be pointing to something that's

missing in your life?" I asked. "Grace, when we talked on the phone yesterday, you were so excited about dressing up and going out. I've never heard you sound so happy. Between work and worries about Jamie's care, you're under constant stress. How long has it been since Jamie's accident?"

"Twenty months. He fell in June. It was three weeks before he woke up. Two weeks after that, he was admitted to Landsdowne."

"Almost two years. Are you really surprised that a little attention from a nice-looking man left you so vulnerable? You're only human. And, Monica, this daily battle to run the restaurant and deal with the kids is wearing on you too," I said.

"Look, I think you've both been doing an amazing job of coping in terrible circumstances. But if you're going to keep coping, you need a bit of joy in your lives."

"But we've got this," Grace said, spreading her hands. "We've got one another, and our Monday nights. I don't know what I'd do without them."

I smiled. "I know. I feel the same. But one night a week isn't quite enough to hang a whole life on, is it? When you were young, before you got married, what did you do for fun?"

"Jamie and I got married at nineteen," Grace said, "so we're talking about high school. Back then, my main hobbies were watching reruns of *The Andy Griffith Show* and eating entire cheesecakes, preferably at the same time. I'm not sure it made me happy—just kind of damped down the depression."

"Cooking *used* to make me happy," Monica said. "As a mostly ignored child descended from a long line of stoic Lutherans from cold climates, I had fantasies about growing up and having the big, happy, vaguely Italian family."

She smiled to herself. "I'd dream of an over-crowded dinner table, people laughing and arguing and yelling, and talking with their hands, devouring huge platters of pasta and veal and sausage, sauces made with tomatoes, and cream, and red wine, all prepared by me, the mother of this big, boisterous brood. When I met Vince, it seemed like a dream come true. Here was this handsome, passionate Italian man with two kids—a good start on a ready-made family.

"But, look," she said in a practical tone, "I didn't kid myself. I knew that Vince and I weren't exactly star-crossed lovers, but we liked each other. I was actually excited about being a stepmother. At my age, I knew it wasn't likely, but I kind of hoped there'd be time for Vince and me to pop out a bambino of our own, maybe even two, before my biological clock struck midnight.

"Well, Vince was passionate all right," she said, bitterly. "Just not about me. While I took care of his restaurant, house, and kids, he was out bedding every blonde in Portland. What a chump I was.

"Anyway," she muttered before taking another swallow of tea, "that kind of spoiled cooking for me. Now it's just a job, an exhausting grind. As far as the kids, if we could manage to sit down at the table without a fight breaking out, I'd still enjoy cooking for them. But I've given up."

"Let's put cooking aside for now," I said. "When you were a kid, what else did you like to do?"

"Anything they told me not to."

She grinned wickedly and I couldn't help but laugh. Monica's sarcasm can be a little hard to take sometimes, but there is something truly lovable about her.

"Hey," Grace said. "I hate to break up the party, but I have to get going. I need to be at the office early tomorrow."

"I should get going too," Monica said, then scooped Nelson gently from her lap and set him down on the floor.

While I got coats from the closet, Grace and Monica put the cups into the dishwasher and tidied up the kitchen. When they were getting ready to leave, Monica turned to me and said, "I totally forgot, you called the restaurant last night. What did you need?"

"Oh, nothing that urgent," I said, and opened

the front door. "I'm just worried about the rescue. End-of-the-year contributions were down and medical expenses are up. We need to come up with a way to raise some money and I thought you might have some ideas. We can talk about it next week."

"Come by the restaurant tomorrow," she said. "We'll do a little brainstorming."

"Thanks. I have to take Nelson to the vet in the morning. We'll drop by after."

Grace zipped up her jacket and looked at Monica. "I almost forgot—what did the doctor say about your headaches?"

"She told me to take some aspirin. Hey! Just because it wasn't serious doesn't mean it couldn't have been," she protested. "Come on, Grace. Quit laughing. I had to put up with enough of that from Hazel."

"Hazel?"

"The Urgent Care doctor. She works the four to midnight shift."

"Wait. You're not only on a first-name basis with the Urgent Care doctor, but you know her work schedule?"

Grace, still chuckling, gave me a squeeze and headed toward her car with Monica on her heels.

"You know," Monica said, "you're going to feel really terrible if something bad ever does happen to me."

"You're right. I will," Grace said. *"If."*

• • •

After waving them off, I went back inside, turning out the lights on my way back to the kitchen. The grandfather clock was ticking steadily, the dogs were snoring, and the house felt too big. It always does after visitors leave. It would pass. It was easier when the kids were still at home. Now I have to work at it, be more intentional. That's what I was trying to explain to Monica and Grace.

I poured the lukewarm tea water down the drain and noticed that the kettle looked dull. I hadn't planned on polishing the copper for another week, but now was as good a time as any and I didn't feel tired. In fact, I was still a little restless, like I had been at dinner. Maybe I ought to stick to herbal tea, eliminate the caffeine entirely? I'd been feeling restless so often of late.

I took my collection of copper down from the pot rack—three pots, two saucepans, and seven gelatin molds that rarely saw use anymore, which was a shame. Gelatin salads are such fun to eat and so refreshing. Unfortunately they'd fallen out of fashion. But fashions come and go, so I held on to my copper molds and polished them every other month. When the gelatin renaissance arrives, I'll be ready.

I mixed up some lemon juice with baking soda, putting the mixture on a clean cloth, and got to work, rubbing the surface of a saucepan in little circles, smiling as the color began showing beneath the layer of tarnish. It's a very satisfying thing, polishing copper.

The phone rang. It was awfully late for someone to be calling. Had Grace or Monica left something behind?

"Hello." There was coughing on the other end of the line, a loose, wet, ragged sound. I knew right away who was making it. "Dani?"

"Mom? I'm sick. I need money for a place to stay."

"Where are you?"

"Under a bridge. It's freezing. You have to give me some money."

I closed my eyes and pressed a fist to my lips.

"Dani, I can't do that."

"But I'm sick! I have a fever! Don't you care? What kind of mother are you?"

She started coughing again. I felt my heart clutch and my resolve begin to crack. But I couldn't crack. I'd been down this road before.

"Dani, I'm not going to give you money for drugs."

"It's *not* for drugs! Why don't you ever listen? I *told* you, I'm sick and need money for a place to stay." Her tone went from demanding to wheedling. "I'm freezing, Mom. It's starting to snow. Bring me some money. Please?"

I looked out the window. It was cold, very cold. But it wasn't snowing. In former days, I would have believed her. Now I knew better. Everything that Dani said required confirmation. She was a habitual liar.

Though, I reminded myself, it wasn't really Dani who was lying to me. It was the drugs. Dani was sick. The absence of heroin in her system resulted in sweating, shaking, weakness, nausea, and even hallucinations. In this state, she was a hostage to her addiction. In some ways, so was I.

"Honey, listen to me. You need help. I've talked to counselors at a very good rehab, a nice place. Tell me where to find you. I'll take you—"

I didn't get to finish. She cut me off, spitting out curses and accusations with the same kind of fury and fear that grips a wild animal caught in a trap. I tried to talk over her, to make her see reason, but it was no use. There was more cursing, then a strangled cry of frustration before the phone went dead.

I stood there, heart pounding, listening to the dull buzz of the dial tone.

I wiped away tears and went back to my copper, rubbing so hard that my arms burned, refusing to stop until every shadow and stain was gone and each piece glowed like the embers of a fading fire.

Chapter 9

Grace

My alarm went off at five the next morning, as usual. After breakfast, I took Maisie for a walk, said hello to Sunny and Z, the homeless couple who lived in the next block, and patted their dog, Kujo, on the head. In the days since my encounter with Luke, I was trying to be more outgoing. It had been a little embarrassing, walking up and introducing myself, but Sunny and Z were very friendly. Why had I waited so long to speak to them?

After changing into my work clothes, I went to Landsdowne to see Jamie. The nursing shift changes at seven, so it was a good time to check in with them. Then I drove to the office, arriving just in time for the monthly companywide meeting.

Those meetings were usually pretty boring and a waste of time. They started with announcements from HR—reminders to clean old lunches out of the break room refrigerator, pitches to sign up for the 401(k) plan, that sort of thing. Then the higher-ups gave the previous month's performance numbers and a speech on doing better in the month to come. After that, they announced the employee of the month and everybody ate bagels.

Theoretically, it was a mandatory meeting, but about a third of the office usually didn't bother to show, or only came in at the end for bagels. This Tuesday, everybody was there. Everybody. And they were dead silent. Something wasn't right.

The chairs were nearly full. My four bosses—Jack Shapiro, Pete Ryan, Mark DeLoitte, and Ava Goddard—were sitting together in the sixth row, but there were no seats with them, so I walked to the back of the room. I found a spot against the wall and stood next to Denise Fine, who worked in accounting.

"What's going on?" I whispered.

"Not sure," she said, talking out of the side of her mouth. "But something. There've been rumors."

"What kind of rumors?"

Denise shifted her eyes to the front of the room and a chair on the far left, occupied by a tall man with a long, thin face. I'd never seen him before. He was sitting next to Mert Hanson, president of the company.

"See that guy? His name is Gavin Nutting. I overheard somebody from HR say that he's going—"

Before Denise could finish the sentence, Mert

Hanson went to the front of the room and thanked everyone for coming.

"Judging from the turnout, I can see that the rumor mill has been working overtime." He smiled, as if expecting people to chuckle, but nobody really did. "Well, the rumors are true. After twenty-two years, I'm stepping down as president of Hewlett and Hanson. It's been a great privilege to—"

Mr. Hanson stopped in midsentence, sniffed, cleared his throat, and looked down at his shoes.

"Sorry. I . . . uh . . . sorry. I didn't mean to get so emotional." He let out a short, awkward laugh, then looked to the front row of chairs and the tall, thin man sitting on the left. "You know, I think it might be better to just let your new boss, Gavin Nutting, take it from here. Gavin?"

Gavin stood up. The two men shook hands and changed places. After a few words of praise for Mr. Hanson and his leadership, Gavin cut to the chase.

"Yesterday, Hewlett and Hanson was purchased by Spector Partners, a division of Carmond-Fox International. As you probably know, Spector is one of the largest commercial real-estate companies in the nation, with offices in twenty-four states."

Gavin smiled, moving his eyes from left to right across the room, as though he was trying to make eye contact with everyone present.

"I'm sure you're all worried about changes that might be coming. Anytime a company is purchased there must be a merging of cultures. But the good news for all of you is that you're now part of the Spector family. As part of that family, you'll be eligible for our generous benefits package and bonus program, and have greater opportunities for advancement.

"Now, I am sure you all have questions and concerns, but believe me when I say there is nothing to worry about. Spector purchased Hewlett and Hanson because we liked what we saw. We have no immediate plans to make any sweeping changes, so the best thing for all of you is . . ."

No immediate plans?

That's when I stopped listening and started worrying. I'd been down this road before, back in Minnesota when the bank I worked for was bought by another bank, and half the teller jobs were eliminated, including mine. There wasn't much work in our little town. I'd had to take a waitressing job with terrible hours and worse pay.

My fingers clenched into fists so tight I could feel my nails pressing into the flesh of my palms. My heart started racing and, for a moment, it felt like I'd forgotten to breathe. I needed this job. I didn't like it, but I *needed* it. More importantly, Jamie needed it. The salary I earned at Hewlett and Hanson paid for groceries, the mortgage, my car payment, and twenty percent of the cost of Jamie's care at Landsdowne. The remaining eighty percent was picked up by company insurance.

If I lost my job . . .

The meeting was over. Everybody got up and started milling around, talking nervously. Denise Fine was wiping away tears. She'd been with the company since the very beginning. I wanted to comfort her, but I was ten seconds away from a full-blown panic attack. I knew I had to get out of there before I lost it.

The aisles were jammed with bodies and there was no easy path to the door. Pushing my way through the crowd, I accidentally bumped into somebody and muttered an apology. Gavin Nutting turned around.

"Don't worry about it," he said, and introduced himself, even though there wasn't a person in the room who didn't know who he was. "And you are?"

"I'm Grace. Grace Saunders."

I took his outstretched hand. His grip wasn't viselike, but close.

"Oh, yes," he said, nodding. "Your husband had a fall, hiking accident. I've heard about you."

The way he said it told me there was plenty to worry about.

• • •

"Grace? Grace, are you in there?"

Ava Goddard knocked on the door of the bathroom stall. I was leaning with my forehead resting against the wall, my heart racing. I felt too breathless to answer. She pounded the door again so hard that I could feel the vibration through the wall.

"I know you're in there, Grace. Open up."

I extended my right arm and released the lock. Ava opened the door.

"Oh, crap. Look at you," she said, her voice a mixture of pity and disgust. "Hang on a second, Grace. I'll be right back."

I didn't care if she came back or not. I was too busy trying to quell the stampede of panic flooding my body to care. I heard a metallic thunk as she locked the bathroom's outer door, then the rustling of paper and the running of water.

"Sit down." She grasped my shoulder, guiding me toward the toilet, then helped me sit down on the lid. "Put your head down and breathe into this, slowly."

Ava handed me a small white paper bag. I held it to my mouth and breathed. When the danger of hyperventilation passed, I realized the bag was meant for sanitary disposal.

"Very resourceful," I said when I could breathe again.

100

"I'm good in an emergency. I used to be a nurse." She frowned. "You still look terrible. Here. Put this on the back of your neck."

She handed me some wet paper towels and I laid them on my neck as instructed. The threat of nausea ebbed, as did the sense of panic and impending doom.

"You were a nurse?" I asked.

Ava was one of my four bosses, the one who hired me, actually, the same week Jamie and I moved to Portland so he could begin his paramedic training. I'd worked for her close to two years, but the only thing I knew about her personal life was that she was single, liked to vacation in Kauai, shop in the Collectors section at Nordstrom—the department with all the designer stuff—owned a penthouse in the Pearl District, drove a Lexus, and took soy milk in her coffee. That was it.

It wasn't that she was a cold person or a bad boss—in fact, she was a pretty good boss. She'd never treated me unfairly or talked down to me. But she was very focused. She worked hard, kept her private life private, and held her cards close.

"I was," she said. "A long time ago and only for three years."

"Why'd you stop?"

She handed me another wet paper towel. I pressed it to my forehead.

"Because I got tired of working all the hours on God's green earth and having absolutely nothing to show for it. Because I like being in control of my life. And because I like having money," she said.

"Women aren't supposed to say that out loud. But I don't know why. We eat, too, don't we? We have mortgages and car payments. And *very* expensive handbags." She smiled at me. "Better?"

I squashed the paper towels into a soggy ball in my fist and nodded.

"Ava. Do you think they're going to fire people?"

Her smile fled.

"Yes."

"Me?"

"I don't know," she said. "The truth is, you're expensive to keep around, Grace. And you missed a lot of work at first, took a lot of personal days—"

"But that wasn't my fault," I protested. "Jamie's accident was . . . an *accident*. My husband nearly died! He was in a coma for weeks. What was I supposed to do? Yes, I know his care has been expensive. But the insurance—"

"Goes up every single year," Ava said. "Like clockwork. When a company has an employee with extraordinarily expensive and ongoing medical bills, then the clockwork moves even faster and the rates climb even higher for the whole company."

The nausea returned. I pressed the ball of soggy paper towels to my neck.

"But Mr. Hanson never said—"

Ava tilted her head to the side. She wouldn't divulge private conversations within management, but she didn't have to. Her face said it all. I'd been a topic of conversation in the past and it was likely that I would be again in the future. The reason I so desperately needed this job, the good insurance coverage that provided for Jamie's care, was the thing that jeopardized my chances of keeping it.

"You really think they'd fire me?"

"I think they'd fire anybody who doesn't add to the bottom line. Including me."

"What should I do?"

She gave me that same look, the deciding-how-much-to-say look.

"The only thing you can do, Grace. Become indispensable."

Chapter 10

Nan

I didn't sleep well, tossing and turning, worrying about Dani. How was she? Where was she?

In the morning, the skies were, if not exactly blue, a lighter shade of gray than usual, so I quickly did my chores, grabbed two leashes from the hook by the back door, and jingled my keys. Blixen, who knew the signal, jumped from her bed and came running, excited to go for a ride. Nelson followed, his legs moving like pistons as he tried to keep pace, excited because his new friend was excited.

Though the famous rose gardens were dormant at that time of year, the bushes cut back and the branches bare, Washington Park was still a nice place for a walk. The grass was green and spongy beneath my feet, the air perfumed by the rich loam of the flowerbeds and a whiff of pine from nearby stands of evergreens. We walked for over an hour, until I was sure both pups got a good workout, then drove over to Hillside Animal Hospital for Nelson's checkup.

Hillside is on the other side of the river from

my place, but I'd gone there for years. Dr. Kelly is a great vet. He's originally from Scotland but doesn't have much of an accent anymore, not unless he decides to put it on, as he often does when he's joking. It's a plus when your vet is smart *and* has a sense of humor. And nice. He gives me discounts on medication and services for all of my foster dogs.

Dr. Kelly clicked the light on his otoscope and peered into Nelson's ears. "Good boy. Thanks for holding still. Uh-oh. That left ear is a little infected." He looked up at me. "I'll give you a prescription for that and we'll give him a rabies booster today. The teeth need cleaning too. Other than that, he looks good. You find a home for him yet?"

"Not yet. You're not in the market for a new best friend, are you, Malcolm?"

"Tempting. As always." He patted Nelson's back. "If I adopted every wee doggie you brought to my office, I'd need to buy stock in a kibble company. But let's take a snapshot of Mr. Nelson and pin it to the bulletin board. Somebody is sure to fall in love with him before long. You're such a handsome lad, aren't you, Nelson?"

Nelson panted in agreement.

"Thanks, Malcolm. Now, about his teeth—how much will it cost for the cleaning? The rescue is running a little low on funds just now—"

"Don't worry about the bill right now, Nan. We'll work something out."

I repeated my thanks and scooped Nelson off of the examining table. Blixen walked over to Malcolm and nosed his hand.

"I'm sorry, Blix," he said, reaching down to give her a pat. "I didn't mean to neglect you. Have you been taking good care of your visitor?"

"Very," I said. "She's always so protective of the new ones."

Malcolm got down on his haunches and rubbed Blixen's head with both hands. Nelson put a paw on Malcolm's leg, demanding his share of the attention.

"All right. A hand for each." Malcolm grinned and started petting both dogs. "So how're you, Nan? How's the family?"

"Fine, everybody's fine. I wish they lived closer, of course. But what can you do? They've got to go where the work is."

"How's Dani doing? Have you heard from her recently?"

"Oh . . . yes. She called the other day. Still backpacking around the country, trying to find herself. You know how kids are."

"Well, if you're going to travel, do it while you're young. You've got your whole life to work, right? Did she ever apply to vet school?"

"She's thinking about it." I shrugged. "But, you know. Hard to get in."

"If she ever wants a recommendation, I'd be happy to help. She was one of the best assistants I ever had. She'd make a great vet."

"Malcolm," I said, smiling in spite of myself, "she cleaned kennels and wrangled cats for you for one summer when she was sixteen."

He disentangled himself from the dogs and got to his feet.

"But she had a feel for it, very gentle she was. And a hard worker. I'd write her a recommendation in a heartbeat." He frowned a little, as if he'd just remembered something. "Say, you have my home phone number, don't you?"

"No, I just call the hospital if I need anything."

"Well, if you ever need to find me at home . . ." He wrote the number on a prescription pad and handed it to me. "Here. Just in case."

I slipped the paper into my pocket, wondering what this was all about. Malcolm had been my vet for fifteen years and I'd never once had to call him at home—if I needed him, the answering service found him.

"Next time you talk to Dani, tell her what I said about vet school."

"I will," I said, clipping on Nelson's leash. "Next time."

After leaving the hospital, I drove to Café Allegro to see Monica, leaving Blixen and Nelson, worn-out from their busy morning, to sleep in the car.

I'd only planned to pop in, say hello, and see if she had a couple of minutes to talk about ways to raise money for the dog rescue, but Monica insisted on feeding me. It wasn't quite ten thirty, but I was hungry after my walk, so I let her. She fixed me a plate of spaghetti Bolognese and set a place for me at the counter so I could watch while she got ready for the lunch crowd.

I couldn't believe how quickly she worked, lifting enormous pots filled with water onto the stove, her knife flashing as she chopped a pile of peppers, a small mountain of onions, then gutted and prepped a whole bucket of fresh and very slimy-looking squid. Disgusting but impressive.

But the most impressive thing was the way Monica and her staff maneuvered around the kitchen and one another—salting sauces, stirring fillings, rolling dough, whisking dressing, tossing salads. It was almost balletic the way each person's movements were perfectly timed to the others, moving expertly through the dance with barely a word of instruction or inquiry. This was a very good thing because Monica had a lot on her mind and needed to talk.

"I'm exhausted. Didn't sleep all night," she said as she seeded and diced a dozen Roma tomatoes with lightning speed. "Zoe and I had a huge fight. I wouldn't let her wear fishnet stockings to school. Apparently, this means I'm out to ruin her life. She called me some terrible names. So I turned around and called her some that were even worse."

Monica swept her knife over the cutting board, scooped up the pile of diced tomato, and dumped it into a bowl, shaking her head.

"Every time she throws out the bait, I snap it up. Why do I do that? Why?"

"Because you care. You're worried about her."

Monica laid her knife on the counter and gave me a searching look. "All she thinks about is boys. Nan, she's not even fourteen years old."

"I know, I know," I said, thinking about Chrissy and Dani and the struggles they'd gone through, growing up without a dad. "She's hurting. She just wants to be loved."

"Doesn't everybody?" Monica started peeling garlic. "Even when he was alive, Vince didn't pay attention to her. He only had eyes for Alex— first-born son and all. I know it hurts. I went through the same thing with my mom and my big brother. Compared to Stevie, I was chopped liver. But Vince was really a jerk, way worse than my mom. To him, the only women worth noticing were bimbos."

"You are not a bimbo," I corrected.

"No, but I could cook. I was useful," she said, bitterly. "This whole boy-crazy bimbo thing is just Zoe trying to find the daddy love she missed. She can't see it, but I do. I'm not trying to keep her from having fun or being popular. I just want her to understand that she's *worth* something! I want her to know that her value as a person isn't based on how many acne-scarred Romeos try to shove their hand down her blouse."

She tossed the garlic into the bowl with the tomato and some herbs, then added salt, pepper, and olive oil.

"The least worst thing that'll happen to her is getting her heart broken," Monica said, her frustration evident in the ferocious way she stirred the tomatoes. "Every time I try to explain that, she yells something at me, then I yell something back, and we're off to the races.

"Why do I do that? I'm supposed to be the adult."

She stopped stirring, put down the spoon, and looked at me. Her gaze was flat and her eyes seemed darker, as if the spark inside them had been suddenly extinguished.

"I'm going to end up ruining these kids, aren't I?"

"No!" I insisted. "No, you're not. Why would you even think that? Monica, raising children isn't easy. Especially teenagers."

"You raised seven and they all turned out okay."

"Every mother makes mistakes."

Monica tasted the tomato mixture, tossed in some salt, and sighed.

"Sorry. I didn't mean to get off on a tangent.

I was supposed to help brainstorm ways to make money for Rainbow Gate, not gripe about my rotten step-kids, right? So. Let's talk fund-raising. But, first—do you want a piece of tiramisu? It's fabulous. You've got to try it."

With my mouth full of spaghetti, I waved a finger in the air, trying to signal that I was too full for dessert. But Monica had turned her back and was heading toward the restaurant's big walk-in cooler. While she was inside, the phone rang. Ben, Monica's sous-chef, answered it, then called out, "Chef? It's for you."

"Take a message."

"She said she's gotta talk to you now. Said it's important."

Monica exited the cooler. "This better not be some yahoo trying to sell me a new espresso machine," she said, scowling at Ben. He handed her the phone.

"Hello? Yes, this is Mrs. Romano."

Monica turned to face the wall, conversing in a voice that was too soft for me to hear. I looked at my half-eaten plate of pasta. I was so full, stuffed. But the sauce was so delicious . . .

As I took another bite, Monica hung up the phone and started barking orders to her staff.

"Ben? I've got to go out. You'll have to take over for a while. Finish stuffing the manicotti, then check the minestrone—it was too bland yesterday. Pound some more chicken breasts for the scaloppine—let's try to get ahead of the game for once, all right? Oh, and order some more oregano, will you? We're nearly out.

"Angela? Did you finish setting the tables? Don't think so; I don't see any water glasses. And update the specials board. We've got manicotti and salad for $11.99 today. I'll be back in a couple of hours. So try not to burn the place down while I'm gone, will you?"

She unbuttoned her white chef coat and hung it up on a hook. "Sorry, Nan. I've got to run."

"What's happened? Who called?"

"The school. They're going to expel Alex."

"You're kidding! For what?"

Monica snatched her car keys from the counter and grabbed her purse.

"Selling drugs."

Monica left. I took the long way home, worrying about her, worrying about Alex, driving slowly beneath a dozen different overpasses and bridges, scanning the ravaged faces of this city's lost and discarded, searching for the one who was familiar to me, the face I would never stop loving.

Chapter 11

Monica

"Right in there, Mrs. Romano." The woman standing at the front desk of the administrative office waved toward a conference room. "They're waiting for you."

This wasn't the first time I'd been summoned to the principal's office on account of Alex, but in the past, the principal, Gerri Lott, and I always met in her private office. When I opened the door to the conference room, I understood why we needed extra space.

Besides Principal Lott and Alex, who was sitting slumped with his head down and his arms wrapped across his body, Bob Smith, Alex's computer teacher and cross-country coach, was seated at the table. So was a Portland police officer.

The sight of that blue uniform and badge made me gasp; I couldn't help myself. Alex looked up. His expression was defiant, and fearful.

Was he under arrest? Would he be? Should I insist on having a lawyer present? But maybe that would make Alex look guilty . . . or guiltier. Or

113

uncooperative. And I didn't know any lawyers. Well, none besides the one who'd handled the probate when Vince died. I didn't think he took criminal cases.

Criminal cases! Oh, dear God.

Alex looked away as I walked into the room. Bob gave me an encouraging smile as I pulled out a chair and took a seat. I was glad he was there. Though I'd only talked to him once at a recent parent/teacher conference, he seemed to like Alex.

"I'm sorry to keep you all waiting. I came as quickly as I could."

"We've only just started," Mrs. Lott said. "I was in budget meetings, Mr. Smith had a class, and Officer Langley just arrived."

I looked at the policeman and smiled, hoping to win him over. He nodded but kept his expression neutral.

"To get everyone up to speed," the principal continued, "earlier today, Mr. Smith observed Alex and another student standing in the court-yard when they should have been on their way to class. When he approached, Mr. Smith saw Alex take some money from the other student and then hand him a plastic bag of marijuana. As required by procedure, Mr. Smith immediately escorted both students to the office. My assistant then notified me of the situation before calling you, Mrs. Romano, and then the police department.

"The other student will be suspended for ten days. But as I'm sure you're aware, this is an extremely serious offense. Selling drugs on school property is—"

"I didn't sell drugs," Alex said. "I *didn't*," he protested when I glared at him.

What was he doing? Lying would only make things worse. He needed to be contrite, throw himself on the mercy of the court.

The court? Oh, crap. Maybe I *should* hire a lawyer.

I felt a little fluttering skip in my chest. As soon as that passed, my head started to pound. I pinched the bridge of my nose. It didn't help.

"Alex, Mr. Smith *saw* you take the money and hand over the bag," I said, not quite hissing but close. Alex glared at me defiantly.

My stepson is a lot of things, but he's not stupid. So why wasn't he taking the hint? Officer Langley looked bored. I doubted he'd signed up to be a cop because he wanted to spend his days collaring idiotic teenagers for selling dime bags of weed. Maybe, if Alex admitted what he'd done, pled stupidity, and apologized, Officer Langley would give him a stern talking-to and let him go? Not likely. The policeman didn't look like the kind who handed out slaps on the wrist. But it was worth a try. Besides, I didn't have any other ideas.

"You're not suggesting that Mr. Smith is lying,

are you?" I said, making my words sound like an inquiry instead of an accusation.

"No," Alex said, using his duh-do-I-look-stupid-to-you voice. "Mr. Smith saw Mike take the money and me give him the bag. But I didn't sell him drugs."

I frowned. Alex sounded so definite about it that I almost believed him.

"I don't understand. If you didn't sell him drugs, what did you sell him?"

He dropped his head and mumbled unintelligibly. I leaned closer.

"What? I can't hear you."

"OREGANO!" Alex shouted. "Okay? Can you hear me now? It wasn't marijuana! It was OREGANO!"

I gasped. "You *stole* my oregano from the restaurant? You ungrateful little—" I smacked the table to keep from swearing. "I can't *believe* you would do something so rotten. And dumb! What were you thinking?"

"I DON'T KNOW!"

Alex dropped his head onto the table with a thunk and covered his head with his arms. I looked at Mr. Smith, then at Principal Lott. Her mouth hung open for a moment before she found her words.

"Oregano?" She looked at Bob. "I don't—"

Officer Langley coughed. "Mrs. Lott, can I look at the . . . uh . . . evidence?"

She pushed the bag across the table. The officer took a sniff, then closed the bag and handed it back to the principal.

"Okay. I'm done here."

He got to his feet and looked at Alex.

"Hey, kid."

Alex picked up his head. His eyes were red.

"Yeah?" he sniffled.

"Yes," the officer said. "Yes, *sir.*"

Alex sat up a little straighter.

"Yes, sir."

"If you *ever* waste my time like this again," Langley said, stabbing his finger toward Alex, "if I get called down here because you've been in a fight, or skipped class, or got caught selling so much as a Tic Tac, I am going to make your life fifty kinds of miserable, got that?" Alex nodded. "Good. And by the way, don't you *ever* yell at your mother like that again. Understand?"

"She's my stepmother."

Officer Langley gripped the top of his billy club and glared.

"Sorry, sir. Yes, sir."

"That's better."

Officer Langley left the room. Mrs. Lott heaved a sigh and closed her eyes. The expression on her face said she was seriously reconsidering her career choice.

"All right," she said finally. "Alex, I'm glad that we don't have to involve the police, but you are still in a lot of trouble. The fact that you weren't selling actual drugs doesn't negate the fact that you were trying to pass them off as such. Plus, you were attempting to trick a fellow student, and you were late for class. And you have wasted the time of every adult in this room.

"So, if you think you're off the hook, think again. You *are* going to be punished for this." She furrowed her brow. "I just have to figure out how."

Mr. Smith cleared his throat. "Mrs. Lott, could I speak with you for a moment?"

"Sure. Excuse us."

The two educators went out into the outer office, leaving me alone with Alex. He looked so miserable that I almost felt sorry for him. Almost.

"Really, Alex, what were you thinking?"

"I don't know. It was stupid. I needed money."

"For what?"

Alex opened his mouth and closed it again, a couple of times, as if he couldn't quite make up his mind to tell me or not. But, finally, he did.

"There's this girl—Gwen Mikesell. She's gorgeous. She's perfect. But she doesn't know I'm alive. So I thought . . . I thought if I could get her something amazing for Valentine's Day, like have a dozen roses delivered to her at school, she might . . . You know. Notice me."

"You needed money to send flowers to a girl? Why didn't you just ask me?"

Alex let out a disbelieving huff of air. "You'd have just said no."

I wished I could have argued the point, but Alex was absolutely right. If he'd asked me for money to impress a girl, I'd have said no. Not because I would have necessarily objected to the request, especially if he would have explained his feelings exactly like he had a moment before.

That poor, dumb, rotten kid. He must be in love. Which, of course, meant he was in agony. In my limited experience, the two generally go hand in hand.

But Alex was right, if he had asked me for money for roses, or anything else, I would have said no. When it came to Alex, no was my default response.

No wonder he hated me.

Mr. Smith and Mrs. Lott came back into the conference room and sat down. The principal folded her hands on top of the table, fixing Alex in her gaze.

"Alex, I cannot impress upon you enough how very, very close you've come to being expelled today, or how closely I am going to be watching your behavior in the future. If you put one foot wrong for the rest of the year, I will have no hesitation about kicking you out of this school. Am I making myself clear?"

"Yes, ma'am."

I twitched. I couldn't help myself. I'd never

before heard the word *ma'am* come out of Alex's mouth, nor heard him speak in such a polite tone of voice.

"However, Mr. Smith has convinced me to give you ten days of suspension and a second chance. During that time, besides keeping up with your regular assignments, you will write a ten-page paper on why deception is wrong. You will also write a note of apology to Officer Langley for wasting his time, and to Mike for getting him into trouble. And, before you ask, yes, I am still suspending him—what matters isn't what he purchased but what he intended to purchase.

"And, Alex," she said, taking off her glasses, "if I were you, I'd steer clear of Mike from here on out. For all the hot water you're in at this moment, you don't really seem like a kid who's bent on a life of crime. I can't say the same of Mike."

"Yes, ma'am."

"Also, you will write one more letter, to your stepmother, apologizing for stealing her . . . herbs." Mrs. Lott looked at me. "I'm sure this goes without saying, but all of these assignments will be completed with careful attention to grammar, punctuation, spelling, and sincerity. Mr. Smith will check them. If he finds them lacking in any way, you'll do them again. Understand?"

Alex bobbed his head.

"Finally, I have asked Mr. Smith to serve as your faculty advisor for the rest of the year. Once you return to school, you'll meet with him once a week."

"Really?"

Alex looked toward his coach and smiled. Mr. Smith didn't smile back, but I had the feeling he wanted to. Everyone got up from the table.

"Mrs. Lott?" Alex cleared his throat and ducked his head. "I'm sorry. Really."

"I hope so, Alex. Because you won't get a second, second chance. Now go home. We'll see you in two weeks."

We stopped by Alex's locker to pick up his books and then got into the car. The bell rang for lunch. Seconds later, the sidewalks were packed with laughing, yelling, jostling teenagers.

"Wow. This feels weird," Alex said, watching the crowd he was exiled from for the next two weeks. "What am I supposed to do now?"

That was a good question. The easiest thing would be to take him home. He was old enough to look after himself, and I really needed to get back to work. But for all of Alex's seeming remorse, I could see that leaving him to his own resources at the house, where there were televisions and video games, might end up being more a reward than a punishment. Plus, he had all those writing assignments. I didn't really trust him to finish them unsupervised.

I started the car. Alex looked at me.

"Where are we going?"

"To the restaurant. You can sit at one of the empty tables and do your homework."

For a moment, I thought he was going to argue with me, but then his expression softened and he buckled his seat belt. I pulled out of my parking spot.

"Hey, Monica? I know that Mrs. Lott is making me write you that letter, but I really am sorry."

"Good. Apology accepted. And since I know you really mean it, after you finish your homework you can keep on being sorry by doing dishes at the restaurant. The pay is five bucks an hour. So, it'll only take six hours for you to pay me back for all that oregano you stole."

"Oh, man! That is so—" Alex let out an exasperated growl and slumped in his seat. "Fine. Whatever. I guess I owe it to you."

"Yes, you do," I said, shooting him a look before turning right out of the lot. "Also, I'm confiscating your cell phone for the next two weeks."

"What!" Alex cried, his eyes practically popping out of his head. "You can't do that! It's so unfair! How will I—"

"And after you've paid me back," I said, raising my voice and talking right over him, "assuming I think you're worth the salary, you can keep the job for the rest of your suspension."

Alex, suddenly quiet, stared at me.

"Well, there's no point in having you sit around my kitchen taking up space all day, is there? Might as well make yourself useful. Now, let's see—when do you go back to school? February thirteenth, isn't it? Right before Valentine's Day. You ought to be able to make some pretty serious coin by then—maybe sixty or seventy bucks."

I looked over to the passenger seat.

"That's about the same price as a dozen roses, isn't it?"

Chapter 12

Grace

Ten minutes after my conversation with Ava, I stood in the hallway, staring at Gavin Nutting's office door. A pounding sound was coming from inside. I tried to think of things that might make me indispensable. None came to mind. I took a deep breath and knocked.

"Enter!"

I poked my head inside. "Mr. Nutting? Can I speak with you for a minute?"

Gavin was wasting no time settling into his new office. Along with a couple of award plaques, he'd already hung several framed motivational posters on the walls, the sort you see for sale in the back of business magazines, with high-resolution photos of redwood forests, eagles in flight, sailboats on stormy seas, and the like. Beneath each picture were urgent, single-word captions that screamed . . .

ATTITUDE!
EXCELLENCE!
FOCUS!

COMMITMENT!
TEAMWORK!

"Have a seat," he said.

While Gavin put down his hammer and rolled down his shirtsleeves, I continued looking over his new office.

He had a personal coffeemaker on his credenza, the kind with plastic pods. Though he wore a wedding band, there were no signs of a wife or kids in his desk photos. Instead, each of the very professional-looking pictures showed him engaged in some sort of athletic pursuit—skiing, surfing, golfing, etc.—and looking so good doing it that I wondered if they'd been staged. There wasn't a single candid-looking snapshot in the bunch, nothing that made him look goofy, or happy, or even particularly human. I'd never seen a desk gallery quite like it.

Still, I wasn't so much concerned with Gavin's office décor as I was with reminding him of why I very much wanted and needed to keep my job. I needed to convince him that I was indispensable, but also figured it couldn't hurt to remind him that I was a woman in dire straits, just in case he turned out to have a hidden streak of compassion. You can't judge a book by its cover, right?

Except, in this case, you could. . . .

When I finished, Gavin stared at me across his

desk, laced his fingers together, and tapped his thumbs. "Yes, I understand that your *personal* situation is difficult. But as I said before in the meeting, I'm not planning on making any immediate changes. Now, what can I do for you, Grace?"

Allowing for variations in vocal tone and inflection, there are about ten different ways to ask that exact question. Probably nine of them are kindly meant. Gavin Nutting asked the tenth way, making two things crystal clear: first, that he didn't give a rat's rear end about my personal problems; and second, that I was one of the first people he planned to fire.

How could I change his mind? What would somebody indispensable say in these circumstances?

"Mr. Nutting, I'm not stupid. 'No plans for immediate change' just means that you're not going to fire me this week. Next week could be a different story. And, obviously, my personal situation is just that—personal. You have a company to run. That is your first, your only priority. And my problems are mine, not yours. And certainly not Spector's. But I . . . what I mean is . . ."

His unwavering stare shook what little confidence I had, made me lose my train of thought. My mind was racing, trying to come up with some way to convince him of my value, but I kept coming up empty. And then, hanging just above his head, I saw the posters and the captions beneath, bold as billboards.

"What you may not have considered is that my personal problems make me a highly motivated and *focused* employee who is eager to learn and willing to work hard. Somebody with an exceptional *attitude* and *commitment* to *excellence.*"

I leaned closer. "What you can do for me, Mr. Nutting, is teach me what it's going to take, not just to keep my job, but to succeed as a member of your *team.*"

"My team?"

My knees were actually trembling. I was afraid he'd fire me then and there. But then he hitched himself up in his chair and I knew I had his attention.

"Do you have an admin yet, Mr. Nutting? If you don't, I'd like the job."

"You?" His face twisted into an expression that was somewhere between bemused and amused. "Huh. Didn't see that coming. Have to say, Grace, I'd already written you off as kind of a . . . Well, a nice girl. And the thing about nice girls is—"

"They finish last."

"Right."

He laced his fingers again, tapping his thumbs together. His eyes became slits. He looked me over like a car he was thinking about buying. I sat very still.

"Huh," he said again. "I planned to tell HR to start looking for my assistant today. But maybe this would save them the trouble," he mused, his voice so low it almost felt like I was eavesdropping on his inner monologue. "If we do it right, it might save the company some money to boot. Can't hurt to try. Can it?"

He sat there for a long moment. I barely breathed. Finally, he unlaced his fingers.

"Okay, Grace, here's the deal. You can stay on as my assistant—"

"Thank you, Mr. Nutting! Thank you!"

"Hang on, hang on," he said, holding up a hand to stave off my flood of gratitude. "Don't thank me until you've finished listening to what I have to say. I want you to continue in your current position, taking care of the administrative work for Peter, Ava, and the rest of that team. In addition, you'll be my assistant."

He wanted me to do my current job and take on a new one? I'd have five bosses instead of four? I bit the inside of my lip. Five bosses . . . Well, okay. Ava and the others were pretty self-sufficient. Mostly I took phone messages, made copies, and followed up on paperwork for closings. Twenty percent more of that should be doable. If that was the price of being indispensable, keeping my job, my insurance, and keeping

Jamie in Landsdowne, so be it. I could do this. I had to.

"That's fine, Mr. Nutting. Won't be a problem."

"Not so fast," he said. "Working for me won't be like working for the rest of them. I get to the office early and leave late. Ten hours is a short day for me, most days it's twelve, even fourteen hours. When I'm here, I'll expect you to be here, too, placing my calls, keeping my calendar, and taking care of all of my personal business— picking up my dry cleaning, taking my car in for service, that kind of thing.

"I know," he said, reading my mind. "It sounds crazy. Nobody has their assistant do all of that anymore. But juggling calendars, organizing conference calls, typing my own memos, and handling domestic chores isn't a good use of my time or the company's money.

"I'm sure this comes as no surprise, Grace, but I make exponentially more per hour than you do. So I make sure that every minute of my day is spent focusing on the big picture, doing the things only I can do, steering the ship. Before I do anything, I ask myself, *Is this the highest and best use of my time?* If the answer is no, I delegate the task to someone else. If you decide you want this job, then a lot of the time, that someone will be you. There would be no salary increase. But you'd keep your benefits, which, as you're aware, are more than generous."

I didn't know what to say. It wasn't the scope of the work that bothered me. What did I care what he wanted me to do, as long as I got paid? Work was just work to me. It always had been. I'd never had a career, only jobs. They weren't fulfilling, but they paid the bills.

But . . . ten-, twelve-, fourteen-hour days? How was I supposed to manage that? I already got up at five every morning so I could visit Jamie first thing, then went back right after work. The staff at Landsdowne was great, but I still needed to keep on top of Jamie's care and be his advocate. And I needed to talk to him . . . *I* needed that. But Jamie needed to stay at Landsdowne, so I had to make this work. But how?

"I do want the job, Mr. Nutting. Really," I assured him, responding to the look of doubt in his eyes. "I won't have any problem doing anything you ask me to. The only thing is . . . the hours. Would it be possible to limit my schedule to, say, ten hours a day? I go to see my husband every evening and—"

He started shaking his head even before I had a chance to finish.

"I'm sorry, but when I'm here my assistant is here. That's the deal. If you want to keep working at Spector, you're going to have to spend less time with your husband and more time at the office.

"I don't mean to sound cold, but you've got a choice to make, Grace. And you're not the only one. Spector is a company that runs lean and mean, always has. That's why we're successful. Anybody who wants to work here has to pull their weight and then some. If they can't, they can't stay."

He laced his fingers again, propped his elbows on the desk, and looked at me. "So? What do you think? Do you want the job?"

"Yes, sir."

What else could I say?

"Good," he said. "I'll be honest—I've still got doubts about you, Grace. If you can keep up with me, then you have a future at Spector. If not? I'm sure there are plenty of places that'd be happy to have a nice girl on the payroll."

He placed his hands on the edge of the desk and pushed himself into a standing position. "You'll start tomorrow morning. Sound good?"

"No, sir." I picked up the hammer he'd left on the desk. "If you don't mind, I'd like to start now. Hanging up posters doesn't seem like the highest and best use of your time."

I stayed at the office until almost eight o'clock that night, hanging up Gavin's pictures, organizing his files, trying to prove my worth. After a quick trip to the condo to pay the neighbor who feeds and walks Maisie every afternoon, then walking her myself, I finally made it to Landsdowne.

"Sorry I'm so late. You wouldn't believe my day," I said after kissing Jamie on the forehead. "Remember my old boss at the bank? The one who used a stopwatch to time employee lunch breaks? Well, my new boss makes him look like Santa Claus."

Jamie grimaced and yelped out a noise that was somewhere between a bark and a laugh. I knew it didn't mean anything—he made similar sorts of vocalizations all the time, usually while I was still speaking. But when his noises came at a break in my commentary, a part of me couldn't help but wonder if he might actually understand what I was saying—not my words so much, but possibly my tone?

"Don't worry," I said, making an effort to sound more cheerful, "he's no match for me. You're looking at a woman who once picked ten bins of apples in a single day."

Jamie let out another yelp.

"Okay, fine. You're right. I was so sore I could hardly move the next day, but the point is, I'm no stranger to hard work. If Gavin Nutting thinks he's going to scare me off with long hours, he'd better think again. I know he thinks I'm just 'a nice girl,' but I'm tougher than I look, right?"

Jamie twisted in his bed, making an undulating motion with his head and shoulders. I bent down, scooped my arms beneath his torso, and rolled him onto his side.

"There you go. Better?" I asked, looking into his eyes.

As usual, he looked right through me, but his expression seemed more relaxed. I sat down and pulled the plastic bag with my quilt patches from my purse.

"Do you remember the year I picked those ten bins? Your dad could hardly find any pickers that year and the fruit was going to rot on the trees, so your mom got on the phone and called every relative within three hundred miles. Everybody worked as hard as they could from dawn to dusk, but nobody harder than you. You picked fifteen bins. Three years before, we thought you wouldn't live to celebrate your twenty-first birthday, but there you were, climbing up and down that ladder with forty pounds of fruit in your picking bag, leaving the rest of us in the dust. It was hot and miserable, but we got it done, didn't we?"

I slipped a length of gray thread through the eye of my needle and smiled, thinking about the satisfaction I'd felt when Jerry, Jamie's dad, drove up on the tractor to tell us that the last bin had been filled and the whole orchard picked. I'd never felt so tired, or so proud.

"Maybe working for Gavin will be like that," I said, looking up at Jamie.

His eyes were closed and his mouth slightly open. He was snoring softly. I was tired, too, but decided to stay and finish my quilt block, one of the Delectable Mountain blocks I was making to represent the many, many challenges Jamie and I had faced since we'd met—the mountains we had climbed and conquered together.

The one I was working on that night was made from a pair of dark blue size twenty pants I owned when Jamie and I first became friends.

He'd been very nice to talk to me that day at the medical center, but I figured that was the end of it. I never expected him to show up at my front door.

"The doctor says I've got to give the knee a rest," he said, "so that's the end of my cross-country season. But I want to stay in shape for spring and he said it was okay to walk, so I was wondering if you felt like coming along? It's kind of boring walking by yourself."

He made it seem like I was doing him a favor, keeping him company and helping him stay in shape, but I'd barely been able to walk a mile on that first day, and huffed and puffed so hard that I couldn't really carry on a conversation.

But the next day after school, there he was again, and every day after. We started with one mile, then two, then three. Pretty soon I was able to talk and walk at the same time. We got to know each other really well, sharing intimacies and inanities with equal enthusiasm, the way teenagers do, as if it was all so important. To me it was. For the first time in my life, I felt like I had a friend, someone who looked at me instead of past me, and liked me in spite of what he saw.

Pretty soon, we were talking all the time, not just on our daily walks but at school and on the phone. One day, about a month after we started walking, I called him at home.

"Jamie, guess what? My blue workout pants were feeling kind of loose so I got on the scale. I lost nine pounds."

"Oh, that's too bad," Jamie said.

"Are you crazy? It's nine pounds!" I squealed. "I haven't even been dieting!"

"But the doctor said you weren't fat enough to be able to get that surgery, right? So this means you've got even more weight to gain before you can lose it all."

"You jerk. I can't stand you," I laughed, meaning the opposite.

Unless I brought it up, we never talked about my weight. But after that first nine pounds, I began paying more attention to what I ate. That was when I got into the habit of dividing things I liked into two portions and saving half for later. Slowly, the weight came off. Whenever I reported my progress to Jamie he was happy, but only because I was. I never felt like his approval or friendship fluctuated along with the scale. By the time we graduated, I'd lost seventy-seven pounds. It wasn't easy, but Jamie was with me for every step of the journey.

Delectable Mountain blocks have a set of increasingly steeper stair steps, up one side of the block and down the other. My plan was to make four blocks and stitch them around the big blank center block, to create a continuous ring of ascents and descents.

It seemed like that was the way things always were for Jamie and me. We'd conquer one mountain only to find another waiting for us. We didn't know then that Jamie's leg pain was an early symptom of osteosarcoma, the bone cancer that was quietly spreading through his body. It wasn't discovered until, weeks before Jamie was to start his freshman year at Minnesota State, he collapsed in pain in his own living room, the leg broken.

At first, everyone in town was talking about Jamie and he was practically overrun with visitors. But when summer came to an end a lot of Jamie's friends went away to college. Not me.

I came to visit every day. I played cards with him, read books to him, and watched movies with him. When he was too worn-out for that, I was just there, in the room, holding his hand or watching him sleep. When he went through chemotherapy, I shaved his head.

When he started radiation, Jamie asked me to marry him and I said yes. It was the happiest moment in my life, also the saddest. No one thought he would last more than a few months, including me.

Jamie had different ideas.

I won't lie; there were days when we wanted to give up, but, fortunately, those days never occurred at the same time. We climbed that mountain, step by step and day by day, together. Three years later, when Jamie picked more apples than anybody else, I was so happy I felt like I was floating, because I knew it was over. He'd climbed the mountain and come down the other side, even stronger than before. It was Jamie's moment of triumph. Mine too.

That's the thing I've learned about mountains: the joy you feel at scaling them is in direct proportion to how high and impassable the peak appears to be once you're on the other side of it.

"Maybe this will be like that," I said again, thinking about Gavin Nutting as I set a final backstitch into the block.

Maybe.

But as I snipped the thread and looked up to see Jamie, eyes still closed, hands fisted and curled under his chin, I couldn't help but recall that it was different this time. This time, I was climbing alone. It was up to me to carry Jamie safely over.

I had to keep going, no matter what. It was all on me. I couldn't fail him.

Chapter 13

Grace

Restaurant Month, when local eateries offer a limited, three-course, value-priced menu, is a big deal in Portland.

"It'll be our first year participating," Monica said when she phoned, "and I need to audition potential recipes, make sure they're up to snuff. Come to the restaurant on Monday night; I want you and Nan to taste test."

This is one of the perks of being Monica's friend. When she changes the menu or caters a special event, she tries out new recipes on us. I always look forward to it. But this time, a week after I'd started working as Gavin Nutting's assistant, I didn't think I could make it.

"But it's support group night. We always get together on Monday."

"But now I can't leave until Nutting leaves. The earliest I've gotten home this week was eight thirty, and that was only because I was so exhausted that I skipped visiting Jamie. Maybe you'd better do it without me."

"No way," Monica said. "I need your opinion,

and your finely tuned palate. We'll just start late. Nan won't mind."

"You're sweet, but I don't think I should. Maisie will have been home alone all day. I'll be tired and she'll be starving."

"So bring her. Zip by the apartment, grab Maisie, and come to the restaurant. We'll bring all the dogs—have a puppy party. It'll be fun."

"Monica—"

"You're coming," she said. "I insist."

When Monica insists, there's no point in arguing. It was almost nine when Maisie and I arrived at Café Allegro. When I opened the door, the canine chorus was so loud it practically knocked me backward.

Desmond, Monica's lumbering Newfoundland, carried the bass line in a series of deep, reverberating woofs. Blixen and Nelson took the tenor, barking in an oddly syncopated rhythm. Two dogs I'd never seen before, a pair of floppy-eared, paddle-footed basset hounds who looked as alike as a pair of bookends, sang the alto, baying in unison. Maisie, always the diva, started yipping in a piercing soprano and wriggling in my arms, anxious to get down and show the big dogs who was boss.

"Hey!" I shouted, trying to make myself heard over all the barking. "Sorry we're late. New boarders?" I asked, indicating the bassets.

"This is Peaches. And this is Cream," Nan

said, pointing toward each hound in turn. "They arrived this afternoon. Their owner has gone into hospice, poor man. They're sisters and very sweet, but I suspect they'll be with me for a while. Bassets are hard to place—baying is an issue—but the owner said they can't be separated."

"Can I put Maisie down?"

"Oh, yes," Nan said. "Their bark is definitely worse than their bite."

I set Maisie on the floor. Mindless of their difference in size, she ran over to Peaches and Cream, gave them a yip and a sniff, then did the same to Nelson, who withdrew behind the safety of Nan's legs. Having asserted herself, she moved on to Blixen, who thumped her tail in welcome, and finally to Desmond. He stopped his woofing and bent down to lick Maisie's face, then calmly lay down on the floor, resting his enormous head on his enormous paws. Maisie circled him with little prancing steps, like a perky pilot boat sailing around a stately cruise ship, then nestled in next to him, settling into the hollow between his head and beefy shoulder.

"Desmond has always had a crush on Maisie," Monica said.

"And why not," I said. "She's a commanding presence."

As soon as Maisie lay down, all barking ceased. The dogs, aside from Maisie and Desmond, who were curled into a lover's knot on the floor, sat in a state of calm expectation. Monica clapped her hands together and addressed them.

"Good. Now that everybody's here, we can get the party started. Who wants a cookie?" The dogs perked up their ears, almost as if they understood what Monica was saying. "Everybody? Okay, good. Now where is my pastry chef?" Monica looked over her shoulder. "Alex!"

"Just a sec! I'm taking the last batch out of the oven."

A moment later, the kitchen door swung open and Alex emerged. He was smiling. Broadly. I didn't gasp at the sight of him, but I could have.

An hour later, after Alex disappeared through the kitchen door carrying an armful of dirty dishes, I leaned across the table and whispered, "Monica, *what* have you done with Alex?"

She grinned. "I know, right? He's polite. He's helpful. He's happy. Hard to believe it's the same kid. I keep looking under his bed for pods."

"The haircut," Nan commented. "How did you talk him into it? And dying his hair a normal color? One that could actually grow naturally out of a human head?"

"I didn't talk him into anything. He asked me to make him the appointment. He wants to impress that girl, Gwen, when he goes back to school."

"He will," Nan said confidently. "He looks so handsome."

"I hope so. Turns out he's a doll when he makes an effort. And he bakes. What girl could resist? And speaking of baking," Monica said, glancing across the room at the pile of dogs, dozing contentedly after having devoured home-made pumpkin-peanut, chicken parmesan, and liverwurst dog biscuits, "the pups obviously approved of their menu selections. But what did you two think?"

"The peppercorn fettuccini with lemon gremolata was good, but the eggplant parmesan was truly inspired," Nan said.

"Agreed," I said. "And roasted rosemary pork—fabulous. I wasn't as crazy about the chicken rollatini. Maybe a little bland?"

Anything Monica cooks is ten times better than anything I make, so it felt odd saying anything negative about her dishes, but I knew she wanted honest opinions.

"I thought so too. Maybe I should add a little more oregano?" Monica said.

"Predictable," I replied. "How about thyme instead? And more garlic?"

Monica nodded and made a note on a pad of paper. "See, Grace? This is why I needed you to be here. Your palate is always spot-on. As much as you love to eat, I've never understood why you didn't really learn to cook."

"Because if I had, I'd weigh three thousand pounds. And it's not like I don't cook at all. I do my basic recipes to keep from starving—chili and soup in the Crock-Pot, turkey meat loaf, tuna salad—then enjoy my occasional treats and the pleasure of being able to button my jeans."

"Turkey meat loaf." Monica shuddered. "I'd rather wear stretch pants. Okay, I still need a chicken dish. What did you think of the piccata? If I pounded the breasts thinner? I thought it was a little tough."

Monica finally settled on four dishes—eggplant parmesan, chicken piccata, roasted rosemary pork, and grilled salmon with fried capers, served on a bed of winter greens. With that decided, we moved on to the important business of catching up.

Monica beamed as she poured wine and told us about Alex's transformation, some of which she credited to Bob Smith, Alex's new advisor.

"He actually came by the house to check on him, then stayed for two hours to help Alex with his homework," she said. "Talk about going above and beyond."

"Are you sure he wasn't checking on you?" I asked, teasing her.

"Not my type at all. I mean, seriously. Bob Smith? Could there be a more generic, less Italian name? He's a terrific teacher, though. I'm so happy he's advising Alex. The kid needs a positive male role model. So, Nan? What have you been up to?"

Nan admitted to feeling a little frazzled with four dogs in residence. "But it's been a good week. I think I finally have an idea to raise some money for the rescue."

"Oh no! I forgot," Monica said, thumping her forehead. "We were going to talk about a fund-raiser. I'm sorry, Nan."

"Don't worry about it. You've been busy. Besides, it worked out. I stopped by the pet shop the other day. Sylvia, the owner, mentioned that the company she buys her dog jackets from had just gone out of business. So I said, what about letting me sew dog jackets for her to sell in the shop, with the proceeds going to Rainbow Gate?

"She loved the idea," Nan said. "If it works, it'd be year-round income for the rescue. And who knows? Maybe we could sell in other shops too."

"So," Monica said doubtfully, "in addition to pet therapy, fostering dogs, and raising money for the rescue, plus all your ten zillion other projects and hobbies, you're going to start a dog jacket empire?"

"Not an empire. A pilot project. Sylvia said she'd take a dozen to start and we'll see how it goes. But I take your point," Nan said, propping her chin in her hand. "It's a big job to take on by myself. If only I had some helpers." She sighed theatrically.

I looked at Monica.

"You know how I'm always accusing you of roping me into things? I'm starting to think Nan is an even bigger culprit," I said.

"Oh, come on," Nan said before Monica had a chance to agree. "It'll be fun. Instead of sitting around and talking every week, we could *sew* and talk. If we do it together, I bet we can make a dozen jackets in no time."

"Don't look at me," Monica said. "I had to make an apron in my eighth-grade Home Ec class. Sewed right over my thumb. Blood *everywhere,* purple stitches showed right through the skin."

Monica lifted the once-wounded digit, tracing a line with her finger where the thread had been. I felt my stomach lurch.

"Okay," I said, "you're not allowed to get within fifty feet of a sewing machine. You can be in charge of cutting. Or maybe just pinning," I said, considering the kind of damage Monica might be able to inflict with a pair of sewing scissors.

"So you'll do it?" Nan asked, her face lighting up. "You'll help me?"

What a question. If Nan had called me in the middle of the night and asked me to paint her house, I'd have grabbed some drop cloths and brushes and headed right over. Of course I'd help. So would Monica.

"Thank you! We really appreciate this!" Nan

said, looking toward the dogs, who wagged their tails in agreement.

Monica started filling our glasses with more of the Chianti she'd chosen to accompany the meal. When she got to me, I placed my hand over the top of the glass.

"Better not. I've got to be at the office by five thirty."

Monica gasped. "You can't be serious. Five thirty in the *morning?*"

"That was the deal I made with Nutting so I could leave 'early' tonight," I said, making air quotes with my fingers.

"Nine o'clock is early?" Nan asked.

"It is in Gavin Nutting's world," I said, and put my hand over my mouth to cover a yawn. "He works constantly, never eats lunch, and has no discernible sense of humor. He may be a robot."

"Oh, Grace," Nan said sympathetically, "maybe you should start looking for another job."

"Believe me, I am. If it was only about salary, I could find a new job tomorrow, but the insurance . . ." I shook my head. "Probably a third of the companies I'd be interested in don't offer it, another third have insurance plans, but really crummy ones, and the final third—with good plans—require a waiting period before the benefits kick in. I can't afford to pay for ninety days of Jamie's care by myself."

Monica bit her lip, the way she does when she's thinking.

"What if they fired you? Spector would have to offer you insurance coverage for a while, wouldn't they?"

"But the premiums would be more expensive and it wouldn't last forever. What if I couldn't find another job? It's too big a risk to take. Besides," I said, tossing back the tiny bit of wine left in my glass, "a part of me wants to hang in there—prove that I can take whatever Nutting is dishing out, like getting through hazing during pledge week. Guess what he had me do on Thursday?"

Nan and Monica shook their heads simultaneously.

"Interview cleaning ladies. For his house." More head shaking, but this time it was the disbelieving sort. "Apparently, it was not the highest and best use of his time."

"You're joking," Monica said.

"Oh, how I wish I was."

"I don't get it. Where's Mrs. Nutting? I mean, it's *her* house, right?"

"Palm Springs." I changed my mind about the Chianti, reached for the bottle, and poured an inch of wine into my glass. "She goes from January to April every year—not a fan of Portland winters. I hope Nutting will cut back on his hours when she gets back." I drained my wine-glass and sighed. "But somehow I doubt it."

"You must be exhausted," Nan said.

"I'm okay. It's worth it to keep Jamie in Landsdowne. He gets such great care there. I've only had time to visit three times last week. Alicia texts me twice a day with updates, but it's not the same as seeing him myself."

"I shouldn't have pushed you to come tonight," Monica said.

"Don't apologize," I said, dismissing her comment. "This is the first decent meal I've had in days. And I needed to see you two. If only to vent a little bit." I reached for the bottle again. "If this is going to be the new normal, I've got to figure out how to have a *little* fun sometimes, right? I'll burn out otherwise."

"True," Monica said. "Say, have you heard anything from Luke?"

I looked at her blankly. "Luke. You mean, Luke Pascal? No. Why would I?"

"No reason. It's just . . . you two had a good time that night. That's all."

The abrupt but too-casual way she'd broached the subject, coupled with the overly ladylike, utterly un-Monica manner in which she was sipping her wine, made me suspicious.

"You didn't tell Luke to call me, did you? You didn't give him my number?"

"Of course not! I was just wondering. Luke is such a nice guy. He'd be—"

I pointed a finger in her face.

"Don't, Monica. I mean it. Don't try to play matchmaker. And do not, under any circumstances, give Luke Pascal my phone number."

"Fine," she groused. "No need to bite my head off. You were the one who said you needed to have a little fun sometimes."

"Right now, I'm too exhausted for fun," I said.

"But you should get out a little bit," Nan said. "You can't spend every waking moment in the office. It's not good for you."

"Don't worry. I get out a little bit," I assured her. "I *never* miss my three o'clock Starbucks run. I couldn't get through the afternoon without it. It's only a two-block walk, but it's nice to breathe a little fresh air and see some daylight."

"Well, I guess it's better than nothing," Nan said. You need to give yourself something to look forward to, even if it's just an afternoon latte."

I shook my head. "Lattes are only for special occasions. A tall drip is all my budget can bear." I sighed. "Maybe I should give it up. Seems selfish to spend two dollars on a cup of coffee I could get free in the office."

"But it's not about the coffee," Nan said. "You said so yourself—it's a little break that helps you get through the day."

"Right," Monica said. "As hard as you're

working, you need to get out now and then—breathe some fresh air, rub elbows with humanity, meet people."

"Why would I need people when I have you?"

I'd intended it as a joke, but Monica didn't laugh. Maybe it was my delivery. I've never been much good at telling jokes. Jamie used to double over laughing when I tried because I was always mixing up the punch lines. For years, all I had to say was, "Then one muffin turned to the other and said, 'Got any grapes?'" and he would laugh so hard tears came to his eyes. Monica's a tougher audience.

"I should go help Alex with the dishes," she said, but then the kitchen door swung open and Alex entered.

"You're too slow," he said. "I already finished."

"Aha! My evil plan worked!"

Monica rubbed her hands together and let out a maniacal laugh. Alex rolled his eyes and set down a plate of chocolate brownies.

"I found the recipe online. Tell me what you think."

"I don't know," Monica said, eyeing the brownies with pretended distrust. "Aren't you the kid who got suspended for peddling suspicious substances outside the library? Is there oregano in these brownies?"

"Ha. Ha," Alex deadpanned. "Did anyone ever tell you that you should consider a career in comedy? No? There might be a reason for that."

Monica grinned. "Too soon?"

"Way too soon," Alex said. But he smiled when he said it.

Chapter 14

Grace

"So, that's a chipotle chicken Panini, a fruit cup, and a grande nonfat latte."

"And a cookie," I said, my stomach rumbling as I peered into the bakery case. "Chocolate chip."

"And a cookie." The girl in the green apron tapped another number into the register. "That'll be sixteen dollars and ten cents."

"Sixteen dollars?"

The girl bobbed her head, looking apologetic. "At least there's no sales tax in Oregon."

True. But sixteen dollars? I thought about canceling my order and going over to Alder Street to see if I could find something cheaper at one of the food carts, but Gavin was on even more of a tear than usual. I had to be back in twenty minutes. What to do?

Once again, my growling stomach made up my mind for me. I dug out my debit card, stuck it in the reader, and keyed in my code. The transaction was rejected—lack of funds.

"No worries," the girl said after I mumbled an apology, explaining that I got paid tomorrow.

"It's tight at the end of the month. Do you have cash? A credit card?"

I pulled out my wallet and handed over eleven dollars in bills, then started digging around the bottom of my purse, searching for change, but was only able to come up with an additional $1.87.

"Cancel the coffee—no, wait! The cookie. I need caffeine more than sugar."

She tapped more numbers into the register. The line of customers behind me was growing longer and more impatient. When she announced the new total, still a dollar and a half more than what I had, someone behind me groaned. Someone else said, "Hang on. I got this."

A man stepped out of line and handed the girl thirty dollars. By this time, my face was bright red. I felt so conspicuous and humiliated that I couldn't bring myself to look up. So it wasn't until he said, "Add another coffee onto that order, please. Tall drip," that I realized the voice belonged to Luke Pascal.

Mortified, I looked up at him and said, "I can't let you pay for my food."

"Well, somebody better do it," said a man wearing red too-short shorts and a pair of Birkenstock sandals paired with white athletic socks, the same man who had groaned before. "Could you move it along? I'm growing old here."

Luke gave him a genuinely withering glance. The man, suddenly quiet, stared at his sandals. Luke turned back toward the girl.

"And if it's not too much trouble," he said in that polite but commanding teacher voice, "I'd like my coffee extra hot. Thank you."

After she handed him back the change and the cookie, Luke shoved two dollars into the tip jar. Two minutes later, we were sitting at a table in a corner, Luke sipping his coffee while I wolfed down my Panini.

"I'm paying you back," I said between bites. "I get paid tomorrow."

"Not necessary. But you can if it'll make you feel better."

He was silent, watching me eat, making me feel even more conspicuous than I had been with the eyes of all those people on me, watching while I grubbed around in my purse for change I didn't have.

"Would you please quit staring at me?"

"Sorry." He ducked his head and took a drink from his cup. "It's just . . . you must be really hungry. Did you eat today?"

I shook my head and swallowed quickly, to avoid talking with my mouth full. "I accidentally left my lunch on the kitchen counter. And my boss just got asked to give a big presentation at a corporate sales conference the week after next. Somebody else dropped out at the last minute.

The good news, at least for me, is that he'll be in Chicago and out of my hair for four whole days. The bad news is, I've got to create thirty-three super-slick slides for his presentation, with all kinds of charts and graphs, and I've never used the design software before."

Luke's eyebrows arched. "Does your boss know that?"

"Not exactly."

"Well, maybe you should tell him. I'm sure he could find somebody else to do it."

"I don't want him to find somebody else to do it. I'm trying to be indispensable."

His brows arched even higher. "Well, that sounds exhausting."

"It is. Hey, do you know what time it is?" I asked, thinking about Gavin.

"Sorry, but I don't wear a watch. Something wrong with yours?" he asked, pointing at my wrist.

"Oh. It's . . . dead battery. Never mind."

I shoved the uneaten half of my sandwich back into the serving bag before ripping the plastic top off the fruit cup and digging in.

"Aren't you going to eat that?" he asked, indicating the leftover sandwich. "You look like you're starving."

"Later." I shoved two big chunks of apple into my mouth and started chewing rapidly. "Thanks for picking up my tab. I'm going to pay you back tomorrow—I insist. It's hard to convince a boss you're indispensable if you pass out from low blood sugar in the middle of the project, so it's lucky for me that we happened to run into each other." I broke the cookie in half, wrapped the first piece up in a napkin, and took a bite of the second. "What are you doing downtown anyway?"

Luke took a long drink of his coffee before answering.

"Yeah, well . . . I didn't quite happen to run into you. Not exactly."

I put the cookie down on the table.

"Monica."

Luke stared into his cup, saying nothing.

"I can't believe it! She *told* you to come down here and wait for me at three o'clock? And you did it? What are you? Some kind of stalker?"

"Hey!" he said, head snapping up, looking offended. "This wasn't my idea, it was Monica's. I just wanted to phone you, but she said you can't take calls at work because your boss is some kind of ogre and that by the time you get home it would be too late, so I should come down and wait for you in the coffee shop. She said you show up here for coffee every day at three and that this would be the best way to get in touch with you."

"And that didn't seem weird to you?"

"Well . . . yes," he said, ducking his head. "But

everything about women seems weird to me. I've learned not to question it."

He looked genuinely sorry and more than a little embarrassed. I couldn't stay mad at him, not once I realized how Monica had played him. However, the length of time I was going to stay mad at Monica for trying to entangle Luke and me in one of her little webs was, quite possibly, an infinite number. How many times did I have to tell her?

"It's okay," I said. "You didn't know. Monica ropes me into a lot of stupid stuff too. And, in a way, I'm glad to see you. I felt bad about running out on you without explaining."

"You don't need to explain. Monica told me all about your husband. And, I . . . well . . . I'm so sorry," he said, stumbling over his words the way people tend to when they hear about Jamie, as if they're not sure whether to offer sympathy, support, condolences, or all three. "I shouldn't have—"

I put up my hand to stop him. "It's my fault. I shouldn't have stayed at the restaurant. As soon as I got Monica's text, I should have told you I was married, said good night, and gone home."

"Why?" he asked, tipping his head to the side. "We didn't do anything wrong. And it was fun, wasn't it? I haven't danced like that in years. You were having a good time, too, weren't you?"

I didn't say anything. He cleared his throat, as if working up to something.

"So listen, I know you have to get back to work, so I'll cut to the chase. There are some dance classes starting up at the Crystal Ballroom. I'd like to sign up, but I need a partner. So I was hoping that you'd—"

The second he uttered the words *dance class* I knew what he was going to ask, but it took a second for me to process the information.

"No, absolutely not," I said, cutting the air between us with the flat of my hand. "Luke, I'm married."

"Yes, I'm aware of that," he said, sounding impatient. "You've mentioned it more than once. Look, I'm just back in the States, haven't even unpacked all the boxes in my new house, and I'm trying to get a new business off the ground. Even if I wanted to, I don't have time for a relationship right now. And why would you think I'd get involved with a married woman? What kind of guy do you think I am, anyway?"

"I didn't mean it like that," I said.

"I'm inviting you to a dance class, Grace. Not a motel room. It's no big deal. All I want to do is dance. There's nothing more to it."

"And you should. But not with me. It's not a good idea, Luke."

I stopped myself. Maybe it hadn't been a big deal to him, but it was different for me. Dancing with Luke had stirred thoughts and feelings that I had no right to.

"I'll give Monica the money to pay you back when I see her," I said, then put my leftovers into my purse, got to my feet, and, once again, walked away from Luke Pascal without really explaining why. This time he didn't attempt to follow me, not even a step.

When I turned the corner, heading back to the office, I caught sight of him through the coffee shop window. Luke was an attractive man, a nice man, but seeing his expression in that unguarded moment made me know I'd been right to turn him down. The sadness of his eyes reminded me of a stray who had seen too much to be surprised by rejection but can't help but search the face of every person passing, looking for the love he's never known.

Luke was as lonely as everybody else. But I couldn't help him.

Chapter 15

Nan

The day after Monica's taste test for Restaurant Month turned out to be busy, and very stressful. It was partly my own doing because when Chrissy phoned that morning, I made the mistake of telling her about Dani's call and how I'd been cruising the bridges and byways of Portland every day since, searching for her.

"Mom, for the ten thousandth time, Dani has made her own choices. Trying to rescue her will only make it worse. You need to let her hit bottom."

Chrissy teaches fourth grade. Maybe that's why she always talks to me like I'm nine years old. But she's always had a tendency to lecture. When she was about six, I walked past Chrissy's bedroom and heard her scolding the teddy bears for not washing their paws before her pretend tea party.

"It's easy to say that. But when I'm lying in bed and it's warm under the covers but freezing outside, and I think of Dani out there—" I felt something brush my leg and looked down to see

160

Blixen leaning against me, her muzzle resting on my knee.

"Mom, you raised seven kids and six of us turned out just fine. Do you know what the odds are against that happening these days? Half of my friend's kids are in therapy, and the other half ought to be. You were a great mother. But Dani is just . . . broken. Beyond repair. Hopeless."

"Don't say that. Nobody is beyond hope, ever. If I could only find her, talk to her. She needs help."

"You can't give Dani money. She'll only—"

"I *know* that," I snapped.

Really, how did I raise a child who is not only bossy but pedantic to boot?

"I packed a bag with food and clothes and a waterproof sleeping bag and put it in the car, in case I see her when I'm driving around town." Chrissy started to argue with me, but I talked right over her objections. "You didn't hear her when she called. She sounded desperate, sick, and weak. I can't force her to get help, but I can keep her from starving or freezing. If I let her know that I'll always be there for her, maybe someday she'll believe me."

"Like she doesn't already," Chrissy scoffed. "The second Dani pulls one of her little dramas, you'll drop everything and run to the rescue. Did it ever occur to you that she might need a little tough love?"

I took a deep breath and counted to five.

"Chrissy, it was thirty-four degrees and pouring rain last night. Your sister is hungry and homeless. She's a hostage to an addiction so strong it makes her forget everything except getting her next fix. How much tougher do you think love should be?"

Chrissy was silent, leaving me space to regret my rebuke. And I did regret it, not my words, but the way I'd said them.

As I was about to apologize, she said, "Well, I don't know how you expect to find her. Or what you imagine would happen if you did. She's had so many chances and thrown them all away. You've done everything for her, Mom. It upsets me to see you feeling bad about Dani when you've done such a good job with the rest of us."

Chrissy is protective of anyone she cares for, including me. She's always been like that—a motherly fussbudget. When she was little, it was sweet. In some ways it still is. But she's more set in her ways than she used to be, and more judgmental. I love Chrissy. I love all my kids. Nothing will ever change that. But some days, liking them can be hard.

"Honey, I'm glad you think I was a good mother. But don't you see? My search for Dani is part of that. It's a big city. I know I probably won't be able to find her, not unless she wants to be found. But I'm going to keep looking. She's my tenth sheep."

"Dani's a sheep?" she asked, sounding confused.

"Like in the parable. When one of the sheep went missing, the shepherd left the other nine in a safe place and searched for the one that was lost. Your sister is my tenth sheep. I'll never give up looking for her, Chrissy. I can't."

Not long after I got off the phone with Chrissy, Donna Gomer, the care coordinator for Rainbow Gate, called. One of the rescue's other volunteers had suffered a stroke and died, leaving behind his own two dogs—a pair of black Labs—and a bulldog he was fostering.

Leaving Blixen and the rest of the pack at home, I dropped everything and drove to Sandy, near Mount Hood, to pick up the orphaned dogs. One of the Labs, Mildred, was holding one eye closed. Though it didn't seem like an emergency, I decided to drop by the animal hospital and ask Dr. Kelly to take a look. But first I drove to the pet shop. Lovey, the bulldog, was on a special diet and needed a particular brand of canned food. And with so many dogs in residence, I was going to need more kibble. Sylvia was glad to see me and happy to hear we were going to move forward with her idea for the dog jackets.

"I thought we'd display them here," she said, walking me to an endcap near the front door that was currently stocked with leashes. "That way people will see them right when they come in."

"You are so sweet to do this. But are you sure you want to donate all of the proceeds to the rescue? You deserve to make at least a little profit."

"A *little* profit is all I've ever made," Sylvia laughed. "You don't open a pet shop because you plan to get rich; you do it because you love animals. Besides, Rainbow Gate does good work. And look at all the business you give me." She pointed to the counter where I'd stacked all my purchases. "You're taking care of seven dogs? I don't know where you find the energy."

"It's just temporary. Hopefully the rescue will be able to find permanent homes for them soon."

Sylvia offered to help carry the dog food to my car, but then the phone rang and she got involved in a conversation about guinea pigs that looked like it might take some time. Though it was cool and cloudy and the car was locked, I didn't like leaving the dogs alone for long. I mouthed a silent farewell to Sylvia, then stacked the bag of kibble on top of the case of food and left.

The car was only parked in the next block, but the load was heavy and my arms were aching even before I got to the corner. As I was about to cross the street, I heard someone call my name. It was Malcolm Kelly.

"Here! Let me take those," he said, relieving

me of my burden before I could protest. "Good grief. Are you feeding every stray in the neighborhood?"

"Almost," I said, then explained about my unexpected guests. "Are you on your lunch hour? I was just about to drive to the hospital. Something is wrong with Mildred's eye."

"I haven't taken a lunch hour in thirty-six years. But I'm not in the office today. Actually," he said, his smile fading, "I've retired, sold the hospital. The new vet, Laura Carey, took over this week. You'll like her."

"Retired?" I clicked the remote to unlock the car. "Why didn't you say anything the last time I came in?"

"I didn't want to tell anyone until the papers were signed. And part of me was hoping for a reprieve. Selling the hospital was my wife's idea, not mine. Well, maybe it was her lawyer's idea." He shrugged, as if it didn't matter one way or the other. "Anyway, it's done.

"Barbara wanted a divorce. The judge ruled that she was entitled to half the business. I couldn't afford to buy her out and so . . ." He shrugged again.

"Oh, Malcolm. I'm so sorry. Are you all right?"

I opened the back door and Malcolm hefted the dog food onto the seat, then straightened up and rubbed his lower back.

"I'm fine. I was going to have to retire eventually. Maybe it's for the best. Barbara moved out once before, after our youngest went to college. I convinced her to give it another chance, went to counseling and all that. For a time it seemed like things were better, but she said she just doesn't like being married. She wants a life of her own, she says. She's training to be a Pilates teacher. Wants to open a studio. But I'm fine," he assured me once again. "And I wish her well. Or well enough."

He smiled a little. "My biggest problem right now is finding ways to keep myself busy. I've reconnected with some old friends from my college days," he said. "That's what I was doing this afternoon, having lunch with some of the Romeos."

"Romeos?"

"R.O.M.E.O.—Retired Old Men Eating Out."

I laughed. Malcolm rolled his eyes.

"Believe me, it's just as bad as it sounds," he said. "The two main topics of conversation were golf and Viagra."

"I thought Scotsmen liked golf."

"I don't *dis*like it," Malcolm said. "But I'm not quite ready to turn it into my reason for living. I'm glad I ran into you. I've been thinking— maybe I could do a little volunteer vet work with the pet rescue?"

"Oh, Malcolm! Would you? Medical bills are one of our biggest expenses."

"And still will be," he said. "Without surgery and lab equipment, I won't be able to do much beyond the basics. Dr. Carey is an excellent vet, but with school loans to pay off, she can't afford to offer discounts. Maybe I can help balance out the costs a bit."

"Malcolm, that would be great. Thank you so much."

"Not at all. You're saving me from spending my golden years trying to tap a little ball into a cup." He shuddered with pretended horror and I laughed. Malcolm always had a good sense of humor.

He walked to the back of the car and peered through the hatch window at the pet crates. "Now, then, which of these wee doggies is Mildred? Oh, I see. The one with her left eye closed." He winced. "That looks sore. But I don't see any seeping or signs of infection. Could be a scratched cornea. Would you like me to take a peek?"

"Would you, please?"

I pressed another button to open the hatch. All of the dogs got immediately to their feet, wiggling and barking in excitement.

"I know, I know," I said. "We're not going for a walk yet, gang. Malcolm is just going to check out poor Mildred's eye. Then we'll head home and have a good romp in the yard. Okay?"

With so many years of experience handling

rescue dogs, I'm always careful to make sure the animals in my care are under control, especially when we're anywhere near a road, and today was no exception. However, I didn't realize that the locking mechanism on one of the crates was damaged.

Mildred, just over a year old, was still a bouncing ball of unbridled energy. As I tried to reach through the bars of the crate to get hold of her collar and clip on her leash, she lunged forward, slamming into the door and snapping open the broken lock. When she bolted through the door, I was knocked backward onto the pavement. Malcolm threw himself between the dog and the street, quickly scooping Mildred into his arms.

"Oh, you naughty brute," he scolded as Mildred licked his face. "You could have gotten yourself killed. Come now, back into the crate. I'll follow Nan to the house and check you there. It'll be safer for everyone. Don't you think so—?"

Malcolm turned around to ask his question and gasped when he saw me sprawled on the pavement. The pain was terrible. Moving quickly, Malcolm popped Mildred back into her crate, closed the hatch, and knelt down beside me.

"Where does it hurt?"

"Everywhere. But mostly—" I tried to sit up and winced in pain.

"Don't move," Malcolm ordered. He conducted

a quick examination, paying particular attention to my neck and limbs, then pulled out his phone.

"What are you doing?"

"Calling 911. You'll be fine," he assured me. "But we're going to the hospital."

Chapter 16

Monica

Still wearing my chef's whites, I raced into the emergency room so quickly that Alex had to run to keep up. When I got to the desk and asked where Nan was, the receptionist said, "Are you okay? Do you need a glass of water?"

"No, I just need to find my friend, Nan Wilja. What have you done with her?"

"Nothing," she said, looking startled. "I mean, we didn't *do* anything with her. She's in exam area four, right through those double doors, left side of the corridor. Don't worry, everything's fine."

Uh-huh. Right. If everything's fine you don't end up in the hospital, do you?

We found Nan sitting semi-upright on the hospital gurney. Her right arm was encased in a blue cotton sling and strapped against her body at an angle, like she was about to recite the pledge of allegiance. There was a bandage on her forehead and a tube coming out of her left arm.

"It's nothing," Nan said in response to my gasp. "A broken collarbone. I shouldn't have called you."

"What are you talking about? Why wouldn't you call me? Nan, you broke a *bone!*" I clutched the bed rail with both hands. "Are they going to operate?"

Alex walked around the other side of the bed and rolled his eyes. "It's a broken collarbone, not cancer. My friend Joey broke his collarbone playing hockey last year and they didn't even put him in a cast—just strapped his arm to his chest so he couldn't move it. Six weeks later, he was good as new."

"You see?" Nan said. "It's nothing."

"Well, not exactly nothing."

A man with dark hair, dark eyes, and a white lab coat walked into the room and stood at the end of the bed.

"Immobility and anti-inflammatories are going to be the primary means of treatment," he said. "Plus some physical therapy. But you're going to have to keep that sling on for at least ten weeks, Mrs. Wilja."

"Ten weeks? Joey got his off in six," Nan said, looking to Alex for confirmation.

Tall-Dark-and-Doctor smiled. "Yes, but Joey's bones are about fifty years younger than yours."

"Gee. Thanks for the reminder," Nan groused, in a very un-Nan-like way. "Monica, Alex, meet Mark Francatelli, spreader of good cheer and pusher of pills."

I gave him a sideways look, asking the question with my eyes.

"She's just feeling a little loopy," he explained. "I prescribed something for the pain. It tends to strip away the social veneer."

He glanced at the embroidered logo on my chef's coat.

"You work at Café Allegro? Love that place. Been there a couple of times. Best Italian food in town, sauce like my Nonna used to make. And the gnocchi?" He clasped his hand to his chest in a gesture of rapture. "Amazing. How is it I've never seen you there?"

The man had gorgeous eyes. Leonardo da Vinci couldn't have had more gorgeous eyes. Mark Francatelli. I said his name in my head, adding an old country accent. Dr. Mark Francatelli. And he'd been to my restaurant and thought it was amazing. How much more perfect could you get?

"I was probably back in the kitchen, rolling out your gnocchi and making the sauce. I'm the chef," I said. "And the owner."

"Really? You run a terrific restaurant. And you're Mrs. Wilja's daughter?"

"Nan is a friend. Her kids all live out of town."

"Oh, I see. Well, she's going to need some help until the collarbone heals. If she doesn't keep the arm totally immobilized, we'll be looking at surgery and all kinds of complications. Maybe one of the children can come and stay with her for a few weeks," he suggested. "Or she could go and stay with them. And I understand there are quite a number of dogs in the home, right? It would probably be best if they were boarded out for the next few—"

"Excuse me," Nan said, raising her good arm and waving it overhead. "You do realize that I'm sitting right here? And that I've broken my collarbone, not cracked my head? I can take care of myself, thank you. The dogs aren't going anywhere. Neither am I."

"But you heard Dr. Francatelli," I said. "You've got to rest and give the bone time to heal." I reached out, intending to pat her arm but changed my mind when I remembered the IV needle. "Do you want me to call Chrissy? Maybe she could stay with you."

"And have her nag me from sunup to sundown?" Nan glared at me and Dr. Francatelli in turn. "You'll have to amputate before I agree to *that*. Don't worry about me. I'll just use the good arm. It'll be fine."

"But how will you dress yourself?" I asked. "And cook? And take care of the garden? The dogs?"

"Why doesn't Nan just come stay with us?" Alex offered.

I'd been thinking the very same thing. There was just one problem. "We just don't have room for the dogs. Nan, could somebody else foster the dogs until you're better?"

Nan shook her head slowly, almost like she was underwater. "Nope, that's why Donna called me. Every foster family is already full up."

"The dogs could sleep in my room," Alex suggested.

"Seven of them? No. Besides, they can't be left alone all day. You're going back to school the day after tomorrow and I'll be at work."

"Forget about the dogs," Nan said groggily, staring at a corner of the ceiling. "Who let all these butterflies in here? Somebody get a net."

"Whoa, Nan." Alex grinned. "You are *so* out of it."

"Hmmm?"

Nan looked blankly at Alex, then shifted her eyes to me. "Hey, did you hear his name? *Francatelli*. Italian." She nodded knowingly. "You got a thing for Italians, right? Plus, he's gorgeous. And single. One of the nurses told me they call him Dr. Dreamboat."

Nan gave an exaggerated wink. Alex laughed out loud, and I planted my face into my palm. Dr. Francatelli cleared his throat.

"All righty, then. I'm just going to reduce the dosage on those painkillers."

He pulled a prescription pad from his pocket and started scribbling. As he was doing so, Dr. Malcolm Kelly pushed open the exam curtain and stepped into the room. He's our vet, so I already knew him. But until he explained what had happened, I didn't know he was the one who'd called the ambulance.

"I'm so glad you're here," he said. "I was worried about leaving her alone, but I had to drive Nan's car back to her place, get the dogs settled, then take a cab back to pick up my car . . ." He flapped his hand, dismissing the details. "Anyway, I'm glad you're here. And that she's okay."

He looked toward Dr. Francatelli. "Broken collarbone?"

"Yes."

Dr. Francatelli shared his concerns about finding someone to help. I was impressed by how patient he was, explaining everything yet again. I was also impressed by his chiseled jaw, Roman nose, and voice like a gondolier. Dr. Dreamboat indeed.

"Well," Malcolm said, "I could take care of Nan and the dogs."

He could? Didn't he have an animal hospital to run?

"Really," he said, responding to my curious look. "Taking care of seven dogs is all in a day's work to me. And since I've just retired, I've got plenty of time on my hands. I can come over every morning and evening to walk and feed the hounds, and take care of anything else that needs doing."

"When did you retire?" I asked. "I brought Desmond in for a checkup just last month."

"It's a recent development. More according to my ex-wife's timetable than mine."

Ex-wife? So Malcolm Kelly was single? I looked at Nan, wondering what she thought about this interesting piece of information, but she was staring at the ceiling with glassy eyes, humming to herself.

"But it does mean I'm available to give Nan a hand. Can't hurt to have someone around with a medical background, can it?"

"You're a physician?" inquired Dr. Dreamboat.

"Animal, not human," Malcolm said. "But if Nan were a border collie, the treatment plan would be pretty similar."

"Oh, how I would *love* to be a border collie," Nan said dreamily.

Dr. Francatelli's pocket started beeping. He pulled out his phone and read an incoming text. "Sorry, but I have to run. Nan can be released as long as there's someone willing to take responsibility for her home care."

"We've got this," Malcolm assured him.

"All right, then, Nan, you rest and take it easy. I'll see you in a few weeks."

Nan stopped humming and waggled her fingers in his direction. "Toodle-loo, Dr. Dreamboat."

Dr. Francatelli handed me Nan's prescription. "Nice to meet you," he said.

"Same here."

My cheeks were already flaming in the wake of Nan's Dr. Dreamboat comment, but since I couldn't possibly be more embarrassed than I already was, I pulled a business card from my pocket.

"Next time you're in the restaurant, give this to the server and you'll get a free dessert. And if you say you know me, maybe I can pop out of the kitchen and—"

Nan, who was still humming, hummed louder. Then she started to sing. "O sole mio, la, la, la, laaaaaa . . ." Proving that there actually is no limit to how embarrassed a person can be. I could have smothered her with a pillow.

Dr. Francatelli pocketed the card. "Thanks. I'll do that."

He smiled and I felt my knees go weak.

"Oh, that was smooth," Alex said after he left, circling his thumb and forefinger into an "okay" sign. "Very subtle."

"Remind me to ground you later," I muttered.

"Well, Nan," Malcolm said cheerily. "What do you say? Should we get out of here?"

Nan blinked a few times. "We?"

"Malcolm is going to drive you home," I explained. "He's going to help take care of you and the dogs until your collarbone is healed."

Nan shook herself, as if trying to clear away the cobwebs.

"Oh, no. I appreciate your kindness, Malcolm, but that won't be necessary. I'm perfectly capable of taking care of myself, even with one hand tied behind my back. Or my front," she said, staring down at the blue sling. "Anyway, I'll be fine on my own. And I'm sure you have better things to do with your time."

"Not at the moment," he assured her. "I'm the most logical choice. And since your doctor won't release you unless there is someone to take care of you—"

"He's right," I said. "It's either Malcolm or Chrissy. You decide."

"No, no. Anything but that," Nan said, and slumped back onto the pillows.

"Then it's settled," Malcolm said. "I'll go see about getting the discharge papers ready. With luck, we'll have you home before dinner."

"That's sounds nice." Nan's eyelids started to droop. "But does anybody have a net? Someone needs to climb up there and get the butterflies."

Malcolm seemed to have everything under control, so Alex and I drove back to the restaurant to get ready for the dinner rush.

As soon as Alex put in his earbuds and started listening to music, I phoned Grace to fill her in on what had happened to Nan, and to try to get the scoop on what, if anything, had happened with Luke.

"Oh no!" Grace said. "Poor Nan. Is she okay?"

"She'll be good as new in a few weeks. And she was definitely feeling no pain when we left," I chuckled. "Dr. Dreamboat prescribed some really nifty meds."

"Dr. Dreamboat?"

"Nothing. Just something Nan said. Not important. I'll tell you later. Maybe." I coughed. "Anyway, how's your day? Anything interesting happen? Did you have any . . . uh . . . visitors or anything?"

"As a matter of fact, I did. Luke Pascal just happened to be in Starbucks at exactly three o'clock today. Isn't that crazy? I mean, what are the odds? Oh, and next time I see you, remind me to choke you."

"What?" I laughed. "You said not to give him your phone number. I didn't."

"Don't play innocent with me, Monica. When I said don't give him my number, you knew that I didn't want to see him or hear from him, period."

I didn't roll my eyes, but I could have.

I mean, sure, I knew what Grace meant when she said not to give Luke her number. But until now, she hadn't been specific about not wanting to see Luke at all, which led me to believe that at least a part of her did want to see him again. And why shouldn't she?

Yes, I understood about being married and that she really loved Jamie and would never want to be disloyal to him. But look at all she'd done for him—making sure that he had the best care money could buy, working all the hours God gave her and then some just to keep her insurance and pay the bills. She hadn't bought so much as a pair of shoes since I'd known her. For Grace, even a latte was a splurge because everything she did, she did for Jamie. Shouldn't that be enough? Did loving Jamie mean that she had to sacrifice even the possibility of happiness for herself? After all, it wasn't like Luke had made an indecent proposal; all he wanted to do was take her dancing. What was so terrible?

The last person who made an indecent proposal to me was Vince. And that was before the wedding. The day we said "I do" was the day the honeymoon was over. At least she had somebody interested, somebody nice. Grace needed to lighten up.

"So . . . when you say you never want to see him or hear from him again, that means you don't want to go dancing with him either? I'm just trying to get some clarity here."

"Monica, you're not as funny as you think you are."

"Oh, come on, Grace. Don't be like that. Do you want me to say I'm sorry? Okay, fine. I'm sorry. I shouldn't have done it. But I was only trying to help. You've been alone for so—"

"I have to go."

"What? You're going to hang up on me just because I told Luke where and when you take your coffee break?"

"No, I'm going to hang up because I have so much work to do that I'll be lucky to get out of here before midnight. But if I needed a reason to hang up on you, the Starbucks stalking incident would be a pretty good one."

"So . . . are you going to be mad at me forever?"

"Not that long."

"How long? A year? A month? A fortnight? I need specifics."

"Seriously, Monica. I have to go."

"Okay. But before you—"

There was a click, then a dull buzz. I took the phone away from my ear and stared at it.

"She hung up on me."

Alex pulled out his earbuds. "Are you surprised? She said she was going to."

"You were listening?"

"Well, it was kind of hard not to. I only paid ten bucks for these," he said, holding up the earbuds. "It's not like they block everything. Plus—nothing personal—but you talk kind of loud."

"Well," I said, feeling defensive. "It comes from spending so much time in the kitchen. I'm always shouting orders."

"Yeah." Alex sighed deeply and faced front, suddenly intent on the road.

"What?" He said nothing. "I'm serious. What were you going to say?"

"It's just that . . . at the restaurant, you're the chef, the boss. You shout an order and everybody goes running to carry it out."

"So what? That's my job. Somebody has to be in charge."

"Right. I get that." He bobbed his head to prove it was true. "But the whole world isn't the restaurant."

"So you're saying I'm pushy?"

He shrugged. I could see he was trying to tread carefully.

"I'm saying that when you have an idea, you go for it. Sometimes that's a good thing. But not always. Sometimes it's better to give people some space."

Before I could comment or question further, he put the buds back in his ears, listening to his music, leaving his words to sink in, giving me space.

I could have smacked him for it.

Chapter 17

Grace

"It's been four days and I'm still ticked at Monica," I said, then gently but firmly pulled Jamie's left arm out from under his chin, pried open his clenched fist, and started to massage his hand.

Severe muscle tightness is one of the many problems patients in a persistent vegetative state suffer from. During my visits, I did what I could to stretch Jamie's limbs and massage his muscles, and to change his position in bed. The staff at Landsdowne was very diligent about doing the same, and I credited their devotion for having helped Jamie avoid painful and potentially dangerous bedsores.

Helping with the exercises made me feel I was doing something tangible to keep Jamie comfortable and as healthy as possible. Also, it helped pass the time during our visits, gave me something to focus on when my conversation was met by silence and Jamie's disconnected stare.

I uncurled his fingers, one by one, then made

a fist and used my knuckles to massage his palm, imagining his response to my comments regarding Monica. He was always so measured in his reactions, so ready to forgive.

"I know, I know. She meant well. You're right. I should forget about it and move on. But I've never been as good about that as you are, Jamie. Do you know that sometimes, I used to get mad because you never did?" I smiled, anticipating his answer. "Stupid, right? I know.

"You're right. I'll phone Monica later. Honestly, I'm surprised she hasn't called me before now—four days without hearing from her is practically a record. It's been kind of a relief, though. No, not because we haven't talked, but because I've been too busy to talk. Or do anything. Even visit you.

"That's what really has me so upset," I said, working my fingers over his, massaging each digit. "All I want is to take care of you, but the only way to do that is to work so hard that I don't even have time to see you. How messed up is that?

"I'm so glad Gavin is leaving for his conference tomorrow. He'll be out of the office for four whole days. Who knows what my schedule will be like when he comes back, but I'll come visit you every day from now through Thursday, honey. Promise."

I lifted his hand and pressed my lips to his

palm, feeling a surge of love that brought tears to my eyes.

I know it's hard for other people to understand why and how my love for Jamie endures undiminished. Sometimes I don't understand it myself. But we've been through so much together, climbed so many mountains. Unless you've been through it yourself, you can't understand the bond that surviving that kind of adversity builds between people.

In books and the movies, it's the sweet times that fan the flame of love—a lazy picnic by the riverbank, the breathless run to the shelter of an ancient oak when the skies roil with unexpected thunder, the passionate kiss in the pouring rain. Jamie and I had our share of romantic moments too. I'm grateful for them. But it's the battles you fight together that make two people one—the hardships, and failures, and occasional triumphs that cement your vows and teach you the meaning and practice of loving someone fully.

I pressed Jamie's palm to my cheek. It was so warm.

Alicia knocked on the door. "Hey, Grace. I just wanted to check Jamie's vitals. Is now an okay time?"

"Sure," I said, and put down his hand. "We're going to watch *The Blues Brothers*—it's one of Jamie's favorites—but it isn't on for another fifteen minutes."

Alicia wrapped the blood pressure cuff around Jamie's arm. "My husband loves that one too. What is it about you guys?" she said, addressing the question to Jamie. "You can watch the same stuff over and over again. I can't get through thirty minutes of a movie without falling asleep. Oh, and I wanted to tell you, Carrie just loves the doll clothes you made for her Barbie. That was so sweet of you. I don't know how you find the time with all you've got on your plate."

"Since I got this new job, I don't. But you know me," I said, tilting my head toward the half-sewn quilt block sitting on the nightstand by Jamie's bed, a Wedding Bouquet block to commemorate our marriage, "if I wasn't doing something with my hands I'd lose my mind. Anyway, it was fun. I haven't made doll clothes for a long time. Gave me a chance to live out my fashion designer fantasy," I said with a laugh.

"Well, Carrie was super excited. She drew a picture for me to give to you. It's back in my office. I'll bring it down later."

I watched quietly while Alicia pumped the black bulb on the pressure cuff, let out the air, then tapped the result into a tablet. Next she took his pulse. When she put a new plastic guard onto the ear thermometer to take Jamie's temperature, I said, "How is he?"

"Fine. His pulse is a tiny bit fast, but it's not a big deal. I bet you're just excited because Grace is here, right, Jamie? You missed her this week."

The thermometer beeped. Alicia pulled it from Jamie's ear, looked at the screen, and frowned.

"What?" I asked, feeling my own pulse quicken.

"He has a tiny temperature, that's all. Ninety-nine degrees. Really, Grace. I'm sure it's nothing. We'll keep on top of it. He might be getting a cold, but this could also be because he's excited that you're here. I see that sometimes, especially in patients who don't get a lot of visitors.

"Listen," she said, seeing the concern in my eyes, "there are worse things than having your husband's heart beat faster when you come into the room, right? The only thing Roger does when I come home is snore. Either that or turn the volume up on the TV. If you think about it, this is actually a good sign. It means he knows you're here."

Alicia said good night and told us to enjoy the movie. After she left I continued the massage, stretching out Jamie's left arm and rubbing the muscles from wrist to shoulders. I worked in silence for a time, my eyes tearing up as I thought about what Alicia said.

Had Jamie felt my absence this week? Did he feel my presence now? The possibility made me feel guilty and elated at the same time—guilty because he might have thought I'd abandoned him and elated because, if what Alicia said was true, it meant that he was still in there somewhere.

Beyond food, water, warmth, and freedom from pain, the first and strongest desire we have is to be important to someone else, to be noticed. If you don't believe me, go to a park or a playground. Watch the children, from three on up, showing off for one another and for their parents, shouting, "Look at me! Look at me!" From the very first, back when no one else could see me or hear me, Jamie did.

I moved to the other side of the bed and stretched out Jamie's right arm.

"Jamie, do you remember Mrs. Babcock? Our civics teacher? She always wore that glittery peacock-blue eye shadow, all the way up to her brows. You remember. Did I ever tell you about what she said to me, just a couple months before graduation?"

I paused for a moment, as I always do, giving him space to respond.

"Well, she stopped me when I was coming out of the library and asked what I was going to do after graduation. I said, 'Get a job,' which seemed obvious to me. When that answer didn't seem to satisfy her, I told her I was saving up for a car too.

"And then she said, 'Grace, listen to me. Instead of working to buy a car, invest in yourself. Use the money to take some classes at the community college. It's much less expensive than a university and later, if you decide to get a four-year degree, the credits will transfer. But even a two-year associate's degree could make a big difference in your life and future.'

"I told her I'd think about it, and she said she hoped I would, that I was a bright girl. Then she squeezed my shoulder and said, 'By the way, I don't know what you're doing, but whatever it is, keep on doing it. You look wonderful!' "

I paused again, not to leave space for Jamie to respond, but because, even now, after all this time, the memory stung.

"In the moment, I was happy. And, of course, I said thank you. Mrs. Babcock was a nice person, a good teacher. But later that night, I started thinking—if I was so bright, why hadn't she said anything before? Why did I have to lose fifty pounds before she took the time to encourage me?

"And it wasn't just Mrs. Babcock. Before I lost the weight, everybody looked right through me, which was a pretty good trick considering how big I was. How ironic was it that, the littler I got, the more people could see me?

"Except you. You were different, Jamie. And I loved you for it. I still do. I always will." I closed my eyes and kissed the top of his head, burying my lips in his thick brown hair, the one part of him that seemed undiminished since the fall.

"I see you," I whispered, lifting my head and looking into his vacant eyes. "Can you see me?

"Because I miss that, Jamie. More than anything else, I miss being visible."

Chapter 18

Nan

You really can't appreciate how dependent you are on a limb until you've been denied the use of it. Without my right arm, I couldn't so much as style my hair properly, or button my own blouse, let alone prepare for my Monday night support group and sewing session with Grace and Monica.

Fortunately, Malcolm was around to lend a hand, two of them actually. I was so grateful. His cooking skills weren't exactly advanced, but he drove me to the grocery store so I could buy fruit, crackers, precut vegetables, and an assortment of fancy cheeses. With a little guidance from me, Malcolm mixed up a batch of delicious homemade hummus to be served with veggies. It wasn't a proper dinner, but no one would go hungry. And while I used my good arm to arrange the food on trays and added some parsley and a few edible pansies for garnish, Malcolm hauled my sewing machine and notions down from the guest bedroom.

He was setting up the ironing board when I

brought in a basket of crackers and put them down next to the cheese tray.

"I set up three work areas," he said, casting his eyes around my huge oak dining table, "one for cutting, one for pinning, and one for sewing."

"Thank you, Malcolm. This is perfect."

"Good. Now, I'll just get out of your hair before your friends arrive."

"Are you sure you don't want to stay? We've got plenty of food."

"No, no. This is your girls' night. You don't need me intruding. Besides, I need to get started on the evening round of walks. Two dogs a session divided by eight dogs—your seven plus my Stuart—means I've got a good two hours of trekking ahead of me. But if you wouldn't mind saving me a bit of that cheese? I imagine I'll have an appetite when I get back."

"I will. I'll save some of everything."

Malcolm put on his coat and took two leashes down from the hook, one for Blixen and the other for Stuart, the shepherd mongrel mix that he had adopted as a puppy. Blixen and Stuart got up and walked to the door.

We were all used to the routine by now. Malcolm arrived every morning at eight, by which time I would already have been down to the kennel to feed the dogs—with so many, I let only Blixen and Nelson sleep inside. He took them for walks, two by two, then stuck around for an hour or two to help me with any errands or chores that needed doing. At five, he would return and do it all again. Malcolm was truly a godsend. But it felt odd, being so dependent on someone I didn't know well, even though I'd technically known him for years.

"You shouldn't have to do all this," I said, frowning at the top of Malcolm's gray head as he bent down to clip on Stuart's leash. "Maybe I *should* ask Chrissy to come."

Malcolm stood up, looking surprised and— possibly a little hurt? Though I may have been reading things wrong. I'm a little out of practice when it comes to interpreting the expressions and actions of men.

"Well," he said. "If you'd rather have your daughter, I certainly understand. But if you're worried that you're imposing on my good will— don't. This is no hardship for me. I far prefer the company of dogs to people." He smiled. "Present company excepted."

Besides being out of practice when it comes to reading men, I was having a little trouble inter-preting my own emotional responses, at least since Malcolm came on the scene. When he smiled I became aware of a strange, anxious, sort of empty feeling in the pit of my stomach.

The only thing I could liken it to was the way I'd felt when James and Leila, his wife, invited me along for a family vacation to Florida. I hadn't set foot on an airplane since Jim died. While waiting to board the flight, I started to feel very strange, almost light-headed, and turned so pale that James insisted I sit down. The Xanax Leila gave me helped me make it through the flight, but I stared straight ahead the whole time, refusing to look out the window.

Malcolm's smile made me feel like I did while I was waiting to get on the plane, but not quite. Maybe I was hungry. Or maybe it was the pain pills Dr. Francatelli prescribed. I'd only taken them for two days, but still. You never knew how long these things stayed in your bloodstream.

"Well . . . I really don't think I could manage this menagerie without help. If you're sure you don't mind, Malcolm."

"I don't mind."

I stood in the doorway watching as he walked down the garden path, following in Blixen and Stuart's eager footsteps. When they got to the gate, he turned to look at me and smiled.

My stomach flew to Florida.

"Be still, Nelson. This will only take a minute."

I knelt on the floor, trying to get Nelson to hold still long enough so Monica could measure the distance between his neck and his rump. We'd decided to make our own dog jacket patterns, using Blixen, Nelson, and Maisie as mannequins for the large-, medium-, and small-sized jackets.

Getting Blixen and Maisie's measurements had been a piece of cake, but Nelson was feeling frisky and kept trying to lick my nose.

"Stop it, you big goofball!" Nelson lunged at my nose again and I started laughing, setting off Peaches and Cream, who began baying gleefully.

"Grace," Monica called out over the din. "Can you take over for Nan? The model's not being very cooperative."

Grace, who had more experience designing garments than I did, not to mention the use of both arms, was sketching out the pattern for a Blixen-sized jacket on a piece of butcher paper.

"Just one second." Grace erased a line and redrew it, then put aside her pencil and got down on the floor. "Uh-uh," she said when Nelson tried to lick her nose too. "No kissing on the first date."

She put a hand firmly on each of Nelson's shoulders. Perhaps sensing she meant business, he stopped wiggling long enough for Monica to get the measurements she needed. Peaches and Cream settled down, too, and we were finally able to get to work.

While Grace quickly drew out the medium-sized pattern, I ironed the fabric to press out any creases, then pinned on the pattern pieces she'd already cut out. It wasn't easy with just one arm, but I managed. Monica was in charge of cutting. By the time she was finished, Grace was ready to start sewing, working so quickly that Monica and I had a hard time keeping up. But before long we fell into a rhythm and were able to work and talk at the same time.

"How are things working out with Malcolm?" Monica asked.

"It's good. But . . . odd. I'm out of the habit of conversing with humans," I said, and reached down to pat Blixen on the head.

"He seems nice," Grace said, reaching for a piece of cheese while she waited for Monica to finish cutting the next jacket.

"Oh, he is. And I am grateful for the help. I couldn't possibly manage on my own, especially with seven dogs in the house. That's a chore even with two good hands. And Malcolm is certainly less intrusive than Chrissy would have been."

"Not exactly a ringing endorsement." Grace brushed cracker crumbs off the sewing machine. "Are you sure you don't want me to come and stay with you?"

"Don't be silly. You're up to your earlobes as it is."

"It's not as bad with Gavin out of town. I had to come into work on Sunday morning, but Gavin's flight took off at two so I spent the rest of the day with Jamie. Tonight I actually left the office at six thirty. Not early enough to go to Landsdowne before I came here, but still . . . It feels good to hop off the hamster wheel for a few days."

"And when your boss comes back, you'll have to hop right back on."

Grace shrugged, but she didn't argue with me. If I had said I needed help, Grace would have found a way. So would Monica. Isn't it a shame that I had to turn sixty before I realized that the words *best friend* could be applied to creatures with two feet as well as four? Monica and Grace were as loyal as any retriever on earth. They would do anything for me and the feeling was mutual.

"Besides, I didn't mean that the way it sounded. Malcolm is a huge help. And we've known each other a long time, so it's not like we have to fill each other in on our life's story. That's a relief. On the other hand, we have a lot in common, too, so there's plenty to talk about—if we feel like it.

"Malcolm's not one who has to talk just to fill the silence. I'm the same. Probably comes from spending so much time with the dogs," I said as I laid a pattern onto a piece of red fabric with blue polka dots.

Monica, who had just finished cutting out a jacket of blue chambray, handed the pieces to Grace and said, "So, if Malcolm were a dog, what breed would he be?"

"What breed?" I laughed, intrigued by the question. "Let me see . . . Definitely a golden. He's calm, not easily ruffled, and goes with the flow. He's also pleasant, cheerful, and a good listener. He's Blixen!" I said. "No wonder I like him."

"That means he's a perfect match," Monica said, "Your spirit animal. Now, what about this isn't working for you?"

"Nothing," I said. "It just feels funny, accepting help from someone else. But I guess I'm helping Malcolm too. I think Malcolm needs to feel useful."

"Sounds like it's a good arrangement for everybody," Grace said.

"Yes," I said, picturing Malcolm at the garden gate. "Yes, I think it is."

"Well, I'm glad we got that settled," Monica said as she took the polka-dot pattern from my hand and started cutting. "Moving on. Are you still looking for fund-raising ideas for the rescue?"

"Definitely," I said. "What did you have in mind?"

"What about a Fairy Dogmother's ball? A dinner dance for pets and people?"

"That's an adorable idea. I love it! Would you do it at the restaurant?"

"I don't think the Health Department would allow it," Monica said. "I was thinking we could have it here, in your garden. You've got so much space. We could invite more people that way, and it's always so pretty in summer."

"It should be a costume party," Grace added,

"with prizes. Maisie and I will need matching outfits. I'm seeing pink tulle and sequins."

"There's not enough tulle in Portland to make a costume for Desmond," Monica said, "but I'll come up with something."

"Monica, this is a brilliant idea. I bet we could raise five or six thousand for Rainbow Gate!" Unable to contain my excitement, I jumped up from my chair and kissed Monica on the top of the head.

"Hang on, hang on," Monica laughed. "Let's not start naming figures until I have some time to crunch the numbers and come up with a ticket price. I'll do the catering at cost, so that will help. And I'm sure I can get some of the vendors I work with to donate at least some of the food and rental equipment. If we have it in June, that should give us plenty of time to plan. And, hopefully, good weather."

Grace turned the jacket she'd finished sewing inside out and carried it to the ironing board to press the seams. "It really does sound like fun. But before we start talking menus and decor, I want to hear about Dr. Dreamboat."

"Dr. Who?" I asked.

"Dr. Dreamboat," Monica said. "You don't remember? The ER doctor—Dr. Francatelli. You pinned the nickname on him, right after you announced to everyone present, including the doctor, that I had a thing for Italian men."

"Oh, no. Did I really?" Monica nodded. "I'm sorry. Those pain meds were too strong. I quit taking them."

"It's okay," Monica shrugged. "Mark has a good sense of humor."

"Mark?" Grace asked. "You're on a first-name basis?"

Monica shrugged again, keeping her eyes on her work, but I could see a hint of a smile on her lips.

"He came around to the restaurant the next day. I brought his dessert out myself and we talked for a little bit, exchanged recipes. He likes to cook. And then I saw him again, day before yesterday."

Grace and I exchanged a look.

"He came to the restaurant looking for you twice in one week?" I asked. "Sounds like things are moving quickly."

"Not the restaurant," Monica said. "I went to the ER on Saturday night. I had this weird rash on my arm."

Grace looked at her blankly. "You went to the emergency room. For a rash?"

"Yes," Monica said, frowning. "WebMD had a picture of a rash that was just like mine. *Exactly* like mine. Do you know what it was? Scarlet fever. It could have been serious."

"And was it?" Grace asked.

Monica's frown deepened, her forehead pleated like a set of shutters.

"No," she muttered. "It was paprika."

"Paprika?"

"I accidentally smeared some on my arm when I was experimenting with a new marinade, okay? But it *could* have been serious! Stop laughing. It's not funny."

One of Monica's many good qualities is that she can see the humor in almost any situation, even when the joke comes at her own expense. Even as she protested Grace's laughter, Monica's own mouth started twitching at the corners. But before her smile had fully bloomed, a cloud crossed over her face. She put down her scissors and hinged her head back, staring at the ceiling.

"I already messed it up, didn't I? I ruined it before it even started." She smacked her hand to her forehead. "What's the matter with me? Why do I always do this? And why with *this* one?

"He's gorgeous. And he's a doctor. Who likes to cook. And he's Italian. A gorgeous Italian doctor who likes to cook. Basically, he's perfect," she said, still talking to the ceiling. "And, for a couple of minutes in the restaurant, when we were talking about cannoli fillings, we had a connection. He *did* like me, I could tell.

"But I had to ruin it, didn't I? Instead of keeping my crazy under wraps until he got to know me well enough to think I was adorable and eccentric instead of nuts, I had to go to the ER with my paprika emergency so Dr. Perfect

Italian Dreamboat would know right off that I am a complete train wreck."

Monica groaned.

"Alex said I'm too pushy and he's right. He said I need to back off a little, give people space. But did I listen? No, of course not. I ruined everything before it even got started."

Grace left the ironing board and went to sit down next to Monica.

"Oh, come on. It's not that bad. Maybe he thought you were just looking for an excuse to see him again and took it as a compliment. Maybe he thought it was cute. And it was, kind of. It's the kind of story that couples tell each other when they go out to dinner for their tenth anniversary."

Grace lowered her chin and her voice, pretending to be Dr. Dreamboat. "Honey, remember how you had such a crush on me that you smeared paprika on your arm and showed up in the ER just so you could see me?"

"Yes," I chimed in. "Grace is right. This is one of those things that will make a great family story someday."

"Not if I never see him again," Monica said glumly.

"I bet you anything he drops by the restaurant again next week. He'll come looking for you. And if he doesn't? Well . . . then he just doesn't deserve you. If he can't recognize all of your wonderful qualities and laugh off a tiny touch of hypochondria, then it's his loss."

Monica stared at me.

"Nan, did I ever tell you about how when I was in the fourth grade and everybody in the class got invited to Hillary Resnick's pool party but me? My mother gave me almost the exact same speech. It wasn't convincing then either."

She heaved a sigh. "Oh, well. I guess it was a little soon to be measuring him for a tux and reserving the wedding chapel. I've only had three conversations with him. So what if he's a doctor? And Italian. And gorgeous. And likes to cook. That doesn't mean he's perfect, does it?"

"Absolutely not," Grace replied. "He might be one of those guys who sucks his teeth after he eats. Or uses toothpicks." She made a face. "I hate that. It's not quite as bad as flossing in public, but close."

"True," Monica said. "He might be one of those guys who spends his entire weekend watching football. Or Three Stooges marathons. He might be a close talker. Or flatulent. He might wear briefs instead of boxers." Monica looked to us for support. "Am I right?"

Grace nodded. "He might drive a car with those big, oversized tires."

"Or worse," I said. "He might hate dogs."

"Yes!" Monica said definitively, holding her hands sideways and chopping the air. "Exactly!

He might be any of those things. Or all of them! I have no way of knowing. But there *must* be something wrong with him. Otherwise, why would a handsome Italian doctor who likes to cook still be single?

"Because he has flaws," Monica said, lowering her voice to an ominous register. "Deep, dark flaws that aren't obvious at first glance, but they're there just the same. They must be.

"You know what? I feel better already. Clearly, I dodged a bullet. Whew!" Monica wiped imaginary sweat from her brow, picked up the scissors, and started cutting again. "So, enough of my drama. Grace, how was your week?"

"Up until yesterday, terrible. Being indispensable is exhausting," she said, sitting down in front of the sewing machine. "I'm really looking forward to these next few days with Gavin out of town. Oh, and did I tell you what Alicia, one of Jamie's nurses, said?"

We shook our heads.

"Well, Jamie's pulse and temperature were a teensy bit elevated. Nothing to worry about. But Alicia thought it was because he knew I was there and—"

Grace's cell phone rang, interrupting her story. She glanced at the screen and quickly picked up.

"Hello? Yes, this is Grace."

She was quiet for a long while, listening to the voice on the other end of the line. From the look in her eyes, I could tell that it wasn't good news. Finally, she said, "All right. Yes, I understand. Thank you, Doctor. I'll be right there."

Grace ended the call. "I have to go."

Monica handed Grace her purse. I got her coat from the closet.

"Jamie?" I asked.

Grace nodded as she slipped her arms into the sleeves of her coat. "His temperature spiked. They're going to take some X-rays, but the doctor thinks it's pneumonia."

"Oh, no," Monica said. "Are you okay? Do you want us to come with you?"

Grace either didn't hear or wasn't listening. She was already halfway out the door. Monica and I stood on the porch and watched her speed away.

In the time that I'd known Grace, Jamie had gone through more than one health crisis. His condition meant he was fragile by nature, but somehow, he always managed to hold on. Grace always said he was strong, a fighter who was determined to live. I was sure she was right.

But no matter how strong the desire to live, death comes for us all in time. Though I hoped I was wrong, something in me sensed that Jamie's time had come.

"Nan?" Monica's voice was uncharacteristically soft. "Do you pray?"

"Every day," I said, my mind turning to Dani.

"How? I mean . . . do you need to say anything special? Read something?"

I shook my head. "I just pour it all out and then leave it in God's hands."

"Does it work?"

"I don't always get what I ask for, if that's what you mean. Am I heard? I believe I am."

Monica reached for my hand and closed her eyes. I did the same. We stood there like that for a long time, joined in a silent plea.

Chapter 19

Grace

"Grace."

I turned around and found myself being hugged by Mrs. Babcock. Her hair was gray and her face was lined, but she still wore the same peacock-blue eye shadow.

"It was a beautiful service, Grace."

"Thank you. Thank you for coming."

I tried to draw back, but Mrs. Babcock didn't seem inclined to let go of me just yet. Over her shoulder, I made an apologetic face to Jerry, my father-in-law, whom I had been talking to before Mrs. Babcock approached. He shrugged to let me know it was fine, then walked off to join Penny, my mother-in-law, who was sitting in a corner, her eyes red from crying.

"I'm so, so sorry for your loss."

Mrs. Babcock squeezed me much too tightly. I took a firm step backward so she'd have to release me.

"Thank you," I said again.

"Such a terrible thing. Pneumonia, wasn't it? That's what I heard. And after all he'd been through." She clucked her tongue. "I hope, at least, that he went peacefully?"

"He did," I said truthfully.

I could have said more and I expect that Mrs. Babcock wanted to hear more, but that wasn't information she was entitled to. In the twelve years of our marriage, Jamie and I had shared countless private and personal moments, but none more intimate than the moment of his death.

For six days, I sat by his bedside. Every day he grew weaker. Every morning, breathing was more of a struggle than the day before. On the final morning, when it became obvious that there was no hope, I asked the doctors to remove all the needles and tubes.

I climbed into Jamie's bed and nestled close to him, lying on my side and stroking his hair, telling him one last time how much I loved him, how happy he had made me, promising him that I would be strong and fine and well, and that it was all right to go before me. As usual, Jamie was staring at the door, now closed to protect our privacy. Though I was lying right next to him, he didn't look at me, or acknowledge my presence.

Somehow I had thought . . . I had hoped he might. After all the months of worry and anguish, I hoped that at the end there might be some brief but miraculous reconnection with consciousness, a sign, and that Jamie would, if not speak, at least look at me in a way that let me know I had not failed him.

It didn't happen.

As the sun was beginning to set, he took a long, ragged breath and then released it slowly, along with his life. In those final seconds an expression of peace and recognition spread across his face. He didn't bid me farewell in any sense that I could understand, but I knew that the one he had been watching for had come for him at last and that was enough for me. The peace granted to Jamie lighted and lingered upon me as well. After so many months of struggle, we were able to rest at last. And then he was gone.

I couldn't explain it to Mrs. Babcock, or to anyone, but it was the most intimate, sacred, and precious moment that Jamie and I ever shared.

"Well, that's a mercy at least," Mrs. Babcock said. "For both of you, I should think."

"Excuse me?"

"I'm just saying that it had to come as something of a relief. You've been so brave, Grace, but it had to be a burden. I mean, first the cancer and then this?"

I felt my jaw clench. "Jamie was never a burden to me. Never."

"No, no," she clucked, "of course not. But now, after all this time, Jamie is at peace and you can move on with your life, poor darling."

She shifted her weight in my direction, as if she

were about to hug me again. I took another step backward.

"Excuse me. But I think my in-laws need me. Thank you again for coming."

"Of course. Of course," she said. "I just wanted to say hello and tell you how sorry I was. You run along and take care of your family." She reached out and grabbed my hand. "But, Grace, can I just say how wonderful you look? It's amazing, the way you've been able to keep the weight off for all these years. When I think about that fat, little girl who used to sit in the back row of my classroom, always dressed in black and too shy to speak, working so hard to be invisible even though she was as big as—"

"Mrs. Babcock, I really have to go."

"Oh, yes. Sorry. I didn't mean to keep you. It's just so good to see—"

I pulled my arm from her grip and walked away.

The crowd was starting to thin out and I was glad of it. I couldn't ever remember being as exhausted as I was at that moment. My encounter with Mrs. Babcock had sucked up the last drops of energy remaining in me. How in the world did the tradition of post-funeral receptions ever begin anyway? As if funerals weren't draining enough, somebody decided that the bereaved family members should host a party after?

It wasn't all bad. I hadn't been home in almost

two years, so it was nice to see my little brothers, Tommy and Skip, and my cousins. And it was good to talk to some of our old classmates and share Jamie stories. Until Mike Zimmerman sought me out, I'd never heard the one about how he and Jamie had driven Mike's beat-up, goner of a Chevy, a rust bucket he'd named Captain America, into the river one night just to see what it felt like to escape from a sinking vehicle.

"Teenage boys are such a bunch of knuckle-heads," Mike said. "But Jamie was the worst of all—thought he was invincible. But I'll tell you, after he beat the cancer and then survived that fall, I kind of thought it might be true."

"Me too," I said, smiling wetly but keeping my emotions in check because, by that point, I didn't even have enough energy to cry. But Mike did it for me and hugged me even longer and tighter than Mrs. Babcock had. I let him.

That was a good conversation, a story I would treasure, and there were many more besides. But I also had to endure a number of less lovely exchanges with people who, though less directly than Mrs. Babcock, hinted that Jamie's death must have come as a relief. They had no idea what they were talking about.

And though I love my in-laws—Jamie and I lived in an apartment over their garage for six years before we moved to Portland—it was hard to see them grieving. Penny was a wreck, had sobbed through the whole service. I felt terrible for her, and for Jerry.

After surviving cancer, Jamie worried about what he might be passing on to a potential child, so we put off the idea of having kids for a few years after we were married. Considering how young and broke we were, it was probably just as well. Later, we were so busy working and going to school that we put it off again. With Jamie only a year away from finishing his paramedic training, the time finally seemed right to think about starting a family. We'd discussed it just a couple of weeks before Jamie's accident and decided to start trying for a baby in the fall.

I'd thought about that a lot, especially in the last few days. If we'd never gone on that camping trip for our anniversary, if it hadn't been raining so hard, if Jamie hadn't tried to be a hero, if, if, if . . . I might be the mother of a chubby-cheeked one-year-old.

How would I feel if that baby, my only son, was taken from me? What special brand of grief accompanied the misfortune of outliving your child? I didn't know. But as I thought about the baby and what might have been and now never would be, I could imagine.

Accepting brief condolences from the few remaining guests along the way, I crossed the room to check on my in-laws. When I sat down next to her, Penny looked at me with tear-stained cheeks and hollow eyes. The look on her face was heartbreaking. I reached out to hug her. The tears I was sure had run dry began flowing again.

"I'm sorry, Mom."

"Honey, you stop that now. What have you got to be sorry about?"

"I don't know. I feel like I should have—"

"Should have what? Never left Minnesota? Stopped Jamie from being Jamie? You could no more do that than keep the earth from spinning.

"You were a good wife to my boy. You stood by him when everyone else had gone; you made him so happy and supported him every minute. Nobody could have taken better care of him. Not even me."

She looked up at Jerry, who was standing behind her chair.

"Now, Gracie, you know Penny well enough to know that it just makes her teeth hurt to admit that," he said, smiling through a sheen of unshed tears. "I sure wish we'd been able to come and help you at the end, but—"

I reached for Jerry's hand. "You drove out at Christmas. I was so happy you did."

"Me too," he said. "Helped a lot to see what a nice place it was. Even if we'd had the money, we couldn't have gotten Jamie the kind of care he needed, not way out here in the country. I know how hard you had to work, keeping him there.

I'm just sorry we couldn't help more. But since we lost the farm . . ."

"I know, Dad," I said, and squeezed his hand. "I know. We all did the best we could."

Penny sniffled. I pulled a tissue out of my pocket and handed it to her.

She dabbed at her eyes. "I know he's in a better place now, but it seems so unfair that he's gone. It just makes me feel sad. But then I remember that we almost lost him once before. I remember when you and Jamie got married. You were wearing a blue dress with little yellow flowers—"

"And Jamie was wearing a yellow dress shirt," I said.

Penny bobbed her head, confirming my recollection, and smiled a little.

"Between the family and all the nurses who wanted to be there for the wedding, I bet there were forty people crammed into that hospital room. Jamie was skinny and pale, not a hair left on his head because of the chemo, but he was grinning from ear to ear," she said as a tear rolled down her cheek. "He was so happy. I remember thinking that he was never going to leave that hospital room. But I was wrong. He got thirteen more years and we got the chance to see Jamie grow up, fulfill his dreams, and find love. He'd never have found the strength to do that without you, Gracie."

Penny gazed up at her husband. "Do you

remember, honey? It was everything we prayed for when he was so sick. In lots of ways, we were blessed, weren't we?"

Jerry nodded and laid a big, workingman's hand on her shoulder.

"He was a good son, a good man. And you've been a good daughter, Grace. We couldn't have asked for better."

After giving Jerry and Penny another hug, I excused myself and went to the bathroom to splash some cold water on my face, an attempt to rally the energy to endure a final hour of condolences before driving back to Minneapolis. I had to catch an early flight to Portland the next day.

Mike and a couple of Jamie's old friends had urged me to stay an extra day; they wanted to take me to dinner. But the funeral and final medical expenses had wiped out what little was left of my savings, so I needed to get back to work.

Exiting the ladies' room, I spotted a woman with white hair kneeling in front of my mother-in-law, holding the leash of a silken-coated golden retriever. The dog's muzzle was resting in Penny's lap, and she was stroking its head and nodding in response to the woman's murmured conversation.

"Nan?"

She turned around, then got to her feet and started walking toward me.

"What are you doing here? I told you that you didn't need to come."

"I know, but I wanted to. Malcolm is taking good care of the other dogs, including your Maisie." She opened her one good arm to embrace me. "I'm so sorry we missed the service. There was some kind of mechanical problem in Portland and our flight was delayed."

"You flew here? You *hate* flying."

"But I love you. And Blixen was with me, so that helped," she said, smiling at her dog, who was sticking close to Penny. "I thought it would be good to bring him. I thought he might be a comfort."

Penny stopped petting Blixen and looked up at me, her eyes still sad, but dry and calm.

A brief bout of light-headedness reminded me that I'd forgotten to eat that morning, so while Nan and Blixen made rounds among the mourners, I visited the buffet table. There wasn't much left by that time, just some cheese and crackers, deviled eggs, a little potato salad, and a few brownies.

My mother, who had been talking to the minister, walked over when she saw me putting food on a plate.

"Are you sure you want all that?"

"All what?" I asked, looking at my plate. It held two pieces of cheese, four crackers, half a deviled egg, a tablespoon of potato salad, and a brownie.

"The only thing I've had today is coffee."

"Well," she said grudgingly, "just so you don't start channeling your grief into food. I'm just saying, you had to work so hard to take off the weight. It'd be a shame if you gained it all back. So many do. The people on that show, the one where they go to that camp and compete to lose all that weight? I read a story just last week saying the winners almost always gain it back."

"Mom, I'm not going to gain back the weight. I've kept it off for thirteen years."

"I know," she said, watching nervously as I ate a piece of cheese. "I'm just saying—people do. And you've been through a terrible loss. You holding up okay, Grace?"

I nodded. "I'm fine. It's been hard, but I'm fine."

"Good." She put her arm around my waist. "You've been so brave, honey. When Jamie had his accident, I didn't think you'd be able to cope. But you did and I'm real proud of you. You took good care of him."

My mother, a glass-half-full person, who believed it was important to keep her children from getting "a big head," was never one to throw away compliments, so her comments surprised me. I was a little curious to know why she thought I might not be able to cope, but decided I was better off not knowing.

"Thanks, Mom."

"So what are you going to do now?"

"Well," I said, "my flight leaves out of Minneapolis at eight o'clock tomorrow morning, so I hope I can get on the road before dark. I'd like to get at least a few hours of sleep. There's a little bit of paperwork I still need to do to get the ashes shipped out to me."

She tilted her head far to the right. "Shipped? Do you mean you're not going to bury them here?"

"No."

"Why not?"

"Because I don't think that's what Jamie would want. I talked it over with Penny and Jerry and they agree."

My mother set her mouth, the way she always does when she's irritated with something I've done. Growing up, I saw that look on her face at least twice a day, sometimes more. It got to the point where I realized that her expression wasn't even necessarily related to my actions. Sometimes, my mere existence irritated her.

That hurt: I won't pretend that it didn't. When I was a kid, I wanted nothing more than to please my mother, but somehow I never could. Jamie said that it wasn't me, it was my mom; that she was the kind of person who just couldn't be pleased with anyone. It wasn't until Jamie and I moved into that little apartment over his folks' garage and I saw firsthand how a happy family operates that I realized he was right.

It wasn't my fault. It wasn't Mom's either. She wasn't wired for happiness.

"Grace," she said impatiently. "Answer my question. What are your plans? When are you coming home?"

"Home? You mean back to Minnesota? Mom, I'm not. My job is in Portland now."

"And your family is here!" She clicked her tongue and set her mouth yet again. "For heaven's sake, Grace. You can always find another job. Family is irreplaceable."

I looked at my mother, the thin woman with the thin smile and the unhappy heart. Then I looked across the room at Nan, whose heart was infinite, who took in strays of all kinds—four- and two-legged—and nurtured by nature, who had swallowed back her greatest fear to fly halfway across the country so I would know she cared, and I realized that my mother was right. Family, wherever you may find it, is irreplaceable.

"I'll call you when I get to Portland. I'll be out to visit at Christmas." I leaned forward and kissed her on the cheek. "I love you, Mom."

Chapter 20

Grace

We hit some mild turbulence on the flight back to Portland. When deep breathing didn't do the trick, Nan, clutching at the armrest, asked me to talk to her.

"About what?"

"Anything. I need a distraction. Tell me what you're working on."

"This?" I asked, looking at the pile of blue and green patches I'd piled on the tray table. "It's just another quilt block."

"It's pretty," Nan said, even though her eyes were screwed shut. "Tell me about it. What's the pattern?"

"Well, I think it's actually called Aimee's Choice," I said. "But I've decided to call it Hero Star. I'm making it with scraps of Jamie's old EMT uniform. He was already working as an emergency medical technician back in Minnesota. He saved the lives of at least a dozen people, probably more."

"I didn't know that," Nan said, opening her eyes.

I nodded. "Originally, even before he got sick, he wanted to be a doctor. He was one of those people who liked helping other people. But he lost a couple of years to cancer; then his dad needed help on the farm. . . ." Nan released her grip on the armrest and laid her hand on my forearm but didn't interrupt my story.

"After a few years, Jamie decided he didn't want to wait anymore, so he signed up for EMT training at the community college. He loved the job but could only get part-time work in our area, and after a while, he decided he really wanted to become a paramedic in a city setting." I smiled. "We closed our eyes and stuck a pin in a map to decide where we were going to move for his paramedic training, but I'm pretty sure he peeked. He'd been talking about Portland all along—mild winters, lots of recreational opportunities.

"At first, I wasn't so sure about moving. I'd never lived anywhere else and I'm not as adventurous as Jamie. He had to talk me into it, but I'm glad he did. I'm glad he got to do some of the things he wanted to do with his life."

"Me too," Nan said. "But what do you want to do with your life?"

I shrugged. "Live, work. Same thing I've always done. I mean, I'd like to find another job at some point, something with a slightly less miserable schedule, but I'll be back at the office tomorrow morning."

Nan frowned. "Are you sure that's a good idea? Maybe you should take some time off, give yourself time to mourn and consider your future before diving back into business as usual."

"I couldn't even if I wanted to; I'm out of vacation days. Plus, I've got bills to pay. Besides, I've been mourning for almost two years. Don't worry, I'm fine. Really."

The plane hit a little bump. Nan let out a little yelp and clutched at the armrest again, her knuckles turning white. Blixen, who was lying quietly on the bulkhead floor and wearing her service dog vest, put her muzzle on Nan's shoe.

"Should I ask the flight attendant to get you some tea?" I asked.

"Vodka tonic," Nan said. "Make it a double."

The next day, I woke up at five as usual. But since I didn't need to go to Landsdowne before work, I decided to take Maisie for a walk and stop by Starbucks for a latte, hoping it would perk me up a little.

When I passed the big cement planters where Sunny and Z hung out, Sunny nodded toward my extra giant coffee cup and said, "Venti size. Did you win the lottery or something?"

"If only," I said, feeling a little guilty.

Maybe I should have bought two smaller coffees and given one to Sunny. Since I'd gotten to know Sunny and Z better, I sometimes bought extra food at the grocery store and gave it to them on my way home. They were always very appreciative—high as kites half the time, but always polite.

When I first moved to town, I'd been shocked by the number of people living on the streets, but I'd gotten used to it. I couldn't do much to tackle the problem of homelessness, but I could help Sunny and Z. Or I could try to. But it was hard to predict if I would find them "at home" or out doing something else. Finding a fix? Riding the bus to stay warm?

"I decided to treat myself," I said, feeling stupid, like I was making excuses.

Sunny nodded dully and slid down to sit on her haunches. As she did, the hem of her dirty gray sweatshirt caught against the wall and rode up to expose a sliver of too-pale flesh. That's when I realized that something wasn't right.

The red wagon was missing, so was one of the sleeping bags, and Sunny looked worse than I'd ever seen her.

"Where's Z?"

"Gone," she said, her eyes glazing over as she stared past my legs.

"Gone where?"

Sunny shrugged. "Woke up three days ago and he was just . . . gone. So was all his stuff. And the dog." She reached out to pat Maisie on the head. "Hey, little girl."

Maisie licked her dirty hand. I squatted down on the pavement.

"You okay? Is there anything I can do?"

"Do you have any money?"

The way she asked quickly, so quickly, and with her eyes suddenly glittering and hungry, made me uncomfortable. I knew that Sunny and Z panhandled to survive, but they'd never directly asked me for a handout. Whether that was because it felt awkward to ask for money from someone who lived right in the neighborhood or because I didn't look like somebody who had any was hard to say.

"I don't have any cash," I said truthfully. "But, here."

I held out my latte. Sunny stared at the cup.

"Go ahead," I urged. "It'll warm you up."

"Are you sick or anything?"

"Totally healthy," I assured her.

She sniffled and swiped at her nose with her sleeve.

"Okay. Thanks."

I watched her drink, feeling better but worse, wishing I could do more but having no idea what more might be. Finally, I stood up.

"You going to be okay?"

"Yeah, sure." Sunny shrugged. "I miss the dog. But Z's just a guy. I can always find another one, right?"

"You think so?"

Sunny held the cup close to her chest, as if trying to warm her entire body from that one small source of heat.

"No, but it makes me feel better to say so."

All of my bosses, including Gavin, were attending an off-site meeting, so the office was quiet and I was grateful, thinking I'd need a day to catch up. But when I actually started sorting through my e-mail and inbox, there wasn't all that much that needed doing.

Gavin had a habit of piling stuff on my desk and attaching yellow sticky notes with terse instructions on each item, telling what he wanted done and when, but the pile he'd left for me was uncharacteristically short, consisting of nothing more than some filing and copying, plus a reminder to schedule a tune-up for his Lexus and an executive physical for himself. Apparently, Gavin had more of a heart than I'd given him credit for. I'd have to thank him when I saw him, then assure him that I was ready to get back to work.

Honestly, I'd have preferred it if he'd heaped my desk with things that needed doing. It would have made the day easier to endure, kept my mind from thinking about Jamie, from trying to imagine how I was going to fill the remainder of my days, and years, and life without him. I made a lot of trips to the bathroom that day, closing myself in a stall to shed a few quiet tears before wiping my eyes with the tissue and going back to my desk.

I did spend a little time updating my résumé. I wasn't planning to look for another job right away, but I wasn't planning on spending the rest of my life being indispensable to Gavin Nutting either. He definitely wasn't my dream boss, but after he'd endured my unexpected leave of absence during Jamie's illness, it didn't seem fair to leave him high and dry. I'd ease out over the next few months, making sure I found a great replacement. There was no rush.

At three o'clock, I went down to Starbucks for my usual small drip coffee. While I was waiting in line, someone tapped me on the shoulder. When I turned around, Luke Pascal was standing there, holding a bouquet of grocery store carnations and daisies.

"Don't worry, I'm not staying," he said. "But I saw Monica yesterday and she told me about Jamie. I just wanted to tell you how sorry I am for your loss."

He handed me the flowers. I briefly buried my face in the blossoms, breathing in the spicy, sweet scent of carnations.

"Thanks, Luke. That was nice of you. Do you have time for a cup of coffee?"

"Yes, but . . . are you sure? I don't want to be accused of stalking."

"It's okay. Besides, I just this minute remembered that I forgot to give Monica the sixteen dollars I owe you."

"Yeah, well. I didn't want to say anything but . . ." He coughed deliberately, then grinned.

Smiling, I walked up to the checkout register. "Two medium drip of the day." I turned to Luke. "How do you take it?"

"Black with three sugars."

"Three?"

"Don't judge."

I ordered two oatmeal cookies in addition to the coffee. When we sat down at a table near the window, I handed one cookie to Luke, then took the other for myself and broke it in half, wrapping the leftover piece in a napkin. It wasn't until I slipped it into my purse that I felt Luke's eyes on me.

"Why do you do that?"

"Do what? Oh, this?" I asked, glancing at the cookie half. "It's kind of a habit. I was overweight growing up, really fat and completely miserable. I tried dieting, but it just didn't work for me. I love to eat too much. Cutting out my favorite foods wasn't a realistic option for me, but portion control was. When I ate out, I started dividing everything I ate in half, saving the rest for another meal. That, along with the addition of regular walking and a few more green vegetables, did the trick."

"You didn't cut the portions in half at The Fish House. You ate everything. In fact, and don't take this the wrong way, but I was kind of impressed. I'd never seen anyone eat that many oysters."

"Oh, well. Oysters are kind of a weakness of mine." I broke a corner off my cookie. "That along with everything else. No kidding, I really do love to eat. Most of the time I work hard not to overdo it. But The Fish House was an exception, a special occasion."

Luke lifted his brows. "Yeah? What was so special?"

"Monica was paying."

Luke's laugh was more like a deep bark, a cross between an enthusiastic seal and a big dog.

"I'm sorry," he said when I didn't join in.

"Don't be," I said, forcing a smile. "I meant it to be funny."

Luke sipped his coffee. "So . . . how are you holding up?"

"I'm fine. Really," I said, responding to his doubtful look. "Nan came to the funeral. That helped a lot."

"She's your other support group buddy, right? Monica has talked about her. She sounds pretty cool."

"She is," I confirmed. "And she's more than a buddy, she's my friend. I'm not sure that I understood what being a friend really meant, and how important it is to have them, until now. Nan's husband was killed in a plane crash, so she's terrified of flying. She flew all the way out to Minnesota anyway, because she thought I might need her. Turns out I did, even more than I knew.

"But, that's Nan. She's so tuned in, so wise. She'd hate hearing me say that, but it's true. And it's not just because she's older. Nan and my mom are about the same age, but my mom—" I shook my head. "Well, let's just say that age and wisdom don't necessarily go hand in hand. But Nan seems to know what I need almost before I do. She never talks at me or lectures. Sometimes she asks questions, but mostly she just listens. And yet, without saying a word, she's able to make me understand where I'm going wrong."

"She sounds like more than your friend. She almost sounds like your guru."

"Oh, she'd *really* hate hearing that," I said, smiling. "But you might be right. Anyway, it was so good to look up and see her there. It helped a lot. And the funeral did, too, in a way, hearing everybody tell their Jamie stories. It was good to know that other people have good memories of him too.

"But," I sighed, "it's good to be home. This has been such a long road."

"I was surprised when Monica said you were going back to work already," Luke said. "You sure you don't need some time?"

"Time for what? To sit home and be miserable?

It's better to keep busy, you know? Get back into a routine."

I bit into my cookie. It tasted like sawdust, sawdust and raisins.

"Hey, do you have the time? Gavin's at an off-site meeting, but I shouldn't stay away from the office too long."

Luke frowned. "You still didn't get a new battery for your watch?"

I opened my mouth and started to make up a story, a lie, but I just didn't have the energy for it, or the inclination. I didn't want to lie to Luke.

And, for some reason, I wanted him to know the story. I wanted him to understand.

"It's not the batteries. It's broken. Jamie gave me this watch, an anniversary present, when we went on our last camping trip together, hiking in the North Cascades. It was drizzling when we started out in the morning, but the rain wasn't that bad. We'd seen worse. But, after we stopped for lunch, it really began to pour. And the wind was blowing so hard, it sounded like a freight train. I'd never seen rain like that. We decided it was too dangerous to keep going, so we turned around, started back down the mountain. But about halfway down, I slipped and fell over a steep embankment and twisted my ankle. Jamie climbed down to get me. I told him not to, that I thought I could crawl back up, but he didn't listen.

"He wasn't being stupid. Jamie was a good out-doorsman and always carried rescue gear in his pack. He tied a rope around the trunk of a good-sized tree and came down to get me. On another day, if it hadn't been raining so hard, it would have been no problem. But it was pouring, just pouring, and the ground was sodden. When he was a few feet away from me, the trail above us collapsed, just peeled away from the mountain. The tree that Jamie had tied the rope to came down too. Jamie fell. He slid right past me, over a cliff onto the trail below, and hit his head on a rock.

"That was how it happened, at 2:18 on the day after our tenth anniversary. It was two days before I noticed that the hands of my watch were frozen. I must have hit it on something when I fell. I've taken it to three different jewelers and none of them were able to fix it.

"When Jamie gave it to me, I told him I'd never take it off and I never have. I never will. I don't ever want to forget him."

Luke was quiet, looking at me. Probably wondering why I wasn't crying. I was wondering myself. But instead of asking about that, Luke said, "Is that what you're afraid of? That you'll forget him?"

His question took me by surprise. "I'm not afraid," I said, my voice sounding a little defen-sive even to my own ears. "I could never—"

Before I could finish the sentence, the door of the coffee shop opened and Ava stepped inside, her eyes searching.

"There you are," she said, crossing the room to our table. "Denise said I could probably find you down here."

"Coffee break," I said, feeling like I'd been caught doing something wrong. "I thought the off-site meeting was going to last all day. Is everybody back?" I asked, though I was really only concerned about Gavin.

"Just me. When you're done, could you come up to my office? I need to—" For the first time, she glanced at my coffee companion and pulled up short. "Luke," she said, sounding as surprised as she looked. "I didn't realize that you two—"

"Ava, nice to see you."

Luke started to get to his feet, but Ava waved him off.

"No, no. I didn't mean to interrupt." She looked at me. "As soon as you're done."

"I'll be right up," I said, and reached for my purse.

"No, it's fine," she said, sounding more flustered than I'd ever heard her. "Take your time. I'll be in my office. Nice to see you, Luke."

She left quickly.

"I should go." I reached into my wallet, took out a twenty-dollar bill, and handed it to Luke.

"Grace, I was just teasing before. You don't need to pay me back."

"I insist."

"I don't have any change," he said, folding the bill and putting it into his shirt pocket. "Guess that means that next time I'll buy the coffee."

I told him to keep the change, but what I really meant was, I didn't plan on seeing him again. Luke was a nice man, there was no doubt about it, but nothing had changed. Jamie was gone, but he had my heart. Luke got the message. When I got up from my chair, he did the same, and reached out to shake my hand.

"I'm glad you're okay, Grace. Good luck to you."

"Thanks for the flowers," I said, picking them up from the table. "Say, I forgot to ask, how do you know Ava? Are you friends?"

"Not friends," Luke said, shaking his head. "But we were married for five years."

To say that was one of the more awkward exits in my life would be an understatement. Luke had been married to Ava? I didn't know either of them all that well, but they just didn't seem like they went together. But obviously, since the marriage had only lasted five years, they didn't.

I said goodbye, thanked him again for everything, and left. When I got to the office, Ava was waiting for me. She got right to the point.

"Grace, I hope you know how sorry I am about your loss, but we're going to have to make a change."

"A change?" I asked, not entirely sure I understood. "Do you mean that you're . . ."

"Letting you go, yes."

My jaw went slack. "You can't be serious. Ava, I . . . If this is about Luke, there's nothing going on between us. I barely know him."

Ava rolled her eyes. "Grace, the amount of time that's passed since I've seen or thought about Luke is longer than our marriage. I was surprised to see the two of you together, but that's not why I'm firing you. I'm just the messenger; Gavin's the one who wants you gone." She heaved a sigh. "I tried to tell you, Grace. The only way you could keep this job was to make yourself indispensable."

"But I did! I worked sixty- and seventy-hour weeks. I came in on weekends. I took his car to the shop. I picked up his dry cleaning, for heaven's sake. I made the slides for his stupid presentation at the sales conference. I stayed up all night teaching myself PowerPoint—"

"And then you disappeared for two weeks."

"My husband was dying! What did you expect me to do?"

"Nothing," she said, her expression softer than I'd ever seen it. "You did exactly what you should have done, went exactly where you were needed. Because you *were* indispensable, Grace, to Jamie. That's how it should have been."

"But, Ava, I need this job. Let me talk to Gavin—"

She cut me off with a shake of her head. "I already tried. It's no use. I did get you two months of severance, but that's the best I could do. Gavin wants you to clean out your desk today. Your replacement starts tomorrow."

Today? They wanted me gone that day? The confusion and anxiety I was feeling must have shown because Ava got up from her chair and walked to the front of her desk, then sat down on the desktop and touched me on the shoulder.

"Listen to me, Grace. You *don't* need this job, not anymore. You never liked working here. Now you don't have to. The timing seems pretty awful, I know, but maybe it's for the best. You need to give yourself some time. Think of this as a chance to assess your strengths and weaknesses, and figure out what you really want to do with your life.

"You were there when your husband needed you most. Nobody could have been more loyal. And I admire you for that, Grace, I really do."

Ava pushed herself off the desktop and into a standing position and put out her hand. The meeting was over.

"Good luck to you, Grace."

Chapter 21

Grace

The pouring rain had softened to a steady drizzle. Walking toward the front door of my building, I spotted an enormous yellow sunflower sitting on the front steps. As I got closer, I realized that it was only a picture of a sunflower printed on an umbrella. Monica was underneath it, shivering, her feet wet, holding a foil-covered pan in her lap.

"What are you doing here?"

"Waiting for you. I brought you some cannoli. I've been experimenting with some new recipes."

"And you couldn't wait until Monday to share? What's the matter with you? You're getting soaked. Come inside."

I unlocked the door, set about turning the lights on and the heat up, then greeted Maisie, who wriggled in rapture over my return.

"Oh, yes. I know," I cooed, squatting down to Chihuahua level. "I'm glad to see you too. How about a biscuit before dinner?"

Maisie let out an approving yip. I picked her up and started toward the kitchen but stopped short when I realized Monica was still standing by the front door.

"Aren't you going to come in?"

"Maybe not. I'm worried about getting water all over your wood floors."

"Oh, Monica. Hang on a sec."

After making a quick side trip to the kitchen for Maisie's biscuit, I grabbed an armful of towels from the bathroom, exchanging them for the pan of cannoli. While Monica dried off, I went into the kitchen, filled Maisie's bowl with kibble, and started making tea.

"Shouldn't you be at the restaurant?" I called across the counter that separated the kitchen from the living room.

"Soon. Ben can handle things by himself for a bit."

Monica walked into the kitchen in her stockinged feet. The bottom few inches of her pants were damp, but she wasn't dripping anymore.

"You got caught in the rain too?" she asked.

I reached a hand up to my hair. After my unexpected ouster from Spector, I'd gone for a long drive, taking my anger and anxiety out on the twists and turns of Portland's West Hills. Without the benefit of a blow-dryer and styling products, my hair had dried into an unruly, frizzy mess.

"I forgot my umbrella when I left the office," I said, lifting the foil off the cannoli.

"There are a couple missing from the pan," Monica said as she pulled up the counter stool that was my only kitchen seating. "A homeless woman came by asking for money. I didn't have any cash so I gave her some cannoli."

"Dishwater blond hair and rhinestone nose piercing?"

"Uh-huh."

The microwave beeped. I pulled out the mugs and tossed a teabag into each.

"Must have been Sunny. Did she look okay? I've been worried about her."

"She looked pale. And skinny."

"That's normal," I said, and pulled two mismatched dessert plates out of the cupboard, then placed two pastries on each one. "Sad, but normal."

"She was starving," Monica said. "I gave her a cannoli and she wolfed it down while she was standing there, so I gave her two more. I thought she might be high."

"Probably."

"Hey," Monica said, frowning as she looked around the apartment, "when are you going to finish unpacking the boxes and actually move into this place? It really does look like a refugee camp. I mean, do you think you could invest in more than one stool? Or maybe even a table? Possibly some plates that match?"

"I'm not too certain about the investment

part, but, as of today, I'll have plenty of time to unpack boxes." I dug two forks out of a drawer and handed one, plus the mug of tea, to Monica. "They fired me."

"You're kidding," she said, sounding surprised, but not quite as surprised as I'd have supposed. "Oh, Grace. That sucks. If there ever was a time that you needed a high-fat dessert, now is that time."

"How true." Standing at the counter, I picked up my fork, took a bite of cannoli, and groaned. "Oh, Monica. Oh, wow. This is amazing."

She beamed. "Pretty good, right? I've been tinkering with the recipe."

"Good? It borders on a religious experience. What's in here?"

"Besides the ricotta and sugar? Marsala, slivered almonds, and a lot of lemon peel. Try the chocolate one," she urged. "That's got hazelnuts and candied orange."

She didn't have to ask twice.

"Oh, wow," I said, closing my eyes in rapture. "This one is even better than the other. How is that possible? And how did you know I needed this today?"

How *did* she know? Okay, sure, I was just back from the funeral, but why would she be sitting on my front stoop in the rain at five thirty when she knows I'm lucky to get home by eight?

"I just had a feeling," she said quickly when I asked her, shrugging and looking very guilty.

"You just had a feeling? Come on. What aren't you telling me?"

Her eyes darted away from mine and she licked her lips.

"Monica," I said in a warning tone.

"Okay, fine. I didn't have a feeling. Luke called me. He told me all about bringing you flowers, and having coffee with you, and then how his ex-wife showed up."

"And?"

"And after you left, it started to rain so he stuck around and finished his coffee, waiting for it to let up. But it didn't, so, finally, he ran out to his truck. That's when he saw you, crossing the street without a coat, getting wet and carrying a box, and looking really ticked off."

"He was watching me!" I gasped.

"Oh, stop it. You act like he's some kind of stalker. Okay, sure," Monica said, spreading her hands a bit, "he showed up in your coffee shop unexpectedly a couple of times. But that part was my fault. Really, Grace, he wasn't watching you. He happened to see you, put two and two together, then called me. That's it. He wasn't stalking you; he was worried about you. Luke is a really great guy, trust me."

I heaved a sigh. "Fine. If you say so. I've bigger things to worry about right now. Anyway," I said, taking another bite of cannoli, "I'm glad you're here."

Monica tsked her tongue. "So Gavin honestly fired you the day after you got back from your husband's funeral? That's one for the Heartless Hall of Fame."

"Technically," I said, "Ava was the one who fired me. But she was following Gavin's orders."

"Wow. He didn't even have the guts to pull the trigger himself?"

I shook my head. "Nope, I'm sure he didn't consider it the highest and best use of his time. As you know, Gavin is very big on delegating the details to people lower in the pecking order."

"What a sniveling little coward," Monica snarled.

For some reason, seeing the disgusted look on her face, like she was about to scrape something unspeakable off her shoe, felt oddly vindicating. I told her about my whole day, from the moment I stepped off the elevator that morning, to the moment I stepped back on it, carrying the contents of my desk in a cardboard box.

"The worst part was that there was a security guard standing there, watching me while I cleaned out my desk. Apparently it's standard procedure now that Spector bought the company, but it was so humiliating. What did they think I was going to do?" I asked, crunching through the cannoli crust. "Steal company secrets? Make a scene?"

"Well, I would have," Monica said. "But you're not the scene-making type. How about a strongly worded letter to HR instead? Or better yet, Gavin's boss? Something starting with, 'Dear Heartless, Soulless Corporate Flunkies . . .' "

Monica hopped off the stool and helped herself to another pastry.

"I actually was thinking about that," I said. "They just brought on a new CEO, a woman. I thought I'd try writing to her. I doubt it'll make any difference, but they might add it to his file. And, if nothing else, it'd make me feel better."

"Good for you, Grace. I think you should. One more?" she asked, lifting a chocolate cannoli from the pan.

"No, thanks."

I hadn't finished even half of the first two, not because I was concerned about the calorie count—today of all days I was entitled to eat whatever I wanted—but because the turn of the conversation had killed my appetite.

I put down my fork and looked at my condo for the first time in a long time, really looked at it, seeing it the way Monica had. Like everything else in my life, it seemed confused and disjointed, a great big mess.

"You know my mom was trying to convince me to move back to Minnesota, but I told her I couldn't because of my job. Now I don't have a job. And look at this place. I've never really lived here, just occupied the space. I'm practically a squatter," I said morosely. "What in the world am I doing here?"

"Well, being my friend for one thing," Monica replied, turning her back to the counter and crossing her arms. "That might not be all that important to you, but it's very important to me. And to Nan.

"But, hey, if you want to run back to Minnesota with your tail between your legs, move into your mother's basement, and milk cows for the rest of your life, I guess that's your business. But if you think I'm going to let you skip town before the Dogmother's Ball, think again. I can't throw a party for a hundred and twenty-five people and hounds by myself. I'm going to need a little help."

"For your information," I said, "I have never milked a cow. And I didn't mean it like that. I'm just . . ." I blinked a few times. "It's been a bad day, Monica. A really, really bad day."

"I know," Monica said gently, crossing the tiny kitchen to stand next to me. "A bad day after a bad week, and a bad month, and a bad two years. I get it. I do. You're entitled to spend some time feeling sorry for yourself."

"Thanks," I mumbled.

"You're welcome." Monica put her arm over

my shoulder and stood with me in silent soli-
darity.

For about ten seconds.

"Okay," she said, removing her arm. "Time's
up."

I shot her a look.

"I'm not kidding, Grace. It's true, you have
all kinds of very good, very real reasons to sit
here and feel sorry for yourself. I'm not trying
to minimize what you've been through. But it's
been like that for close to two years now. It's
enough."

I tried to speak, to remind her about what Nan
said, that there's no timetable for grief, but she
wasn't having any of it.

"Maybe there isn't," she said, "but maybe
there should be. Do you remember the night we
met at the community center? All those weeping
widows who'd been coming to the group for
years and years without graduating? I wouldn't
want to see that happen to you. Okay, sure," she
said, countering my argument before I even had
a chance to speak, "you could say it hasn't been
that long, but if you really think about it, you've
been in this exact same spot, grieving, for almost
two years.

"Jamie's fall left him stuck halfway between
one world and the next. You've been stuck too.
But now, finally, Jamie is at peace. He's moved
on. I know it's sad and hard. But nobody knows

better than you that life is short, precarious, and precious. It's time for you to figure out what you want to do with yours. Find the thing that makes you excited to get out of bed in the morning."

"Everybody keeps saying that."

"Well, maybe everybody's right. And, I hate to pull rank, but if Jamie were here, I bet he'd say the same thing."

I didn't like to say so, but she was probably right.

"Did I ever tell you how I got to be a chef?" Monica asked. "I was working at this restaurant, waiting tables. The food wasn't very good and, you know, shrinking violet that I am"—she grinned—"I kept giving the chef suggestions. Just by way of being helpful.

"One day, I told him his marinara sauce needed more garlic. He started screaming, said I was fired and that he didn't need some stupid, scrawny, mouthy *girl* telling him how to run his kitchen and that if I thought I knew so much about cooking, then maybe I ought to open my own damned restaurant. Then he threw a colander at my head. And as I ducked, I thought, You know something? Maybe he's right.

"Six weeks later, I was enrolled as a student at Oregon Culinary Institute and the rest is history. I've loved my work ever since."

"Ever since? Two months ago you said that you

didn't like cooking anymore, that it was just a job."

Monica waved her hand dismissively. "That was just because I was frustrated with the kids. Once Alex quit spending every waking moment figuring out how to make my life miserable, I started loving my job all over again—especially when he was at the restaurant with me. That was really fun. I mean, Zoe still keeps me awake at night, but I was actually starting to feel like I had the stepmother gig down.

"But," she sighed, "since Alex recently decided he hates my guts again and has gone back to being a card-carrying jerk, I'm sure that's about to change. We've reverted back to our old roles. Once again, he is my Rotten Stepson and I am the Evil Stepmother, Cruella De Vil in chef's whites."

"Why? What happened?"

She swiped a finger across her plate, capturing some leftover cannoli filling.

"Oh, it's that girl—Gwen. She dumped him. He's heartbroken and miserable. And since misery loves company . . ." She shrugged. "He'll be fine. But I kind of miss having him around the kitchen."

She licked the filling off her finger. "Speaking of the kitchen, I've got to get back to work."

I walked her to the door. She put on her jacket and gave me a hug.

"Are you going to be all right?"

I nodded. "Thanks for the cannoli. It was just what I needed today."

"And the advice?" she asked, smiling wryly. "Listen, I know I'm being pushy, but I really think a push is what you need right now. That being said—" She paused abruptly and took a big, somewhat dramatic breath. "I owe you an apology. That stunt I pulled, trying to throw you and Luke together, wasn't just pushy, it was stupid, and misguided, and really, really thoughtless."

I tried to interrupt, to say that I knew her heart—if not her head—had been in the right place, but Monica shook me off.

"No, Grace. I was wrong. And I'm sorry. Watching the way you cared for Jamie in the last days of his life, never leaving his side for a moment, helped me finally realize just how wrong. You tried to make me understand how sacred your love—and your marriage vows—were to you, but I just didn't get it.

"Or," she said, her voice lower, her tone sincerely remorseful, "maybe I didn't want to get it. The love you shared with Jamie—pure and totally unselfish—I've never known that kind of love. I probably never will."

"Oh, Monica. Don't say that. You'll fall in love someday. You will," I insisted, responding to the doubtful look on her face. "Probably when you least expect it."

"Yeah, sure. Maybe," she said, then grabbed her umbrella, which she'd left leaning against the wall to dry. "But we'll worry about me another day. Right now, my concern is you.

"I know this is the very last thing you want to year, but Ava could be right, you know. Getting fired might turn out to be the best thing that could happen to you right now. Okay, sure. It would have been nice if they waited a week or two to can you, but it is what it is.

"The good news is, you're still getting paid. The clock is ticking, Grace, but you've got two months to figure this out.

"So, for the rest of this week, you get to take it easy. Sleep till noon, play with your dog, eat stuff you shouldn't, and watch a really, really sad DVD. Something that will make you want to cry, yell, shake your fist at the universe, and get it all out of your system. Then get back to work and decide what you want to do with your life."

"Easy to say, but how? Where do you expect me to start?"

Monica pointed the tip of her umbrella toward a corner near the front window.

"How about that box?"

Chapter 22

Grace

When Monica left, I sat down on the floor and opened the box. It was filled with books.

Maisie trotted over and lay down next to me, resting her tiny head on her even tinier paws, her big brown eyes shifting from the box, to my face, and back again as I pulled out book after book, used my sleeve to dust off the covers, and read the titles, one by one:

Little Women
The Devil Wore Prada
Jemima J
Harry Potter and the Sorcerer's Stone
The Hardy Boys: The Haunted Fort
The Hardy Boys: The Vanishing Thieves
Little House in the Big Woods
Little House on the Prairie
Dune

"Oh, Jamie," I murmured, smiling to myself as I leafed through the pages, spotting passages underlined, sometimes twice, some with stars and exclamation points.

A tear came to my eye. I wiped it away, thinking about the day we'd packed that box.

I could see why my mother thought we were going off half-cocked, moving halfway across the country to a city we'd never even visited, putting a bid on a condo we'd never actually seen, but she didn't understand how much you could do on the Internet, and we really did have a plan.

We'd arranged for three months temporary housing and storage of our stuff until we could close on the condo. As soon as we arrived in Portland, I would get a job and Jamie would go to school full-time, finishing his paramedic training in a year. Then it would be my turn. For what, I honestly didn't know. I wanted to start a family; we both did. But beyond that? I had no clue. But even though the condo was smaller than our garage apartment, after all those years of scrimping and saving, I was thrilled about finally having a home of our own.

Our furniture was mostly borrowed or made of particle board, so we left it behind. Even so, we needed to weed out some possessions. Since both of us had pack-rat tendencies, it wasn't easy— especially when it came to books. When we got to the sixth box, Jamie gave me a look and said, "Come on, Grace. Do you really need the entire Little House on the Prairie series?"

"Grammy gave me those for my ninth birth-day."

"Okay, fine. But do you still read them?"

"Do you still read the Hardy Boys?" I asked, picking up a tattered copy of *The Haunted Fort*.

"Hey, those were my dad's books. I can't throw them away. Besides," he said, grabbing the book before I could toss it into the giveaway pile, "this book has everything—a stolen art collection, death threats, and ghosts. The Hardy Boys are going to Portland. All of them."

"Then so are Laura and the rest of the Ingalls family."

Jamie picked another book out of the box. "What about this? You've read it so many times you must have the story memorized by now."

"No way. Jo March is the sister I never had." I held up another volume. "What about this one?"

Jamie's eyes bugged out of his head. "Are you crazy? *Dune* is like the greatest book of all time. A classic! *Dune* insists that magic and fact are knit together in everything. It urges us to examine the miraculous alongside the mundane and see they are all of a piece. Plus, it has sandworms!"

"Okay, fine. So we'll bring that one too. And all the Harry Potters," I said. "We both love those."

In the end, we packed them all.

To make up for the weight, I left behind a lot of the dishes. They were mostly mismatches anyway, things I'd picked up cheap at yard sales. It was a good thing I'd never been much of a cook.

That entire box was packed with books that Jamie and I had read and loved, familiar titles we just couldn't leave behind. However, at the very bottom of the box was a pristine, unread volume given to me by my cousin Melody not long before we moved, *Me Before You* by Jojo Moyes. I set it on top of the stack of books before flattening the box for recycling.

Later that night, I picked it up and brought it to my bed—a mattress and box spring on the floor—planning to read just a few pages before falling asleep. At 2:38 after Maisie opened one eye and let out an irritated snuffle to let me know I was disturbing her beauty sleep, I finally turned out the lights.

The next day, I woke up at noon, pulled on some yoga pants, and took Maisie for a walk. I didn't even bother to brush my hair, still frizzed and frightening from my trek through the rain. Returning home, I climbed back into bed with my dog, a bowl of Peanut Butter Cap'n Crunch, and the book.

That was pretty much the agenda for the next two days—I hid under the covers with Maisie snuggled up beside me, ate stuff that was salty-sugary-crunchy-creamy and devoid of all nutritional value, and read the heart-wrenching tale of Louisa Clark and Will Traynor.

Upon closing the cover, I sobbed and shook my fist at the universe, cursing its cruelty to star-crossed lovers whose love is cut short. But mostly, I cried. For another three days, between trips to the bathroom and walks for the dog, I lay in my bed, a tangle of sheets and blankets sanded with crumbs from carelessly consumed snacks, and in a way I had never allowed myself to do in those whole two years since Jamie's fall, I mourned, finally letting the truth of Jamie's death sink into my soul.

When I woke on the third day I had no more tears but a strange sense of being . . . grounded, reattached to the earth and my life upon it. But what did that life look like if Jamie wasn't in it? What was I going to do now?

I had no idea. But I decided to begin by taking Maisie for a walk.

Come June, Washington Park would be a riot of roses. That was one of the first sights Jamie and I saw upon moving to Portland, because everyone said you should, and they were right. Mid-April was too soon for flowers, but the subtle rise of temperature and lengthening of days had roused the rosebushes from sleep. The branches were as high as my waist and lush with leaves. While Maisie snuffled the grass and pranced along the edge of the flowerbeds, yipping at lackadaisical, utterly unimpressed squirrels, I leaned close and studied the green rosebuds, closed but plump, edged with delicate, almost imperceptibly thin ribbons of red, yellow, pink, and white, a whispered clue, a promise of summer and longer, warmer, better days to come.

All that snuffling, prancing, and yipping wore Maisie out, so I picked her up and carried her home, down Twenty-third Street with the trendy boutiques and shops I still couldn't afford to enter, especially when I considered the limits of a two-month severance and how far I could stretch it.

To avoid temptation, I altered my route and took a street that was new to me. The church that I passed, a turn-of-the-century cut stone structure with heavy oak doors and a squat, square bell tower, housed a thrift shop, open 10 a.m. to 2 p.m. on weekdays.

The shop was dusty and the aisles were narrow. The shelves were disorganized and filled with bric-a-brac, musty books, and painted portraits of other people's relatives. Far in the back, shoved up against a wall and partially hidden under a faded flower sheet, I spied a glimpse of blue. Pulling the sheet aside, I discovered a love seat with rolled arms and weirdly oversized ball feet. The lines were pleasing, but the light was dim so it was hard to judge the exact color or condition of the upholstery.

"Excuse me," I called to the white-haired woman who had cooed over Maisie's "sweet little face" a few minutes before, saying it was fine to bring her inside. "Are there any more lights back here? I'd like to get a better look at this love seat."

"Well, let me see," she said, making her way toward me, navigating a labyrinth of old upright vacuums, dressers with missing handles, and children's toys. "I only just started volunteering, so I'm not sure where everything . . . Oh, wait. Here's a switch."

The room flooded with fluorescent light, harsh but bright. I thumped my palm against the armrest. The love seat coughed up a cloud of dust. It was dirty, no question, and those ball feet were absurd, but the velvet upholstery was untouched by moths and was a surprisingly beautiful sapphire blue.

"How much is it?" I asked.

"Well, let me see," she said again, craning her neck up, down, and sideways, searching for a price tag, finding none. "My goodness, I really don't know. But I think they'd be glad to let it go, it takes up so much space. Let me think . . ." She did for a full minute, then cautiously asked, "Would fifty dollars be too much?"

In the end, I paid $122.50. But for that price I got the love seat, a chair with a cushion and a curved wicker back, a generic floor lamp, a bed-frame with a fake brass headboard, some battered floating shelves, a small pine desk, and an eight-place setting box of dinnerware that was missing only two salad plates. The dishes were so cute and cheery—raspberry pink with turquoise circles and a band of white dots along the edge.

The woman agreed to hold everything for a few days, so I'd have time to unpack more boxes, and called the church secretary, who called the youth group leader, who arranged for a pickup truck to deliver everything I'd bought.

It started so simply, with a half-hidden glimpse of velvet, blue bright and brilliant, that roused my craving for color and need to nest, hungers long silenced by the urgency of caregiving and the single-minded focus on simple survival.

When I got back to the condo, I tore into the boxes, sorting and stacking the contents, figuring out what to toss, what to keep, and where it all should go.

Some choices were easy.

Opening the door to my closet, I spread my arms as wide as I could, corralled every item in my black-gray-charcoal-brown-navy work wardrobe, and stuffed them all in the trunk of my car, along with every pair of toe-pinching pumps, before depositing them at the drive-through donation center of the nearest Goodwill store. When I opened a big plastic bin with yard after yard after yard of bright cotton dress goods, fabrics I'd bought on sale and stowed away, and then found the box containing my sewing machine, notions, scissors, and thread, I immediately carted them over to the "keep corner" with the rest of the stuff I couldn't live without.

Other decisions were harder to make.

No matter how much I loved them, there simply wasn't room for all those books. I weeded out a few of my own and quite a few of Jamie's, holding on to his Hardy Boys collection and, of course, his copy of *Dune*, before donating most of them to the downtown library for their annual used book sale. But I slipped one of each of our favorites, including much-read but well-preserved copies of *Pride and Prejudice* and *The Great Santini*, onto the shelf of a "Little Free Library" I spotted on my way back from the thrift shop. Though I thought I'd been pretty ruthless when sorting through and weeding out our possessions when packing the boxes in Minnesota, I was amazed by the number of knickknacks, minor memorabilia, and just plain junk we had transported clear across the country.

Why did I think we would need six bud vases? Five boxes of rubber bands? A broken VHS player? A yogurt maker?

Well, that one I did understand. Sort of. It had been a birthday present from my mother, one of her constant and not particularly subtle reminders to watch my weight. I had no intention of using it, but since it was brand new and she'd only given it to me a couple weeks before the move, I felt guilty getting rid of it.

But two years had passed since I'd opened it, which, I was pretty sure, was beyond the gift guilt statute of limitations. And my mother was almost two thousand miles away, so I put it in the Goodwill pile.

Some choices were close to impossible.

A medium-sized box sporting the ubiquitous "Miscellaneous" label contained a mélange of papers, folders, flyers, a kitchen towel, picture frames, and a blue plastic water bottle—and that was just the stuff I saw from the top. It was just too much to deal with at that moment, so I closed the lid and shoved it into the front coat closet, promising myself I'd sort through it all later.

Another, much larger box labeled with a big question mark, because it had apparently been taped shut before I had a chance to list the contents, was filled with Jamie's winter clothes, things we hadn't thought he'd need until after we closed on the condo. The moment I opened the lid, the air filled with a scent both strange and familiar—a mixture of ripe grain, sandalwood soap, detergent, and strong coffee. Familiar because, the instant I breathed it in, I knew it was Jamie's smell, and strange because, until then, I'd never been aware of its existence. But there it was, Jamie's smell. Packed away for all that time, still it clung to every article of his clothing, permeating every thread.

I lowered my head, breathing deep. I wanted to dive in headfirst, burrow into sweatshirts, sweaters, and flannel shirts, immersing myself in the last vestiges of his particular perfume. For a moment, I considered hanging them up in the too-cramped closet, next to my things. But I stopped myself, imagining what Jamie would have said on the subject, something like, "Don't be so sentimental. There's a lot of good wear in those clothes. I don't need them anymore, but somebody else does. If Z was still living with Sunny, think how happy he'd be to get that warm sweater, or that shirt. They're practically new."

Jamie always had more than his share of practical, Midwestern good sense. I made another drive-through donation, but not before sorting through the box and picking out a few items to include in my quilt.

In the morning, I called Monica to tell her I wouldn't be at our support group.

"Are you depressed? Should I bring more cannoli?"

"No, it's okay. I'm just busy. I'm painting."

"Painting what?"

"My bedroom wall. And some shelves. Maybe a chair. I haven't decided for sure, but I'm kind of on a roll. I don't want to lose my momentum."

"Do you want help? I can come over and give you a hand. I bet Nan would too. We could have support group at your place this week."

"How about next week? I should have every-thing finished by then."

"Sounds good. I'll tell Nan. Are you sure you don't need anything?"

"Not right now. I'm okay," I said.

And I was.

I still missed Jamie. In the days that followed, I experienced moments of sadness and even tears. In time, I came to realize I always would. That was okay and so was I. Just okay. But it was a start.

Monica would have approved. So, I realized, would Jamie.

Chapter 23

Grace

It's hard for me to explain, but turning the condo into a real home did more to help me handle Jamie's loss than months of therapy could have.

Sorting through the trash and treasure of our life together and combining it with new treasures gave me a sense of moving forward while honoring the past. Seeing our old things in this new setting brought so many good memories to the surface, reminding me that, in spite of everything, Jamie and I had had a wonderful, even enviable life together.

It also helped me to fulfill one of his final wishes.

When Jamie decided to give up the idea of medical school and become a paramedic instead, he said he wanted to use the money we'd been saving for his someday tuition as a down payment. Though I had long dreamed of having a home of our own, I wasn't so sure. It bothered me to think that Jamie might be giving up on his dream just so I could have a house.

"I'm not," he'd assured me. "My dream was

always working in the medical field and helping people. I'm getting to do that, only a lot faster. I don't want to wait anymore, Grace. The other part of my dream is giving you a home and family and all the things you've wanted. I want you to have an amazing life, but the house is just a down payment on that. I love you more than anything, Grace, and I meant what I said. As soon as I finish school, it's your turn."

"Turn for what?" I'd laughed. "I already have you. What more could I possibly want?"

"More," he'd said.

Until I opened that first can of paint, I'd forgotten about that conversation. The trauma of Jamie's accident, followed by the months of constant tension that came from worrying about his care, had crowded so many good memories into the far corners of my mind—including the fact that, on the drive out from Minnesota, he'd talked about wanting to use that exact color on the walls of our new bedroom. Turquoise was Jamie's favorite. He had three shirts in that color, one of which I had cut up to use as cornerstone patches in his quilt.

For the next week, I worked from first light until last.

Painting was cheap and made a big difference. I painted the living room walls a beautiful pearl gray, and the bedroom and bath the lovely light turquoise Jamie had talked about and that I had unwittingly chosen when I went to the paint store. It made a nice contrast against the white molding and cabinets. When the furniture arrived, things really started to take shape.

To start with, for the first time in two years, my mattress was off the floor! And when I made up the bed with a white eyelet bed skirt I'd found for sixty percent off on the discount table at Target and the turquoise and coral quilt my mother-in-law gave me for my thirtieth birthday, it looked pretty and so inviting. Maisie, however, wasn't as thrilled with the changes as I was. After I finished making the bed, she stood next to it and gave me a look that said, "You're joking, right? Where's the escalator?" I went back to the thrift shop, bought a wooden step stool for three dollars, and spray-painted it white. The minute I set it down, Maisie hopped up on the bed, curled up into a ball on my pillow, and went to sleep. Problem solved.

The bathroom didn't need much besides paint. However, I did splurge on a new set of coral-colored towels and completed the look with a little bouquet of silk daisies in a tiny galvanized tin bucket. The whole thing looked fresh and pretty and feminine—too feminine for Jamie's taste, but I don't think he would have minded.

The kitchen didn't need much either. Giving the cabinets a good scrub cheered things up a lot, but I also changed the old wooden knobs for some new polished chrome pulls. The difference was amazing. Next, I removed the mismatched plates and plastic cups from the glass-front cabinet and replaced them with the raspberry dinnerware and a set of six blue glass goblets that I found, also on sale, which made it even better. There's something incredibly satisfying about grubbing through a discount bin and finding a pretty something you absolutely adore.

Besides the goblets, I found a ceramic salad bowl that wasn't precisely the same raspberry as the dishes but close, which I put on the counter and filled with fruit. I also nabbed a vintage-style mason jar caddy—like you'd use for canning—then filled the jars with some gravel and potting soil and planted them with parsley, rosemary, cilantro, and thyme. I've never had much space or talent for gardening, so I wasn't sure how long the plants would survive, but that little spot of green on my kitchen windowsill looked very pretty and homey.

Nan, I thought, would be thrilled. She was always saying, "It takes living things to bring a room alive." I was starting to see what she meant.

My final and largest project was the living room. My downstairs neighbor let me borrow her portable upholstery steamer. By the time I finished cleaning the velvet, removed the weird black balls from the bottom, and screwed on four new natural wood-colored wooden legs, the sofa looked brand new. That big splash of blue velvet against those pearl gray walls was elegant but so vibrant.

Two apple crates from Minnesota topped with a rectangle of thick glass made a cute coffee table, and I jazzed up the floor lamp by hot-gluing some gray, pink, and white chevron fabric over the old shade. They turned out great and cost me $13.67 to make. It had become something of a competition, trying to see how little I could spend while still getting the look I wanted.

Spray paint is the best friend of a girl on a budget. I used it to freshen up the ugly floating shelves before bolting them to the living room wall to hold books, knickknacks, and family photos. I mounted some smaller shelves on either side of the little bow window that overlooked the street.

That bow window added so much to the space. It was just big enough to hold the pine desk, which I also painted white. I put my sewing machine on the desk and some mason jars filled with thread, buttons, trim, pins, and other sewing notions on the floating shelves and—voilà! Instant sewing studio. It was compact for sure, but efficiently laid out, and I had always wanted a dedicated sewing room.

The final, and if I do say so myself, most ingenious addition to my living space was the idea I had for refurbishing the wicker side chair. Once again, I broke out the spray paint, but this time I used a very pretty green, a color like leaves of birch trees in the early days of spring. Once the paint was dry, I removed the seat, ripped off the old fabric, and recovered it with a yard of sturdy white twill. Then, with yarn from a needlepoint project I started but never finished, I stitched through the evenly placed holes in the wicker chair back to create a pretty pattern of blue flowers with bright pink centers growing on dark green vines. The total cost of the project was only twenty-one dollars, but when I put it next to the sapphire love seat it pulled the whole room together.

In terms of physical exertion, I'm not sure I ever worked as hard as I did during those five days when I was decorating the condo, but the results were worth every drop of sweat and way more than the $530 I put into the decorating. I felt proud of my accomplishment and knew that Jamie would have been proud of me too.

I placed the last picture on the bookshelf—a photo of Jamie and me on our canoeing and camping trip to Bear Head Lake State Park, a honeymoon delayed by a year and a half because of Jamie's cancer—and stood back to admire the completely transformed and absolutely beautiful space.

"Thank you, honey," I said, turning in a circle and smiling. "It's just what I always wanted, a real home."

Of course, no decorating project is ever truly finished. Throw pillows and drapery panels could come later, when I found a fabric I loved at a price I was willing to pay. And I would keep my eye out for a nice, inexpensive rug to define the living room area.

The biggest ticket item on my wish list was a table, something that could do dual duty for both dining and crafting—I didn't have room for one of each. It would be nice, too, if there was some kind of storage included, a place to stow crafting tools. But even if I could find one to meet my needs, the table would have to wait. Considering all I'd accomplished, $530 wasn't much, but until I had a steady source of income, I wouldn't spend one more unnecessary dollar.

Monica was right—the clock was ticking. Two weeks had already passed since my unceremonious termination from Spector. In two more days, right after Monday night's Big Reveal for Nan and Monica, I'd start my job search in earnest. In the meantime, there was one more project I wanted to tackle, something I'd been thinking about ever since the conversation in my head, when Jamie told me how happy Z would have been to get his old sweater or hand-me-down shirt.

I went to my bedroom closet, which now finally had space enough so my twirly skirts wouldn't get wrinkled, pulled out the box of my old fabric, and started searching through the contents until I found just what I was looking for—rosy pink background printed with pastel, pop-eyed owls.

"Perfect!"

"You're joking," Sunny said, as if she really believed I was playing some sort of trick on her. She held the dress up to her shoulders, looking it over carefully. "It looks brand new."

"It is."

"Oh. Was it too small for you? I bet the store would let you return it."

"Well, it *is* too small for me. I wear a twelve and I'm guessing you're about a four. But I didn't buy it, I made it. For you."

"You . . . you made it for me," she said. Then, as if she was sure she'd gotten it wrong, she said, "For me? Why?"

"Because I thought you'd look nice in pink. Because I thought you'd like something new. And because, for some reason, I thought you'd like owls."

"I love owls!" Sunny exclaimed. She covered her mouth with a hand as her eyes began to fill, only to move it a moment later and say, "Look! Even the buttons are little owls!"

I grinned, excited that she was so excited. "I know! Aren't those fun? I know it's not very practical. You'll probably want to wait until summer to wear it. Oh, hang on. I almost forgot."

I reached into the bottom of the shopping bag I'd brought to hold the outfit. "Here's a sweater to layer over the dress when it gets chilly. It's used and probably kind of big for you. But the color is perfect and I washed it so—"

Sunny lunged toward me and threw her arms around me so forcefully that I not only couldn't finish my sentence, I dropped the bag and the sweater onto the sidewalk.

"Thank you, Grace! Thank you so much!"

She smelled like weed, and sweat, and dirt. I hugged her anyway.

"People walk past me every day and they look right through me like I don't even exist. Or if they do look at me and I catch them, they shift their eyes away fast and pretend they weren't, you know? You're not like that. You look and talk to me the same way you'd talk to anybody in the neighborhood, like I belong here. But with most of them," she said, shaking her head as she finally let go of me, "it's like they're embarrassed for me."

Sunny's eyes started to fill again and she put her fist to her mouth, pressing hard against her lips until she regained her composure.

"And I know I'm an embarrassment, I get that. And I know it's probably my own fault. I mean, sure. I've got a sad story to tell. But so does everybody else, right? So why am I here?" she asked, spreading her hands and glancing over at the concrete planters, the cardboard floor, and dirty sleeping bag. "What's wrong with me?

"Nobody wants to end up like this," she said, then let out a short, bitter laugh. "Nobody grows up dreaming about living on the street and being an addict. I'd like to stop, but I just . . . I can't. It's too hard.

"But that doesn't mean I'm not a human being, you know, a ghost you can see right through. I'm a person," she said, pressing her fist to the middle of her chest, directly over her beating heart. "Maybe I'm a failure, and a disappointment, and an addict, but I'm still a person. I want what everybody else wants, you know? I just want—"

"To be seen," I said, and nodded my head. "I get it, Sunny. I know."

Chapter 24

Grace

For the first time in my life, I entertained friends in a home of my own.

Monica supplied a pan of spinach and ricotta stuffed shells with marinara for the main course, and Nan brought cold grilled asparagus and a salad of baby lettuce, the first fruits of her spring garden. Over Monica's objections, I handled the appetizers and dessert. Maybe I couldn't cook, but anybody can shop, and in Portland, home of artisan everything, finding fresh, delicious, gourmet food is as easy as taking a walk in the park.

On Saturday, Maisie and I went downtown to the Farmers' Market in the Park Blocks. After wandering through the stalls, admiring piles of artfully arranged produce that was so fresh and bright and beautiful it seemed almost too pretty to eat, I bought a box of artisan crackers sprinkled with sesame and poppy seeds, three slivers of delicious, locally made cheese, and ingredients for a strawberry-rhubarb sangria recipe I'd found online. On the way home, I stopped by Salt &

Straw and picked up two quarts of ice cream for dessert—Almond Brittle with Salted Chocolate Ganache and Strawberry Honey Balsamic with Black Pepper.

The evening was a great success. The meal was delicious and the sangria started things off on a festive note. I was very gratified when both Nan and Monica asked for the recipe. But most gratifying was the way they kept oohing and aahing over what I'd done to the place. It was the first time Nan had ever been to my condo, but Monica made sure she was able to appreciate the full nature of the transformation by providing a vivid description of what the place had been like before.

When she described my bedroom as looking like "a cheap dorm in a badly run youth hostel," I said, "Oh, come on. It wasn't *that* bad." Monica laid her hand on my arm and said, "Yes, it was, Grace. It really, really was."

The ice cream was almost as big a hit as the decorating.

"Salt and Straw!" Monica exclaimed. "I love that place!"

Nan, who was sitting at the counter on my single stool, said, "I usually get the Honey Lavender, but this strawberry is delicious." She put down her spoon and looked around the room. "And, really, Grace, the whole place looks fabulous."

"Thanks," I said, sitting down next to Monica on the love seat. "It's still a work in progress. I'd like to find the perfect table, a nice rug, and make some fabric shades for the windows, but I should hold off on doing anything else until I find a job.

"Oh wait!" I cried, springing to my feet and quickly putting my ice cream down on the coffee table. "I forgot to show you my other project!"

I ran into the bedroom closet and pulled out the second dress I'd made, same pattern but a different fabric—pale blue background printed with pen-and-ink style drawings of the Eiffel Tower and bright red and blue suitcases. Showing it off to my friends, I explained about the owl dress I'd made for Sunny and how her reaction had inspired me to run right home and make another dress that I intended to donate to a nearby homeless shelter.

"It's only a dress," I said, when I realized I'd been gushing. "It's not like it's going to change her life or anything. In fact, she hasn't been around since yesterday, so I'm sure she's off on some kind of bender. She does that sometimes. But the look on Sunny's face . . . I'll never forget it. Is it crazy to hope that getting a new dress might not just help her feel seen, but actually convince her she's worth something?"

"It's never crazy to hope," Nan replied. "Whoever gets this dress will love it just as much as Sunny did."

I folded the dress over my arm. "I hope so. It's the most satisfying thing I've done in a long time. I hope my new job, whatever it is, leaves me enough spare time to make a few more. I've got yards and yards of fabric stowed in my closet. It'd be nice to put it to good use."

Nan, who was only halfway done with her ice cream, put down her spoon. She stared at me for such a long time that it started to feel uncomfortable, like when somebody sees you've got spinach in your teeth and can't look away but doesn't tell you either.

"What?" I said, covering my mouth with my hand. Those stuffed shells did have a lot of spinach.

"The dresses. Don't you see?" she asked, turning from me to Monica and back again, her expression suddenly bright. "*That* should be your job!"

My heart beat a bit faster when Nan said that, but it didn't take long for me to start thinking of reasons it couldn't work. I mean, I would have had to sell a *lot* of dresses to actually make a living doing it. Those dresses took me half a day each to sew. And, as Monica pointed out, opening a business from scratch was risky; it required capital and experience. I had neither.

"She'd need to hire employees," Monica said. "Open some kind of workshop or factory. She can't mass-produce dresses with one used sewing machine, cutting them out one by one on her kitchen counter. Besides, the reason Grace found this so satisfying is because she was giving the dresses away, not selling them. It could end up being a nice hobby, but"—Monica shook her head—"I just don't see how this could be a business."

Neither could I.

And yet, I couldn't stop thinking about it. I couldn't sleep either. Around three in the morning, I finally gave up trying and got out of bed. Maisie gave me a bemused look, then scooted herself onto the warm spot I'd left on the mattress.

I went into the living room, got out my sewing basket, and stitched a couple of seams in the Lemoyne Star block I was working on, made from Jamie's red flannel shirts. Sewing normally relaxes me, but that night I just couldn't settle into it. I kept thinking about the conviction in Nan's voice when she said that dressmaking should be my business and then Monica's voice, equally insistent, saying there was no way it could work. Since Monica is the only one of us who'd ever run a business, she was probably right.

After a few minutes, I put my stitching aside and opened the coat closet, thinking I'd sort through the miscellaneous box I'd shoved in there earlier. Now was as good a time as any.

Like so many of the other boxes I had unpacked in the previous days, this one contained a lot of junk, stuff I couldn't believe we'd bothered to pack and ship halfway across the country. But there were some things that mattered, a copy of our marriage certificate, some pictures I was glad to find, including one of Jamie in the orchard when he was about nine years old, sitting in the top branches of one of the apple trees. I put that aside, deciding to get a copy made to send to Penny.

Near the bottom of the box I found a sealed envelope with my name on it. Seeing Jamie's handwriting, that jagged, cramped script only I could decipher, my heart beat faster.

The card had three watercolor hearts in shades of blue and green on a white background and a printed inscription inside that read, *You're the woman I love, making life beautiful, filling my years with joy, and the world with light.* Opposite the inscription, he had written a note.

My beautiful Grace,

Ten years is a pretty long time, more than a third of our lives, but the only regret I have in life is that I wasn't able to marry you even sooner. Although, if I had, I guess we'd probably have been breaking the law—

Feeling my throat tighten, I stopped reading to wipe my eyes, remembering our tenth anniversary, the camping trip, that magical day, our last full day together. So many people, after losing someone they love, look back and think if they'd known that day was the last day, they'd have done or said something different. But when I think of my final day with Jamie, I have no regrets. It was perfect.

We'd closed on the condo the day before. Leaving the boxes unpacked, we went on an anniversary camping trip to the North Cascades of Washington State. Sitting on a boulder at the top of Mt. Pilchuck, panting from the effort of the ascent, I held Jamie's hand and was awestruck by the beauty of the world at our feet, a carpet of green and granite that stretched to the edge of everything and felt like it belonged to us alone.

I turned to look at Jamie. His square jaw was peppered with the stubble of a missed morning shave. His lips were red and chapped from the chill wind but smiling still.

"God, it's beautiful," he'd said, his voice a clear and reverent whisper. "The edge of heaven. Even the air is just . . . Can you smell that?"

I could—juniper and ice, sunlight and pine, and the mineral-flavored bite of dust in a cold and freshening wind—the clean perfume of life above the tree line. I squeezed his hand.

A fringe of brown brows peeked out over the top of Jamie's sunglasses. He lifted his arm, inviting me to move closer. I did and put my head on his shoulder.

"I've got an idea," he'd said. "Let's stay here forever."

"Okay. Let's."

We sat there, not forever but for a long time, until the sun started to dip toward the horizon.

At our trailside camp, after a dinner of freeze-dried stew and wine, Jamie gave me my anniversary present, the beautiful watch, silver and gold with a mother-of-pearl and three small, sparkling diamonds floating behind the glass.

"Do you like it?" he'd asked, laughing when I'd gasped and threw my arms around his neck in answer. "I bought it months ago. I wrote you a card, too, but I can't find it now. I think I might have accidentally packed it into one of the boxes."

I hadn't really heard that part, not then. All I'd said was, "I love it, Jamie. I love you. And I am *never* taking this off."

And now, after all this time, here it was in my hand, the message he'd written to me. Jamie was bothered that he'd mislaid it. I remembered him saying something about it as we were starting off the next morning, on our last hike. But his message to me, hidden from view for so long, was more precious to me now than it could possibly have been back then because his words came to me fresh and at the moment I most needed to hear them.

Ten months after we got married, I was pretty sure that I wouldn't live until our first anniversary, so I wrote you another note and gave it to my mom to give to you if I died. I wrote to say how much I loved you, and how I didn't want you to be sad after I was gone, because you made me happy and my life amazing, and how I wanted you to find someone else to love after I was gone, someone who would love you the way I did—one hundred percent, all-in, forever and ever.

I'm so grateful that you never had to read that note. In spite of all my brave talk back then about beating the odds, I didn't really believe we'd get to this day. But you gave me a reason to keep going when I thought I couldn't. You made me want to live and, because of you, I did. Every extra day I've had with you has been a gift, like opening a great surprise package every day for ten years.

The great thing about almost dying is that you are constantly aware of how incredibly priceless and completely uncertain every moment is and that, when you find what you really want out of life, you've got to go for it because you might not get another chance.

But, come to think of it, maybe I knew that even before I got sick. From that first day we talked, I also realized we were supposed to be together. But you were so shy and self-conscious, and it seemed kind of crazy, even to me. I knew it wouldn't be easy to convince you, but I'm glad I didn't talk myself out of trying. You've made me so happy and I love you so much. Every mile I walked to make you mine was worth it a thousand times over.

If tomorrow were my last day, I'd have no regrets. That's the gift I really wish I could give you, a life with no regrets. But that's something you have to do for yourself, so I'm giving you this watch instead, to remind you of all the good things I want for you and that I love you—

"One hundred percent, all-in, forever and ever. Jamie," I said, reading the last lines aloud. I clutched the card to my heart and looked up. "Thank you, babe. Message received."

A few minutes later and more awake than ever, I climbed back into bed, bringing my laptop with me. The sound of the computer booting disturbed Maisie. She opened one eye and glared at me.

"Sorry, punkin. I just had an idea," I said, typing the words "business plans" into the search bar. "Go back to sleep. This shouldn't take long."

Twenty-seven hours later—only five of them spent sleeping—I couldn't stand it any longer. I had to tell somebody, somebody who actually knew something about running a business. It took six rings for her to answer.

"Monica? Are you up?"

"That depends," she said groggily. "What time is it?"

"Six o'clock."

"I would have been, in about half an hour. Are you okay? What's wrong?"

"Nothing's wrong. It's just . . . I had an idea."

"An idea? You woke me out of a dead sleep to tell me about an idea?" Monica groaned. "This better be good, Grace."

"It is," I said. "I really think it is."

Chapter 25

Monica

"Twelve dollars a pound. For branzino? You're kidding, right?"

Tony, my seafood wholesaler, shook his balding head.

"It's been a bad year. The catch was way down, so the prices went up." He shrugged. "What can I tell you, Monica? Supply and demand. At twelve bucks a pound, I'm practically losing money on that fish."

"Sure, sure, Tony. I get it. Everybody's got to make a living. But the median price point for my customers is around twenty dollars a plate. So, at twelve dollars a pound," I said, glancing at his so-far empty order slip, "branzino isn't on the menu. And the way your prices have been going up, neither is shrimp, cod, crab, or salmon.

"But, hey, no hard feelings. I understand. I'll just stick to chicken and beef. Most of my customers prefer it anyway. Or, maybe I'll give St. Clair Seafood a call. They might be willing to give me a break, a new customer discount or something. But I'll miss you, Tony. I really will.

How many years have we been doing business now? Four? Or is it five?"

Tony crossed his arms over his chest. "Eleven fifty a pound."

I shook my head. "Ten dollars even."

"Ten seventy-five. Final offer."

"Ten fifty."

Tony rolled his eyes. "Fine. Ten fifty. You're killin' me here, Monica. How am I supposed to keep food on the table selling you branzino at ten fifty a pound, eh?"

"Oh, somehow I think you'll manage," I said, looking pointedly at his ample waistline.

Tony started laughing and I grinned. It was the same every week—the sparring, the back-and-forth, the bickering and bargaining. He enjoyed it as much as I did.

"So how much do you need, Monica? Fifteen pounds?"

"Make it twenty. Twenty-five pounds of shrimp. And twenty-two pounds of salmon—filets not steaks." He wrote down the numbers. "Oh, and listen, Tony, I'm catering this big fund-raiser in June, a dog rescue benefit. Think you could give me a deal on about fifty pounds of salmon?"

"Yeah, sure," he said. "I like dogs. I'll do it at cost. Must be a pretty big party if you need fifty pounds."

"Should be," I said. "That's not even counting

the vegetarians. We just started advertising and they've already sold sixty tickets. It's a Fairy Dogmother's Ball. You and Brenda want to come? Should be a fun night. You can bring Bruno."

Tony looked intrigued. "Dogs are invited? Even St. Bernards?"

"Sure, as long as he doesn't try to eat the Chihuahuas or anything."

"Naw. Bruno's like me, a real marshmallow." Tony laughed, patting his belly.

"Here, take a look." I handed him a hot-off-the-press flyer from a stack near the mixer. "Second Saturday in June. It'll be outside, but we'll have tents and heaters, just in case the weather doesn't cooperate. The food, of course, will be fantastic."

"Seeing as you're making it," Tony said.

"Exactly. And we're going to have a dance band and a costume contest."

"Dancing, eh?" Tony mused, reading the flyer. "Our anniversary is that weekend—thirty-eight years. Brenda always says I never take her any-place nice. This might be good. I could get out of buying an anniversary present and get her off my back at the same time."

"And it's tax-deductible. Which, you know, always adds that extra touch of romance." I grinned. "Take it home to Brenda and see what she says. Tell you what, I'll send you home with some cheesecake to sweeten her up.

"Hey, Ben," I said as my sous-chef walked in the door, "can you wrap up a couple of pieces of cheesecake for Tony to take with him?"

"Sure," he said, then gestured toward the dining room. "Luke Pascal is in there. He brought the new tables and stuff."

"Already? I didn't think they'd be done for another two weeks. Tell him it's fine. I'll be out there in a minute."

Tony handed me a pen so I could sign the purchase order.

"Monica, you okay? Your hand is shaking."

"I'm just tired," I said, yawning and waving off his concern simultaneously. "Dining month was great—brought in a ton of new customers—but keeping up was a killer. Now the kids have all their spring activities—Zoe's on the dance team and Alex has cross-country, so I'm hauling them back and forth to practices and meets and trying to run a business at the same time. Plus, I've got this big fund-raiser coming up and I'm catering a wedding the week after next.

"I'm fine," I said. "Just too busy."

"I don't know how you do it," Tony said, shaking his head. "You cook, run a business, raise a family—and you're gorgeous." He sighed. "If only I was twenty years younger . . ."

I flapped my hand at him. "Bah. More like thirty. And if you were, *paisano*, I'm sure you'd figure out a way to break my heart like all the rest of them. Besides, what would I want with a broken-down old fish salesman who never takes his wife anyplace nice?"

Tony grinned, slipped his pen back into his shirt pocket, and picked up the container of cheesecake Ben had placed on the counter.

"Monica, you're a good girl," he said, and patted my cheek. "You take care of yourself. See you next week."

"See you next week. Tell Brenda I said hello."

Ben and a couple of the dishwashers helped bring the tables and banquettes in from Luke's truck. After the guys hauled out the old stuff, Luke and I arranged the new furniture.

"Take a load off," Luke said once the seating was in place. "I can do the rest."

He didn't have to ask twice. I sank down onto the closest banquette bench and ran my hand over the luscious, rich, honey-colored wood. "It's so smooth," I said. "It's like silk. How do you do that?"

"Pick a really good piece of wood and then sand it and sand it and sand it some more," he said, picking up one of the smaller, two-seater tables, then setting it in a corner and pulling two chairs up next to it.

"It's beautiful. Exactly what I wanted—real furniture, like you're having dinner in some-body's home instead of a restaurant. But how'd you finish so quickly? You said it'd be two more weeks."

"Well," Luke said, grunting as he hefted one of the larger tables. "I'd rather promise late and deliver early than the other way around. And I've got another couple of orders behind yours, so I was motivated—a standup desk for an architect and a very custom, carved sleigh bed for a couple in the West Hills."

"Oooh," I cooed. "Sounds fancy. I hope you're charging them an arm and a leg."

"Not an arm and a leg," he smiled. "But it'll be a good project for me and they have a lot of friends, so, hopefully, it'll lead to other orders."

"Sounds like you're off to a good start. I'm glad."

"Me too. So, how've you been?"

"Fine. Busy. You know how it is."

He placed another two-seater next to the first table, lining them up, then pulling out a tape measure to make certain there was sixteen inches between the tables. Some restaurants put their tables twelve, even ten inches apart, but I like to give my customers a little breathing room.

"How are ticket sales going for the Dogmother's Ball?"

"Good," I said. "Sold sixty so far. I was worried at first—new event and all, you never know how it'll go until you do. But Bob designed these cute flyers—"

"Bob?"

"Bob Smith, Alex's cross-country coach and advisor. He also teaches tech. Not only did he design the flyers and posters, he got some of his students to make a website for us where people can buy tickets online. Saved us all kinds of headaches doing it that way and the kids got extra credit—everybody wins."

"Bob sounds like a good guy."

"He's a good coach too. Alex shaved a full minute off his 5K this season. And Bob drops him off at the house after practice, which is a big help. Saves me a trip at my busiest time of day. It's good for Alex too. Bob's a good influence."

While I'd been talking, Luke added two more tables to the lineup under the windows. Now he crossed the room and started repeating the process on the long wall, near the gas fireplace I'd installed over the winter.

There's something so romantic about dining in front of a fire. We'd already had three proposals in front of that fireplace. In fact, the wedding I was catering later in the month was for the first couple to become engaged in the glow of that fireplace.

That was the really good part about my job, the part I truly loved. Running a restaurant was more work than I could ever have imagined, but it was worth it because I got to be part of my customers' lives. When I did my job right, my restaurant was more than a restaurant—it was the place memories were made, happy ones. I couldn't think of a better reason to go to work every day.

Luke put the final two small tables in place.

"Thank you. It all looks so beautiful."

"Thank *you* for being my first order."

He pulled up a chair and sat down, puffing a little. It was a lot of work for one person. If I'd had more energy, I'd have insisted on helping. But I woke up at six and hadn't stopped since. In another hour, we'd open for dinner. I needed a break.

"So how's everybody else?" he asked. "Support group still going strong?"

"Oh, yes. Everybody's good. Nan will get her sling off just in time for the ball. She was a little annoyed to be immobilized for the spring gardening season, but Malcolm rototilled the vegetable patch and helped harvest the asparagus. Crisis averted.

"We met at Grace's condo last week, first time ever. You wouldn't believe what she's done with the place—and for practically nothing. Well . . . five hundred dollars. It's still pretty impressive.

"But, you probably don't want to hear about that," I said, remembering what Grace had told me about Luke showing up with flowers on the day she'd been fired, how she'd shut down his not-so-subtle hint about getting together again. "I'm sorry about the whole matchmaker thing. I just thought you two might hit it off. You might have if the circumstances had been different. But in retrospect it was kind of a dumb idea."

"Don't worry about it."

"I really *am* too pushy," I said, my mind flitting to Dr. Dreamboat, who I would probably never hear from again. "I've really got to work on that. Hey, were you able to find a partner for your dance class?"

He shook his head. "Maybe someday. They run new sessions every couple of months. I'm busy, so it's probably just as well. But tell me about Grace's place," he said, shifting his weight forward and putting one elbow on the table. "Why'd she suddenly decide to dive into redecorating?"

I told him all about what had happened after he'd called to give me the heads-up about Grace needing a friend on the day she'd been fired. I told him about the cannoli and our very frank conversation. I told him about what a wreck her place had been before my visit and the complete transformation Grace had wrought in just a few days and that it seemed to extend to Grace herself.

"See?" Luke said. "Sometimes it's good to be pushy. Sometimes that's what friends do."

"Well, if that's true, then I'm the best friend on the planet. But I really think it's helping her deal with her grief. That and the quilt—the one she's making from Jamie's old clothes."

"Grace makes quilts?"

"Among other things. Grace is super crafty. Remember that dress she was wearing when you met her?"

"The one with those crazy flamingos?" Luke asked, smiling curiously.

"Made it herself," I informed him. "Once upon a time, Grace sewed all her own clothes. But wait, I haven't even told you the best part yet. She dug out her old machine and some fabric that she brought from Minnesota—I bet she has sixty or seventy yards, when it comes to fabric she's practically a hoarder—and made a brand-new dress for a homeless girl who lives in the neighborhood."

"You're kidding. That was really nice of her. Probably good for her, too, therapeutic. But you said she only had two months of severance, right? Has she started looking for a job yet?"

"Yup, as of this morning, she has two."

"Two?"

I was about to launch into the story when the door to the kitchen swung open and Ben stuck his head out.

"Chef, what do you want me to do with that salmon?"

"What do you *think* I want you to do with it?" I spat, rolling my eyes. "Take it to the movies? Filet it!"

"Hey!" Ben barked. "I'm not a mind reader, you know. Last week you wanted to roast it whole, two days ago you chunked it up for risotto." Ben glowered at me. "What's wrong with you? You're acting like a real witch lately. If you want to fire me, then go ahead and do it. Because I do not need this crap."

"Okay, okay." I sighed and held up both hands. "Sorry. I shouldn't have snapped at you. Just filet the fish, please. We're going to keep it simple tonight—grilled with a balsamic glaze."

"Fine," Ben said, though his tone of voice said otherwise. "We open in less than an hour."

"I'll be there in five minutes," I said, trying and failing to keep the edge from creeping back into my voice. I didn't need Ben reminding me of the time.

Ben disappeared behind the door. I could hear him yelling, taking out his frustration on the rest of the staff.

"You should go," Luke said.

He was right and I knew it. But I also knew that it was Friday, that the reservation book was full, and that for the next five and a half hours, I'd be on my feet, so busy I wouldn't even have time for a bathroom break. It was going to be a long night. Before I was ready to face it, I just needed to rest a few more minutes. Besides, I was the boss here, not Ben, and the story of Grace's two jobs—not to mention my role in helping her secure them—was too good not to share.

"In a sec. Anyway, Grace phoned me this morning, *before* the alarm went off. If she hadn't been so excited, I probably would have slugged her," I said, then went on and told him the rest of the story, or tried to. Luke interrupted me more than once with questions.

Just as I finished, Nan came breezing through the door, accompanied by Blixen and Nelson. I got up and gave her a hug, asked her if she wanted something to eat.

"No, no," she said. "We're on our way to the park. I just thought I'd pop in and say hello, see how the ticket sales are coming."

"Sixty so far," I reported proudly.

"Sixty!" she exclaimed. "That's wonderful! Bob's flyers are really doing the trick. When you see him, be sure to tell him I said thanks."

"Will do. Have you met Luke Pascal yet? I told you about him," I said, not mentioning the Grace connection but seeing a flicker of recognition in her eyes, "he built all our new tables. Luke, this is Nan Wilja."

"I was about to say how beautiful everything looked," Nan replied, reaching out to shake Luke's hand.

As Nan and Luke exchanged pleasantries, Ben

stuck his head out of the kitchen and growled, "Chef. Thirty minutes."

"My master's voice," I said, faking a laugh to cover my irritation.

I *knew* what time it was. If it hadn't been so close to opening, and if Nan and Luke hadn't been standing there, I'd have had it out with Ben then and there.

"Are you sure you don't want something to eat?" I asked, looking at Nan and Luke in turn. "We've got eggplant parmesan on special today. Come on into the kitchen and I'll fix you a plate."

"Can't. I'm meeting Malcolm for dinner at six." Nan reached into her pocket for her car keys. Both dogs got up from the floor, tails wagging. "See you Monday," she said, then gave me a hug and said goodbye.

"I should go too," Luke said, his head turning as Nan walked out the door.

"Are you sure?" I asked. "Let me wrap something up for you to take with you. It's the least I can do after all your hard work."

"Thanks, but I've got to run," he said.

"Twenty-*eight* minutes!" Ben's voice bellowed.

"All right, already!" I bellowed back, yelling toward the kitchen door. "When I need the time, I'll ask for it!"

I turned around, ready to apologize to Luke for my outburst, but he was already gone.

Chapter 26

Nan

"Okay, you two. Ready to go to the park? Yes?" I opened the hatch on my car. Blixen and Nelson immediately jumped in, eager to get going.

"Good dogs. Let's go," I said, and closed the hatch.

"Nan? Hey, Nan?"

I turned around. Luke Pascal had come through the door and was trotting toward my car. I wasn't all that surprised. He'd been looking at me pretty intently inside the restaurant and when I turned to leave, I'd felt his eyes follow me.

"I've been hoping I might run into you. Do you have a second?"

"Not really," I replied, glancing at my watch.

"Right. You've got a dinner date. But you're taking the dogs to the park first, right? Would you mind if I came along? I could follow you in my car. I'd really like to talk to you about something."

Luke didn't say what he wanted to talk about, but he didn't have to. The subject, I knew, was Grace. I could see it in his eyes, the desperation of unrequited love. I was going to say no. But then I said yes, because the other thing I saw in his eyes was determination.

This wasn't a man who could be brushed off easily. I was going to have to explain to him, in clear and certain terms, why he needed to leave Grace alone, if not forever, at least for a good long while.

"All right," I said, opening the door to my car. "Follow me."

Laurelhurst Park is much smaller than Washington Park, only about twenty-five acres, but it's a quiet oasis on the east side of the river, green and a bit formal, designed by the Olmsted Brothers, the same firm that designed New York City's Central Park, with a lovely little lake in the center. Such a peaceful spot. Even the dogs seem to sense that, trotting calmly along without tugging at their leashes, which was a good thing since I still only had the use of one hand.

Blixen, Nelson, Luke, and I were on our second lap around the lake and I was no closer to convincing Luke to let Grace be than I was when we started. He was a *very* determined man, even more than I'd taken him for, and he was in love with Grace. How did I know this? Because he kept saying so.

Every good and sensible reason I gave him for leaving Grace alone, at least for now, was met with, "I get it. I know. You're probably right. But I love her."

He was so earnest and, I think, very sincere. It was hard not to like Luke Pascal.

"I know it doesn't make sense," he said, shoving his hands into his pockets as we strolled past a big willow tree, the dogs walking much more slowly now, their energy beginning to wane.

"But I do. I love her. I've tried to talk myself out of it, believe me. Do you have any idea how inconvenient this is for me? I'm trying to get a business off the ground. That's what I should be focused on. Instead, I spend all my time thinking about Grace.

"When I first met her, that night at The Fish House, I liked her. A lot. But that was all. We had a really good time and I hadn't danced in forever. I was having fun and so was she, but that's all there was to it. But then, during that last dance . . . I don't know. Something happened."

He stopped in the middle of the path and pulled his hands out of his pockets. Blixen, who was looking a bit tired, immediately sat down, her tongue lolling from her mouth. Nelson sat down beside her.

"It's ridiculous, I know that. This shouldn't be happening to me, not now. I'm thirty-seven years old. This is the kind of thing that should have happened to me when I was eighteen, or twenty-three. But it never did. When Ava and I got married, it was because she was smart, attractive, and it was time. I just figured I was one of those guys who couldn't fall in love. And that was fine with me. I'd watched a couple of my friends go through it and they looked miserable.

"Now I know just *how* miserable. Come on, Nan. You've got to help me. Please."

Poor Luke. He really did look miserable. A part of me really did want to help him, but I wasn't sure I could.

"I'm sorry, Luke. I know this is hard. But you've got to understand, Grace and Jamie—"

"Were deeply in love," he said, finishing my sentence for me. "I realize that. And, listen, when Monica told me that Grace was married and all about Jamie's accident, I backed off. Yes, I went to find her at the coffee shop, but only to invite her to take the dance class. She really had fun that night and I thought dancing might help her. She was carrying such a load.

"But I would never have laid a hand on her," he said, raising one of those hands. "Scout's honor. Miserable or not, I would never touch another man's wife, Nan. You've got to believe me."

I did believe him. I'm usually a pretty good judge of character and in the previous half hour, Luke had shown me he was a man with plenty of it.

"Luke, don't you see? Grace needs time to

mourn. It might take a year. Or more. There's no way of knowing. Grief has no timetable—"

"If that's true, then why does it have to be a year? Why can't it be a month? Two months? I'm not trying to replace Jamie. That would be impossible, even if I tried. But if I think I can make Grace happy now, why should I have to wait? Why should she? Give me one good reason," he said. "Just one."

But when he put it that way, I couldn't think of one. Sure, there was the "decent interval" argument, but Luke asked for a good reason. Satisfying the expectations and judgments of people outside the situation didn't qualify.

And Luke had a point, if he could make Grace happy now, what was the virtue of waiting until some far-off tomorrow? How many nights should Grace have to spend alone, how many too-quiet rooms had to press in on her, how many copper pots was she supposed to polish, trying to erase the ache of loneliness, before she was allowed to love again?

Where did these rules come from? And why did we suffer to abide by them?

"Luke," I said helplessly. "What is it you expect me to do? Grace is the one you need to convince. Why come to me?"

"Because Grace loves and respects you," he replied. "And because you know her better than anyone. She said so herself. I'm in love with her, but I hardly know her. If I show up at her door and declare my undying love, she's going to slam it in my face. Even if she doesn't, there's no way she'll believe me. Tell me what I should do to convince her I'm for real? What should I say?"

"Nothing," I answered. "Don't say a word."

Luke frowned and shoved his hands in his pockets. Obviously, he wasn't finding my suggestion very helpful. I gave a little tug on the leashes. Blixen and Nelson got to their feet. We began walking again.

"Two weeks before I left for my freshman year of college, my boyfriend broke up with me. We'd met on the first day of junior high and had been together ever since. I assumed that we'd be getting married after college, so the breakup really, really hurt. It also made me determined not to make the same mistake twice. I decided I wasn't going to date at all in freshman year. After that, I was going to play the field, not commit myself to any one boy until at least the end of my junior year.

"But on my first day at Oregon State, a tall, skinny boy sat down next to me in freshman English. He had a really goofy grin," I said, smiling. "And he wouldn't stop looking at me, but I refused to look back. Every day for the next two weeks, he took the seat next to mine, even after I moved to another row. He asked me out twice. Both times, I said no, pretty forcefully.

"But he didn't give up. I didn't know until later, but he figured out who my roommate was, waited for her outside the library and talked to her, trying to find out everything he could about me. After that, he changed his tactics.

"He didn't sit next to me anymore. But when my roommate told him my car wouldn't start and I was upset because I wanted to go home for the weekend, he replaced my alternator. When I got a terrible case of the flu and couldn't come to class, he took notes and gave them to my roommate to give to me. And not just for my English class, but all my classes. He actually sat in on my classes, courses he wasn't even enrolled in, and took notes for me.

"It went on like that for three months. Every time I needed help, sometimes even before I knew I needed it, Jim Wilja was there. He didn't tell me he loved me," I said. "He showed me. And then he waited for me to figure it out. He waited for me to come to him.

"One day in December, I did. I sat down next to him in English class. When class was over, I asked if he wanted to go to the Christmas concert with me that night. He said yes, and that was that. Three weeks after graduation, we were married."

My eyes had been fixed forward, looking straight ahead. Luke walked alongside me, silent as the dogs the whole time I was talking. Now I turned to look at him.

"Don't say anything," I said. "Be there for her. Be her friend."

"And then?"

I shrugged. "And then who knows? Maybe she'll fall in love with you. Maybe she won't. But one thing I do know: Being in love with your best friend is the best thing that can ever happen to a person."

Chapter 27

Grace

At the end of my redecorating project, every freshly painted room in my home was pristine and tidy, every surface free of clutter, every corner and counter a pleasure to look at, adorned with a carefully chosen and placed collection of accessories and artwork, like something out of a magazine. It was beautiful.

And after I finished discussing my business proposal with the very groggy Monica, it stayed that way for—let me see—about ten minutes.

Three days later, the place was an absolute wreck. My beautiful blue sofa was invisible under piles of fabric; the fruit bowl and cute counter accessories had been unceremoniously shoved aside to make room for my cutting mat, scissors, pins, and patterns; and the floor was so littered with stray thread that it looked like somebody had thrown a ticker tape parade in the living room.

I'd been sewing pretty much nonstop since getting off the phone with Monica, sleeping and eating only when I had to, not leaving the house except to walk Maisie. I was tired but still energized, thinking about how amazing it would be if I really could make this work. I'd already finished seven dresses and three skirts, each one a little more quickly than the one before, but there was still a lot to do. So I wasn't exactly thrilled when I heard the doorbell ring—I didn't have time for interruptions—and even less so after I opened the door.

"Oh. Luke. Hi."

"Hi. I don't want to disturb you. Just thought I'd drop by and say hello. I had some errands to run on this side of town," he said, smiling and gesturing toward his white panel delivery truck, which was parked at the curb.

"Oh, well. That was nice of you."

I stood there for a second, feeling awkward, wishing I hadn't answered the door, wishing he'd go away. But then that Midwestern politeness that is woven into my DNA kicked in and I asked if he wanted to come in for a minute.

"Can't. Thanks anyway," he said. I tried not to look relieved. "But can you come out to the truck for a second? I'd like your opinion on some-thing."

I couldn't imagine what he could possibly have in his truck that would require my approval, but how could I say no? After a moment of hesitation, I followed him to the curb and stood on the street while he rolled up the truck's metal door.

"Well? What do you think?" he asked, waving his hand toward the compact but handsome farmhouse table standing in the middle of the truck bed, its light-honey finish fresh and gleaming.

"It's gorgeous," I said sincerely. "Who's it for?"

"Well, that kind of depends. I won't know for sure until I get your opinion."

He hopped up into the truck, then turned around and reached out his hand to help me up. I grabbed it and climbed inside.

"Is it new?" I asked, walking around the table, admiring the pristine finish, the richly etched grain of the wood that shone through it.

"Yes and no. When I moved into my house, I found it in the garage. It's good, solid oak, but there were about three different colors of paint on it. I stripped the paint, sanded the top, and refinished it. Do you like the color? I kept it nearly natural. I always think it's nice to let the grain show through on old pieces like this."

"Me too," I said, running my hand over the tabletop. "So smooth. But it's tall for a dining table, isn't it?"

He nodded. "I put on new legs to make it counter height and redesigned the drawers underneath, added extra space to hold rulers, scissors, pins. Stuff like that."

"So . . . it's a craft table?" I asked, my heart beating a little bit faster.

"Yes, but also a dining table. See?" He pointed to some backless counter stools at the back of the truck. "When you're done with your crafts or sewing or whatever, you just pull the stools out and you've got seating for six."

He grabbed one of the stools and pushed it under the table. "They're just the right size to fit underneath so they won't get in the way when you're working or take up extra floor space. I wish they swiveled," he said. "But I knocked them together in kind of a hurry. Still, they'll do the job."

Yes. Yes, they would. But the table—that was what really intrigued me. My kitchen was teeny. Under normal circumstances, considering how little I cooked, that wasn't a problem. But now trying to use that two foot by three foot counter as a place to cut out patterns was really slowing me down. A craft table like this one was exactly what I needed. In fact, it was almost exactly what I'd imagined having—someday, when I could find it and afford it.

But now, here it was in front of me, the very table I'd imagined, but much, much prettier. I'd have been satisfied with something assembled together with particleboard and elbow grease, an Ikea special, as long as it did the job. But this table was more than serviceable; it was an heirloom, something anyone would be proud to have in their home.

"How big is it?" I asked, my eyes glued to that beautiful piece of furniture.

"Forty-four by sixty inches," he said. "Wider than the average dining table, so there's plenty of room for crafts and cutting, but shorter, so it'll fit in a small space. Say, an apartment or condo. Well? What do you think?"

"I think it's fantastic," I said, my voice almost a whisper. I looked up at him. "Luke, I don't have enough money right now, but later . . . Do you think you could make another one of these? This table is perfect."

"Sorry. Can't do it," he said, and my shoulders drooped with disappointment. "It's a one-of-a-kind piece," he explained, "custom-made for a very specific person—you."

My head popped up. I stared at him doubtfully. I must have heard him wrong.

"Really. It's for you." When I didn't respond, he said, "No kidding, Grace. And no cost. It's a gift."

"A gift? No," I said. "You have to let me pay you, Luke. I'm kind of short right now, but maybe I can . . ."

I paused, thinking about my shaky finances and the giant project I was about to undertake, a project that might not see fruition for years, or ever. Oh, man. This really wasn't the time for me to be buying anything new, especially a custom-made piece that probably ran into the thousands.

But that table would really help speed up my production time. Plus—it was gorgeous.

I had to have it.

"How about . . . a hundred a month?" I asked hopefully, certain it wouldn't be enough but knowing that was the most I could spare right now. "And more later, once my finances are a little more settled? Luke, I really, really love this table. It's just what I need. See, I'm about to start a little—"

"No payments," he said, cutting me off. "It's a gift. And I already know why you need it now. That's why I made it. Monica told me all about your new business and I think it's great. I want to support what you're doing."

"Monica!" I exclaimed, instantly irritated. Of course. When she and Nan had come over for support group, I told her exactly the kind of table I wanted someday. And Monica, in turn, had told Luke. The snitch.

"Why is it whenever you pop into my life uninvited, Monica is always involved somehow?"

Luke frowned and scratched his ear. He looked like he was trying to keep himself from saying something he'd regret.

"Look, do you want the table or not?"

"Yes," I said. "But only if—"

"No buts. And *no* payments," he said, his eyes as serious as his voice sounded. "It's a gift. I don't want anything from you, Grace.

308

No dancing, no coffee dates, no quid pro quo. Nothing. But either accept this as a gift or don't accept it at all."

I bit my lip, thinking things over. How could I accept something so expensive? He must have spent hours and hours on it? On the other hand, how could I say no? This was exactly what I wanted. And needed. It would make my work so much easier.

"Well? Do you want to help me haul this thing inside? Or do I drive back to my workshop and chop it up for firewood? Up to you, Grace."

It's a good thing I'm stronger than I look because that table, though compact in size, was really heavy. Luke said it was because good oak is a strong, dense wood.

While I carried the stools in from the truck, Luke reinstalled the drawers, finishing up just as I brought in the last two. I pushed them into place underneath the table.

"It's perfect, Luke. Just perfect. I don't know how to thank you."

"You don't need to," he said, putting his screwdriver back into the toolbox he'd brought with him, then closing the lid. "Well, I should get going."

"Oh. Do you have to?" I asked, feeling awkward but also a little guilty. Just because he said I didn't need to repay him didn't mean

I didn't want to. It seemed rude to just take his table and close the door behind him. "You must be thirsty. Can I get you a glass of water? Coffee? Wouldn't take me a minute to make some."

"I'm good. Thanks anyway. I should get back to the shop. And out of your hair."

"Oh," I said. "Sure. I understand."

"Unless," he said, sounding a little bit hesitant, "is there something else you need, Grace? Something I can do for you?"

Was he serious? After everything he'd already done? And yet, the moment he said it, I realized there was something more I wanted Luke to do for me. In fact, the day before, even prior to him knocking on my door, I'd briefly considered calling to ask for his help but immediately rejected the idea. It would have been too awkward, especially after the way I'd brushed him off that last day in the coffee shop. Also, I wouldn't have wanted him to get the wrong idea about why I was calling. But now, here he was, standing in my living room. . . .

"Are you sure you don't mind? Monica said it sounded good to her, but I'd like a second opinion. Since you've owned two businesses now—"

He grinned, "Yeah, but remember, that first one failed."

"I know," I said. "But I consider that a plus; you already know what doesn't work. And you

310

were a lawyer. I don't want to keep you from your work, but . . ." I grabbed a stack of papers from the seat of the wicker-back chair. "Are you sure you don't mind?"

"Not a problem," he said. "What are friends for?"

Thirty minutes, a bowl of ice cream, and two cups of French roast later, I sat down on one of my new stools, looking at Luke across the table, waiting to hear his verdict.

"Well? What do you think? Can it work?"

"Well, before we get into details," he said, putting down his coffee cup, "I want to say how impressive this is. It's hard to believe you've never written a business plan before."

I narrowed my eyes. "Wow. You really sounded like a lawyer right there. Why do I feel a 'but' coming on?"

"Because you're smart," he laughed. "But honestly, Grace. I really am impressed. Before we get to the 'buts,' let's discuss what's good in your plan."

"Okay."

"To begin with, let's talk about your mission statement—'Twirl and Whirl Clothing Company merges fashion and philanthropy. When customers make a purchase from Twirl and Whirl, they will receive not only a fun, flirty, fashionable item of clothing, but also the satisfaction that comes from knowing a similar item will be donated to a needy woman in the local community.' That's really good," he said, lowering the paper and looking me in the eye.

"I don't know," I said, wrinkling my nose. "Now that I'm hearing it out loud, it sounds kind of long. And there are too many words that start with F."

"You can edit later if you want to," he said, "but this is really just a roadmap, a way for you to figure out where you want to go and how to get there. The basic concept, connecting fashion with philanthropy, is genius. That feel-good angle will separate you from the competition."

I nodded. "Plus, it's a good thing to do. That's the part that really has me excited."

"And that comes through in your plan. This is something you feel really passionate about. And I can tell you from experience, that's the *only* reason to start your own business."

He paused and took another drink from his coffee cup.

"This is where the 'but' comes in, right?"

"This is where," he said, putting down the cup. "Grace, it's never a mistake to follow your heart, but be sure to bring your brain along."

"Meaning?"

"Meaning your projections are overly optimistic."

I frowned and he lifted up his hand.

"Hang on," he said. "Don't get discouraged. It's a workable plan—with some adjustments. Starting a business with zero capital means you have to watch every penny."

"But it'll hardly cost me anything to start," I protested. "I already own the fabric, enough to make twenty-five dresses and thirty-five skirts. With the money I make from them, I can afford to buy more fabric and keep going."

"But you have other costs," he explained. "Getting a booth at the Saturday Market is a smart idea. The booth fee is fairly reasonable and you'll be surrounded by shoppers who want handmade goods. But if you found somebody to share the space, you could cut that cost in half."

"Oh. Good idea," I said, wondering why I hadn't thought of that myself. I grabbed a piece of paper and a pen from off the table and started scribbling notes. "What else?"

"Well, in general . . . I just think it's going to take longer to turn a profit than you think it is. You'll need outside income—"

"But that's why I'm going to work two jobs," I said, interrupting him. "I'll sew during the day, wait tables at Café Allegro at night, and sell clothes on the weekend."

"Right," he said. "But living on tips is dicey. Until you know how much you're really bringing in, I'd plan on picking up more hours."

I thought about that for a second. Remembering

my past waitressing experiences, I saw he had a point.

"Okay. I'll ask Monica if I can work Saturday nights too. Tips should be better and I know she's short on staff."

"But that's a lot of hours. Are you sure it won't be too much for you?"

"Are you kidding?" I laughed. "When I was working for Gavin, seventy hours was a short week. One thing I'll say for that job, it built up my stamina. And this time, I'll be working for something I care about. I got this," I assured him, adding another note to my list. "What else?"

"Right," he said, and the way he said it made me know that he was preparing to tell me something I didn't want to hear. "The thing is, Grace—donating a dress for every dress you sell? It's a big-hearted idea. But it won't work. If you're serious about making this a viable business over the long haul, there's just no way you can do it. At least not yet."

This *wasn't* something I wanted to hear. Being able to donate dresses was the whole idea behind the business, the thing that would set it apart from other companies, and the reason I wanted to do it in the first place.

Seeing the look on Sunny's face when I gave her a pretty dress, made just for her, had somehow opened up my world, made me think that I really did have something to offer,

314

something that mattered. I knew my company had to make a profit to make the idea viable, but donating a dress to a woman in need for every dress we sold, that was my dream.

"Yeah, and I get that," he said when I finally took enough of a breath. "But you keep talking about what you *want* to do, and I'm telling you what you *can* do. If you're serious about making that dream a reality—getting to the point where you can actually afford to donate thousands of dresses in a given year—then you need to plow your profits right back into the business. This can't be a hobby, Grace. If you're serious, you're going to need to buy equipment, hire employees, rent warehouse space, build a website. . . ."

When I started arguing with him again, he raised his hand to cut me off and said, "Grace. Follow your heart, but bring your brain. That's the only way this works. First make your company profitable, then make it philanthropic."

I didn't like hearing that. At. All.

But the look on Luke's face told me he didn't like saying it either. He wasn't trying to squash my dream. He was just trying, honestly and at the risk of ticking me off, to give me his very best advice, based on his experience. I didn't like it, but I'd be stupid not to listen.

"Okay," I said at last, "thinking with my head *and* my heart—you said that the philanthropic part of the mission was what would help me stand out from the competition. So doesn't eliminating that element also mean I'm eliminating a potential advantage in the market?"

"Well, yes. Potentially."

"Then what about starting smaller? Donating one garment for every two sold." He shook his head. "Four? Five? Ten?"

"How about every hundred."

I grinned. "Okay, now you're just being cheap. But, seriously, what if I use a percentage of each sale to make donated clothes? That could work, couldn't it?"

He admitted that it could, but said the difference between success and a pipe dream would lay in figuring out the right percentages. After some discussion that sometimes verged on argument, we came up with a system of graduated donation levels that Luke thought could work—two percent of the first thousand, three percent for up to five thousand, five percent up to ten thousand, and so on, until the company was strong enough to support the one-to-one donation goal.

"But it'll probably take five or six years," he said. "Plus every ounce of energy you've got. And even then, it might not work. Are you sure you're ready for that?"

Was I?

Five or six years was a long time. But, one way or another, those years were going to pass. Why not spend them doing something that mattered?

Something I believed in? And sure, it was a long shot, I knew that. Even if I worked as hard as I knew how, the chances of my success were pretty slim. But, if I failed, at least I'd have failed trying to do something I believed in, right?

But it was a risk. The biggest risk I'd ever considered taking in my life. *Was* I ready? If Jamie had been there, sitting next to me, what would he say?

"Yes," I said. "One hundred percent. All-in."

I picked up my pen and looked at Luke.

"Now, what else?"

Chapter 28

Grace

I put off starting work at Café Allegro until after my opening day at the Saturday Market. The only way for me to have enough dresses ready in time for that first day of sale was to sew from daylight to midnight, seven days a week. But when Alex qualified for the regional finals in cross-country, I took a couple hours off to go to the meet and cheer him on. Nan came too. Unfortunately Monica got caught in traffic and missed the start of the race.

"Where is he?" she puffed, winded and a little frantic-sounding after jogging from the parking lot.

"There," Nan said, pointing to a brownish head in a sea of other heads on the far side of the field. "In the middle of the pack."

Monica squinted in the same direction as Nan's finger, then swung her fist over her head and shouted, "Go, Alex! Woot-woot! You can do it!"

When he rounded a corner and disappeared she turned toward us. "He looked good, don't you think?"

"Really good," I said.

"I couldn't run that fast even if something was chasing me," Nan said.

Monica, still winded, laughed. "Yeah, I know what you mean. He's had a really good season, but only the top three will qualify for state, so it'd basically be a miracle if he made it. But you never know."

Bob and the other coaches, who had been standing a few yards down the course, cheering their runners on, started trotting toward a grove of trees on the opposite end of the field, where, presumably, the runners would reappear in a few minutes. Spotting Monica, he swept his arm over his head and waved. She waved back.

"Bob has a strategy," she informed us. "He wants Alex to lay low in the middle of the pack, reserve his energy, and then break hard in the last half kilometer. Alex has a heck of a kick. The tricky part is figuring out when to use it. Anyway, thanks for coming. This is kind of a big deal for Alex."

We sat down on a nearby bank of bleachers and Monica's smile faded.

"I can't *believe* I missed the start of the race," she said, rubbing her forehead as if she were trying to scrub the furrows from her brow. "I left the restaurant half an hour early to make sure I was here in plenty of time. Everything was going fine until I got to the tunnel and then—bam!

Dead stop. How did you two manage to get here on time?"

"I took the light rail," Nan said.

"And I took surface streets instead of the highway, drove over the hill. It's faster from my neighborhood."

Monica sighed. "I should have done that. I was just sure that there'd be enough time."

"Will you quit beating yourself up?" I said. "It's not like he didn't have a cheering section. The two of us made a ton of noise. We were actually kind of obnoxious. Did you know that Nan can do that thing where you stick your fingers in your mouth and whistle super loud?"

Monica's eyebrows popped up as she turned to look at Nan.

"Very helpful for calling dogs," Nan said.

"I don't believe it. Prove it," Monica demanded.

"Not now," Nan said self-consciously, glancing around at the other spectators. "Not until he's getting close to the finish line."

"How long will that be?" I asked, staring toward the clump of coaches on the far edge of the field.

Monica glanced at her phone. "About eleven minutes, give or take. So, let's get to it. Tell me everything. I feel like I haven't talked to you two in forever."

Eleven minutes divided by three friends isn't much time, so we all tried to do a sort of bullet-point version of our usual conversation, just hitting the highlights.

Nan was thrilled that seventy-two Dogmother's Ball tickets had been sold so far and that three college kids from the neighborhood had offered to help park cars for the event. With the advent of spring, the chickens were laying more eggs, and she was down to only three dogs. Mildred and Morgan, the black Labs, as well as Peaches and Cream, the basset hounds, had all been adopted.

"I miss them," she said, "but they went to very good homes."

"So that just leaves Lovey and Nelson. Poor Nelson," Monica said. "Isn't anybody ever going to adopt him?"

"He's already spoken for," Nan said. "I called Donna on Tuesday and told her I wanted to keep him. He's such a sweet boy. I just couldn't give him up."

"With only three dogs is Malcolm still coming to help?"

"Oh, yes," Nan replied. "Every morning and evening."

"So you're adopting him too?"

"Very funny. Your turn," Nan said.

"Same old, same old," Monica replied.

The restaurant business was busy, Alex was still rotten, her sous-chef was acting like a prima donna, and the mothers of the bride and groom at the wedding she was to cater the following weekend couldn't agree on the salad course.

"And," Monica said wearily, "Zoe got sent home from school for wearing a T-shirt with an inappropriate slogan."

"What did it say?" I asked.

Monica closed her eyes and moved her head from side to side. "Let's not even go there. The shirt has been burned and now, every morning, I check Zoe's backpack for contraband. But there's at least a little good news. Guess who dropped by the restaurant yesterday?"

"Hmm . . ." I tapped my chin with my finger, pretending to think, but Monica's smug little smile was a dead giveaway. "Could it be . . . Dr. Dreamboat?"

"Bingo! And he is still so, so dreamy." She sighed and clapped her hand to her heart. "He showed up just before closing, we shared a plate of linguini and a bottle of Chianti. He's got another late shift on Thursday and is going to drop by after to take me to a movie."

"Oh." Nan, who had been watching the grove of trees for sight of the returning runners, turned to look at Monica. "Really?"

Monica tipped her head to one side. "Yes, really. Why do you sound so surprised?"

"Oh, no reason," Nan replied.

"Nan," Monica said flatly. "You're a terrible liar. What is it?"

"It's nothing, only that I thought . . ." Nan

looked toward the grove of trees again and the cluster of coaches who stood nearby, waiting to cheer their runners to the finish line. "You know . . . Bob."

"Bob?" Monica's eyes widened. "Bob is a nice guy and everything, but . . . he's Bob. He's good to Alex. And good to me, too, I guess. But I don't think about him like that. He's just a friend. He's . . . Bob."

"You said that before," Nan reminded her. "Fine. If you're happy, I'm happy. Forget I mentioned it."

Nan turned her attention back to the trees. Monica looked at me and rolled her eyes, shooting me a sort of can-you-believe-her glance before changing the subject.

"So, Grace? What've you been up to?"

"Besides sewing?" I laughed. "Not much, including sleeping. But Luke . . ."

They already knew about the amazing sewing table and the adjustments he'd helped me make to my business plan, but they didn't know about the accounting software he'd recommended to help me keep track of my expenses, or the great, inexpensive website design company he'd steered me to, or how he'd helped walk me through the process of finding and buying a domain name.

Most importantly, he got me thinking about how to speed up my production. Even though I was running a factory with only one worker, I had to start thinking in terms of an assembly line.

Now I spent every morning cutting, making only one size that day—small, medium, large, or extra large—and layering fabric so I could cut two garments at once. Also, I cut all the individual pieces at the same time—the sleeves, then the yokes, then the skirts. Working that way enabled me to have six garments ready for sewing by lunchtime. Sewing took longer and by chain stitching all six pieces, one after the other, I'd cut hours off my garment production time. Luke was the one who'd pointed me in the right direction, gotten me to think like a businesswoman instead of a hobbyist. Without him, I'd never have been able to do it.

"My, my," Monica said, batting her eyelids. "Isn't he helpful? Sounds like Luke is trying to worm his way into your affections."

"Stop," I said, batting away her insinuation. "I feel about Luke the way you feel about Bob. He's a friend."

Nan looked like she wanted to say something, but a distant whoop from the cluster of coaches interrupted the thought and had us all on our feet, eyes glued to the trees as we waited for the first of the runners to emerge. We didn't have to wait long. A boy with impossibly long legs, wearing a blue and white jersey, sprinted toward the finish line. Several moments passed before two more racers appeared, another boy in blue and the other in green, running almost neck and neck. Alex wasn't among them.

Monica jumped up and stood on top of the bleachers, craning her neck and yelling, "Come on, Alex!" even though she couldn't see him. The fourth, fifth, sixth, and seventh racers came into view. The boy in blue crossed the line, taking first. Still no Alex. But then, all of a sudden, there he was—dashing through the trees and pounding across the field. By this time all the spectators, including me, were on their feet, yelling and cheering or, in Nan's case, whistling.

Monica leapt off the bleachers and jogged toward the finish line clapping her hands and screaming, "Go, Alex, go!" as Alex, his face red and contorted, seemed to find another gear. Legs and arms pumping like pistons, he passed the seventh racer and then the sixth. The battle for fifth place was intense and the crowd was cheering on both boys as they sprinted toward the finish. If the course had been twenty yards longer, Alex might have pulled it off. As it was, he crossed the finish line three paces behind his competitor.

"Woot! Way to go!" Monica hollered, and hugged me when the race announcer gave out Alex's time. "A personal record!"

The remaining racers were crossing the line so quickly and thickly now that the announcer couldn't keep up. Monica jogged over to congratulate Alex, who was standing off to one side of the course, bent over and with his hands on his knees, shoulders heaving as he tried to catch his breath.

She bent down near him. "Did you see your time? It was amazing, Alex! Way to go!"

Beaming with pride, Monica patted Alex on the back. He didn't say anything, just lifted his right arm and stretched it out, pushing her away.

"Hey," she said, moving in closer, "I know you wanted to go to state, but you've improved so much this season. You'll make it next year, Alex. You'll see. Really, honey, you should be proud."

With the last of his racers coming in, Bob was walking toward Alex, presumably to congratulate him. As he approached, Alex straightened up, glared at Monica, and said, "Shut up."

Monica's jaw slackened a little. I could see she was surprised, and hurt, but she reached out to put a hand on his shoulder anyway, saying, "Alex. It's okay. I know you're disappointed."

"Shut up!" he snapped, shaking her off. "I'm not your honey and I don't need your advice!"

"Hey!" Monica protested. "I was just trying to be supportive."

"When I need your support, I'll ask for it, okay? And if you're so interested in supporting me, maybe start by showing up on time."

Bob arrived on the scene.

"Alex! Knock it off! That's no way to talk to your mom."

Glowering and still red in the face, Alex turned on his coach. "She's *not* my mom. Just because my dad was sleeping with her—" Alex shouted, except he didn't say "sleeping with," resorting instead to a more vulgar and wounding vernacular that brought tears to Monica's eyes.

"Alex!" Bob boomed. "That's enough! You are way, way out of line!"

I didn't really know Bob, but I'd been under the impression that he was an affable, mild-mannered sort. So when his face contorted with fury and his voice thundered, I was taken by surprise.

Alex's face turned even redder. It looked like he, too, was fighting back tears.

"But, Coach!"

Bob shook his head, raised his arm, and pointed toward the field.

"Take a lap, Alex. You need to cool down."

By this time everyone was staring, including Alex's teammates. Shamefaced, Alex swallowed hard but didn't budge. Neither did Bob. He stabbed his finger toward the field a second time.

"I am serious, Alex. Take a lap. Now. Other-wise, you're off this team—and I mean forever. It'll be the end of your running career."

Alex hesitated a moment longer, then dipped his head low, and finally jogged off toward the far edge of the field. When he was out of earshot,

Bob placed his hand on Monica's shoulder, seeking out her eyes.

"You okay?"

"I'm fine. Just another day in the life of an Evil Stepmother," she said, pretending to laugh as she swiped at her eyes.

"You sure?" Monica sniffled and nodded. "Don't let this get to you, okay? Teenagers are idiots—big, colliding bags of hormones held together by skin and self-absorption. I ought to get hazard pay for the crap I put up with from these guys."

Monica smiled a little.

"Listen," he said gently. "I got this. After Alex finishes his lap and takes a shower, I'll chew him out, buy him a hamburger, and drop him at the house. You go on back to work, okay?"

"Okay," Monica said. "Thanks."

"You're welcome."

Bob went off to check in with the rest of his runners. Nan and I walked Monica to her car. When we got to the parking lot, Nan said, "That's a very nice friend you've got there, Monica."

"He is," Monica said. "He really is."

Chapter 29

Nan

"You didn't have to do this. I can still drive," I said, looking at Malcolm, who was sitting in the driver's seat of my car.

"I know," he said. "But it's no trouble. Besides, I need to pick up kibble and some better chew toys. Stuart shredded the last two."

Malcolm backed into a tight spot directly in front of Pet Parade, managing the maneuver on the first try, then hopped out of the car and jogged around the car to open my door.

There were definitely some advantages to being chauffeured about. It would have taken me three or four tries to fit into that space, if I'd have attempted it at all. I hate parallel parking. And it was nice to be fussed over a little bit. Most of the time.

Sometimes I felt that Malcolm went a little too far in his attempts to be helpful. Apart from the broken collarbone, I was a healthy, independent woman, and I liked doing things for myself.

In just four more weeks, I could. As soon as the

sling was off, I'd be able to cook a proper meal, bake something more complicated than oatmeal cookies, and dress in clothing with buttons and zippers instead of shapeless elastic-waisted pants and pullovers. I'd be able to fix my hair properly, and prune the hedges, and mulch the vegetable patch.

Of course, Malcolm would have gladly handled the pruning and the mulching if I asked. He loved gardening as much as I did and had a particular talent with hostas. Only the day before, he'd ordered some miniature varieties that he felt would do particularly well in the shady bed under the front window. I'd never had much success with that planter before and could hardly wait for the new plants to arrive. The week before that, he'd raked out all the rotted winter leaves. I was so grateful.

I wanted the garden to be in tip-top shape for the ball, and spring cleanup was always such a big chore. But not being able to do it myself was frustrating. Even so, I knew I would miss Malcolm's company once I was out of the sling. Funny how quickly I'd gotten used to having him around.

"What?" Malcolm asked, giving me a curious look when he opened the car door.

"Nothing," I said, quickly shifting my gaze. "I was just thinking how much I appreciate your help. You're good company, Malcolm."

"Well, thank you," he said with a matter-of-fact little nod. "So are you."

The bells on the pet shop door jingled to announce our entrance. Sylvia, who was kneeling down on the floor, stocking a shelf with kitty litter, got up to greet us.

"Just in time," she said. "I was going to call you later today."

She walked behind the counter, opened the register, pulled out two envelopes, and handed them to me.

"What's this?"

"The first one is a check for one hundred forty-five made out to the rescue, proceeds from the sales of eight dog jackets."

"Oh. We only sold eight?"

"Only? Nan, this is a very small shop. That's about a thirty percent increase for my jackets sales in the same month last year. My customers, few though they are, love your dog jackets."

"You're right, Sylvia. Every little bit helps, doesn't it? But it's a good thing the Dogmother's Ball is coming up. I don't think we can balance Rainbow Gate's budget by selling dog jackets."

"The ball will be a big success," Sylvia said confidently. "Good thing you brought more flyers, we went through the first batch so quick. A few of my customers said they're planning to come. That other envelope has two checks for tickets. One is from the Olneys, sweet old couple, but they don't have a computer so I said I'd give you their reservation. Mine's in there too."

"That's great, Sylvia. I'll add three more tickets to the list. Or is it four?"

"Oh, no," Sylvia said. "Just three. Unfortunately, I'm between boyfriends. Have been since . . . let me see now." She tapped her finger against her chin. "I believe it was the Reagan administration. But, hey, if any nice, single, animal-loving guys of a certain age show up without a date, feel free to seat them next to me."

"Will do."

Sylvia laughed. "I'm just joking. I've been alone so long that if you actually did find me a date, I doubt I'd know what to do with him. At this point, I've decided that dogs are better company than most men—so much more obedient. I never could train my husbands to sit, let alone stay. Should have had all three of them fixed on day one."

She laughed again and closed the drawer on the cash register.

"What about you, Nan? Do you have a date to the ball?"

"A date? Me? Oh, no—"

"She does," Malcolm said, heaving a twenty-five-pound bag of kibble onto the counter. "She's going with me."

• • •

Leaving the pet shop, we drove a good two miles before I worked up the nerve to say anything.

"Malcolm, when you told Sylvia that we were . . . going to the ball together. I was—" I cleared my throat. "What exactly did you mean by that?"

Malcolm glanced toward me with an amused expression, like he was someone waiting for the punch line of something he'd just figured out must be a joke.

"Well," he said slowly, "I meant we were going to go together. You are going to the ball. And I am going to the ball. And, this being the case, it only makes sense that we'd go together. Doesn't it?"

"Yes, but . . ."

I stared at him for a moment, waiting for him to state the obvious instead of forcing me to spell it out. He didn't.

"Malcolm," I said, "you know what I mean. There's together, as in two people being at the same location at the same time, and then there's, you know, *together.*"

"Ahh . . ." He looked over his shoulder before moving into the left turn lane. "I see. Well, I was thinking we could go *together,*" he said, mimicking my emphasis and intensity. If I wasn't so flustered, I might have thought it was funny.

"Oh, I see."

Frowning, Malcolm glanced at me again before making the turn. "Is that a problem? I've really enjoyed your company and getting to know you better over these last few weeks. I assumed you felt the same. But if I misread the situation—"

"No, no. But, well . . . It's like Sylvia said. I haven't been involved with a man since the Reagan administration—in a romantic sense, I mean. I assume that's what we're talking about?"

"It is," Malcolm confirmed.

I felt my heart flutter, more from anxiety than ardor.

"Right. I see."

"You said that already."

"Sorry. It's just that . . . I don't quite know how to respond. I've been alone a long time. And I . . . well, I'm sixty-two years old."

"I'm sixty-three. Why should that make a difference?"

I was quiet for a moment. "Maybe it shouldn't. But this is a lot to wrap my head around, Malcolm. It's been so long since I even considered the possibility of a . . . ."

"Romance," he said, supplying the word. "Go ahead. You can say it."

Even with Malcolm's urging it took a moment for me to summon the word, as if the syllables were somehow too sticky to utter.

"Romance," I said finally. "I thought that ship had sailed."

"Think again," he said. "Because it hasn't."

Malcolm's tone was practical, just as even and matter-of-fact as it had been when we'd been discussing which hostas might do well in that shady spot in my yard. I found that reassuring.

"Fine. Let's say it's true. Let's say that, after two decades alone, I'll be able to adjust to the idea and practice of a romantic relationship." I hesitated briefly at the end of the sentence, but the R-word came more easily this time. "Let's assume that, all right? Just for argument's sake."

"Good. Let's," Malcolm said, nodding deeply to indicate that he was with me.

"You were married for over thirty years. Your divorce was only finalized a few weeks ago. On top of that, you've been forced into retirement sooner than you'd planned. Your whole life has been turned upside down this last year. You're trying to sort out what your new life is going to be like, looking to fill in the holes left in the wake of all this, which is understandable, admirable even. It's great, the way you're handling everything, staying positive and trying to move forward and all that. But I'm not sure how I feel about being . . . well, cement."

"Cement?" Malcolm smiled as he pulled the car into my driveway.

"Cement, caulking, grout—whatever it is you use to fill holes in with." I flapped my hand impatiently. "It's a masonry analogy."

335

"Oh, right," he said slowly, then set the parking brake. "Sure. Masonry."

"Okay, fine. Now you're making fun of me. But this is serious," I said, even as a smile tugged at the corners of my mouth. "I don't want to have my life upended and my heart broken just because you're . . ."

"On the rebound?"

Malcolm turned off the car.

"Look, Nan, helping out during your recovery has been a good distraction while I'm adjusting to all the changes in my life. But I'm not an aimless man or an indecisive one. With or without you, I'd have figured out a new direction and purpose in life. And much as I find you lovely, and fascinating, and great fun to be with, I can assure you that I am not about to make you, or anyone, my reason for getting up in the morning.

"I'm a man of many interests and inclinations. I've never been bored a day in my life. From what I've seen, you're the same. That's part of the attraction. Seems to me we might be able to find lots of wonderful ways to share our lives but still be able to maintain the independence that each of us values. And, along the way, we might each of us learn a few things from the other."

I found myself nodding as he spoke, especially when it came to the part about being able to share life even while maintaining our identities. That was what had been so wonderful and so very special about my marriage to Jim. We could not have been closer and yet, we were able to give each other space to operate as individuals.

"As far as me being on the rebound?" Malcolm shook his head. "I'm not. Yes, my divorce came through just recently, but the marriage was over a long, long time ago. Marriage wasn't a commitment I made lightly; I tried everything I could to salvage my relationship with Barbara. If I ever marry again, I'll be just as committed. But you can't be in a marriage by yourself, and Barbara made it clear that—"

Malcolm stopped in midsentence at about the same time I realized I had stopped breathing.

"Uh-oh. I'm scaring the hell out of you, aren't I? Sorry. An unfortunate by-product of a scientific mind. I tend to mentally walk through all the potential outcomes before choosing a path. You're right. One step at a time."

Malcolm unbuckled his safety belt and twisted toward me, pulling one leg up onto the seat so he was looking right at me. As he reached out, placed his hand on my shoulder, and leaned in, I felt my face get hot.

"What are you doing?"

"Well, before we get too far into this, I thought I'd kiss you."

His words were as straightforward as ever, but his voice had dropped to almost a whisper and his Scottish burr became simultaneously thicker and softer, a voice that sounded like velvet feels, soft as a sable brush caressing my cheek.

"That is, assuming you have no objection. And then, if you like it, you can decide if we should go to the ball together. What do you think? Does that seem like a good first step?"

My stomach flipped in that same way it had when he turned around at the gate and looked at me.

"Oh. If you put it that . . . I mean . . . Yes. Yes, that makes sense."

"Good," Malcolm said. "Because it's something I've wanted to do for a long time."

Like so many things that would happen that day, his admission came as a surprise, but it was a good one. That said as much as anything about my feelings toward Malcolm. I've never liked surprises. But this was different. So was Malcolm.

It was a long kiss. I suppose you could have described it as lingering. And, based on the cloudy comparisons I was able to summon from the recesses of my oh-so-distant memories, it was a very, very good one. During the first moment or two, I actually tried to assess it, contrasting Malcolm's kiss to those of my Jim, so many years before, but I gave up pretty quickly.

Jim was the best of men, an ideal partner. Malcolm was like him but not. Yet he, too, was the best of men. An ideal partner? It was too soon to tell. But I kept thinking about what

Monica said when she told us that Bob was "just a friend." If the crowd hadn't started to cheer on the first racer at precisely that moment, I would have told her the same thing I told Luke, that falling in love with your best friend is one of the best things that can happen to a person. I knew from experience. Jim Wilja wasn't just my husband, he was my best friend. Had fate not deemed otherwise, he would have remained so for life.

Now, there was Malcolm. Certainly he was my friend. Could he be my best friend? Could I love him?

With Malcolm's lips on mine, sweet and soft and searching, and his arms pulling me into an embrace that made me melt, I understood that there was more than one kind of kiss, just as there was more than one kind of man, and that each could be the best and oh . . . so lovely.

Finally, at the end of that long kiss, which was still far too short, Malcolm loosened his grip and looked into my eyes.

"Well?" he asked. "What did you think?"

It was the voice of a man who was bracing himself for the best or the worst, the kind of anxious but stalwart tone people use to question a physician about the outcome of a potentially life-altering lab result. Hearing it, I couldn't help but smile.

"I think we should definitely go to the ball

together. Definitely. And . . . I think you should kiss me again."

He didn't wait to be asked twice.

The second kiss was just as good as the first. Even better, in fact, because this time I kissed him back. I slid my fingers slowly along his shoulder and the length of his neck, up into his hair. I admit to feeling tentative at first, hesitant, like a musician who is trying to remember the exact position and placement of her fingers on the keyboard after a years-long lapse at the piano. Even so, it was an elating sensation, the thrill that comes from breathing an old ember into new flame.

When we finally broke apart, I was smiling.

"Like riding a bicycle," I laughed.

"All comes back to you, doesn't it? Just imagine if the emergency brake wasn't standing between us," Malcolm said, glancing down at the console with a grin. "We might spontaneously combust."

"But . . . maybe we'd better keep the brakes on for a bit? I'm no prude, Malcolm, but I—"

"You don't need to say more, Nan. I understand. And I agree. One step at a time. The Scottish Book of Common Prayer says that marriage is to be entered into 'reverently, discreetly, advisedly, soberly, and in the fear of God.' That was my mind-set when I married the first time. Though I know we are miles away from taking any steps in that direction, if I were ever to marry again, I'd be just as committed and would enter into that union just as soberly, just as reverently."

"Oh, Malcolm," I laughed.

He shrugged. "I know. Hopelessly old-fashioned."

"Well, if that's true, then we both are. But . . . we can still kiss, can't we?"

"Aye, that we can, lass," he said, purposely thickening his brogue and making me laugh again.

He reached for me again and I leaned toward him eagerly, my hands arching over his shoulders. And then, just as our lips were about to touch, someone rapped sharply on the back window of the car.

Startled by the sound, I quickly pulled away. Malcolm jumped, too, swiveling his neck in the direction of the noise. A moment later, a face with sallow skin, sunken eyes, and dirty blond hair appeared in the frame of the passenger's side window.

"Sorry," she said. "I didn't mean to scare you."

My breath caught in my throat and my hand flew to my heart. I reached for the door handle, but Malcolm grabbed my wrist to stop me.

"Wait. Who is that? Do you know her?"

"It's my daughter," I said.

He looked at me blankly and I pulled from his grasp.

"It's Dani."

Chapter 30

Nan

Malcolm and I had fallen into the habit of sharing a pot of tea after he finished the evening round of dog walking. When he heard my footsteps on the back stairs after I finished checking on Dani, he called out, "Chamomile or Earl Grey?"

"Chamomile. Not that I'll be able to get a wink of sleep tonight. But . . ."

Malcolm scooped tea into a strainer and placed it in the pot to steep. I took a flowered plate out of the cupboard and filled it with a half-dozen oatmeal cookies.

By this time, Malcolm knew my kitchen so well that we were able to complete the preparations in silence. Though this wasn't the normal procedure, I was glad he left me to my own thoughts. I had so much on my mind.

When everything was ready, Malcolm carried the tea tray into the dining room. Blixen, Nelson, and Lovey padded along behind him, then curled up in a pile in the corner.

"Is she asleep?" Malcolm asked after pouring the tea.

"Out like a light. She didn't even bother drying her hair after her shower. The pillow was soaked so I slipped another one under her head. She didn't even stir. But she'll feel better in the morning after a good sleep and a good breakfast. We need to get some weight back on her," I said, more to myself than Malcolm.

I sipped my tea. Malcolm reached for a cookie, chewing in silence for a time.

"But you know it's going to take more than that, right?"

"Sorry?" I looked up. For a moment, I'd forgotten he was sitting there.

"You know it's going to take more than a shower, a good night's sleep, and a bit of a weight gain to put her back to rights, don't you?"

"I know," I said, trying to keep the tension from my voice.

Malcolm was just trying to watch out for me, keep me from getting hurt. I appreciated that, but I'd been handling this situation on my own for a long time. If Malcolm hadn't happened to be in the car at just that moment, he would never have known about Dani's addiction and I'd still have been handling it by myself.

"I called some of the rehabs I'd been in contact with before. There's a bed available in Newberg starting tomorrow. I'll drive Dani out first thing in the morning."

I closed my eyes, took in a deep breath, then

exhaled in a long, slow whoosh, feeling the tension drain from my body.

"This is an answer to prayer, Malcolm. An answer to prayer. All those nights I've lain awake, wondering where she was, worrying that she was freezing, or starving, or had overdosed. You have no idea. . . ."

A tear of relief rolled down my face. I pressed my hand to my cheek and wiped it away, then opened my eyes. Malcolm was watching me.

"I'm sorry I never told you, Malcolm. You were always so good to Dani. Every time you asked about her, I wanted to tell you—"

He shook his head and lifted his hand, stopping my explanation.

"It's all right, Nan. I understand. It was a private matter. You and I haven't known each other very well for very long."

"It's not just you. I haven't told anyone outside of the family."

"Not even Grace and Monica?"

I shook my head.

"I think about Dani all the time, day and night, but talking about it is just too painful. That's why, until I met Monica and Grace that night in the parking lot and asked them home for tea and turnovers, I had no real friends. I cut off contact with almost everyone who knew Dani before. I felt like, if they knew what had happened to her, they'd think it was my fault."

"Nan," Malcolm said, his voice chiding. "You were a wonderful mother and Dani is a wonderful girl. If she made a mistake, a bad choice along the way . . ." Malcolm reached across the table and took my hand.

"Don't cry. Don't. The drugs that are out there today are so powerful," he said. "No matter how much you try to warn them, kids do all kinds of foolish things. It doesn't take long to go from experimentation to full-blown addiction."

"It wasn't just that," I said, my voice catching as I tried to stem the tears. "Dani was only five when Jim died. It was terrible for all the kids, but Dani took it harder than the others. She was the baby and I'd had two miscarriages before she was born. At that point, we realized we probably wouldn't have more children. I babied her, we all did. But she and Jim were so, so close. Everybody kept saying, 'Oh, kids that age are so resilient, she'll get over it,' but she didn't. Not ever.

"She'd always been such a sweet little girl, so sunny and eager to please. But after Jim died, she changed. Looking back, I really think she was depressed. You don't think of a child that age suffering from depression, but . . ." I placed my hand over my mouth and looked away, collected myself so I could continue with the story.

"And, the thing is, sometimes there were glimpses of the old Dani, especially when she was interacting with people outside the family.

Sometimes I felt like there were two different Danis—the person she was and the person she wanted people to think she was. That's the side you saw."

Malcolm nodded. "She was always capable and responsible around me, upbeat. And so good with the animals."

"That part *was* real," I said. "Dani adored animals, related to them better than she did people, I think. That was the reason I started keeping chickens and then got the goats. Taking care of them seemed to calm her. But the part you didn't see was the moody, manipulative Dani. She used to lie about"—I shrugged—"well, everything.

"When she was twelve, I noticed that the door of the liquor cabinet was open. When I checked, the key was hidden in my great-grandmother's copper kettle, where I always kept it. The bottles were at the same level they had been when I put them away after the holidays, once I'd finished baking fruitcake and had the neighbors over for New Year's Eve. But when I opened the brandy bottle, I realized that somebody had watered it down and added food coloring so I wouldn't suspect anything. I blamed the boys. They swore up and down that it wasn't them, but I grounded them for two weeks. Back then, I just couldn't make myself believe that a twelve-year-old girl would be sneaking liquor."

"Self-medicating," Malcolm said, nodding.

"That was the beginning. When Dani was sixteen, Kyle got injured playing soccer, damaged the knee ligaments. The doctor prescribed Percocet. Kyle didn't like the way it made him feel, so he didn't finish the prescription. Dani took the bottle from the medicine cabinet and . . ."

Nelson and Lovey were asleep, but Blixen, who had been watching us the whole time, got up from the floor and passed across the room to rest her muzzle on my lap. I stroked her head, took in big, slow breaths. Malcolm picked up the teapot and added more tea to my cup.

"My mother always said a cup of tea makes everything better."

"Wouldn't it be great if that were true?" I tried to smile. "Anyway, things went downhill pretty quickly after that. She held it together at school, but home was a different story. We had terrible fights. She stole money from me. I caught her red-handed so she couldn't lie about taking it, but she told me she'd spent it on her friends, treating everybody to dinner. I punished her, but I believed the story. Maybe I wanted to. Of course, the truth was she used the money to buy illegal prescription drugs."

I sighed, drank some tea. It was getting cold.

"Chrissy was the one who finally figured it out. One day, Dani and I had a huge fight. She packed up her bags and said she was going to live with her sister. Honestly, it was a relief to see her go. I was just worn-out with her. And I really thought that spending some time with her sister might be good for Dani. They were very close when Dani was little. For a few days, it seemed like it was going to work out, but then Chrissy caught Dani raiding the medicine cabinet and, well . . ."

I let the rest of the story lie. There was no need to say more, at least not right then. It wasn't like the story of Dani's spiral into addiction and homelessness was all that singular. Thousands of parents across the country could have told a similar tale. Malcolm squeezed my hand.

"This wasn't your fault. You know that, don't you?"

I bobbed my head obediently.

"So Chrissy keeps telling me. And I've said it to myself, a million times or more." I pressed my lips together. "Saying it is one thing. Believing it is something else entirely. It's hard, Malcolm. Every single day.

"About a year after Dani disappeared, I went to the liquor cabinet and realized that the vodka bottle was nearly empty and that I was the one who had emptied it. After that, I started stepping up my volunteer work, spent more time gardening and helping out at Rainbow Gate. In theory, I was supposed to be rescuing the dogs, but I think it was the other way around." I lowered my head, gazed into Blixen's beautiful brown eyes. "Whoever said that diamonds are a girl's best friend never had a dog."

Malcolm nodded. "Sometimes I think they're the only truly selfless creatures on God's earth. Well, some of them," he said, reaching out to scratch Blixen's head. Blix closed her eyes, sighed her contentment, then tipped her head to one side, making it clear that her ears needed attention as well. Malcolm obliged.

We sat there for a few minutes, sipping tea in silence. When, at last, all of Blixen's itches had been thoroughly scratched and she went back to the corner, Malcolm took a final sip of tea.

"Would you like me to drive you to Newberg in the morning? It's a bit of a trek."

"Thank you, but no. I think Dani would feel more comfortable if it was just the two of us."

"All right. But if you change your mind, all you need to do is call." He got to his feet. "I suppose I should be going."

I walked him to the door. After kissing me good night, chastely this time, on the cheek, he dropped into his thickest Scottish brogue and said, "It's a lang road that's no goat a turnin'."

I smiled. "What?"

"Something my mother used to say—It's a long road that's got no turning," he said. "You've walked this road a long time, Nan. I imagine you'll be walking it a long time yet.

Come tomorrow, God willing, you and Dani will be walking in the same direction, the right direction."

"I hope so."

"So do I."

He placed one hand on each side of my face and kissed me once again.

"Sleep well."

I didn't sleep well.

I lay awake wondering how long Dani would need to be in rehab and how I would pay for it. It wasn't cheap and Dani didn't have insurance. It could add up to thousands. But if that's what it took to save her, then I'd find a way. Somehow. I'd sell the house if I had to.

I worried, too, about the detox phase of treatment. It was bound to be rough, and Dani seemed so frail. I worried about whether or not to tell the other kids but decided against it, at least for the time being. I worried about what would happen once Dani completed the program. Would she move into a place of her own? Into a halfway house of some kind? Would she be better off coming home for a few months? Or should she get as far away from Portland as possible?

Finally, sometime after two, I fell asleep and woke up again around six thirty when Nelson started scratching at the bedroom door, demanding to be taken out for his morning wee.

Nelson didn't have the most reliable of bladders, so I put on my bathrobe and crept down the hall.

On the way, I poked my head into Dani's room, relieved to see her tangled blond hair on the pillow. I tiptoed downstairs, let the dogs out, then started brewing coffee and making toast. Later, I'd make some eggs. In the meantime, a good, strong cup of coffee and a piece of raisin toast should help ease Dani into the new day. She'd never been a morning person.

Once the toast was buttered and the coffee poured, I let in the dogs. They bounded into the house and up the stairs. I followed, carrying the tray. It wasn't easy with only one arm, but I managed. I could hear the shower running in the guest bathroom and saw the light shining out underneath the door. I carried the tray into Dani's room and set it down on the dresser.

"Think they'll be able to teach you to make your bed when you're in rehab?" I muttered, seeing the rumpled sheets and the quilt lying on the floor. "God knows I never managed it."

I went back into the hallway and stood next to the bathroom door.

"Dani? I made raisin toast and coffee to get you started, but how do you want your eggs? Omelet or scrambled? Dani? Honey?"

Hearing nothing aside from the hiss of the shower, I pressed my ear to the door and called her once again, louder this time.

Nothing.

I knocked as hard as I could, waited a moment, then opened the door and pushed aside the shower curtain. Steam billowed out, but the shower was empty.

I walked quickly down the hallway, opening each door, checking each room, with Blixen and Nelson close on my heels, calling Dani's name. Blixen let out a series of barks as if he, too, were calling for Dani.

Heart pounding, I raced down the stairs. The front door was open. Dani was gone. So was my purse and all the money inside.

Chapter 31

Grace

Though I had hoped to have thirty-five dresses in stock for my opening day at the Saturday Market, when I finished the thirty-fourth, around three o'clock on the afternoon before, I shut down my sewing machine. Saturday was going to be a long day and I needed a break.

I slipped on my tennis shoes and took Maisie for a walk around the neighborhood, concerned when we passed the concrete planters and saw no sign of Sunny. She did that sometimes, disappeared for a day or two, or even as long as a week, and always turned up. What if, one day, she didn't turn up? Who would I call? Who would even care? She was an adult, of course, free to come and go as she willed, and there was nothing I could do to keep her from it, but I couldn't keep from worrying about her.

I was worrying about a lot of things that day. In particular, I was worried about what Saturday would bring.

I'd spent the last three weeks sewing dresses, beautiful dresses, any one of which I would have loved to wear. But just because I loved them didn't mean other people would love them, or buy them. What if I'd put in all this effort, put my search for a real job on hold, and nobody bought anything?

What if I failed?

Back at home, I ate half a turkey sandwich, leftover from my lunch the day before, then sat down on the sofa and turned on the television, surfing channels and trying, unsuccessfully, to find something to watch that would hold my attention and silence the questions and doubts that kept circling my brain. Finally, I shut it off and got out my sewing basket.

I'd been sewing nonstop for weeks, but I hadn't touched my quilt blocks at all. Hand sewing always calmed me, quilting especially. Sewing the seams, stitch by stitch, I would quickly fall into the rhythm that allowed me to focus on the task at hand and clear my head of worry. And it was such a pleasure, after putting in the last stitch, to unfold the patches like the pages of a book and reveal the pattern, see the colors and contrast between the patches, and how pretty they looked together. It was a small sort of accomplishment, I realized that, but satisfying nonetheless.

I took out a bag with triangles for a star block I'd cut out just before immersing myself in dress-making. The patches were blue and red plaid, cut from a shirt I'd always thought brought out the blue of Jamie's eyes. I threaded my needle and started stitching, but halfway through the first seam, for the first time in many days, I dissolved into tears.

What if I failed? What if?

Tears gave way to sobs. Hearing them, Maisie ran to the sofa, yipped and fussed, then jumped onto the sofa and started licking my face. Another day, it would have helped, maybe even made me laugh through my tears. Not then. I felt afraid, and lonely. And homesick, more homesick than I'd ever felt in my life. Which was pretty ridiculous, considering I *was* home.

What was I doing here? What if I never felt at home anywhere ever again? What if I failed?

Eventually, I'm not sure when, I fell asleep on the couch.

I dreamed I was walking in downtown Portland, in the Park Blocks, and Jamie was walking with me. We were holding hands and I was wearing one of my twirly skirts, the one with the flamingos, and I felt so happy.

It was Farmers' Market day and there were people everywhere, walking across the bright green grass, wandering among booths, sampling cheeses and fresh baked bread, picking through produce to find the sweetest strawberries, the freshest lettuce, buying pizza and tamales and bowls of noodles, finding a bench and picnicking under the high, green canopy of sheltering trees.

We strolled past the college library, into the cool shadow of the giant copper beech tree, and were suddenly surrounded by people, by women. They were all wearing bright cotton dresses and skirts, patterned with fruit and flowers and birds, with polka dots and paisley and bright cheerful plaid, dresses I had made, and they were old and young and fat and thin and beautiful. And smiling.

Jamie was smiling too. He squeezed my hand. "Look what you did, babe. Look what you started."

I'd planned to get up at five and arrive at the market well before seven, but I fell asleep on the couch before setting my alarm. Fortunately, the weather was fine on Saturday. The sun beamed bright rays through the pane of my bow window and shone on my face, waking me a little before six.

Fifteen minutes later, I was slipping my feet into a pair of red pumps that perfectly matched the clusters of cherries on my new dress. I spun around in a circle to test the twirl and looked down at Maisie.

"Well? What do you think? Cute, right?"

Maisie, whose dog jacket was made from the same cherry print and mint-green polka-dot fabric as my dress, sneezed and let her tongue loll out of her mouth.

"Absolutely. If there was such a thing as a cuteness meter, we'd be breaking it right now."

I put on some red lipstick, looked myself over in the mirror one last time, and took a deep breath. Maisie stood up on her back legs and pawed at my calf.

"You're right. No need to be nervous. If we're not ready now, we never will be. Let's go."

The Portland Saturday Market was founded in 1974 by two women: artists who envisioned a nonprofit, open-air venue where artisans could sell handmade crafts and food items. In the early years, the market was smaller and more free-form in terms of setup. Now, it's a well-oiled machine.

Every Saturday from March through Christmas, vendors line up early, awaiting the seven o'clock allocation of over 250 eight foot by eight foot booth spaces, before setting up their booths and organizing their displays in time for the ten o'clock opening.

Maisie and I arrived at Waterfront Park just before seven, got our booth allocation, and were back at the car by seven thirty. The flat bed dolly that Luke had loaned me made hauling everything a lot easier. Between display tables, a chair, a tent, my sign, a cash box, Maisie's dog bed, and all my products, there was a lot to carry. Besides the dresses and skirts, my booth would also carry dog jackets. That, too, was Luke's suggestion.

When I called Nan and offered to sell the

jackets for Rainbow Gate if she'd split the cost of the booth, she was thrilled. Thinking it would be good marketing, I quickly stitched up a new dress for myself and matching jacket for Maisie. Pairing my dress with the red pumps was probably not the most practical choice—by the end of the day my feet were killing me—but I felt pretty and fresh and happy in my new dress. Judging from the way Maisie pranced around in her little jacket, I think she felt the same.

The pop-up shade tent I'd found used on Craig's List turned out to be trickier to set up than I'd anticipated. Lucky for me, Diane, one of the other vendors, who'd been selling her ceramics at the market for nearly ten years, stopped and gave me a hand. I was ready by nine fifteen, but when I looked around at my neighbors' booths my heart sank. Compared to the other vendors, my display—a wheeled clothing rack and table, where I'd laid out the dog jackets—was kind of primitive and not very conducive to encouraging sales.

As I was rearranging everything for the fourth time, Luke arrived, carrying a white paper bag and a cardboard coffee tray with two cups.

"Well, hi," I said, smiling as he approached. "I wasn't expecting you."

"I couldn't miss your debut, could I? Thought you might need a little sustenance," he said, reaching into the bag and pulling out two fresh, flaky chocolate croissants, then handing one to me. "I brought lattes, too, just plain. I wasn't sure what flavor you liked."

I bit into a croissant and groaned with pleasure.

"Oh. So good," I said, taking a grateful slurp of my latte. "I woke up late and didn't have time for breakfast. Once again, Luke Pascal saves the day. Thank you."

Maisie yipped and pawed at Luke's pant leg.

"Maisie!" I scolded. "Stop that. Have some manners."

"It's okay," Luke said, reaching into the pocket of his jeans and pulling out a little plastic bag. "She just smells the leftover chicken. I thought Maisie might need some breakfast too."

He fed Maisie a tiny piece of chicken and I shook my head. "Luke, you think of everything."

"I try."

While Maisie scarfed down the rest of the chicken, I showed Luke around the booth, sharing my concerns about displaying my merchandise.

"You can't really see anything unless you actually come into the booth," I said.

"I was thinking about that a couple of nights ago," Luke replied. "Can I borrow the dolly?"

"Sure. It's yours anyway. But why do you need it?"

"You'll see. Be back in a flash."

A flash turned out to be twenty minutes. The closer it got to ten, the more anxious I felt, so nervous and preoccupied that I kept looking at my wristwatch, forgetting about the frozen hands.

Even so, as the minutes I couldn't track ticked by, the doubts returned. What if no one bought anything? What if, at the end of the day, I had to take home every one of these dresses and skirts? Okay, sure, I could give them away. But . . . then what? When I woke up this morning and remembered the dream, I'd felt so certain that everything would be fine, that Jamie had returned to give me his blessing. But that could have been wishful thinking, couldn't it? After all, it was only a dream. If Jamie had been there, what would he really have thought about all this?

I stopped fussing with the hangers and closed my eyes. Always in the past, it had been easy to imagine Jamie's response to any number of questions or observations, but today he was silent. His expression was blank and his features less clear to me than before. Was I losing my memory of him? Or just his approval?

"Grace? Are you okay?"

My eyes flew open. I fumbled with the hanger, nearly dropping the dress before finally placing it back onto the rack. "I'm fine. I was just . . . thinking."

I turned around. Luke was standing next to the dolly, which was loaded with a weird-looking assortment of lumber, hooks, and other odds and ends, and looking very pleased with himself.

"What's all this?"

"Your new display system," he said, and started unloading the cart.

The weird assortment of lumber turned out to be a pegboard that hung at the back of the booth, with hooks that would hold three dog jackets each, all at eye level, and two revolving wooden clothes trees with four screw-in arms that held a half-dozen dresses each, all face-out so they were easy to see.

Luke finished assembling everything quickly, then took down the unneeded rolling rack and table, loading them back onto the dolly while I hurried to rehang the dresses and place the dog jackets on the pegboard. By the time I finished, it was five after ten. When I turned around, Luke was halfway down the aisle with the loaded cart, steering his way upstream through the trickle of early shoppers.

"Luke!"

He looked over his shoulder. "I'll put this in my truck for now. Good luck!"

It didn't seem right, letting him leave without saying a proper thank you. I scooped Maisie up in my arms and started after him. As soon as I did a woman with big sunglasses and blond braids stepped right in front of me, blocking my path.

She looked me up and down, pulled off her glasses, then squealed and clutched at my skirt. "Gina!" she cried, looking over her shoulder.

"Holy crap! Gina! Come over here and look at this!"

Gina, who, apart from having brunette braids instead of blond, could have been the other woman's twin, stuck her head out of a nearby booth selling diffusers for essential oils.

"What?" she asked, her voice bored.

Her friend pointed toward my dress, making big, stabbing motions with her index finger. When Gina pulled off her own sunglasses, her jaw dropped. She immediately left the diffuser booth and walked toward me, mouth open, like she was being drawn by some invisible tractor beam.

"O. M. G. Is that not the cutest thing ever? Love this. So retro. And look!" Gina gasped. "The puppy has a matching outfit! Seriously, Aria? How stinkin' cute is that?"

"Too cute," Aria said. "Cutest dress *ever*. And the cherries. And the rickrack on the pockets. How fun is that?"

"*So* fun. But you know what my favorite part is? The skirt." Gina pulled the fabric out wide from my body. "Look how it moves."

Aria nodded deeply. "And with that fabric and the fitted waist, it'd really hide your butt."

"Exactly. Shows off your curves." Gina picked up her head, as if finally realizing I was a person instead of a mannequin, and said, "Where did you buy this?"

"I didn't buy it. I made it."

"You *made* it?" Their mouths dropped open again, simultaneously.

I nodded. "My booth is right over there. Would you like to take a look?"

If somebody asked me how to make a success in your first attempt selling stuff at a craft fair, I'd tell them to have an adorable animal model their product and, if at all possible, have two sisters visiting from New Jersey with voices that really, really carry be the first customers of the day.

Gina and Aria bought two dresses, two skirts, two dog jackets, and took two of the business cards I'd thought to have printed only the day before.

"Would you do mail order to New Jersey?" they asked anxiously.

"Sure," I said. "I mean . . . I guess so. Shoot me an e-mail."

"Oh, we will," Gina said earnestly, as another customer tapped me on the shoulder, asking if the medium would fit a size twelve, only to be interrupted by still another customer who wanted to know if I had the cherry print available in extra large.

Luke came back to check on me around one o'clock, bringing a chicken wrap and a lemonade for my lunch. I didn't have time to eat it, or to deal with the steady stream of customers who kept pouring into my booth. By the time he arrived, I'd already sold fourteen dog jackets, eight skirts, thirteen dresses, and taken full-payment deposits for three more dresses with matching dog jackets. If I'd had more help and more stock, I'm sure I would have sold even more.

Seeing my predicament, Luke jumped in and gave me a hand—making change, bagging up product, and answering questions. It was pretty funny, hearing him launch into his sales pitch.

"That's the thing about this dress—it looks good on any body shape, but especially women with curves. The fabrics are all one hundred percent cotton, so you can toss them right into the washing machine. And they're really fun to wear. Hey, Grace?" he'd call out. "Do that thing you do."

Then I would smile and spin around in a circle, making my skirt flutter and twirl, and he'd look back at the customer and say, "See? Fun, right?"

"So fun," they'd answer, and hand him their money.

Three times that day customers looked at Luke, then me, and asked, "Is he your husband?"

"Just my friend."

"Really?" they said, looking impressed. "Nice friend."

When the market closed at five, my unsold stock included fourteen dog jackets, nine dresses, and zero skirts—we'd sold every one of them. In addition to that, I had eight special orders that needed to be filled. It didn't take nearly as long to pack up as it had to set up. When we were done, Luke and I went to a nearby bistro with dog-friendly, outdoor seating for souvlaki, beer, and a post-market briefing.

"Okay," Luke said, after tossing a bit of lamb down to Maisie, who gobbled it down and looked up at him, hoping for more. "Here's what we learned today. One—you need to rig up some kind of curtain in the corner so people can try on the dresses. Two—you need a full-length mirror so they can see how they look. Three—you need more ones and fives in the cash box so you can make change—"

"And a system for accepting credit cards," I added.

"Right," he said. "Four—everything I told you about starting small and going slow was completely wrong."

He shook his head slowly, as if he was still trying to wrap his brain around everything that had happened that day. I didn't blame him, I was feeling the same—excited but overwhelmed and a little bit dazed.

"You can't do this part-time, Grace. No way can you work for Monica and run Twirl and Whirl. This is a full-time job and then some. In fact, you need to hire some help and soon. There's no way you can do all the sewing by yourself."

"Hire some help. As in an employee? Luke, you can't be serious. We took in a lot of money today, but, like you said, I need to put it back into the business. Fabric for the first batch of dresses was free—from here on out I'll have to buy it. Plus, I need to eat and pay my mortgage. How am I supposed to support an employee if I can't even support myself?"

"Grace," he said earnestly, "moments like this don't come along often. When they do, you've got to grab them. Either you go big, or you go home. That's all there is to it."

"Okay, fine. But how?"

Luke picked up his beer bottle and took a swig.

"You have to borrow some money. There's no other way. But I've got—"

"No!" I held my hand up flat, cutting him off before he could say anything more. "Thank you," I said more gently, "but no. I won't borrow money from you. You've been great, Luke. You've been a lifesaver. And this day has been . . ."

I took in a breath and lifted my head, examining the clouds in the clear May sky, searching for words that might express all I was feeling, coming up short.

"Amazing. More than amazing. And it might not have happened without you, so thank you. Thank you so much. But what to do next is *my* problem."

"Okay," he said. "Fair enough. But can I just make two more observations?"

"Sure," I said, spearing a tender, delicious bite of souvlaki with my fork and dipping it into cucumber sauce before popping it into my mouth. "Go ahead."

"Number one," he said, leaning in and raising an index finger to begin the countdown. I started to laugh.

"Do you always talk in lists?" I asked, giggling and taking a sip of beer.

"Do you always interrupt?" he countered, grinning.

"Yeah, pretty often. If you're going to hang out with me, you'd better get used to it. You were saying?"

"Number one," he repeated. "As problems go, this is an *awesome* one—"

"Isn't it? I still can't believe it! Did you see the way they were—" Luke cleared his throat and shot me a look. "Sorry. I got excited. I'm actually feeling a little giddy. Go on. You were saying?"

"Number two—you don't have to solve this problem tonight. Tonight, just bask in the glow and enjoy your success. You were terrific today, Grace. Really. I'm so proud of you. And, by the way, if I haven't mentioned it before," he said, lifting his beer bottle and tilting it toward me in a silent salute, "you look terrific too. Where'd you get that awesome dress?"

"What? This old thing? It's just some rag I bought off the rack. But do you know what's great about this dress?"

"Hmmm . . . Let me guess . . ." Luke tapped his chin, pretended to think. "One hundred percent cotton, machine washable?"

"Yes, but more importantly, it moves. In fact, I'd say that this is a dress that's just made for dancing. Or would be, if only I knew how to dance. Such a waste. Especially with the Fairy Dogmother's Ball just a couple of weeks away."

I heaved a sigh, picked up my beer glass, and took a drink.

"Say, Luke? You don't happen to know of any place around here that gives classes, do you?"

Chapter 32

Monica

The crowd was light on Sunday night and I was worn-out from catering the wedding the day before, so when Bob showed up to have dinner around eight, I sat down to join him. Over his objections, I insisted on picking up the bill—a small token of thanks for putting up with rotten Alex and helping him have such a great season—then ordered insalata caprese, linguine with clam sauce for two, a bottle of Pinot Gris, and proceeded to drink and talk way, way, *way* too much.

"I shouldn't be jealous," I said, filling my glass for a third time. "And I'm not. I'm not!" I insisted, responding to Bob's doubtful look.

"Okay," he said, twirling linguine onto his fork, a skill I had taught him earlier in the evening and which he had quickly mastered. "Good. Because it would be terrible to be jealous of Grace. She's your best friend."

"Right. Which is why I'm not jealous. I mean, so what if she hit the ball out of the park her very first month in business? So what if Luke is clearly mashed on her and bent over backward trying to help and she doesn't even get it? So what if she's doing so great that she doesn't have time to work here and left me short a waitress? So what? I can always find another waitress, but I'll never find another friend like Grace."

"No, you won't. What you, Nan, and Grace have is very special."

"Right. Which is why I'm thrilled that her condo has shot up in value since she bought it and she's going to be able to take out a second mortgage, even though she isn't getting a pay-check now, and that her rich aunt Rickie in Milwaukee was willing to cosign so she could borrow fifty grand to get her business off the ground without having to grovel to the bank for financing like the rest of us poor slobs. Good for Grace. I'm happy for her. I am!"

"I know you are," Bob said, swallowing his linguine. "Because you, of all people, know how much Grace has gone through."

"Yes," I said, twirling a single noodle around my own fork. "So sad. Tragic, really. But . . ." I sighed. "At least Jamie really loved her. She might not have him, but she has that.

"Nobody has ever loved me. Ever. Not my parents. Not Vince. Certainly not my rotten step-kids," I said, reaching for my wineglass. "Never."

"Well, I can't speak for Zoe, but I think Alex loves you."

"Ha! If he does, he's got a pretty weird way of showing it."

"Teenagers usually do. And anyway," Bob said, "never is a pretty long time. How old are you?"

"Forty-three," I said. "Just turned."

"That's nothing. You've got plenty of time to find the right guy."

"Never going to happen," I said, moving my head back and forth. "You know why? Because I am never attracted to the right guy. I'm only attracted to bums. Handsome, heartbreaking Italians whose sole purpose in life is to humiliate me and make me miserable."

"Monica," Bob chuckled. "Come on. You're a very attractive—"

"Nope," I said, sticking out my index finger and putting it against his lips to keep him from saying more. "I'm not. I'm an idiot. I'll prove it. But only if you promise not to tell anybody. Promise?"

I lifted my finger from his lips. Bob raised his right hand.

"Okay. I'll tell you. Do you know who I went out with on Thursday?"

Bob shook his head.

"Dr. Mark Francatelli—also known as Dr. Dreamboat. He's tall. He's Italian. He's gorgeous. He's a doctor. What more could a girl want? He's the perfect man. Even my mother would approve of him. And *my* mother?" I tipped my glass to my lips. "She doesn't approve of anything—especially me.

"Anyway, Dr. Dreamboat came to the restaurant on Thursday, real late, after his shift and mine, to take me to the movies. It was fun, a romantic comedy with that blond girl. What's her name? You know the one I'm talking about. The blond girl, the one with the face."

"With the face?"

"Yeah, anyway," I said, waving my hand, "doesn't matter. So Dr. Dreamboat and I are watching the movie and splitting a bag of popcorn and a box of Junior Mints, and everything is going great.

"And I'm thinking, 'Yes! This is good. This is going to work. Why? Because I finally had the sense to wait for the right guy, the perfect match, and then hold back and wait for him to come to me. I wasn't pushy—well, except for that one time. But after that, I just let things lie. I didn't call him. I didn't e-mail or forward memes or funny animal videos. I stayed away from the ER, even when I was feeling like crap, because I didn't want him to think that crazy, hypochondriac lady was stalking him. For once in my life, I just played it cool and laid low, and it's finally paying off.'

"So, about halfway through the movie, when it gets to the steamy part where the girl is getting involved with the really good-looking guy who is totally wrong for her and everybody knows it but her, Dr. Dreamboat puts his hand on my thigh. And, Bob," I said, leaning in, "I gotta tell you, I didn't mind. At. All. It's been a really long time, you know?"

"Uh-huh," Bob said, looking down at his plate as he spun his fork around. He'd been doing that for a while.

"So, after the movie, we get into the car and we start making out. So, after a while, things are getting pretty hot and heavy, you know?"

Bob didn't say anything, just kept spinning his fork. By this time, he had a bite of linguine about the size of a tennis ball, so big he'd have had to unhinge his jaw like a boa constrictor to be able to eat it.

"Then, just as we're kind of getting to the point of no return, his phone rings. And he answers it. At first I didn't think that much about it because he's a doctor, right? He's gotta answer the phone, right? It's in the Hypodermic Oath or something."

"Hippocratic Oath."

"Whatever. I should have suspected something right off. When his ringtone started playing the theme song from *The Brady Bunch*, I should have known something wasn't right. But I didn't. Why? Because I'm an idiot."

"*The Brady Bunch*? So he's married."

"*So* married." I tossed back some more wine, hoping, unsuccessfully, that it would wash the taste of humiliation from my mouth. "Five kids. Five! And you know what the worst part was? He didn't even try to lie about it.

"He just looked at me and said, 'Hey, that was my wife. The twins picked up some kind of flu bug, so I have to go home and help her out.'"

"And he's definitely married?" Bob asked. "Not a divorced dad who's really involved in his kids' lives?"

"Definitely married. And for some reason, he thought I'd be fine with that. In fact, right before he took off—leaving me to take a cab back to the restaurant, I might add—he said, 'Hey, this was fun. We should do it again soon.'"

"Really?" I said, throwing out my hands. "Why would he think I'd be okay with helping him cheat on his wife and five kids? Do I *look* like a home wrecker?"

"Not to me," Bob said, putting down his fork and the tennis ball's worth of pasta. "To me you look like a very caring, considerate, thoughtful, and loyal woman. Cute as hell to boot," he said, raising his glass.

I was so ticked off that I didn't really hear him.

"Why does everything always happen to me? I mean, apart from me being an idiot. I'll tell you why—because I'm hunting for unicorns, that's why?"

Bob scrunched up his face and tilted his head to one side. "Unicorns?"

"Unicorns. Mythical creatures that don't exist outside of fairy tales, just like perfect men. There's no such thing. Never was, never will be. I don't believe in them, not anymore."

"Neither do I," Bob said. "Nobody's perfect, men or women. But you know what I do believe in?"

"What?"

"Perfect matches. I believe that every now and then, two flawed, messed-up, imperfect people can come together and all their chips and cracks and broken bits match up in such a way that, together, they're perfect. Or pretty close to it.

"Actually, that's the reason I came over here tonight, Monica. I've been watching you for a while now, getting to know you, your kids, your past and your personality. I've got an idea that you and I might turn out to be a perfect match, or something close to it. And I think that warrants further investigation."

"Excuse me?"

Bob reached across the table to hold my hand.

"Monica, would you be my date for the Fairy Dogmother's Ball?"

I looked at his face, then down at his hand and mine in it, then at Bob's face once again.

At that point, I was tipsy enough that I didn't entirely trust my own observations, but he gave every appearance of being serious, not just about asking me to go to the ball, but, if I was reading the signs correctly, about exploring the possibilities of a real relationship.

I didn't know what to say.

I liked Bob, I did. He was easy to be around, funny, kind, calm, considerate, athletic, an excellent listener, great with kids, hardworking, dedicated, and—for a guy with Anglo Saxon roots and a lot of consonants in his last name— pretty good looking.

But.

He had nothing in common with anybody I'd ever dated or considered dating—not Mark, or Johnny, or Joe, or Anthony, or Rob, and certainly not Vince.

On the other hand, given my track record, was that such a bad thing? Still.

Bob. Bob Smith.

I sighed. "It's nice of you to ask. I like you, too, a lot. But, Bob—"

He plucked a red rose from the vase on the table and placed it in my hand.

"Call me Roberto."

Chapter 33

Grace

The Crystal Ballroom. The name seemed a little overblown for an old three-story brick building in that particular part of Portland, so near to the freeway.

The neon sign near the door, topped with an image of the moon as a grinning, disembodied face, coupled with the fact that the lower floor was occupied by a pub, made me think the place had probably seen better days and added to the generalized anxiety that had been hovering over me all afternoon.

The quip about my dress being made for dancing had sort of popped out unexpectedly. It wasn't that I hadn't understood what I was getting into, committing to four weeks of dance lessons with Luke. But I'd done so in the excitement of the moment, giddy from my unanticipated success and grateful to Luke for helping to make it all possible. It wasn't until I woke up the next morning that I realized I might have left Luke with the wrong impression.

Though it was awkward, I felt like I needed to call and make things clear.

"Sure," he said casually. "We're just going to dance, as friends. I got that."

"Okay, good. I mean . . . I just. You know. I wanted to make sure we were on the same page."

"We are," he confirmed. "Not a problem. I'll meet you there, right?"

"Right. Thursday, seven o'clock. See you then."

Though it had to be said, it was a weird conversation and left me feeling unsettled. Fortunately, work kept me so busy that I hadn't had much time to think about it—especially since Aunt Rickie had agreed to cosign my loan so I could get Twirl and Whirl off the ground more quickly.

Two more wildly successful Saturdays had proven to me that my debut at the market hadn't been a fluke. The demand was there. People loved my twirly skirts. But I wouldn't return until I had a chance to hire some reliable help and build up the inventory so I could keep up with demand. However, apart from the eight prepaid special orders, I hadn't sewn a thing that week and I was so busy I'd even skipped support group. At that moment, my whole focus was on planning the future of Twirl and Whirl and turning it into a proper business.

Already I had bank accounts, a company

logo, a website in the works, and accounts with a fabric wholesaler. I had purchased another sewing machine, and was searching for someone who knew how to use it—my first employee. For some reason, that part seemed especially daunting.

I was incredibly busy. So busy that, until Luke called that afternoon to ask if I needed directions, I'd forgotten about the class.

I looked down the street in both directions, hoping to catch sight of Luke. I'd feel less awkward if we could go in together. Where was he? I looked at my watch, then remembered the frozen hands and checked my phone instead. It was only 6:44. Luke wasn't late; I was early.

When it started raining, I reluctantly went through the doors alone and climbed the stairs to the third floor, expecting . . . Well, I don't know what exactly. But definitely not what I found.

Entering the doors of the Crystal Ballroom was like entering another world, another time, like walking onto the set of one of those old black-and-white movies I loved so much and seeing it come alive with color and sound.

I stood just inside the doorway, drinking in the atmosphere, breathing deep of the scent of wood, and spent candles, and dust, as I watched a few couples who had arrived early and were already practicing some steps. They looked so graceful, so beautiful. Were they always like that, I wondered. Or had they become so when they entered this room?

"It's really something, isn't it?"

Luke's voice, coming from behind, startled me a bit, but I was happy to see him.

"The windows are amazing," I said, looking toward the four enormous palladium windows on the street-side wall, each one outlined by white marquee lights. "But the chandelier . . . I've never seen anything like it."

I walked into the center of the room and stood beneath the four-tiered crystal chandelier from which the ballroom took its name. It was part Palace of Versailles, part carnival midway; a fanciful, glittering jewel, embellished with blown glass flowers of vibrant coral and turquoise that straddled the border between dazzling and garish.

"Did you see the murals? That's my favorite part."

Luke pointed to one of several large medallions, also outlined with marquee lights, and painted with an assortment of fantastical scenes. In one, a couple waltzed among the clouds as angels looked on in envy. In another, a silhouetted female form wearing a crown of sunbeams balanced a moon and planet in her outstretched arms.

"It's not often you get to dance in a space that truly was designed for dancing," Luke said, "back in the days when dancing and courtship were the same thing. My grandparents met here, at a USO dance."

"Really?" I smiled. "That's so romantic."

He nodded. "They were married for fifty-seven years. After World War Two, it became more of a concert venue than an actual ballroom—same as now. It was closed for almost thirty years because the town was worried that rock music was corrupting the city's youth. Some people say that Little Richard fired then unknown guitarist Jimi Hendrix in the middle of a gig they played here." Luke grinned. "But I think that's just a story."

"Kind of a good one, though," I said as more couples filed in.

"But the best part is the floor. Feel that?" Luke bounced up and down on his toes, signaling me to do the same.

"It's kind of . . ." I searched for a word to describe the sensation of lightness under my feet, as if the laws of gravity didn't quite apply here. "Springy?"

Luke nodded. "Exactly. It's a sprung floor, some people call it a floating floor, specially designed to absorb shocks. There are only a few like it in the whole country. That's—"

Luke's explanation was interrupted when an old man walked to the front of the room and started clapping, slowly but deliberately, summoning everyone's attention.

Judging from the lines on his weathered, overly tanned face, our instructor, Florian Hybels, appeared to be in his eighth decade. He wore a blue spandex jumpsuit that looked like it belonged to a 1950s fitness guru, but I had to say, he wore it well. After welcoming everyone, Florian explained the basic format of the class. Every week for the next four weeks, he would teach a different dance—waltz, fox trot, swing, and tango.

"Don't worry if you've never danced before," Florian said, speaking loudly so everyone could hear. "We're going to start at the very beginning with every dance and walk you through it step by step. This course is meant to be an overview. If you want to sign up for advanced classes later or take some private lessons, I'm at your service."

He made a small but courtly bow and came up smiling.

"But even if this is the only ballroom class you ever take, in the next four sessions, it's my goal to give you the skills, confidence, and desire to keep dancing. The important thing to remember," Florian said, pointing his finger and tracing an imaginary line slowly through the air, touching every couple present, "is to relax and enjoy yourself. Have fun."

Luke gave me a sidelong look. I nodded. Message received.

"Having fun is what I've been doing," Florian

continued, "over the past sixty-two years of my dancing career. The last forty-five of which, I have been lucky enough to share with my partner in dance and in life, my wife, Victoria, who will now help me demonstrate this evening's dance, the waltz. Darling?"

He made a graceful arc through the air with his arm, extending his right hand to a woman who had been standing alone near the outer fringes of the group.

Though Victoria appeared to be a decade younger than her husband, her hair was completely white. Her platinum tresses were drawn into an elegant twist that emphasized her long neck and beautifully balanced shoulders. Everything about her was elegant, even her walk. She all but floated across the room toward her husband and when she took Florian's hand, the look in her eyes was a perfect mirror of his.

There could be no doubt in the minds of anyone watching that the years had done nothing to decrease the ardor they felt for each other. They were still very much in love.

Florian and Victoria walked toward the center of the ballroom. Stopping directly under the crystal chandelier, they turned to face each other, the fingertips of her right hand resting lightly on his shoulder, his left hand making contact at the base of her shoulder blade, their free hands clasped and held at shoulder height, looking directly into each other's eyes. Someone hit a button on the portable CD player and the music began to play.

Florian and Victoria stepped off at exactly the same moment, their movements so perfectly synchronized it was as if they were thinking the same thoughts. They continued that way throughout the dance, like two people who were one, twirling in each other's arms, floating across the floor, creating a large oval around the room. They were fascinating to watch. I couldn't have taken my eyes off them if I'd wanted to.

They were true to the rhythm of the music, but also played with its possibilities. Sometimes they moved slowly, even sinuously, hesitating briefly to strike a pose, Victoria's back arching like a bowstring as she turned her head to one side, emphasizing the long, supple line of her body. Sometimes they moved quickly and with sudden energy, Florian pulling his wife close before they stepped off into a series of dizzyingly rapid spins.

As they spun and dipped and twirled, the crepe and chiffon layers of Victoria's blue dress fluttered like a flag in a fresh breeze. It really was a dress made for dancing.

Finally, the music slowed and Florian guided his wife back to the place where they'd begun, right under the chandelier. Once again, Victoria arched away from her husband, her movements slow and languorous. She lifted her arm lightly from his shoulder, tracing an elegant arc above her head as her beautiful and smiling face turned toward the audience.

In that breath between the final note and the ringing burst of applause that came after, I had two connected and conflicting thoughts. First, that I could never in a million years imagine myself being able to dance like that. Second, that I really, really wanted to try.

Breathing heavily from the exertion of their efforts, Florian and Victoria bowed and curtsied to acknowledge the applause. I was clapping so hard my hands hurt.

"Doesn't that look like fun?" Florian asked. "I bet you can't wait to try. So let's get started. Face your partner and let's stand in the closed position. Like this."

Victoria turned toward him and they connected at shoulder, back, and hand, as they had before. There was a noise of shuffling and some awkward laughter as the students, including Luke and I, assumed the position. When everyone was set, Florian and Victoria walked around the room, offering advice and adjustments.

"Very nice," Victoria said when she came to check on us. "Just lift your arm a bit," she said, touching me on the elbow, "and keep that nice curve in your arm, like you're getting ready to hug an enormous oak tree. That's it. Lovely."

"All right," Florian said after every couple

had been inspected and corrected. "I think we're ready to learn the basic waltz step, yes?"

"But," he said, lifting his chin high, sounding suddenly serious, "before we begin, it is only fair to warn you that the waltz made me fall in love with my darling Victoria. It's a beautiful dance, but a powerful one, eh? So. Unless you're ready to fall in love for a lifetime, perhaps you should sit this week out."

A murmur of laughter passed through the crowd. Luke, who had been watching Florian, laughed too. But when he turned back toward me and saw the look on my face, his expression became solemn.

"He's kidding, Grace. It's only a dance."

I shifted my eyes from his face to my feet. He was right. It was only a dance.

I took a breath and looked up. Luke clasped my hand and smiled.

"Ready?"

"Ready," I said.

The music began.

Chapter 34

Monica

With only a couple of weeks remaining until the ball, it was time to think about costumes, so on Monday, instead of our usual support group meeting, I suggested a field trip. I held the door so I could get a good look at Grace's face when she walked inside. Her reaction was all I thought it would be.

"Oh. Wow." She blinked a few times.

"What did I tell you? The Fabric Depot— forty thousand square feet of retail space, twenty thousand different fabrics. If you don't find something you like for your costumes here, you never will."

"How did I not know about this place? It's amazing," Grace said, her voice almost reverent as her eyes scanned the brilliantly hued horizon, row after row and bolt after bolt of satin, silk, wool, taffeta, tulle, chintz, chenille, chiffon, chambray, corduroy, cotton, and broadcloth in every imaginable color, pattern, texture, and weight. "How are we even going to figure out where to start?"

"Maybe with actually getting everybody inside the building," I said, looking back through the doorway to the parking lot. Zoe was walking toward the door at a snail's pace, shuffling toward the entrance while she thumbed a text message into her phone.

"Were you planning to join us anytime this year?"

"This was your idea," she grumbled, "not mine. Isn't the whole point of being grounded that you have to stay home?"

"Don't think of it as being grounded so much as punished," I said. "When I can trust you to stay home, then you *get* to stay home. But since I can't and since your brother is at a basketball game, you *have* to go with me. See how that works?" I asked, flashing a fake smile.

"I hate you," Zoe glowered. "Do you know that?"

"I don't care. Do you know *that?*"

Zoe all but hissed as she slunk through the door, still texting, staring into her phone but holding it at an angle that made it impossible for me to see the screen.

"And since you hate me anyway, I really don't feel bad about doing this."

I plucked the phone from her hand. She started to howl. "What? No! Give it back!"

I turned my back to Zoe, blocking her frantic attempts to recapture her phone. As I scanned the texts, waves of disappointment, weariness, and frustration washed over me, but when I spotted the picture, frustration turned to fury.

"That is *it!*" I spat. "Zoe, I have had it! You are thirteen years old. Ryan Plummer is almost seventeen. In case I hadn't already made it clear, when I punished you for sneaking out of your bedroom window to hook up with Ryan and said you couldn't see him anymore, that *also* meant you couldn't text him anymore."

Honestly, I felt like shaking her. Instead, I pushed my face up into hers, desperately trying to get her attention, if not her understanding. It wasn't working. She turned her head away and I grabbed hold of her shoulders.

"Zoe, you have *got* to listen to me, this boy is way, way too old for you."

"Only three years," Zoe countered, finally looking at me. "Daddy was five years older than you."

"Zoe, five years in your forties is a whole different thing than three years when you're barely out of grade school. Besides, look how that worked out."

"That's because Daddy never loved you," Zoe spat as tears sprung into her eyes. "But Ryan loves me!"

Zoe's observation wasn't exactly breaking news, but that didn't mean it didn't hurt. Like her brother, Zoe knew the location of all my vulnerable spots and how to strike to inflict maximum damage. Did she do it by plan or by instinct? I wasn't sure, but it didn't matter at that moment. I was the adult here. I was the mother. And this girl, this rotten, selfish, stupid girl was my responsibility. It was my job to protect her from all threats, including herself.

I turned the phone around so Zoe would be forced to see the screen the way I was seeing it. "I see. He loves you? Is that why he's texting you pictures of himself in his underwear?"

Zoe's cheeks flushed red. She looked down at her feet.

"Zoe, a guy who wears briefs that say, 'Unleash the Beast,' is looking for a lot of things, but love isn't one of them. If you've had sex with this boy . . ."

Her head popped up. "I haven't!" Zoe raised her hand out flat, as if she was taking an oath.

"Really, I haven't. I swear. All we've done so far is just . . . fool around a little." She paused, her cheeks flaming anew. "I let him touch my boobs."

I closed my eyes and rubbed my forehead. My head was pounding. What was I going to do with this girl?

"I just want him to like me," Zoe said, her voice a whimper.

"Oh, Zoe . . ."

The irritation of a moment before drained away instantly, replaced by pity.

"Honey, I know. We all want that. But that's not the way to do it." I held the phone up again. "This isn't just fooling around, or it won't be for very long. Ryan knows exactly where he's trying to lead you."

For a moment, it felt like I was getting through to her, but then her eyes glazed over again. I wanted Zoe to like me, to make her understand that I was acting in her best interests. But if I couldn't do that . . .

"Zoe, you are thirteen years old," I said. "If Ryan gets what he wants, the state of Oregon calls that second-degree rape and I will absolutely press charges."

Zoe's jaw dropped. "But he never made me—"

"Your consent means nothing here," I said. "I know you don't like hearing this, Zoe, but you're still a child. The law is there to protect you. And whether you like it or not, so am I. That's why I'm keeping your phone."

"Monica!" she cried, tears spilling over. "You can't! What if there's an emergency? How will I talk to my friends? What am I supposed to do all day?"

"Since you're going to be either at school, at home, or with me, there will be someone to help if you have an emergency. You'll see your friends at school. If you want to talk to them after school, then you can call them on the house phone. As far as ways for you to keep busy . . . we'll think of something. Now, come on."

I put Zoe's phone in my purse and started walking toward Grace, who was standing at the far end of the store, looking through bolts of sateen. Zoe trailed along, dragging her feet and weeping.

"I hate you, Monica," she said, sniffling and gulping air.

"I know."

"Why are you trying to ruin my life?"

"I'm not," I said, keeping my eyes straight ahead. "I'm trying to save it."

Chapter 35

Grace

"You're sure this time?" Monica asked. "Because you've put that same blue silk in the cart and then taken it out again three times now."

"Yes, absolutely. The green satin was too heavy. And blue is a good color on me. Plus, it's on sale," I said. "Yup, blue. Final answer."

Zoe, whose face was a study in boredom, sighed dramatically. "About time. Can we go now?"

"No," Monica answered. "I still need to pick out fabric for my costume. You'll help me sew it, won't you, Grace? I just need some kind of gingham jumper or pinafore. Nothing fancy."

Though my decision to postpone my return to the Saturday Market until after the ball had taken off some of the pressure, I was still very busy. But so was Monica.

The Dogmother's Ball was nearly sold out. There was no way she could run the restaurant, cater a dinner for 125 people, and make a costume for the event. I doubted she'd be able to leave the kitchen long enough for anybody to see her costume, but still. She deserved to get in on the fun.

"Sure," I said. "A pinafore won't be hard. What are you going as?"

"Little Miss Muffet. I found a hilarious spider outfit for Desmond online, so he's all set. I planned to buy mine online, too, but all I could find was 'Sexy Miss Muffet.' " She stuck a finger into her mouth, pretending to gag. "Really? Sexy nursery rhyme characters? Since when did Halloween and costume parties get to be one more excuse to objectify women and cater to bizarre male fetishes?"

"You're going as Miss Muffet?" Zoe made a face. "That's so lame."

" 'That's so lame,' " Monica parroted, making her voice a whine. "Fine, Miss Fashionista. What do you think I should go as?"

"A Kardashian."

The set of Zoe's mouth and rapid-fire response told me she'd prepared her answer in advance specifically to annoy Monica. Surprisingly, Monica didn't take the bait.

"I'm serious, Zoe. If you were going to a ball and could have any costume you wanted—any costume that won't get you arrested, I mean—what would it be?"

Zoe, who seemed surprised to be asked for her opinion, took a moment to think.

"Pirates," she said finally. "From France. But

girl pirates with a big hat with feathers, and strings of pearls, and a ruffled blouse, and a big, swooshy skirt. You'd need to tuck the skirt up into your belt so you could fight, and a sword on the belt, too, a gold one. And black boots."

"Wow," I said. "That seems pretty specific."

"I was reading this book about pirates," Zoe said. "Turns out a bunch of them were girls, from all over the world. I thought it was pretty cool. Usually in the adventure stories the guys are the only ones having fun. The girls either stay home and wait for them to come back, or get kidnapped and wait to be rescued. Boring.

"But these girl pirates? They were in charge of whole ships and crews, and they sailed all over the place, and robbed treasure, and fought in battles. And they were *real*. Sometimes, they got captured or killed. So that kind of sucked. But at least they had adventures. And I bet the French pirates had really cool clothes. Because, you know," she said, and shrugged, "France."

"Right," Monica said. "Because that's where all the cool clothes come from. Okay. You've convinced me. We're going to the ball as French girl pirates."

"We?"

"I'm going to need a crew, right? You can't be a pirate if you don't have a pirate band." Zoe shot her a suspicious look. "Hey, you don't *have* to go. I can always ask Alex to babysit."

After an eye roll, probably her fiftieth of the evening, Zoe said, "Okay, fine. But can I bring a friend?"

"That depends. This is an all-girl crew," Monica reminded her.

"Not Ryan. Zinnia Applegate. She's in my English class."

"Sure, but . . . Zinnia?"

"I know, right?" Another eye roll. "Her parents are crazy too. I'm going to go look at that purple stuff over there," Zoe said, pointing to an entire shelf of violet-hued fabrics. "Purple is good for pirates."

Once Zoe was out of earshot, I said, "Five minutes ago she hated your guts, now you're the leader of the All-Girl Pirate Band."

"Don't be too impressed," Monica said. "In another five minutes she'll probably hate me again. But at least she's speaking to me. If I ever get Zoe *and* Alex speaking to me at the same time, then you can be impressed."

"Ha! Well, I guess we better start looking for swooshy skirt fabric," I said, trying not to think too hard about the fact that I now needed to make two warrior pirate outfits instead of one and come up with something for Desmond as well— maybe just a hat and eye patch?

But pirate costumes would definitely be more fun to make than a Miss Muffet outfit, and if it meant Zoe and Monica might start getting along better, then it was more than worth the effort. I steered my cart toward a promising-looking aisle of taffeta. Monica came along.

"I was surprised Nan didn't come tonight. Is she okay?"

"I talked to her a couple of days ago," Monica said. "She's fine. Just has a lot going on, trying to get the garden in shape for the ball. And she said she's all set for costumes. They're going as the cast of *The Wizard of Oz*. Nan will be Dorothy, Malcolm will be the Tin Man, Blixen will be the Cowardly Lion, Stuart will be the Scarecrow, and Nelson will be Toto."

"What about Lovey?"

"Adopted by a nice family who lives in the country and already has one bulldog. What about that?" Monica said, pointing at a bolt of purple, green, and gold plaid taffeta.

I pulled it off the shelf and held it up to Monica's face. "That's actually kind of perfect. I'll make your skirt from this and Zoe's with whatever fabulous purple thing she finds. I think we're going to need petticoats too. Just plain cotton, but we'll need lace to trim the hem." I plunked the plaid bolt into the cart.

"*The Wizard of Oz* costumes were Malcolm's idea," Monica reported as we headed toward the ribbon and trim section of the store. "He's so much fun and he couldn't be more perfect for Nan—the whole 'must love dogs' thing to begin with. He's as excited about raising money for the rescue as Nan is. Besides helping with the gardening, Malcolm booked the band, figured out the lighting and sound . . . such a good guy. And the brogue," she said, clapping her hand to her chest. "Is there anything sexier than a man with an accent?"

"They do make a great couple," I agreed.

"But if I were Nan, I think I'd rather he come to the ball as a Highland warrior. There's just something about a man in a kilt."

"Speaking of men in costume," I said, examining some eyelet lace that was on sale. "How is Bob going to feel about joining the All-Girl Pirate Band?"

"Shoot. I hadn't thought about that. Maybe he can be our hostage. Actually," she said, raising and lowering her eyebrows, "he might like that."

"Okay . . . yeah. Too much information. Do the kids know about you two yet?"

Monica shook her head. I shot her a look and put the eyelet lace back onto the shelf, rejecting it in favor of a two-tiered white cotton lace that somehow seemed more pirate period to me.

"I'm not avoiding the subject," Monica said. "Honestly. I've just been so crazy busy. When I get home at night, I'm so tired I fall into bed. Don't tell Nan I said so, but I'll be glad when the ball is over. I've just got too much on my plate."

She did, it was true. So did I. So did Nan. But Monica looked so tired.

If Monica hadn't been Monica—i.e., the biggest hypochondriac in Portland and therefore prone to panic over all things medical—I might have suggested she go in for a checkup. But she'd been in the ER not that long ago with the scary rash that turned out to be paprika. If there was something wrong, surely they'd have caught it then. And it wasn't like she didn't have cause for fatigue.

"I get it," I said. "When all this is over, we all ought to go away for a few days—rent a condo at the beach or something."

"Wouldn't that be great?" Monica sighed. "My cousin Lisa has a big beach house in Lincoln City. She's offered to let me use it a bunch of times, but I've never taken her up on it.

"Maybe I should," she mused. "I could just close the restaurant for a week in late August. It'd cost me some money, but I really need a break, so does the staff—Ben is such a pain right now." Monica looked at me. "What do you think? Could August work for you? Or will you be too slammed?"

"I might not be able to take the whole week, but maybe a couple of days. It kind of depends on how things work out with my new employee." I stopped, thought about what I'd just said, and laughed. "Boy, those are two words I never thought I'd hear coming out of my mouth."

"Hey," Monica said, correctly reading the undertone of anxiety in my laughter, "every entrepreneur feels like that when they're starting out. You're going to be good at this, Grace. You already are. And you'll be a good boss. You know why?" I shook my head and she grinned. "Because you know how miserable it is to work for a bad one."

"Oh!" I exclaimed, "Speaking of bad bosses— Denise, who worked in accounting at Spector, called me yesterday and said Gavin got fired!"

"Really?" Monica said, her eyes lighting up in the same way mine had when I heard the news. "So your letter to the CEO worked?"

"Oh, I doubt that was the reason," I said, while secretly hoping it was, "but it couldn't have happened to a nicer guy. Ava is taking his place, which is great. She'll be a great boss."

"She really liked you, didn't she?" Monica asked. "Any chance of her asking you to come back?"

"Well . . ." I said slowly, "I think that's why Denise called me. She didn't come right out and say so, but she kind of hinted at it. But I told her I'm happy doing what I'm doing." I laughed. "Of course, I might end up regretting that later; there's a very good chance this whole thing will turn out to have been a terrible idea. But I'm going to do everything I can to make it work. I really feel like this is what I'm supposed to do with my life. And I'm having a great time doing it."

"Good for you," Monica said. "That's how it should be. So, who's your employee? And how is she working out?"

"Billie Dawson," I said. "She starts next week. Nan found her at the grief support group— another misfit. Her husband died of a heart attack about six months ago; he was only fifty-six."

"And she needs a job?"

"Yes, but she also needs something to do. She's kind of . . . squirrelly," I smiled, recalling the rapid-fire way she talked and her fidgety hands. "She said she hadn't sewn since high school but five minutes after I sat her down at the machine, it all came back. She sews like lightning. I like her. I think it'll be a good arrangement for both of us. And—"

The sudden catch in my throat caught me by surprise. I swallowed quickly and plucked a roll of blue tulle off a nearby shelf.

"What do you think of this for Maisie's tutu? If I glued on some sequins?"

"Cute," Monica replied without even looking at it. "Grace, what's wrong?"

"Nothing." I swiped at my eyes. "It's stupid."

"Grace?"

"It's nothing bad, really," I said, smiling to prove I was telling the truth. "In fact, it was

401

kind of sweet. When Billie came over for the interview, she saw my quilt blocks. She asked me about them, so I started telling her stories about Jamie. Then she started talking about her husband, Pete. It was just . . . it was really good. Billie's decided to make a quilt for Pete, too."

"Oh, Grace." Monica grabbed me and hugged me hard. "That's great. It sounds like you really helped her."

"She helped me more. If Jamie and I had had a baby, I'd be telling our child all those stories but—" The dam in my throat broke and I started to cry in earnest, clutching her shoulder like it was the only solid thing in the world. "Oh, Monica. I'm so afraid I'm going to forget about him."

"Forget Jamie?" Her eyes went wide. "That is never, ever, ever going to happen. The things you and Jamie learned together and went through together will be part of you always; he's a part of who you *are*. Nothing and no one will ever change that."

Monica squeezed me even tighter, making sure I was steady before putting her hands on my shoulders and pushing me back so she could look into my eyes.

"Is this about Luke? It's all right for you to care about him. It doesn't mean you didn't love Jamie, or will ever love him less."

"It's not that," I said, swiping at my eyes, putting the lid back on. "I just get emotional sometimes. I miss him. I think I always will."

"Sure," Monica said. "Why wouldn't you? He deserves to be missed."

"He does," I said, clear-eyed again. "And Luke's just a friend."

"A pretty good friend, I'd say."

I nodded. There was no denying it.

"So, if you're going to the ball as Cinderella, will Luke be Prince Charming or the frog? Oh, wait," Monica frowned. "The frog is a whole different story, right?"

I shook my head. "Maisie is my date for the ball."

Monica tilted her head to one side and looked at me the way she would have if she'd caught me in a lie.

"Luke and I are just friends," I said again. "We dance. We have fun. And then we go home. That's it."

"Okay," Monica said. "So if you're just friends, then what's the big deal? You like to dance, he likes to dance, and there's going to be a really good band. It'll be just like class—you'll dance, you'll have fun, and then you'll go home. Shouldn't be a problem." She waited for me to speak. "Unless you're afraid of what happens if Luke becomes more than a friend?"

Monica drew her face close to mine. Her

normally brash voice was almost a whisper. "Grace, listen to me. You're not doing anything wrong. You can love Luke and love Jamie too. It doesn't change anything."

Doesn't it?

Chapter 36

Grace

As the introductory measures played, I mentally checked my dance position, making sure my shoulders pressed down and my neck was long, that I was standing just off center from Luke with my back just slightly arched.

Florian counted off the final beats—five, six, seven, eight—and everyone stepped off to the rhythm of the castanets.

"Slow, slow, quick-quick, slow," Florian chanted as we moved across the floor, performing two basic tango steps, then a progressive link to point us in the right direction before we transitioned into our promenade step.

"Better," Florian said when we got to the end of the combination. "But remember, tango is about attitude, and power, and passion," he said, pronouncing the *s* with a dramatic hiss. "Let's try it again."

Good ballroom dancers make dancing look as easy and instinctive as taking a walk. If you're doing it right, that's how it *looks*. That's not how it is.

We practiced the combination over and over. I knew the steps perfectly well, but I was stiff and awkward executing them. Florian kept saying, "Relax, Grace. Quit thinking so much. You're supposed to be enjoying yourself." But the more he said it, the more I did the opposite.

On the next attempt, when I tried to make an inside turn instead of an outside, we got so tangled up that it's a miracle we didn't fall. It was embarrassing. I was sure everyone was staring.

Florian called a five-minute break. I grabbed my water bottle and stood by the wall, feeling disgusted with myself. Luke came over and leaned against the wall, standing next to me but staring straight ahead.

"Do you know what ballroom dance really is?" he asked.

"Something I suck at?"

I was trying to be funny, sort of. But Luke wasn't in the mood for banter.

"It's a conversation," he said. "A dialogue between a man and a woman. Dancing lets you use your body to express all the thoughts and feelings that you can't, or won't, or shouldn't, or don't know how to say. It's one of the earliest, honest, most universal forms of communication. If you can see it, you can understand it. Here," he said, pressing his fist to his chest. "But only if you trust your partner."

At last he turned toward me.

"Grace, forget about everybody else. Forget about what you think you're supposed to feel or be. This is a conversation between you and me, nobody else. Okay?"

I looked up at him, finally meeting his eyes.

"Okay."

"Good," he said. "Let's dance."

When Luke's fingers closed around mine, I felt a shudder run the length of my spine, through my arms, and all the way to the end of my fingertips, a sensation that seemed to connect us at every point of contact, like an electrical current. And this time, when the castanets rattled and the accordion trilled, I didn't need to count anymore, or to think about which steps came next, or which direction to turn. I saw it in Luke's eyes, felt it through the skin of his hand.

Our bodies only connected within the space of a palm print, but it felt like there was only one pulse between us, and one set of intentions. We led *each other,* followed *each other,* moved and breathed in perfect sync, like two sides of a mirror, the reflection and the reflected, at once the same, yet utterly opposite. We pivoted into the promenade position and the look in Luke's eyes stole my breath. I saw in them all the things he had been trying to say and that I had been trying to deny, to him and to myself.

He lifted his arm and touched my waist, sent me spinning into one, two, three circles as he strode alongside. We hadn't rehearsed that, but we didn't have to. I knew what Luke wanted me to do because it was what I wanted as well.

On the third turn Luke lowered his arm and swept it sharply to one side. I responded, spinning across the floor and flinging my arm out wide for just a breath before spinning back into his embrace.

He pulled me close, our bodies meeting from breast to hip, as our steps rocked back, and forward, and back again as the music began to slow. I lifted my arm and arched my back, bowing my spine so fully that I could feel my hair brushing against the floor. Surely I would have fallen if Luke hadn't been holding me.

But he was holding me.

At that moment, that's what I wanted, that's all I wanted—for Luke to hold me up, hold me close, and never let go. I wanted it more than anything in the world, more than what was good, more than what was right. And I let him see that. I hid nothing.

The music ended and we stood there for a moment, breathing heavily, struggling to fill our taxed lungs with necessary air and our brains and bodies with the truth of our separateness, fighting and losing the battle to remain in the wordless world, remembering who we were.

We stepped back from each other at the same moment and dropped our hands. The room burst into applause and we remembered there were other people in the room. They were staring at us. I didn't care.

Florian walked toward us, beaming and clapping, then placing a hand on each of our shoulders. "That is what I was talking about, ladies and gentlemen. *That* is the tango—attitude, power, and passion!"

It was our fourth and final class.

We thanked Florian and Victoria and said good-bye to our fellow students. As always, the hour being late and the neighborhood a little sketchy, Luke walked me to my car. But when I turned the key in the ignition, the engine wouldn't turn over. Luke got out of his car to investigate.

"Dead battery," he said. "Don't worry. I've got jumper cables in my trunk."

As he reached for the door handle, I touched him, curving my palm over the spot where his wrist became his arm.

"Leave it here," I said. "Take me home."

Chapter 37

Monica

On the Wednesday before the Dogmother's Ball, I didn't get home from work until after midnight and was so stupidly tired that I spent a good minute and a half fumbling with the front door lock before I realized I was trying to use the wrong key.

Inside, the lights were dim and the house was silent, which was just what I'd expected. What I didn't expect—and what made me almost jump out of my skin—was a voice coming from the shadows saying, "Where the hell have you been?"

"Geez! Don't do that," I said, clutching my heart when Alex got up from the sofa and walked into the light. "You scared the crap out of me. And you sounded just like my dad when I used to break curfew. What are you doing up?"

"Waiting for you," he said, still sounding *exactly* like my dad. It was kind of eerie. "Where were you?"

"At work. Where else would I be?"

I went into the kitchen and dumped my stuff

on the counter. Alex was right behind me.

"I've been trying to call you for two hours. I called your cell and the restaurant. I thought something happened to you."

"Oh, Alex. I'm sorry. The battery on my cell must have died and we don't answer the restaurant phone after closing. I'm sorry," I said again, and walked over to the sink for a drink of water. "It was a crazy night. Ben and I had a fight and he walked out in the middle of his shift, so I had to do his job and mine, too, and then one of the dishwashers didn't show up for work. . . . It was miserable. But I'm sorry you were worried. What did you need?"

"What did I need?" he asked incredulously. "I needed for you to be *here* for once!"

"Hey! That's not fair!"

I spun around, ready to remind him that when I wasn't *here,* nine times out of ten it was because I was quite literally slaving over a hot stove to provide for the family, but Alex cut me off before I could.

"Ryan Plummer showed up here," he said. "I caught him out in the yard, throwing gravel at Zoe's bedroom window, trying to get her to climb down."

"No!" I shouted, my heart pounding, thinking about an open window, Zoe getting into that boy's car. "Where is she? She better not have—"

"She didn't. She's upstairs asleep," Alex said.

"But Ryan wouldn't leave. We got into a fistfight and the neighbors called the cops."

"What? The police were here?"

For the first time, I noticed a scratch on Alex's right cheek.

"They were going to take me and Ryan in." Alex's eyes grew bigger, angrier, and even more frightened, reminding me that he was still just a kid. "Mrs. Patterson from next door told them I lived here, but they wouldn't listen. Why aren't you ever here when we need you? Why? I called you and called you—"

"Oh, Alex . . ." I paused, not so much because I couldn't find words but because, just for a moment, I couldn't find my breath. "Honey, I am so, so sorry. You must have been so scared."

"I was!" he shouted. "Where were you, Monica? If that cop from school hadn't shown up and said he knew me, they'd have taken me to the station. They almost put me in handcuffs. Where *were* you?"

"Alex, I . . . I . . ."

My breath was gone again. The pounding of my heart became a lurching. Dots of black danced before my eyes. I slumped to the floor.

I don't know what happened next; I'm not sure how long I was unconscious.

But I do remember being in the ambulance, Alex sitting next to the gurney, tears streaming down his face, and him babbling, "Don't die, Monica. Please, don't die. I didn't mean to yell at you. I didn't mean what I said. I love you, Monica. So does Zoe. Don't die, Monica. Please, don't leave us."

Honestly, I don't remember if I actually said the words or just thought them. An oxygen mask was covering my face, so I'm not sure he could have heard me anyway. But I do remember squeezing Alex's hand so he'd know that I loved him, too, and that I wasn't going anywhere.

The emergency room was a blur as well, a montage of people in white coming and going, asking questions and sticking needles. They admitted me to the hospital and ran some tests. By the next morning, I felt—well, a long way from one hundred percent, but better. Or I did until the door to my room opened and Dr. Dreamboat walked in.

"Monica," he said, swooping to my bedside. "How are you feeling?"

"I'm fine. Why are you here?"

I pulled my hand from his grasp and Alex, who had been snoozing in the recliner next to my bed, blinked and sat up straight in his chair.

"Just checking on you," he said. "I was on duty when they brought you in last night, don't you remember?" I shook my head. "That's okay. I'm glad you're looking so much better this morning. I felt terrible about having to leave before I knew how things turned out with you. But it was the end of my shift and the twins—"

"Get out," I said, pointing to the door. He just stood there. "I'm serious, Mark. Get out. I don't want you in my room."

"Hey," he said, looking offended. "I'm a doctor in this hospital."

"You're not my doctor. Or, if you are, you're not anymore. I'm firing you. Go."

Alex, now fully awake, practically catapulted from the recliner and put himself between me and Mark.

"You heard her; my mom wants you out of her room."

His mom?

Dr. Dreamboat didn't move. Alex's fingers curled into a fist.

"Did you hear what she said, you . . ."

The very descriptive words that came next were the sort of thing that, in other circumstances, might have forced me to dock Alex's allowance. But in this instance, I was totally fine with it. And it wasn't like he said anything inaccurate.

As he was walking out the door, the Bad Doctor looked over his shoulder and snarled, "Real nice kid you've got there, Monica."

"Thank you," I said, lifting my hand and resting it on Alex's shoulder. "I think so too."

Chapter 38

Monica

Nan was the first person Alex called after dialing 911. She'd arrived just a few minutes after the paramedics and took Zoe and Desmond home with her for the night.

She was also the first of my visitors on Thursday morning. She entered my room carrying a basket she'd woven herself, filled with fresh-baked maple scones with organic butter, hard-boiled eggs from her chickens, a thermos of home-brewed pomegranate kombucha, and a tiny vial of lavender oil, a few drops of which she immediately placed on the hospital pillowcase. "It'll help you relax."

I'm sure she was right, but I was more excited about the food. That gray hospital oatmeal they'd sent up for breakfast looked like something you'd use to paste up wallpaper.

Zoe came right behind her, carrying a bouquet of roses she'd cut in Nan's garden. The second she saw me, Zoe burst into tears and threw her arms around my neck. The rose thorns pricked my shoulder, but I didn't mind.

"Monica, I was so afraid you were dying!"

"Of course I wasn't dying." I kissed the top of her head. "Only the good die young, don't you know that?"

"Zoe," Alex said, prying away his sister's arms. "Let go before you choke her."

"It's okay," I said, patting her on the back. "I can take it."

Malcolm came in next, carrying a potted hosta plant and advice on where to plant it once I got home. "Cool and shady, but don't let the feet get wet," he said, and then, in response to my blank look, "The soil should drain well."

"Oh, right," I replied, though I wouldn't know drained from undrained and have managed to kill every houseplant that has ever been unlucky enough to come into my possession. Still, it was a nice thought.

Bob arrived a couple of minutes later. He brought a bouquet of balloons from the hospital gift shop, including two big silvery Mylar globes that shouted, "It's a Boy!" and "It's a Girl!" respectively.

"Sorry," he said after kissing me hello. "They were out of the 'Get Well' kind."

I smiled up at the bobbing balloons. "These are nice. And seem oddly appropriate."

Five minutes later, Grace and Luke walked in, arriving together in spite of the early hour. I took that as a sign that things were going pretty well between them, but the expression on Luke's face was a pretty good tip-off as well. He couldn't keep his eyes off her. They, too, had stopped in the gift shop before coming up, and brought me a bouquet of spring flowers in a white wicker basket and a bag with ten bars of gourmet chocolate.

Grace hugged me. "I take back everything I ever said about you being a hypochondriac."

"Ha! That's what I'm engraving on my tombstone—See? I told you I was sick."

"Just don't engrave it anytime soon, okay?"

"I'm fine."

Grace looked skeptical. "Oh, yeah? Then what are you doing here?"

"Fulfilling my insatiable desire for attention, of course. And collecting presents." I looked into the bag of candy. "Dark chocolate?"

"With almonds."

"I love you *so* much right now."

Grace grinned. "I know."

A few minutes later, a petite blond woman wearing a white coat came through the door and said, "Hey, hold it down in here. Don't you know this is a hospital?" She smiled and stuck out her hand "Hi. I'm Elsie Pringle, staff cardiologist."

"I have a cardiologist?"

The thunk-bump in my chest answered the question even before Dr. Pringle bobbed her head.

"Don't worry. The prognosis probably isn't as dire as you think. Is this a good time to discuss it?" she asked, looking around at my visitors, her tone suggesting it would be a good time for them to leave.

"They can stay," I told her. "This is my family."

The news that I hadn't had a heart attack came as a huge relief. But atrial fibrillation, a condition in which the upper chambers of the hard beat irregularly and can keep the blood from moving well, possibly resulting in heart failure or stroke, can be a serious condition too. Symptoms can include fatigue, fluttering sensation in the heart, shortness of breath, light-headedness, and even fainting. Over the last days and weeks, I'd experienced all of those, but especially fatigue.

"I've had so much going on," I told the doctor after explaining about the demands of my business. "I just thought I was tired."

"And I think you were right. Causes of atrial fibrillation, A-fib, can include heart disease or defect, lung disease, high blood pressure, or an overactive thyroid. The tests we ran didn't show signs of that.

"And so, especially in a patient under sixty, we start looking for other, less chronic causes—like exhaustion," she said, inclining her head. "Also alcohol and caffeine use."

"I have been drinking—not a lot of wine but more than usual," I admitted. "And I've been downing coffee by the potful. It's the only way I've been able to keep up."

"Well, you've got to cut down on both. Way, way down. And what about sleep apnea?" she asked. "Do you snore?"

I shook my head. Alex and Zoe started laughing.

"Yeah, you do," Alex said, happily sharing this little tidbit with everyone present, including Bob. "Monica, you snore like a buzz saw. I can hear you all the way from downstairs, even with my door closed."

"So can I," Zoe giggled.

"Well, okay then," Dr. Pringle said, tapping something into her electronic tablet. "Sounds like I need to order a sleep study. But I'm guessing this episode is the result of a sort of perfect storm of the causes I mentioned—apnea, alcohol, caffeine, and fatigue—emphasis on the latter. We can release you tomorrow, but only if you promise to take care of yourself when you get home—no wine, no coffee, and no work for at least a week—two would be better. You've got to get some rest."

"A week?" I let out an incredulous laugh. "You've got to be joking. Who's going to run my restaurant? My sous-chef just quit. I can't just close the place down for an entire week."

"Yes, you can," Grace said. "You were planning on doing it in August anyway. Just

419

move things up a couple of months. I'm sure your cousin would still let you use her beach house."

"But the ball!" I protested. "One hundred and twenty-five people who paid big bucks for dancing and a gourmet dinner are going to be trampling all over Nan's garden in two days. What are you going to do? Call out for pizza?"

For a moment, the space of a heartbeat—or, in my case, a heartbeat and a half—the room was silent. Then Alex said, "I can do it."

"Alex—"

"I can," he protested. "I've spent a ton of time at the restaurant with you, I know my way around the kitchen. Besides, you already did the tough part—planned the menus, ordered the food and everything."

"Alex, you are very sweet and yes, very capable. But feeding that many people is a huge under-taking. You can't take it on by yourself."

"Well, he wouldn't be by himself," Nan said. "I know my way around a kitchen. I can help."

"So can I," Bob said. "I don't know if I told you, but I barbeque a mean steak."

"I can help too," Luke said. "You don't spend three years in France without picking up a few things."

One by one, they chimed in, offering to help. It was really touching. However, I drew the line at Grace.

"No," I said. "Nothing personal, Grace, but

you're a terrible cook. You can set the tables."

For a second it looked like Grace was going to argue with me, but then she shrugged and said, "Fine. I can set the tables. And arrange the flowers."

"Oh, can I help with that?" Zoe chirped, raising her hand.

"Sure," Grace said.

"Well, then," Dr. Pringle said, looking at the assembly, "if that's all settled, all we need to do now is discuss the procedure."

I reached out and clutched Bob's hand.

"Procedure?"

Chapter 39

Grace

I didn't blame Monica for looking alarmed when the doctor explained the procedure. If somebody said they wanted to stop my heart and start it again, I'd have been alarmed too. But Dr. Pringle assured her it was a straightforward procedure, describing it, in layman's terms, as "a kind of cardiac reboot," the hope being when Monica's heart started beating again it would return to a normal rhythm.

Monica was hesitant, but with Bob's encouragement and the doctor's promise that they would absolutely, definitely, without question be able to restart her heart, she agreed to undergo the procedure.

It worked! Monica was under anesthesia for less than ten minutes and when she woke, her heart was beating normally and she already felt much better, so much so that she felt sure she could handle the catering for the Dogmother's Ball. But Dr. Pringle was having none of that and neither were we.

"Monica," I said, "you heard the doctor. If you

want to prevent another episode, you've got to rest!"

"And I promise I will," Monica said. "After the ball."

Bob leaned down and stopped her protests with a kiss. "We've got this," he said firmly.

After much moaning and groaning, Monica agreed to close the restaurant for ten days, and then allow Bob to drive her, the kids, and Desmond to Lincoln City the day after the ball. Bob would stay for the whole week to make sure Monica really was resting. Once that was settled, we all got to work.

Nan and I immediately got on the phone to call customers with current reservations at Café Allegro, then explain what happened and help them either reschedule or make reservations at other good restaurants. The outpouring of concern and good wishes they asked us to convey was really touching. We only had two complaints out of sixty-six customers, and so many people sent flowers to the hospital that when Monica went home on Friday the nurse had to find a cart to get all her presents down to Bob's car.

Ben's abrupt departure had definitely complicated things, but the response of the remaining staff made their devotion to Monica obvious. As soon as Monica woke up and Alex knew the procedure was a success, he asked Luke to drive him to the restaurant so he could speak to the staff.

"You should have seen him," Luke reported when he came over to Nan's house a few hours later, filling me in while Zoe and I dipped dog biscuits in glue and silver glitter, creating decorations for the flower arrangements. "Alex was calm, and mature, explaining the situation and asking for everybody's help while making it clear that he was running the show. That boy is a real leader.

"When he finished talking, the whole team sat down together and came up with a plan. They're going to make it a buffet instead of sit-down service, serve cold poached salmon instead of hot, carve a beef tenderloin in the line, and serve an eggplant parmesan casserole instead of preparing individual portions, and replace the hot vegetables and potatoes with salads they can make ahead and serve cold.

"Oh, and instead of chocolate lava cake, they're going to set up a make your own sundae bar. Nan said she knows a great new ice-cream shop in Southeast that wants to get the word out and will give us a discount."

"That sounds like it will make everything a lot simpler," I said. "I just checked the weather report—should be clear, sunny, and in the low eighties on Saturday—so cold foods will be nicer anyway. And what's not to love about making your own ice-cream sundae? Where's Alex now?"

"I left him at the restaurant," Luke said. "He and Angie, one of the line cooks, wanted to get to work right away. When I left they were making a cold sesame noodle salad and Angie was calling Alex 'chef.' " Luke grinned. "They've got things under control. Now, what can I do to help?"

For the next forty-eight hours that pretty much summed up the attitude of everyone in our group—what can I do to help?

Nan, who had finally been released from her sling, finished up the last of the trimming and gardening, planted four flats of beautiful purple and yellow pansies along the front walk, and filled two hundred white paper bags with kitty litter and votive candles to make luminarias. Zoe and I made twenty flower arrangements for the tables, spraying twenty plastic Halloween pumpkins with silver spray paint, then filling them with white daisies, pink carnations, and the silver glittered dog biscuits we'd wired onto floral picks, and topping each one off with a "Fairy Dogmother's Wand" with a sparkly silver star and hot-pink ribbon streamers. They looked pretty cool, if I do say so myself.

Alex was at the restaurant supervising the food preparation, assisted by the entire kitchen and waitstaff. It was all hands on deck.

Malcolm and Luke got out ladders and strung thousands of fairy lights on anything that didn't move—trees, bushes, even Nan's chicken coop. After the rental company arrived and set up the tent and dance floor, they strung up even more lights, winding them around the tent poles and over the dance floor. Bob, who spent the morning at the hospital to make sure Monica was doing all right, came over to help in the afternoon. However, he spent so much time fielding calls from Monica, who was trying to micromanage everything remotely, that we sent him back to the hospital to confiscate her phone and keep her calm.

On Saturday morning, a dozen volunteers from Rainbow Gate showed up to help with the setup at almost the same time that the restaurant crew, led by Alex and Angie, descended en masse and took over Nan's kitchen. It was organized chaos—everybody moving fast, working fast, talking fast, racing the clock—but chaos just the same. And there was still so much to be done.

When I got into my car at five o'clock, rushing home to change into my costume, the ice cream still hadn't arrived, the water goblets had spots, a heap of mulch was still sitting in the middle of Nan's driveway, and Luke and Malcolm were still in the backyard, muttering and cursing because every time they tried to turn on the fairy lights, they blew out the breakers.

"Maisie," I said, glancing into the back seat, "I don't mean to sound negative, but there is no way in the world they're going to be ready by seven."

Two hours later, I took it back.

"Wow," I said, turning the corner onto Nan's street. "Maisie, are you seeing this?" I asked, calling over the back of the seat. Maisie reared onto her hind legs, put her paws on the window, and yipped. "Nan's house looks like something out of a magazine."

The newly washed windows sparkled. The flowerbeds, burgeoning with mounds of freshly planted pansies, showed nary a weed or stray blade of grass. And the two hundred luminarias, lit and lined up along the curb and driveway at two-foot intervals, cast a soft, magical glow over everything. It was about as close to Cinderella's castle as you could find in Portland, Oregon.

If the front of the house was beautiful, the garden was breathtaking. The thousands of white lights that Malcolm and Luke had sweated, fussed, and cursed over turned Nan's garden into a fairyland, a charmed kingdom populated by costumed people and pets.

There were any number of kings and queens, as well as knights and fairies and sprites. I counted four dinosaurs and two unicorns. There were also cheerleaders, superheroes, and various Star Wars characters. A lanky greyhound wearing a white tunic and a pair of braided Princess Leia earmuffs was one of my favorites. But I also liked Peter Pan, who was accompanied by Princess Tiger Lily, a spaniel wearing a buckskin skirt and feather headdress, and Heidi, in her dirndl and blond braids, who strolled across the grass with a St. Bernard, simply clad in his natural fur and a collar with a little wooden beer barrel.

Dinner wouldn't be served until eight, so people were milling around the garden, talking and taking selfies, nibbling on appetizers and sipping glasses of champagne or sparkling cider as they checked out each other's costumes. Everyone had been handed a ballot upon entering. After dinner they would be collected and tallied to determine the winners of the costume contest. Judging from the way people were oohing and cooing over Dorothy, Tin Man, Cowardly Lion, Scarecrow, and Toto, it looked like Nan, Malcolm, and company were the team to beat.

A passing waiter with a tray of home-baked dog biscuits stopped to ask if Maisie would prefer chicken or beef. I broke a beef biscuit into Maisie-sized bites and started feeding them to her when the blue silk drawstring bag on my wrist started to vibrate. I tossed the last piece of biscuit onto the grass, then reached into the bag and took out my phone.

"Monica? Why are you calling? Where's Bob?"

"He's in the bathroom," she whispered. "I've only got a minute before he comes back. How is everything? Did you try any of the appetizers? The crab cakes. Are they crispy? Do they have enough crab?"

"Monica. Hang up and go back to bed. You're supposed to be resting."

"Resting," she huffed. "Do you know how boring that is? Now, quick—tell me about the gorgonzola puffs. Are they puffy enough? Because sometimes, if you add too much cheese, they turn out gooey."

A man emerged from the shadows. Maisie yipped, ran toward him, then started jumping and pawing at his leg.

"Sorry, Monica, have to go. I just spotted a handsome prince."

"What? Wait! Grace, just tell me about the crab—"

I hung up and slipped the phone back into my purse. Luke bent down, scooped Maisie up with one arm, and used the other to encircle my waist and pull me close for a long, lingering, tender, and utterly delicious kiss.

"Oh my," I murmured when he released me at last. "Maybe I should have come as Snow White instead. That kiss definitely would have broken the spell."

Luke took a step back and made a show of looking me up and down. "Mmmm . . . I think I like you better this way. But I can't be sure until I get the whole effect."

Laughing, I took two more steps back and spun in a circle. The layers of sapphire chiffon lifted and fluttered in the soft summer air.

"I like that dress," Luke said, appreciation evident in his eyes. "You know why?"

"It moves?"

"Exactly." He pulled me close again, kissed me again, lightly but no less tenderly. "You look beautiful, Grace. Really, really beautiful."

"And you look—"

"Like a complete idiot," he said, looking down at his costume. "The sequins are one thing, but these tights?" He groaned. "There's no one on earth I would do this for besides you, Grace. No question about it; I must be in love."

At the far end of the garden, under the twinkling canopy of lights Luke had hung himself, the band began to play a waltz. Luke kissed me again.

"Let's dance."

He grabbed my hand and I ran alongside him down the path and across the grass, excited and already a little breathless, my heart hammering and my mind reeling.

He loves me?

Chapter 40

Grace

Let's dance.

I was beginning to think those were the two most wonderful words in the English language. The band was fantastic. Luke and I danced, and danced, and danced to that beautiful music. But I had the feeling that even if there had been no band, no waltz, no sweet, soulful trumpet or tinkling piano, still we would have danced. We would have danced in silence, in darkness, and perfect happiness, as long as we danced together.

There was dinner at some point, and breaks for the band, and speeches, thank-yous, and appeals for the rescue, pictures and prizes, too—Nan, Malcolm, and company won, of course, and there were two runners-up, but I don't remember who they were or what they wore.

There was dancing, and Luke, and me. And the question.

He loves me?

When I looked back, I realized I'd known it was true for a long time, maybe even as far back as our accidental date, the dinner and the dancing that left me giddy and breathless, the surge of emotion I wasn't prepared for. Maybe I knew then. But if not, then the coffee shop encounters should have tipped me off. And if even that didn't do it, then the table should have.

Luke was a good, kind, and considerate man, but he wasn't perfect and far from a saint. Already his little cracks and flaws had been exposed—he was grumpy in the morning, a bit of a perfectionist, very stubborn and determined almost to a fault. When he wanted something badly, he kept after it until he got it. And what he wanted was me.

He loves me.

Was I ready to love him back?

The love I felt for Jamie was a fact. I loved him deeply and eternally for always and forever. Nothing would change that. I didn't want it to. There was no question there.

The question was this: Is it possible to experience true, deep, eternal love twice in one lifetime? Is it possible to wholly commit your heart to one man without diminishing the love you bore and always would for another?

That was the question I had been wrestling with and running from since that first night on the dance floor, when my head dropped onto Luke's shoulder and I felt deep desire, but also profound peace. It felt like coming home.

And that scared me.

When Grammy taught me how to sew, all those years ago, I had to concentrate as hard as I could to get my brain and needle to cooperate. But now, twenty some years and thousands of stitches later, the moment I pick up that needle, muscle memory takes over. My fingers just know what to do and I hardly have to think at all. That's what I love about it. It feels so easy and natural, and results in something so beautiful.

Maybe love is like that, too, an emotional muscle memory, something that comes more easily if you've been lucky enough to know it before.

He loves me. Do I love him? Can I? Should I?

It was late, drawing closer to midnight and the end of the ball. The band played a fox trot, "Just in Time," an old standard that's been covered by every crooner from Bobby Darin to Tony Bennett. The lead singer, with his black tuxedo and crisp white shirt, channeled Frank Sinatra, leaning into the mic and singing about the kind of love that comes just in time, just when you need it the most, the unexpected, undeserved, unplanned-for love that changes lonely lives in one lucky day.

"Was that supposed to be a message?" I asked, laughing and flirting with Luke when the song ended.

"No, but this is," he said, then bounded up onto the bandstand and whispered into the piano player's ear.

A moment later he was back on the dance floor, holding me in his arms, and we were dancing again as the pianist played and sang alone. The song was "Make You Feel My Love," a lovely old Bob Dylan lyric that's tender and vulnerable and brave, like a love letter written in secret and finally read aloud, a pledge that risks rejection, knowing that the desired beloved hasn't made her mind up, yet exposing his heart in the most raw and unguarded way possible.

That night, it was more than a song. It was a message from Luke to me, a prayer for love requited, a promise of love unending, a pledge of protection in the raging storm, of constancy, presence, and persistence for a million years and more, a vow to do whatever it took, to travel to the ends of the earth and back again, so I would feel his love.

Luke held me close as we swayed and turned in time with the music. As the notes pulsed and slowed into the final phrases, I began to believe his message was true and to think that maybe, just maybe I could promise the same to him. In a minute more I might have. Then the lights went out.

There were no screams—the moon was out and the stars were bright, so everyone could still see—but there were whoops of surprise followed by titters and nervous laughter. It wasn't just the lights that went out, all the electricity did, including the power to the electric keyboard, interrupting not only the song, but a romantic and potentially life-changing moment for Luke and for me.

"Well, this is awkward," Luke said, trying to sound funny but coming off as ticked. "Hang on a second. I'll try to figure out what happened. Malcolm? Did you check the breakers?"

A second became a minute and then several. The breakers were fine. Luke, Malcolm, and a couple of other men emerged from the house with flashlights and started checking plugs and connections.

I left the dance floor and found a chair near Nan. Blixen, Nelson, and Stuart were curled up near her feet, sound asleep. So was Maisie. After the first few dances, when I'd carried her in my arms, Maisie's wriggling made it clear she'd had enough, thank you. She'd pranced off to join her buddies in the dog pile.

Malcolm shone a light up high onto one of the tent poles and yelled, "I see it! There's the problem. Hey, Luke, bring me a ladder—the big one."

The ladder was produced and steadied, Malcolm climbed to the top, muttered and cursed and fumbled with cables, eventually finding the loose connection. When he pushed the plug back in place, the lights re-illuminated. At the same time, a spark flared.

The spark didn't shock Malcolm, but it startled him. He jerked backward, a reflexive response, then lost his grip, fell ten or twelve feet, landed on the ground, and didn't move.

This time there was screaming, screaming and shouting and chaos. Nan catapulted from her chair and was kneeling next to Malcolm before most people really understood what had happened. A crowd closed in around her, making it impossible to see what was happening. Luke was there, too, hidden inside the scrum of bodies, but I had spotted him kneeling next to Nan before the curtain of onlookers closed. I could hear him telling people to move back, give Malcolm some air, and call 911.

I got to my feet, picked Maisie up from the ground, and held her to my chest—fighting panic, hearing voices.

"Move back! Give us some room!"

"The ambulance is on the way."

"He's not breathing. Oh my God! He's not breathing! Who knows CPR?"

"I do!"

"Wait, wait. Hold on a second. He's breathing!"

"Malcolm! Malcolm, can you hear me? Are you all right?"

"Yes . . . I . . . I'm all right. I just got the wind

knocked out of me. I'm fine. Really. Somebody help me up."

Then there were cheers of relief and applause, probably because Malcolm did indeed get up from the ground, seemingly unharmed, but I couldn't be certain because I didn't see it myself. By that time I was already running across the lawn and up the path to the front of Nan's house, clutching Maisie close, running as fast as I could from the sounds and voices and frightening scene.

As I jumped into my car, I thought I heard Luke calling my name. I pulled into the street and drove away just as an ambulance and a firetruck arrived. The luminarias were still burning.

Looking into the rearview mirror through a blur of tears, I saw Nan's house growing very small and Luke on the lawn, watching me leave, backlit by the flame of two hundred candles and a strobe of lights, pulsing blue, red, and white.

Chapter 41

Nan

"Grace?"

I turned my head to press my ear against the door. I couldn't hear anyone moving inside, but her car was parked on the street. I knocked again, insistently enough, I hoped, so she would realize I wasn't leaving until she answered.

"Grace, open the door. You can't spend the rest of your life pretending you're not home."

At last, I heard movement, footsteps, the yip of a little dog, the click of a deadbolt lock. Grace opened the door. She was wearing a bathrobe and had a towel wrapped around her head.

"Hi," she said. "I wasn't avoiding you. I just got out of the shower."

"But you've been avoiding my calls. And Luke's. He's been calling me instead. He's worried about you. So is Billie. She called and said you told her not to come in to work this week. Are you all right? You're not sick, are you?"

She shook her head and then waved me inside.

"What are those?" she asked as I put down

my bag and set a foil-covered plate down on the dining-sewing table Luke had made for her.

"Peach turnovers," I said, removing the foil. "I just baked them."

Grace smiled wryly. "The grief prescription, huh? Is it as bad as that?"

I pulled one of the stools out from under the table and sat down. "You tell me."

She paused for a moment, then took a turnover from the plate.

"I should make some tea."

Grace carried two mugs in from the kitchen and sat down at the table.

"I haven't been avoiding you," she said. "I've been busy working."

I looked around the apartment. Everything looked very tidy, no pins or needles or fabric scraps strewn about, and Grace's sewing machine was inside its case.

"Not on the dresses," she said, answering the question before I could ask it. "I've been working on the blocks for Jamie's quilt. I'd like to finish it."

She gestured toward a small stack of blocks on an end table, lying next to a wicker sewing basket and a small white cardboard box.

"Jamie's ashes," she said, indicating the box. "They were delivered a couple of days ago."

The ashes. I nodded. Now I understood.

"Grace, do you know why I started doing

pet therapy, volunteering to help people work through their grief?"

She gave me a curious look. "Well . . . because of Jim, I assumed. Because you'd been through it yourself."

I shook my head. "It was because of Dani, my youngest daughter."

Grace tipped her head to one side. "You've never really talked about her."

"No," I said quietly. "I never have."

For the next few minutes, I told Grace all about the daughter I never really discuss. I told her about how Dani and Jim had been joined at the hip, how deeply Jim's death impacted Dani, and how the intensity of her grief, and my inability to help her move through it, started her on a path to chronic depression, self-medication, and addiction.

I told her everything, about Dani and about myself. When I was finished, Grace reached for my hand.

"It wasn't your fault, Nan. You did everything you could for her."

"Did I? I tried. But could I have done something more? Something different? If I had, would it have made any difference?" I shrugged. "I'll never know for sure. I try to help other people because I couldn't help Dani. Because I know what can happen when people are unable to confront their fears and feelings in the wake of loss.

"I'm not saying that what happened to Dani will happen to you. But when a deeply loved one dies, sometimes the people left behind want to die too. They might not say so out loud, they might not even be aware of what they're feeling, but it's there just the same. They start pulling back, turning inward, disconnecting from people and things they used to enjoy before or might enjoy now, living in the past and hiding from the future because they are so afraid of what it might bring."

Grace turned her head, staring out the front window of her condo. Outside, two girls wearing pink bike helmets cycled past, but I'm not sure she really saw them.

"When Malcolm fell," she whispered, her voice rasping and her eyes distant, "it was like I was right back there again, on the mountain, watching Jamie fall and not being able to stop it or help him. Life is so uncertain, and cruel. You can do everything right and still everything can go wrong. If something happened to Luke . . ." Grace swallowed hard and turned to face me. "I can't go through that again, Nan."

"Yes," I said. "You can. And if you inhabit this earth for any length of time, chances are you will.

"Jamie took a long time leaving this world. He fell down that cliff and started dying by inches, and because you loved him so much, because what the two of you had was so wonderful and rare, you tried to die by inches too. But you couldn't do it. Because there's too much life in you, Grace—too much life, and love, and joy—and all of it is meant to be shared."

I looked toward the coffee table to the plain white box with Jamie's ashes and the quilt blocks lying next to it, scraps of cloth and memory stitched into a story.

"Grace, when you're sewing those blocks, thinking about Jamie and how much you miss him—do you ever stop to think how lucky you are to have had someone to miss? Do you ever think about what your life would be like if you'd never met him, never loved him, never let him love you back?

"That's the thing that truly does kill people by inches, Grace—the lack of love. For all that you've gone through, that's one thing you've never suffered from."

"That's true," she said softly. "Not since Jamie. He loved me. I don't know why, but he did."

"I bet Luke could tell you."

Grace looked at me with liquid eyes. She smiled sadly but didn't speak.

"Every love story turns sad eventually, Grace. If someone loves you and you decide to love them back, at some point you are going to get hurt. The only way to avoid it is never to love in the first place. That's the deal. I know that and so do you. That's why this is so hard.

"Luke truly loves you, I have no doubt about that. Do you love him? If you do, we both know it'll be worth it—a hundred, a thousand times over. But that's a question only you can answer."

Grace walked me to the door and I said I'd see her on Monday. "Monica should be back by then. It'll be interesting to hear how she handled a whole week of rest."

"Oh, I forgot to tell you. I can't come next week. Don't worry," Grace said, reading the concern in my eyes. "There's just somewhere I need to . . . something I have to do. I'll be back the week after. Promise."

"Okay. But you call me if you need anything."

"I will. Tell Luke I'll call him in a few days."

"You don't want to tell him yourself?"

She shook her head. "Not now."

After Dani stole my purse, I had to buy a new one. It's much bigger than my old one, too big really. So when I left Grace's house and I reached into my purse to find my keys, I couldn't. I started walking with my head down in the direction where I'd left the car, rooting around in my bag in search of the missing keys.

Finally, a block and a half later, I found them inside a small, interior pocket I'd never known existed until that moment, and looked up just in time to avoid tripping on a homeless woman with dirty blond hair and a vacant expression, wearing a full-skirted dress of a very familiar style.

"Dani?"

Her movements were so slow and her reactions so delayed, it was almost like watching someone who was underwater. Finally, her eyes cleared enough to recognize me.

"Hi, Mom."

I squatted down so I could speak to her at eye level.

"Dani, what are you doing here?"

"I live here," she said, spreading her arms wide, her fingers stretching toward two concrete planters. "Sometimes. I've been gone for a few days, maybe a couple of weeks. A friend of mine had some—"

She stopped in mid-sentence. I wasn't sure if it was because she'd lost her train of thought or because she decided that whatever she was going to say wasn't any of my business.

"What are *you* doing here?" she asked.

"Visiting my friend, Grace. In that building, in the next block."

A smile slowly spread over Dani's face. "You know Grace? She's really nice. I like her."

"So do I. Dani, did Grace make that dress for you?" She nodded. "And does she call you Sunny?"

"Everybody calls me Sunny. Remember how I always liked that stuff, that drink? SunnyD."

444

"The orange drink. I remember."

"When I first got out on the street people started calling me D, then SunnyD, then just Sunny. Everybody calls me that now."

"Would you rather I called you Sunny?"

"No," she said, answering quickly for once. "To you, I'm Dani."

"Okay."

Dani started to cry, her eyes filling and spilling over so suddenly that it was like someone had turned a spigot on inside her. She covered her face with her hands.

"I stole your purse, Mom. I'm sorry. I am. It's just . . . I get so sick. Sometimes I feel like I want to rip off my own skin. And if I don't get—I'm sorry, Mom. I'm so sorry."

"I know, Dani." I laid my hand on her shoulder. "I forgive you. Do you want to get well? Can I help you?"

She lowered her hands. Her eyes were dilated pools of pain and shame. "I want to get well. But I don't want to quit. I can't. I wish I could. I wish I were somebody different. If Daddy saw me like this—"

"He would love you," I said. "Just like he always did, like we both did and I still do. I hate seeing you in such pain, baby. And I hate thinking of you in danger. But I will never, ever stop loving you."

I reached inside my new bag, into a pocket I'd

never had occasion to use but knew very well, and pulled out a card I had been carrying with me for weeks.

"Here, Dani. Put this somewhere so you don't lose it. This is my cell phone number."

After staring at the card for a moment, she slowly lifted her head.

"You hate cell phones. You always said that anybody who knew you would know enough to call you at home."

"But I'm not always at home." I pulled my new phone from my new purse. "Dani, I'm going to keep this with me day and night. There's only one person who has the number, and that's you.

"But I need you to understand, I am never, ever going to give you money. And unless you're clean and sober, you can't stay at my house. But if you're ever in trouble or hurt, you can call me. If you're hungry, I'll bring you food. If you're cold, I'll bring you warm, clean clothes. And if you ever, at any moment of the day or night, decide you want to quit, I'll be there. I love you."

Her eyes swam again. She looked so hopeless and defeated.

"Why?"

"Because I do. Love isn't something you negotiate. It just is."

Dani leaned forward and I wrapped her in my

446

arms. She smelled of dirt, and pot, and sweat, and God only knew what else. And I never wanted to let go of her.

Because love just is.

Chapter 42

Grace

"Let's stay here forever."

That's what Jamie had said to me, two years ago to the day, as we sat on this same ledge, gazing at a vista of gray, and green, and granite to a spot on the horizon that might be the end of the world or the beginning, a scene so majestic it felt like the threshold of heaven itself. For Jamie, it was.

"Let's stay here forever," he'd said as the sun, cut in crescent, flamed orange, red, and gold, halfway between the old day and the new, a day we knew nothing about, when our two paths, blessedly converged for so many years, would finally part as we journeyed toward the far horizon by two different roads, one direct but delayed, the other delayed but circuitous—at least so far.

I don't know what tomorrow will bring. None of us does. That's why we get up and go on because, until forever comes, you can't stay where you are.

Jamie said, "Let's." I squeezed his hand and

said, "Okay." And then we got up anyway. Though we had no way of knowing the distance, we knew we weren't there yet and so we had to get up and walk on, continue the journey.

Jamie said, "Let's." We both understood it was kind of a joke. But it was also a wish, the kind you murmur under your breath because if wishes were horses, beggars would ride and the beggarly, sensible side of your soul doesn't really suppose that wishes come true.

I'd decided some weeks ago, ever since Jamie slipped over the horizon, that I wanted to come to this beautiful place, on this day, and grant the wish that neither of us realized was his last.

The longer I live, the less I am certain of what will happen and the more I understand what can happen. For so long that frightened me, left me living in an emotional crouch, worrying about problems I knew I could never see coming. The curse of living like that, bent low and bowed down, is that you can't see anything else either.

On the first night of my pilgrimage to retrace my last happy days with Jamie before saying a final farewell, I couldn't get the tent to stay up—one of the poles was bent. It was dark and hard to see and, after driving so far alone, I was tired. The third time the canvas collapsed, only minutes after I'd put it back up, having tripped, fallen down, and whacked my wrist on a rock in the process. I crawled out from underneath the canvas, dragged my sleeping bag to a flat spot, and slept in the open, under a canopy of stars as bright as diamonds scattered on velvet.

They were so beautiful. I'd never seen stars like that before. If I had stayed in the tent, curled up in a false wall of protection that kept falling in on me, I'd have missed them.

Lying there, looking up, allowing my vision to expand and my mind to travel the universe and memory, I became a cartographer of my own life, recording the events with a wider scope, standing back to see, not just the mile markers, elevations, and descents, but the entire map of my existence up until that moment, and discovered something I'd missed before. I discovered many somethings.

At every impassable peak, unfordable stream, and impossible canyon, in the moments when I had been most tempted to turn back or give up, there had always been a rope, a boat, a bridge, an ever-present help in times of trouble, a means of moving on.

Sometimes I got stuck, or traveled in circles, or lost my way. When I did, it was only because I distrusted the path, refused to grab hold or step out. But at every crossroad and crisis, the rescue always arrived, just in time, at the instant I needed it most, not a moment before.

When I thought I was nothing and no one, invisible and unlovable, Jamie stepped into my path, walked by my side, and exposed the lie.

When I was going under for the third time and didn't even know it, Nan and Monica pulled me into the boat. Losing the job I hated, I stumbled upon my purpose. Believing that love was behind me, Luke came along to prove I was wrong, that it really was possible to find the love of my life, twice in my life.

Nan was right—every love story turns sad eventually, but if you love, truly love, then it's worth it. Looking back, looking forward, it's all worth it. And when the hard road comes, help will, too, just in time. Sometimes I will need a bridge. Sometimes I will be a bridge. I see that now.

The time is short, the day is ending. Only a sliver of sunlight is visible above the horizon, just a small and succulent slice, a last brilliant blaze of orange and gold, a sunset I will never forget, a love I will always cherish.

"Let's stay here forever."

I came to grant his final wish. But as I climb to my feet, open the box, tip it forward, and watch as the wind carries away what remains, I realize that the part of Jamie that *was* Jamie, that soul and spark, doesn't reside in this box, this ash.

We can't stay here forever. Staying is not what we are created for.

I lower the arm holding the box, now empty of ash, and I catch a glimpse of my watch, Jamie's final gift to me, strapped to the wrist that hit the rock in the dark of the night. Its hands are moving again, steadily ticking the passage of time. I lift my face skyward, to the orange, gold, red of the fading day.

Message received, babe.

Two Years Later

Chapter 43

Monica

Twenty-two hours in transit is enough to take the shine off any bride. But when the bride is almost old enough to be the mother of a bride? Well, it's not pretty.

"Oh, geez. Look at me," I said, staring into the compact I'd pulled from my carry-on bag after Bob and I stepped onto the first of many moving sidewalks that would carry us to baggage claim, and seeing my own bloodshot eyes staring back.

"Why did I bother to bring a suitcase? I could have packed two weeks' worth of clothes in the bags under my eyes. I look like a bride all right. Bride of Frankenstein."

"So that makes me the monster?" Bob asked as we stepped onto the next moving sidewalk.

I lowered the mirror and looked at my husband. His chin was stubbly, a chunk of hair was sticking out at a weird angle from the top of his head, and his rumpled shirt, sporting a stain from marinara sauce he'd consumed somewhere between Rome and New York, looked like he'd slept in it—which he had.

"No, you look great. And very handsome," I said. And to me, he was.

"Well, I think you look beautiful," Bob said. "Like the *Mona Lisa* and *Venus de Milo* rolled into one. Except with arms."

"Well, that's a relief," I said, wrapping both of mine around his neck before giving him a kiss. "I love you, Mr. Smith."

"And I love you, Mrs. Smith. In fact, I love you so much," he said, lowering his voice into that sexy little growl that he knows melts my butter, "that when we get home, I am going to make mad, passionate love to you. It'll be the best you've ever had."

"Really? Better than that first night in Rome? Better than the boat on Lake Como? Or the balcony in Portofino? Better than in Naples, in Florence, in Milan, in Venice?"

"Better than all of them," he said, pulling me close, staring hungrily into my bloodshot eyes. "Better than all of them put together."

"Wow," I said, a smile tugging at the corners of my mouth. "And when are you going to do this?"

"Right after I get home," he said, "and sleep for a week."

He groaned and all but collapsed in my arms, limp as a rag doll. I laughed out loud and kissed him again. And when we exited the door from the gate area to the terminal, I laughed again. We both did, so hard.

Alex, Zoe, and Jean Smith, Bob's mom and the best mother-in-law on earth, who had come up from San Diego to keep an eye on the kids and Desmond while we were on our honeymoon, were standing just outside the door, wearing bedsheet togas over their clothes and waving little Italian flags over their heads. Desmond was there, too, panting and thumping his tail, wearing a circle of plastic leaves on his head that was supposed to be a crown of laurels.

They were so cute and funny and silly. And, best of all, they were mine. My family. My kids.

Seventeen-year-old Alex, now two heads taller than me and with legs that went on forever, had survived his morose and moody phase. He and Bob went running together every Saturday morning, then went to the Screen Door for fried chicken and waffles. Alex still ran cross-country and had qualified for regionals in his sophomore year, gone to state in his junior year. He'd just returned from a week-long running camp at the University of Oregon. Alex was a good athlete, a good student, a good boy. Most of the time. And even when he wasn't, I was proud of him.

Zoe, now fifteen, could still be a royal pain in the butt, but not as often as before. She was actually starting to think about life after high school and was more sensible about boys now, less needy and prone to heartbreak. That was a good thing because there were a ton of them pursuing her. I was glad to have Bob in the picture. Any boy who wanted to take Zoe out first had to meet and pass muster with Bob, who pulled them aside and, with a heavy hand on the kid's shoulder and menacing smile on his face, explained exactly what would happen to him if he disrespected or hurt Zoe, and didn't have her home by ten.

Zoe ran toward me, waving her flag over her head and shouting, "Ciao, Bella!" She hugged me so hard I could barely breathe.

"Wow!" I said when she let me go and threw herself into Bob's arms, hugging him just as hard. "That was some greeting. Did you miss us?"

"*So* much," she chirped. "What did you bring me?"

"Uh-huh. I see how it is. Don't worry," I laughed, "we've got presents for everybody. Jean, your son picked out a Fendi handbag for you that's going to make you drool."

"Oh, honey," she said, grinning as Bob hugged her hello, "you didn't have to do that. What color is it?"

Alex, who had been hanging back a little, came forward, gave Bob one of those manly handshake-backslap things, then one-arm hugged me before taking my bag from my shoulder and carrying it toward the escalator.

"How was camp?" I asked as we walked.

"Good," he said. "Really good. And I've got some good news."

"Oh, yeah? What?"

"I'll tell you later, in the car. First, how was Italy? Bet you were sad to leave, eh?"

I looped my arm loosely around his waist.

"Italy was fantastic. Amazing," I said. "But it's great to be home. Really, really great."

Chapter 44

Nan

Brianna, Emily, and I were sitting at the patio table, splitting a bottle of wine and eating bruschetta made from the first of the summer tomatoes and basil. James and Dan were ferrying back and forth from the kitchen to the deck, carrying platters, plates, pitchers, and bowls to the table. Matt and Kyle were standing by the barbeque, conferring about the doneness of the steaks and burgers, which I reminded them mustn't touch my veggie burgers. Barefoot grandkids and barking dogs were galloping all over the yard, hooting and whooping and sometimes somersaulting across the wet grass, having the time of their lives.

So was I.

The second weekend of July has always been our Homecoming Week, when all my kids and grandkids—well, almost all—come to Portland for eight days of food, fun, and family time. It's my favorite week of the entire year, now doubly so because, during last year's Homecoming Saturday barbeque, Malcolm and I were married.

The ceremony was casual and perfectly lovely. I wore a simple white sheath overlaid with crocheted lace and carried pink roses from the garden, Malcolm wore a khaki summer suit with a white shirt and pink tie, Blixen wore a pink silk bow around her neck, and Nelson and Stuart had baths.

Later, after the champagne had been poured and the pictures taken, Malcolm changed out of his suit and joined in the grandkids' annual game of tag. When he suggested the addition of sprinklers and dogs to the game, the kids started calling him Grampy.

They just love Malcolm. So do I.

Our life together is incredibly rich and full. But, unlike before, when I filled my days with activity as a means of staving off loneliness, now my life is filled with activities I truly enjoy, including "vegging out" as Malcolm calls it. Yes, with Malcolm's help, I have actually learned the value of sitting still and doing absolutely nothing. But that's not all we do. We travel quite a bit, Malcolm has a little teardrop trailer that we've taken on camping trips to the beach, the mountains, and Glacier National Park in Montana. For our honeymoon, we took it down to Ashland and spent a whole week at the Oregon Shakespeare Festival. That was fantastic. I can't wait to go back. In the fall, we're planning a trip to Scotland to visit Malcolm's relatives. It will be my first overseas trip. I'll probably need a prescription for some antianxiety medicine, but with Malcolm's help, I know I can do it. I'm very excited.

We do a lot here in Portland too. Stuart and Nelson are both certified therapy dogs now, so we visit local hospitals and nursing homes and are on call in crisis situations. And, of course, we're both still involved with Rainbow Gate.

The third annual Dogmother's Ball raised close to ten thousand dollars. We moved it to an outdoor event venue in Oregon City for the second year. That way we can accommodate more people, and we have a whole staff of professionals to handle the actual event—meaning Malcolm doesn't have to climb ladders to deal with dicey electrical wiring anymore and we have more time to do other things we enjoy. I bought Malcolm a little eighteen-foot sailboat as a wedding present and we both took lessons. Sailing with your husband, I have learned, is a real test of a marriage. But, in spite of that incident with the jib sheet, and the yelling, and the boom, we're still together. And, in spite of the results of Malcolm's recent prostate biopsy, results that we aren't ready to share with the kids just yet, we're incredibly happy and fortunate. If someone had told me three years ago that I would be happily married to the most wonderful man on earth, I'd have said they were dreaming. Now,

I'm living that dream. Whatever we have to face, we'll face together. Life is good.

Malcolm waved his arm over his head, beckoning me to leave my comfortable seat on the patio and join in the game. "Come on in, honey! The water's fine!" And immediately, the grandkids started chorusing, "Come on, Grammy! Come play!"

"After lunch," I promised, looking down at the pink bundle in my lap. "I'm having a pretty good time right here at the moment."

When we married, I had eight grandchildren and Malcolm had three. This new addition, Ellie, gives us an even dozen. Yes, life is very good.

Chrissy, who was in the kitchen making a salad, poked her head out the door. "Mom? Are you getting tired of holding her?"

"Never," I said, looking down at this perfect little person, placing my finger in her palm and smiling as the five tiny fingers curled around mine.

"We should be ready to eat in about fifteen minutes. What time do you think Monica and Bob will show up? Should I hold off serving until they get here?"

"Well, Monica said they were coming, but they only got home last night. I'm sure they're so jet-lagged they'll probably sleep right through the barbeque—but hopefully not Grace's opening."

For a moment, I considered getting up,

calling Monica's house, and leaving a message reminding them about the opening, but decided I'd wait a few more hours before disturbing the honeymooners. The opening started at five. There was still plenty of time.

Baby Ellie stirred in her sleep, yawned and stretched, clenching her tiny fists as she lifted her arms over her head, then opened her eyes and blinked, gazing at me with a solemn expression.

"You're awfully serious for someone who's only six weeks old," I said, lowering my face closer to hers. "You don't look as if you approve of me one bit."

Ellie blinked again, as if confirming my observation. I looked at my daughters. "Honestly, have you ever seen a baby so serious? I think she's sitting here right now, judging every one of us, and wondering when her real family is coming to claim her."

Emily laughed, then got up from her chair and looked over my shoulder at her newest niece. "Sorry, kiddo. It's not a bad dream. We really are your family."

Brianna grinned "Jake was like that. Don't you remember, Mom? He always used to—"

My cell phone, which was sitting on the table, rang. Brianna stopped in the middle of her sentence. Emily held out her arms. "Here, Mom. I'll take her."

In the two years I'd had my phone, it had rung

less than a dozen times, but I continued to carry it with me everywhere I went, making sure it was always charged and within arm's reach, the ringer turned up as high as it would go. Everyone in the family knows why. Of those dozen calls from Dani, probably half were requests for food or clothing, and once for a ride to the doctor when she caught bronchitis. The others, in spite of the conditions I'd laid out to Dani, were stoned, panicked, often incoherent conversations in which she either demanded or pleaded for me to give her money. Those calls were hard to take, painful to listen to, but I was grateful for every call because at least I knew that Dani was still alive.

I was sure this call would be the same as all the others, brief and largely uneventful, but my heart was hammering just the same. It always does when Dani calls. Hope dies hard in a mother's heart.

I handed the baby to Emily and picked up the phone, walking quickly toward one of Malcolm's hosta beds before answering the call, turning my back so the girls wouldn't be able to overhear my conversation.

"Dani?"

"Hi, Mom."

She sounded nervous, subdued, and anxious, but coherent.

"Hi, sweetheart. How are you? Do you need something?"

"No, I . . . I just . . . Mom, I overdosed yesterday."

"Oh, Dani. Oh, my God," I said, my words a prayer, tears springing to my eyes.

"It's okay, Mom. Really, I'm okay. That's not why I'm calling. The policeman who found me, the one who called the ambulance, came around today and said there was a rehab spot open for me if I wanted to take it. I decided I do. I want to stop, to get my life back."

"Oh, honey . . . Dani, that's wonderful. . . ."

"Mom, it's okay. Don't cry."

"It's all right," I said, wiping my eyes with my sleeve. "It's happy crying."

"Well . . . don't start dancing a jig just yet," she said, and I could hear the smile in her voice, the first time I'd heard that in years. "It's going to be hard. A lot of people who go into rehab still don't make it."

"I know. But you will, Dani. You're strong. And you're ready."

"I am," she said quietly. "I really think I am."

"Honey, do you want me to come get you? I could drive you there, bring you some clothes."

"No, Mom. Not right now. You can visit in a few weeks, but . . . I need to do this on my own, okay?"

"Okay," I said, bobbing my head and blinking back tears. "I'll be praying for you, sweetheart. So will Malcolm."

"Thanks, Mom. I'll need it."

"Can I tell your brothers and sisters? Everybody's here."

"Oh, that's right. It's Homecoming," she said, the sound of her smile making my heart sing. "Yeah, you can tell them. Tell them that I said hello and that next year I'll be at the barbeque."

"I will, Dani. I'll tell them."

Chapter 45

Grace

"Grace? Is this good, or do you want it higher?"

I turn from the table, where I have been pouring bottles of ginger ale and pink lemonade into the punch bowl, and look up to see my husband standing on a ladder and holding a rope.

"Can you bring it up about a foot? I think it looks better when they're hanging at different heights." Luke pulls the rope, raising the bar and the quilt that's hanging on it, then turns and looks at me again. "That's perfect. Thanks, honey."

Luke ties off the rope and climbs down the ladder. I come over and stand next to him.

"That's the last one," he says. "It looks good, Gracie. Really good. You should feel proud of yourself."

I turn in a circle, looking at the twenty quilts hanging along the brick walls of the warehouse. The quilt I made for Jamie, with the stars and stories that always make me smile, hangs next to an extraordinary quilt, a portrait of a man's face pieced entirely from neckties by a woman who was married to an executive. On the opposite

468

wall, I see a quilt of red, white, and blue by the wife of a veteran, another made entirely from race T-shirts and embellished with medals and blue ribbons by the husband of a woman who ran marathons, and a crib-sized quilt with pastel pink angel blocks, embellished with rosebuds and ribbons, made by a young mother. So many quilts, all different, all beautiful, all made to celebrate the life and memory of someone deeply loved and never forgotten.

Looking at them, I can't help but smile, but I don't say anything. Portland truly is my home now, but the mark of my Midwestern upbringing will stay with me for life. Where I come from, you don't brag about your accomplishments and you don't say you feel proud of yourself—even when you do.

"I'm proud of us," I say, rising up on my toes and kissing Luke on the cheek.

And I am. It's a big day for both of us.

Three months ago, Luke and I bought this building, a three-story, twelve-thousand-square-foot warehouse in East Portland. Even though Luke and I got a good return on my condo and his bungalow, we had to take out a mortgage, a big one. When we went to sign the papers, my hands were shaking I was so nervous, a feeling that didn't dissipate for about a month.

But now that the remodeling is finally done and we're only an hour from opening our doors to one hundred friends, associates, and family members, I feel happy and completely at peace with our decision. We're doing the right thing, for ourselves and a lot of other people as well.

The top floor of the building has two loft apartments. Luke and I live in one and rent out the other. That's where most of the remodeling took place. Honestly, I thought it was fine as it was, not a palace but definitely habitable, but Luke . . . Well, let's just say that we now have the most beautiful kitchen cabinets and built-in bookshelves on the east side. The bottom floor has a storage space, a big industrial-sized garage, and Luke's workshop and showroom. He employs two other carpenters now and is looking to hire another one, or maybe take on an apprentice. Though he has more orders than he can fill and could definitely make more money if he had more help, Luke won't compromise on the quality of his work. He's starting to think training apprentices is the only way he'll be able to maintain the standard of workmanship he insists on.

The second floor, where we are now, houses my workshop and offices. Twirl and Whirl Clothing Company, now Twirl and Whirl Workshop, has six employees, including me. Billie is in charge of the actual workshop floor, sewing dresses and supervising three additional seamstresses we were able to hire after we got into the space. Janet works in the office with me. I brought her on about a year ago to help with online marketing, order fulfillment, shipping, bookkeeping, and anything else that needs doing. Janet and I have pretty much the same job description. We have a really great team in place. They're not just good workers, they're good people who really believe in the mission.

Every person who works here gets a vote on where our donated dresses will go. So far, we've made one thousand dresses to encourage women in need or transition. By this time next year, if our projections are right, that number will be five thousand.

Some are sent to homeless shelters, others to shelters for victims of domestic violence, some to the Red Cross to be given to women who lost everything after a house fire or natural disaster, and some to an organization that helps women reentering the workforce by making sure they have something nice to wear to job interviews. Kim, one of our new employees, recently came up with a new idea. It meant a little extra design work on my part, but I'm really excited about it. Twirl and Whirl is now making children's dresses. In September, we'll donate seventy-five dresses so girls in foster care can have something new and nice to wear on the first day of school. It's just a pilot project, but it feels like the start of something pretty wonderful.

I still have a sewing machine on the workshop floor, a much faster industrial machine than my old one, and manage to spend a few hours there each week, but not as much as I'd like. I'm not complaining. There are worse problems for a business to have than being so overwhelmed by demand that you have to bring on more people to make the product. Besides, it means I have time for some of the other things I care about.

Billie and I have gotten to be really good friends. After we finished our quilts, she told me about another woman at her grief support group and asked if we could help her make a quilt. Of course, I said yes. Things just kind of grew from there. Now, every Thursday from six to nine at night, we meet here on the workshop floor to help people make quilts and tell stories of the people they love and miss. Sometimes, Nan and Blixen drop by. I think it helps people. The way I can tell is, though people are welcome to come for as long as they want, once they finish their quilts, they gradually stop coming. That's why we decided to have this little quilt exhibition in conjunction with our building opening—so people who've moved on have a chance to keep in touch. I think it's good that we need a reunion. Staying isn't what we're created for.

Besides the business and the quilting group, the other focus of my time is, of course, Luke. With two businesses growing by leaps and bounds, it's very hard for us to make time for each other. We really have to work at it. That's been the biggest challenge in our sixteen months of marriage. Part of the reason we decided to take the leap and buy the warehouse is because we thought being able to live where we work would make it easier to spend time together.

So far, it's working out, but some of that is Luke's doing. When we first moved in, he said, "I have an idea for a project. Let's make love in every single room of this building."

"All twelve hundred square feet?" I asked.

"All twelve hundred square feet. Including this stairwell," he said, then sat on the bottom step and pulled me down on top of him.

It's gotten to be our little joke—every time we make love, we talk about The Project. Sometimes, when we're out to dinner with friends or visiting their house, Luke will say, "Well, we'd better get going. Grace and I have this project we're working on." It's really kind of cute and also kind of sexy. It's fun sneaking off like that, having people think we're going off to work, but knowing that the second we get back to the house, we're going to jump on each other.

It's our inside joke, but to tell the truth, I think people are catching on. A few weeks ago, Monica said, "Boy, Luke sure has a lot of projects in the works," then winked at me.

Well, what can I say? It's a big building.

473

• • •

Billie, Janet, and Ed, one of Luke's carpenters, came early to help us set up. The guests started arriving promptly at five. Nan, Malcolm, and their clan, including kids and grandkids, showed up first. Nan immediately pulled me aside to share the good news about Dani.

"Oh, Nan. That is wonderful," I said, and gave her an enormous hug.

"It is," she said. "But pray for her, will you? It won't be easy."

"I will," I promised. "Every day."

The kids were running all over the place, bouncing with energy. We didn't mind; we'd put the sewing machines in the storage room, so there really wasn't anything they could break. James, Nan's oldest son, organized a game of sardines so that kept them busy. Once things settled down, I asked Chrissy if I could hold baby Ellie.

"She's gorgeous," I said, cooing over Ellie's tiny fingernails and breathing in that sweet milk and baby shampoo smell.

"She is," Chrissy agreed. "Really, I thought Bill and I were done with kids, but, you know." She shrugged. "Sometimes life has other plans. She's the best surprise we ever got."

I'll say. I could have held that little sweetheart all night. But when I heard a booming voice from the door yelling, "Grace! Ciao, bella!" I handed the baby back to Chrissy and ran to give Monica a hug.

"Ciao! How was the honeymoon? Was Italy all you hoped for and more?"

"*So* much more," Monica gushed. "Rome was great, but oh, Grace! Venice and Verona! Portofino! So romantic. And the food! Grace, the food was just phenomenal. You have never in your life had pasta this good. And the sauces! I don't know what it is—either the tomatoes, or the olive oil, or the atmosphere—but you haven't eaten marinara until you've eaten it in Italy. Wait until we show you the pictures. We only took about a thousand."

"All of food," Bob joked, putting his arm around Monica's waist. "We really did have a great time. We've already decided to go back for our third anniversary and bring the kids."

"Oh, and we came home to some very good news," Monica said. "One of the coaches from U of O pulled Alex aside at his cross-country camp and invited him for a campus visit in the fall."

"Really," I said. "You think they might offer him a scholarship?"

"Well, first he has to get in," Monica said practically. "But you never know. Oh, and Zoe wanted me to ask you—could you use an intern this summer? Unpaid, of course. She's thinking about studying fashion—at least this week,"

Monica laughed. "I thought working with you might help her figure out if she's serious about it or not."

"Sure," I said. "Have her call me. I can always use an extra pair of hands."

My mom and Aunt Rickie were next to arrive. I flew them out for the opening and booked them into a nice hotel downtown for the weekend, to be followed by a tour of the Oregon wine country and two more days at the beach. They hadn't had a sisters' getaway in years and seemed to be having a terrific time. Mom couldn't wait to tell me about their visit to Blue Star Doughnuts.

"Gracie, they were so delicious, but they had the strangest flavors. Blueberry Bourbon Basil. Would you believe it? Bourbon! In a doughnut!"

"Personally," Aunt Rickie said, "I've always preferred my bourbon in a highball glass. That's why I'm in charge of tomorrow's field trip. We're going to the Multnomah Whiskey Library. It's right near the doughnut place. Want to come?"

"Thanks, Aunt Rickie, but I've given up drinking. How about Luke and I take you and Mom for an early dinner. Tasty and Alder doesn't take reservations, but it's worth the wait. I've actually had dreams about their skillet corn cake and the radicchio with bacon lardons and egg is so good, I've been known to order one as an appetizer and then order it again for dessert."

"You always did know the best places to eat," she said. "Even after you lost all that weight. Why don't you let me pay for dinner? You and Luke have already done too much—the airline tickets, the hotel."

"No," I said. "This trip is our treat. Thanks to you, we can afford it."

"Oh, posh. All I did was co-sign for the loan. I knew you'd be good for it." Aunt Rickie craned her neck, looking all around the workshop. "And I was right! You must be doing well to afford all this."

"Most of this is mortgaged," I laughed. "But we are doing well. But that first loan helped me sell enough dresses so the bank would loan us money to expand. We could never have done it without you. I think that's probably worth a trip and a dinner, don't you?"

It was a wonderful party. I felt so happy, for so many reasons.

Dianne Maestro, the woman who made the quilt from her husband George's ties, came and brought her sister-in-law. They stood in front of George's portrait and cried, but they were good tears. Becky Jones and her husband, Roger, came and brought their parents to see the crib quilt Becky made. It was sweet to see Becky and Roger standing together in front of the quilt holding hands.

After a few minutes, Luke came up behind me

and whispered in my ear, "Should I get Becky a chair or something? She looks like she's going to deliver that baby any minute."

"She's okay," I said. "Still has a month to go."

Luke wrapped his arms around my waist, then kissed me on the neck.

"You are one incredible woman, Grace. Do you know that? Look at all these people you've brought together. Look at all these lives you've impacted."

"You mean the lives *we've* impacted. If you hadn't stalked me in Starbucks, or built me a sewing table, or taught me to dance, it would still be just me and Maisie, living in the condo and hiding from life. Credit where credit is due, mister."

"Okay, fine. I helped with some of it," he said, squeezing me. "But the quilts are all you. I can't even sew on a button."

"Yes, I know," I laughed. "But you have other skills." I placed a hand on top of his and moved it low, over a small, new swell at my waistline. "I was thinking, I might want to make another quilt. One about that size."

I pointed to Becky's pink and white crib quilt, then waited for Luke to pull the pieces together. Honestly, it took a little longer than I thought it would. Finally, after about six seconds of silence, he let go of my waist and took hold of my shoulders, turning me toward him. His eyes were wide.

"Wait. What? Grace, really?"

I nodded and my face split into a goofy, joyous grin that mirrored his.

"Really?" he said again. "How?"

I laughed. "What do you mean how?"

"No . . . I meant . . . You know, when?"

"Well . . . I can't be entirely sure—you've been pretty aggressive about The Project—but I'm pretty sure it was in the stairwell."

"The stairwell? You mean the very first night?" Luke wrapped his arms around my waist, lifted me off the floor, and swung me in a circle. "What did I tell you when I first saw this building? Didn't I tell you it was lucky?"

I looped my arms around Luke's neck and laughed, laughed for joy, and life, and complete, perfect, incandescent happiness.

"You know what else is lucky?" I asked, then kissed him again. "Me."

Dear Reader,

Just in Time was one of the most challenging books I have ever written. Perhaps because she is a bit shy, Grace in particular took some time to reveal herself to me.

But the more I got to know Grace, Nan, and Monica, the more they began to feel like friends, the kind of women I would love to have for a next-door neighbor. After reading their story, I hope you feel the same way.

If so, I would so appreciate it if you'd help spread the word about this book! Please tell your friends, family, and book club about *Just in Time*. Word of mouth from passionate readers is the very best form of advertising and the greatest compliment that any author can receive. It can make a huge difference in helping a book find an audience.

I do love hearing from readers. I read every note personally and do my best to make sure each note receives a response. If you have a moment, drop me an e-mail at marie@mariebostwick.com or by regular mail. Please note, after spending my entire writing career in Connecticut, I have recently moved back to my home state of Oregon, so I have a new mailing address . . .

Marie Bostwick
18160 Cottonwood Road
PMB 118
Bend, Oregon 97707

These days, social media is the easiest, fastest way for me to connect with readers. You can find me on Facebook at https://www.facebook.com/mariebostwick/ and on Twitter, Pinterest, and Instagram by searching @mariebostwick.

Also, please take some time to visit my website, www.marie bostwick.com. While you're there you can sign up for my monthly newsletter, check my calendar to see if I'll be making an appearance in your area, enter the monthly reader giveaway, and download free recipes and quilt patterns created exclusively for my readers. To find them, go to the Quilt Central tab on my website and choose Patterns and Recipes from the pulldown menu. (Please note, these patterns and recipes are for your personal use only and may not be copied to share with others or published by any means, either print or electronic.)

I've been pretty busy writing the actual story, so I haven't been doing a lot of quilting or cooking lately. However, you can be sure that I'll have a new companion pattern available for this book, based on the memory quilt that Grace makes in the story. I have been in discussion with Deb Tucker, the extraordinary designer and dear friend who has created so many of the companion patterns for my book, and we are both very excited about the possibilities for the next free, downloadable quilt project!

Deb has also created many companion patterns for purchase to go with my books. To check them out, visit www.studio180design.net, click the Shop tab on the menu, and look for the Cobbled Court section under Specialty Collections. There are some beautiful patterns here!

Besides the quilt pattern, I'll have a crop of new book-based recipes available for my food-loving readers, which I'm guessing includes everybody. I'm not yet sure which recipes we'll publish, but given Monica's love of all things Italian, I'm guessing pasta will be involved. We might need to have the recipe for Nan's peach turnovers as well. And I think that Grace's strawberry rhubarb sangria is a must. Wouldn't that be a fun beverage to serve to your book club when they get together to discuss *Just In Time*?

It's not a coincidence that this book is titled *Just in Time*. The longer I live, the more cognizant I am of the fact that time is the most finite and precious commodity we possess. The fact that you have chosen to spend some of your valuable time with me and with my characters is a tremendous honor. Without you, my readers, I would not have been able to become a writer.

That's why I say, with all my heart, thank you for your time and for the opportunity to do this work I love so much.

Blessings,

Marie Bostwick

Discussion Questions

1. Grace, Nan, and Monica are close but unlikely friends connected by a common experience with grief. Think about your circles of friends. . . . What are the connections that brought you together? Is that still what keeps you together? Grace, Nan, and Monica became close later in life. . . . Are your best friends from long ago or more recently made?

2. As an overweight teenager, Grace's response to the bullying she experienced was to try to blend in and go unnoticed, yet, she says, "No one truly wants to become invisible. Everyone, no matter how fat, or slow, or tall, or ugly, or beautiful, wants to be important and loved." Can you think of people in your life or community who are "invisible" or go unnoticed? Have you ever felt invisible? What are some adjectives to describe how being "invisible" might make someone feel? What are some adjectives to describe the feelings that person might experience when they are "seen" and appreciated for who they are?

3. The issue of homelessness plays a part early in the story and becomes very personal toward the end. Is homelessness a concern where you live? If so, discuss ideas of how you and your community can help the homeless in your town. Consider the big picture for the population as a whole as well as the needs and dignity of the individual, taking into consideration the thoughts you discussed in question 2. For personal reflection, what are some concrete steps you can take to positively impact the lives of homeless people in your town?

4. Though married at a young age, Jamie and Grace endured many hardships and struggles. Grace says, "Unless you've been through it yourself, you can't understand the bond that surviving that kind of adversity builds between people." Do you agree that life's difficulties can create particularly strong bonds between couples? If so, how has that played out in your life or the lives of people you know?

5. Nan said, "Whoever said diamonds are a girl's best friend never had a dog." What has "rescued you" or "saved you" when times were tough? Share favorite dog/cat/pet stories.

6. Monica is a fiercely loyal friend with a good heart and the best of intentions, but isn't the most emotionally sensitive member of the group. How did those two conflicting personality traits play out in the story? By the end of the story, do you think that Grace really did thank Monica for her interference? Do you have a Monica in your life? Does the goodness of her intentions make up for the ham-fisted way she goes about trying to help?

7. Nan has a lot of children, but one "lost sheep. . . ." Dani's issues seem to have begun when her father died. Nan seems to think she could have done more to help Dani. Do you agree? Discuss the epidemic of depression and drug addiction in family members. In what ways was Nan handling things correctly? What might she have done differently?

8. Grace says, "Sometimes I need a bridge and sometimes I will be a bridge." Share with your group a time when you either needed a bridge and got it or were able to be a bridge for someone else.

9. Looking back on her life, Grace says, "At every crossroad and crisis, the rescue arrived

just in time, the instant I needed it most, not a moment before." Has this proven true in your life? If so, did you or do you see this as a coincidence or part of a larger plan?

10. In different ways and to varying degrees, Grace, Nan, and Monica each experienced moments of being "stuck" in their grief. How was that evident in each of these characters? Who or what finally helped each of them move through their grief and embrace life more fully?

11. Each of the friends found love again (or love found them)! What love story did you enjoy the most? Share the moment you knew your love was "the one." Was your story one of love at first sight? Did you find love after a series of "moments"? Or did your love grow over time?

12. Speaking of love, Nan said, "In silence and presence, love is spoken most truly." Do you agree? What does this mean in your life?

13. Ms. Bostwick sets her novels in various parts of the country. Connecticut is the backdrop of her Cobbled Court Quilts series. Texas, of course, is home to the two "Texas books." We were in Wisconsin for *The*

Second Sister and Seattle for *The Promise Girls*. Now we visit Portland, Oregon. Where is your favorite part of the world? In what city or town would you set your own "Great American Novel"?

14. Grace, Nan, and Monica's life looks completely different on the last page than it did on the first. Grace said, "Staying is not what we are created for." Talk about your hopes and dreams for yourself and the ones you love most. Did this story make you start thinking about any new career ideas? Travel plans? Love interests? New hobbies to try? Languages to learn?

15. We witnessed each character in the role of care giver: Grace with Jamie, Nan with Dani, Monica with her stepchildren. . . . What are the challenges each one faced and can you relate to them? How do you care for yourself while caring for others?

Books are produced in the United States using U.S.-based materials

Books are printed using a revolutionary new process called THINKtech™ that lowers energy usage by 70% and increases overall quality

Books are durable and flexible because of smythe-sewing

Paper is sourced using environmentally responsible foresting methods and the paper is acid-free

Center Point Large Print
600 Brooks Road / PO Box 1
Thorndike, ME 04986-0001 USA

(207) 568-3717

US & Canada:
1 800 929-9108
www.centerpointlargeprint.com

Center Point
5/15/18
38,95